TEMPESTUOUS REUNION

"I told you I would return to claim you one day. It has taken a good deal longer than I would have wished."

Eden's mind screamed at her to flee, but her traitorous flesh refused to obey. "I'm not afraid of you, Roark!" she asserted breathlessly.

"Ah, but you should be, my love," he whispered. "You should be."

He kissed her, gently at first. Then, with a low groan sounding deep in his throat, he brought his warm lips down upon the startled softness of hers with an impassioned, ever-deepening thoroughness that demanded a response.

Her head spun dizzily beneath the unexpected fury of his assault, and she found herself swaying closer to his hard, virile warmth. . . .

Passion's Chains

CATHERINE CREEL

ZEBRA BOOKS
KENSINGTON PUBLISHING CORP.

For my beloved son, Caleb,
whose sweet smile and dancing
blue eyes set my heart aglow

PINNACLE BOOKS

are published by

Windsor Publishing Corp.
475 Park Avenue South
New York, NY 10016

First printing: January, 1991

Printed in the United States of America

One

Barbados, 1814

Lady Eden Parrish was neither saint nor sinner.

She had strayed too far to be the former—and had enjoyed too little to be the latter. Of course, those of her acquaintance took it upon themselves to place her in one category or the other. How utterly mistaken they were.

They, and Eden herself, were on the very brink of enlightenment.

Sunlight blazed across the sky. Alive with the fresh smells of sea spray and sugar cane and the heavy perfume of jasmine, all mingling together with other scents to be borne aloft on the gentle trade winds, the morning issued a promise of yet another humid, sun-drenched day on the island. This tiny speck in the Caribbean, bearing a marked and inglorious resemblance to a leg of mutton, was considered by many of its inhabitants to be a tropical paradise. For others, however, it was a living hell.

Had she been asked, Eden would no doubt have employed *both* descriptions to characterize her own existence during the past eight months.

"Please, mistress, come away!" an aproned maid-servant implored from the wide, arched doorway of the great house. Aghast at the scene taking place, the young woman hastened forward to declare in a breathless tone laced with apprehension, "Your uncle, my lady! He be down any moment now!"

Eden ignored the well-intentioned caution offered by the plump, genial Betsy. She determinedly pushed her lace-trimmed sleeves above her elbows and sent a luxuriant cascade of raven curls tumbling back over her shoulder with a toss of her head. Her eyes, which had on occasion been so eloquently likened to "twin pools of liquid emerald fire," flashed with a wholly *un*ladylike enthusiasm when she bent to her task again.

"You must pull the cinch until it is quite snug, Jonah, or else the saddle will not remain in its proper position," she directed the new stable hand. A visibly nervous boy of fourteen, he watched with rapt attention as his beautiful mistress, not so much older than himself, took a firm grip on the leather strap and gave it a brisk tug. "There," she said, straightening again, "now you try it."

The young slave did as he was bid, taking hold of the cinch and tightening it in the same manner Eden had just demonstrated. Her smile brought a rush of warm color to his smooth-cheeked face.

"I daresay even Old Sangaree will not criticize your methods once you have practiced a bit," she pronounced kindly.

"No, mistress," Jonah murmured in gratitude—and perhaps a touch of youthful adoration. His guileless brown eyes shone with pleasure, and he suddenly no longer minded the hot, stiff clothing he was forced to wear in his new position.

"And you must also make certain the reins are looped up in readiness before the rider takes mount." Oblivious to the prospect of creasing her elegant white cotton gown, she reached out for the reins.

"Eden!"

The sound of that familiar, ever-rigorous voice caused her to start guiltily. Giving an inward groan, she forced a smile to her lips and pivoted reluctantly about to face the stout middle-aged gentleman whose forbidding expression matched his mood.

"Are you ready at last then, Uncle?" she inquired with all innocence. Casually scooping up the hat she had tossed aside, she was betrayed only by the merest spark of defiance in her emerald gaze.

"I employ a stable master to instruct the slaves in their duties!" William Stanhope reminded her tersely, his long angry strides leading him out of the Jacobean-style mansion. He transferred his unamiable gaze to Jonah. "Get back to the stables at once, do you hear? And tell Old Sangaree you are to remain here from now on!"

"Uncle, please!" Eden attempted to intervene as she watched the terrified boy beat a hasty retreat. "I was only—"

"Do not dare to cross me in this, Eden," he warned, "for I am already of a mind to deny you the honor of accompanying me into Bridgetown!" His aristocratic features were suffused with a harsh glow, and

7

his eyes were fairly snapping with displeasure.

"Why?" Eden challenged bravely, lifting her chin and meeting her guardian's wrath without flinching. "What other 'transgressions' have I committed of late?"

"Take care, my dear," advised William, "or else you'll find yourself confined to your room for an entire fortnight!"

He spared her one last glare, as he directly signaled to have the waiting carriage brought round. The Bajan driver, well accustomed to the older Englishman's formidable temper, prompted the matching pair of grays to draw the conveyance up to the front of the house without delay. A tall, uniformed footman hurried to open the carriage door.

Eden preceded her uncle up into the open vehicle, then quickly settled her skirts about her and tied the blue satin strings of her straw bonnet. Her silken brow creased into a frown as she watched William hoist his considerable, black-clad girth upward.

"I suppose you are referring to this morning's visit by Donald Parkington-Hughes," she remarked with a heavy sigh once the stern, balding master of the plantation had taken a seat opposite. "Who played the spy for you this time, Uncle?"

"Don't be impertinent! When a man of young Parkington-Hughes' caliber honors someone with a call, he deserves to be treated with a high degree of regard! But it seems you have once again refused to grant him the merest civility!" Eden's mother's elder brother yanked on his buttersoft leather gloves. His eyes, similar to his niece's and yet at the same time so vastly different, narrowed in a renewed burst of annoyance. "Donald's familial connections are beyond reproach, his financial prospects are excellent, and he is obviously quite besotted with you. What the devil more can a young woman, particularly a *troubled* one such as yourself," he added pointedly, "ask for in a husband?"

Eden bit back the scathing retort which rose to her lips. There was no use in being drawn into the same tiresome quarrel, she thought unhappily, no use at all. She couldn't possibly win. And heaven help her, there was no way she could hope to make such a cold, heartless man like William Stanhope understand that it required a good deal more than connections and prospects to enhance a suitor's—*any* suitor's—chances for success. As for Donald's being "besotted," well, there was little she could do about that. She had certainly never encouraged him. No indeed, she mused with another inward sigh, her conscience was entirely clear on that point.

But not on another, a tiny voice at the back of her mind tormented. Her frown deepened.

"Heed me well, Eden!" her uncle insisted, leaning a heavy hand upon his gold-topped walking stick after rapping out the command for them to be off. With his starched white shirt, severely tailored tailcoat, and perennial scowl, he looked every inch the dour old bachelor he was. "Your parents sent you to me for a reason, and we both know what that reason was—to find you a husband."

"That is not true!" she adamantly denied. Provoked by his deliberate bluntness, she found that her resolve to be silent had fled. "It was because of—"

"Because your reputation had been compromised

9

beyond repair," he supplied in a tone edged with distaste. The carriage lurched forward a bit as the driver cracked the whip above the horses' heads. William resettled himself on the cushioned leather seat and continued, "There is no need for us to speak of the shameful incident, for it is in the past where it belongs. But you've only yourself to blame for the misfortune which befell you, just as you've only yourself to blame for the regrettable fact that even after eight months' time you are not yet betrothed."

"Even if I desired such a thing, a betrothal would be impossible!" she reminded him, her eyes bridling with anger and resentment. "Or have you forgotten a certain small matter of legality?"

"I can assure you I have not," he bit out. His gaze bored into hers. "Your disgrace is shared by the entire family. And lest *you* forget, my dear Eden, might I remind you that you will never again be allowed the freedom you once enjoyed? You have sealed your own fate with your actions. Your father, however, has promised to bring the matter before the courts at the first available opportunity. Were it not for the war—"

"Were it not for the war, I would not have suffered a 'fall from grace' at all," she remarked, a telltale note of bitterness creeping into her voice, "nor would I have been sent halfway around the world to live with a kinsman who bears little affection for me and who apparently believes I should . . . should *sacrifice* myself on the altar of matrimony in order to pay for the mistake of falling in love with the wrong man!"

"Love?" William Stanhope, though always having taken great pride in his impeccable breeding, gave what sounded suspiciously like a rude snort of disgust. "Call it what you will," he sneered, "but the fact remains that you have brought dishonor upon yourself, upon your parents and your brothers, and, yes, even upon me!"

"And how, pray tell, have I done that?"

"Come now, you cannot expect me to believe you are completely unaware of the gossip. Why, the tongues had set to wagging within a week of your arrival. News travels quickly, even in wartime, and most particularly when it is news of a scandal involving the daughter of Lord Grayson Parrish! Of course," he added, more by way of congratulating himself than comforting Eden, "you need have no fear that any member of polite society here on the island will ever be so bold as to offer you insult. No, my own estimable position demands that you are treated with the utmost respect at all times. But that does not prevent the rumors from flying about!" He cast her yet another look designed to excoriate.

"Let them fly!" retorted Eden. "Do you think I care a fig for what others say of me?" She *did* care, of course. The thought of her disgrace being so well known hurt more than she was willing to admit. But not for the reasons anyone else would have supposed. . . .

"I can see you are determined to be foolish," William now spoke in a chilling tone that had a distinct ring of finality to it. "Well then, so be it. You are a headstrong, ungrateful little chit, but you are apparently what Donald Parkington-Hughes wants, and by damn, he shall have you!"

"No, Uncle, he shall *not*!" Her full young breasts

heaved with fiery indignation beneath the tight, high-waisted bodice of the muslin gown. "You cannot force me to wed him!"

"Can I not?" His mouth curved into a slow, cryptic smile that struck a sudden chord of fear in Eden's heart. "We shall see about that, my girl. We shall see."

He settled himself more comfortably back against the cushions and turned his self-satisfied gaze upon the green, windswept beauty of the passing landscape. It was evident that he considered the subject of his ward's future closed for the moment—closed and in his own mind neatly settled.

In Eden's mind, however, there was no order. Both her thoughts and her emotions had been thrown into utter chaos by her uncle's stated intention to see her married off to a suitor who, though entirely respectable and well-mannered, would no doubt prove to be the most *un*exciting and *un*fulfilling of husbands. The mere thought of having to endure Donald's presence, not to mention his "attentions," for the remainder of her life was enough to make her wish she had never come to Barbados.

She shuddered involuntarily at the memory of the chaste but annoying kiss her would-be fiancé had pressed upon her lips when taking leave of her that morning. It infuriated her anew to think that Donald Parkington-Hughes, or any other of the gallant young swains who had relentlessly paid court to her these past eight months, should believe her willing to lend herself so readily to tiresome notions of romance. Romance was something she had no desire whatsoever to cultivate. None whatsoever, she reiterated in angry silence.

Her eyes narrowed, hurtling invisible daggers at the stern master of Abbeville Plantation before she looked away. She turned her head to watch as the stately, plastered coral mansion and numerous outbuildings grew smaller in the distance.

All were sheltered by native palms and English evergreens, bordered by immaculately trimmed shrubs and flowers, and surrounded by lawns carpeted with thick grasses. A formal garden unfolded its lush, colorful brilliance beneath the rear gables of the three-storied house, while the nearby fields of ripening sugarcane took on the appearance of gently rolling seas of gold. A windmill marked the location of the spot where the cane would soon be crushed to make the precious sugar and molasses, and the even more precious byproduct, rum.

Eden closed her eyes and raised her face toward the sun, defiantly risking the freckles so despised by the creamy-complexioned young women of social standing. A faint smile, an ironical one, tugged at her lips as she envisioned her mother's reaction to such willful and rebellious behavior. The smile faded when she felt a sudden, sharp pang of homesickness. She opened her eyes and stared despondently toward the beckoning waters of the Caribbean, wishing for all the world that she were back in London.

The carriage traveled down a neat, tree-shaded avenue, which would have looked eminently more at home in England than in this far-flung colonial outpost. "Little England" and "Bimshire" were affectionate nicknames for the island, whose growing resemblance to the mother country had been

13

brought about mainly by the prosperity of the sugarcane plantations. Two hundred years of British rule had ensured its civilization, but nothing could change the fact that it was, and would always remain, a special kingdom in its own right. While the English had managed to lay claim to its fertile shores and enslave a good many of its people, they could not entirely vanquish the spirit of exuberant independence which rested within each Bajan's heart.

It was this spirit that never failed to intrigue Eden. She felt a strange kinship with the natives, as if she, too, possessed a secret inner passion for life and all it held, a *joie de vivre* just waiting to burst free. But freedom was a privilege now denied her . . . and she had only herself to blame. It was just as her uncle had said, she mused with another inward sigh of discontent. She had ruined her chances for a life of her own choosing.

And her heart had been broken in the process.

Her gaze darkened again before sweeping back to where the land met the calm turquoise waters of the Caribbean. Here on the western side, the coastline was gracefully indented. Several charming little fishing villages lay perched on the edge of the sea. Children cavorted in the gentle waves, women chattered amiably with one another at the local market, and men either tended their nets or passed the morning in a leisurely, rather half-hearted game of cards.

Such sights were rare on the opposite side of the island, a wild and rugged place where the roaring surf of the Atlantic pounded the white sands lying beneath jagged, towering cliffs and etched out the caves so valued by smugglers, runaway slaves, and any others desirous of concealment—by those seeking escape of one kind or another.

Escape. Yearning for a release from her own less than satisfactory existence, Eden stole a glance at her uncle. His attention was riveted for the moment on the small, black leather account book he had drawn from the pocket of his waistcoat. She watched the pensive frown creasing his broad, aristocratic brow while he studied the most recent entries made by his manager, Edward Tallant—entries which concerned a human cargo instead of sugar. Eden was all too familiar with the book's contents.

"Surely you do not intend to purchase more slaves today?" she demanded, her voice full of mingled disbelief and disapproval. She set aside her personal troubles and took up the banner on a subject which never failed to elicit a fervent response from her. "I should think there were already enough poor souls to—"

"I did not seek your opinion," William had cut her off without looking up. "Nor do I intend to do so."

"Nevertheless, I shall offer it!" she retorted. Then, striving to adapt a more reasonable tone, she pointed out, "We've scarcely the space for those who live at the plantation now. Even your precious Edward would agree with me on that particular point. And was it not only last week that I heard you telling him there would be no need for extra field hands until harvest time?"

"Spare me your noble protestations, my dear." He finally met her gaze, his eyes every bit as cold and calculating as his heart. "They will avail you

15

nothing. I run the plantation as I see fit, and I will tolerate no interference on the part of some spoiled, overly imaginative young miss who should limit her thoughts and energies to household matters."

"Household matters?" Eden's green eyes bridled with indignation. "In the event it has escaped your notice, *dearest* Uncle, I have a mind, a mind which my father and mother encouraged me to use!"

"Therein lies the problem," William countered, scowling again. "I blame your mother, of course. She was always too flighty and self-willed for her own good, even as a child. Not that your father hasn't been amiss as well. No indeed, he should have beaten such nonsense out of you long before you reached a marriageable age."

"Intimidation is your solution to everything, isn't it? It is little wonder your slaves are so terrified! Well, I refuse to be bullied by you or anyone else!" As usual, her outrage made her brave—and reckless. "Whether by choice or not, I am a part of Abbeville Plantation! I have certainly witnessed enough of its 'workings' in these past several months to form my own opinions. And rest assured that I shall continue to speak out upon matters involving the treatment of my fellow human beings. You've no right to command my silence about this or anything else, no right at all!"

She was pushing him too far, and she knew there would be the very devil to pay for it later, but she could not hold her tongue. Not when the issue was one of such importance. And not when her temper had already been pushed to the limit by his stated intention to marry her off to some self-righteous

16

young fop who would bore her to tears before the wedding festivities had even commenced. No, thank you every much, she had already had *quite* enough of matrimony and the heartache it brought with it.

"You claim that slavery is necessary," she continued, determinedly steering the conversation back to the subject at hand, "but I say it is a barbarous practice that should be outlawed—"

"Never make the mistake of repeating such inflammatory nonsense in public," her uncle warned in a low, seething tone. "You will find no one of any consequence who shares your views. And you will very likely alienate our friends and associates to such an extent that you will no longer be received into their midst. Not even your connection to me will be able to save you should you decide to fancy yourself a proponent of emancipation!"

"But the slave trade was abolished almost seven years ago!"

"Abolished," he echoed disdainfully. "Come now, Eden, even you must know that ridiculous edict carried little weight here."

It was true, she reluctantly conceded in silence. Nothing had really changed. There were fewer slaves imported for auction in Bridgetown, of course, but the planters simply saw to it that all young females were "encouraged" to produce offspring on a yearly basis. And there were always a goodly number of ships' captains willing to risk fines or imprisonment by continuing to engage in the highly lucrative practice of transporting slaves.

"We'll have no more of these childish outbursts," decreed the man who held Eden's life in his hands.

"You are far too passionate for your own good, my dear girl. Either learn to control your emotions, or suffer the consequences." He thereupon returned his gaze to the book in his hands, leaving his beautiful young niece to glare helplessly across at the unyielding hauteur of his countenance.

Eden caught her lower lip between her teeth and looked away again. A dull, rosy color rode high on her cheeks, and her eyes fairly snapped with a mixture of resentment and angry frustration.

Just once, she told herself, she would have liked to have told William Stanhope precisely what she thought of him. She settled instead for maintaining a proud, obstinate silence for the duration of the journey.

They arrived at the outskirts of Bridgetown soon thereafter.

"To the market, Ezekiel!" William brusquely instructed the driver. "And do not tarry this time!"

The Bajan responded with a quick sideways nod and a murmured "Yes, master," then proceeded to guide the team of grays toward the whirlwind of activity that was Broad Street—a misnomer, since it was actually the narrowest of the city's avenues.

Crowded with horses and carriages and a veritable mass of humanity, this main thoroughfare was lined with a potpourri of architectural styles. Here could be seen public buildings constructed of locally hewn coral rock, houses built in the English style with glazed windows, a magnificent cathedral whose spires were often the first landmarks noted by approaching ships, and an endless array of shops, taverns, hotels, and other "establishments" whose employees were more than happy to provide solace

18

for the lonely sailors streaming ashore.

Eden always looked forward to these Saturday visits to the island's capital, for they were her one link with the outside world. During the week, her life was a continuous whirl of social obligations, filled with the same faces and the same small talk and the same fervent desire for something—*anything*—to happen. Bridgetown offered a glimpse of vastly different cultures, of places and people who had little in common with the planters' aristocracy. She reveled in the contrast.

Smiling briefly at the monument to Lord Horatio Nelson standing tall in the center of the island's own Trafalgar Square, she allowed her sparkling gaze to travel past the bronze statue to the Careenage, so named because of the fact that its sloping, warehouse-lined banks resounded with the clamor of boat repair. It was also the berthing place for small ships arriving from various territories of the Caribbean. Cargo was loaded and unloaded at all hours of the day in the miniature harbor, while passengers hurriedly made their way along its congested wharves to immerse themselves in the bustle of the city, or to secure passage on an outbound vessel.

Farther out, where the larger ships were anchored, the waters of Carlisle Bay shone crystal clear and beautifully calm. Tides and currents made the island easily accessible; until the war, it had not been unusual to see American ships among those in the harbor. The escalating conflict had actually brought about an increase in trade throughout the Caribbean, in spite of the ever-present danger of attack.

"Dolphin! Dolphin!"

19

"Fish, hey!"

"Nuseful limes!"

The piercing cries of the sidewalk vendors rose in the aromatic breeze as the carriage continued on its way. William, growing increasingly impatient with their slow progress, proceeded to deliver a sharp, undeserved word of rebuke to Ezekiel. Eden turned her head and spied a well-dressed young woman, parasol in hand, standing alone before the Royal Navy Hotel. It was obvious from the look on this woman's softly feminine features that she was a bit overwhelmed by all the commotion going on about her.

"Jamaica!" Eden called out a greeting. Smiling warmly when the pretty, fair-haired vision caught sight of her, she leaned over the edge of the carriage to inquire above the surrounding din, "Where is your father?"

"Oh, Eden, I am afraid he has gone inside to speak to that odious Mr. Pettigrew!" replied Jamaica Harding in distress. "He should have been out ages ago!" She brightened in the next instant and asked Eden, "Will you be in attendance at the Stewarts' tonight?"

"Yes! Will you?"

"Of course! I am to help Charlotte and Mary present the entertainment! I daresay you will be much surprised!"

Eden smiled again and lifted a hand in farewell. She watched as Jamaica's father, Colonel Harding, suddenly emerged from the hotel to collect his daughter. He was a gruff, often imperious man, but basically a good-hearted one. Widowed more than twelve years ago, he cherished his only child above everything.

Jamaica was entirely worthy of his intense regard, Eden mused fondly. She was both kind and charitable, almost to a fault. The petite blonde had been a true friend to her from the very beginning; unlike the vast majority of the other young ladies, Jamaica had never once pressed her for information about the scandal which had forced her into exile upon these shores.

Exile, her mind repeated. An apt description for her present circumstances. And as long as the war continued, there could be no possible hope of deliverance. . . .

Her uncle's voice broke in on her thoughts. "You will do me the favor of remaining silent."

"Remaining silent?" She turned to him with a frown of puzzlement.

"While we are at the market," he elaborated tersely. "I've no wish to be embarrassed by any further demonstrations of your misplaced loyalties." His thick, gloved fingers tightened their grip upon the walking stick, as if he were wrestling with the temptation to give his anger full vent. "I have not forgotten what happened the last time. Had I believed there would be a repetition of the distasteful incident, I would not have allowed you to come along. If you dare to interfere—"

"Am I not at least allowed to speak to our 'esteemed' acquaintances then?" she inquired, her voice laced with noticeable sarcasm. "Surely it would be unforgivably rude for me to ignore them altogether. Indeed, Uncle, I cannot think you would find it at all agreeable to have your own niece labeled a *poseur.*"

"Mind your tongue, damn it!" William ground out. His face had turned a dull shade of red, and his narrowed gaze promised retribution. "Your parents have charged me with your care. The arrangement is one neither of us sought. Nevertheless, I have agreed to do my duty. As long as you continue living under my roof, you will do as I say. And you will not—you will *not,* do you hear?—make a spectacle of yourself each time I deem it necessary to purchase additional slaves!"

Eden started to reply, but the angry retort which rose to her lips was never granted release, for Ezekiel was already pulling the team to a halt beneath the lofty, heavily branched shade of a tamarind tree. They had reached their destination.

"Hold there, you spranksious beasts," Ezekiel murmured to the two lively grays. His voice was low and pleasantly tinged wih the evidence of his Caribbean heritage. To William, he announced with all due reverence, "The market, master."

"I can see that, you fool!" William waited impatiently while the young footman hurried around to open the door, then pulled his considerable girth upright and alighted from the carriage. It was obvious he meant for Eden to remain seated. "You will wait here until my business is completed," he instructed her, glowering anew as he tugged the front brim of his hat well forward.

"Wait here?" she echoed in disbelief. Her emerald gaze made a hasty sweep of her surroundings before returning to her stern-faced guardian. Then, bridling with annoyance, she inquired, "Would you have everyone think me so faint of heart?"

"Better that than wanting of sense!" Without another word, he pivoted about and marched stiffly away.

Eden glared at the ample, retreating target his back made, torn between the urge to defiantly give chase and the desire to sit and enjoy his absence for the next half hour or so. She settled back against the leather cushion with an audible sigh of displeasure.

Eyeing the numerous other carriages and their occupants, she couldn't help but be reminded again of home. The gentlemen in their top hats and tail-coats, the ladies in their white, high-waisted frocks and fashionable bonnets, the liveried drivers and footmen—all were so indelibly British. There was little to indicate, at least from outward appearances, that they realized themselves to be strolling elegantly about on a tiny spot of land in the West Indies instead of in the midst of a summer garden party at a country estate near London.

There was, however, nothing too pointedly British about the market itself, Eden reflected as she looked toward the center of activity a short distance away. Crowded with people from many different nation-alities and walks of life, the broad, grass-carpeted grounds lay just beyond the city proper. Wooden stalls, topped by brightly colored canvas awnings, had been set up to provide a sizable army of merchants with the means to ply their wares. Here were offered for sale fruits and vegetables, fresh fish, strong spirits, silks from the Far East, locally made garments and tapestries, baskets large and small, books, jewelry, perfumes, and a dizzying assortment of other articles and services.

The market was as popular with the lower classes as with the planters. On this one day out of seven, a lowly fisherman could mingle with a lord and his lady. It was this rare circumstance of equality that gave Eden a sense of excitement; today was no exception. She certainly wasn't going to pass up an opportunity for adventure, however brief it might be.

"Ezekiel?" she rose purposefully to her feet.

"Yes, mistress?" He shifted about to gaze down at her.

"If my uncle should return before I do, would you please tell him I have taken it in my mind to pay a visit to a few of the merchants?"

"Oh no, mistress," advised Ezekiel, his countenance displaying extreme worriment, "don't trouble trouble till trouble troubles you."

"I shall keep that in mind," she replied, trying hard not to smile at this peculiar bit of wholly Bajan philosophy. "But I *am* going." She extended her hand to the young footman, who favored her with a quick, respectful nod before assisting her down. "Thank you, Zach."

"My Betsy, she say Mistress Della's conkies be the best," he offered with a twinkle in his eye. Referring to a steamed, breadlike concoction made with cornmeal, coconut, sweet potato and spices, he made no effort to disguise the hope that Eden would see fit to bring a sampling of the popular cakes back with her.

"Then Mistress Della's shall be the first establishment I visit," she promised, her mouth twitching and her own eyes aglow with merry humor.

Shaking out her skirts, she made a slight adjustment to her bonnet before setting off across the wide, tree-dotted expanse of lawn. Social convention made it necessary for her to pause and exchange a few polite words with the women, most of them older, who had accompanied their husbands to town and were now perfectly content to sit within the shaded comfort of their carriages and gossip with their nearest neighbor. They were only too happy to inquire about Eden's health, about her family's health, and about her future plans with Donald Parkington-Hughes. She was only too happy to turn their more personal questions aside with a forced smile and a polite good day.

It took considerably longer than she would have wished to reach the market. Another successful run of the gauntlet, she thought, breathing an inward sigh of relief when she finally approached the first line of stalls. It wasn't that she disliked her sister Englishwomen; quite the contrary. Some of them had been very gracious to her, very gracious indeed given the fact that she was tainted with more than a hint of notoriety. The irony of it all was that her parents had hoped to avoid a scandal by packing her off to this faraway tropical outpost.

Her gaze clouded with pain for a moment, then sparkled to a vibrant, clear emerald hue once more. The sights, sounds, and smells of the market provided a veritable feast for her senses. She could not possibly remain downcast.

The swirling breeze teased at her skirts while the leisurely stream of market-goers made a path around her. She reached up to tug the bonnet from her head, initially unaware that in so doing she prompted several gentlemen to stop dead in their tracks and fasten their appreciative masculine gazes upon her loveliness. When she did notice their rapt attention, she colored faintly and turned away.

Never having considered herself a great beauty— her nose tilted up too much for her own taste, and her figure was almost indecently curvaceous—she was in truth oblivious to the sort of impact she had upon the opposite sex. She knew only that men had courted her with a vengeance since her first introduction into society nearly three years ago; she had always suspected that their ardor was due more to her father's wealth and influence than to her own charms. Her suspicions had ultimately been proven correct. . . .

"Dash it all, don't start *that* again!" she muttered in furious self-recrimination. Her fingers threatening to crush the straw bonnet, she resolutely squared her shoulders and immersed herself in the commotion at hand.

As promised, she first sought out Mistress Della's stall and purchased a generous supply of freshly made conkies for Zach. The delicious aroma had been a beacon, reminding her all too well that she had eaten little for breakfast. She willingly surrendered to temptation and sampled one of the cakes as she pressed onward through the jubilant melee.

Vendors and merchants called out to her, some holding up their wares to better display them while others tried to entice her patronage with a cheerful singsong of information.

26

"Pudding 'n' souse!"

"Cou cou here, mistress!"

"Chick and pepper wine!"

"Come and see what I have for you, fairest of the fair!" one bearded tradesman hailed her with a flourish of shimmering fabric. "Silks from Madagascar! The most beautiful in the world! A fitting tribute to your beauty, lovely lady!"

Eden smiled and shook her head, musing to herself that the fellow no doubt employed the same outrageous flattery with every woman that walked by. For some, vanity was the key; for others, it was greed. Life had already taught her that.

She took her time browsing amongst the stalls. Pausing whenever something caught her eye or whenever someone she knew happened to recognize her in the midst of the crowd, she was blissfully ignorant of the fact that she was moving ever closer to where her uncle stood waiting for the weekly slave auction to begin.

"We've a special bargain for you today, me lords!" the auctioneer announced in a loud, rasping tone that was full of avarice and excitement. Perched atop a narrow stone platform which had already witnessed more than a century of human anguish, Honest John Biddles was a small man whose close-set eyes darted with calculating swiftness over the faces of the prospective buyers. "A special bargain!" he reiterated, his grimy fingers curling about the whipstock in his hand. "A special bargain to tempt the devil 'imself!"

Hoping to build suspense and thereby increase interest, he did not immediately continue. His mouth curved into a broad, yellow-toothed grin. Several long moments passed. Finally, when the crowd of planters had grown restless and an irritated murmur was starting to rise above the other sounds of the market, Biddles hastened over to the edge of the weathered stone block. He motioned to the two burly, coarse-featured men who waited there to do his bidding.

"Bring 'im up!" he growled by way of command. He watched as the two obediently hurried behind the platform.

Having already designated which of the prisoners would be offered for sale first, he could only hope he wasn't making a mistake. These fancy bastards he dealt with every week could be a troublesome lot. It might just turn out they'd not like it, the best being auctioned off in the beginning and all. Could be they'd be disappointed that the others weren't nearly so strong and pleasing to the eye? Still, he reasoned silently, there was something to be said about whetting their appetites for more. His beady little eyes gleamed with black-hearted pleasure at the thought of the pretty profit he'd make that day.

"Caught right off the north coast, 'e was!" Biddles gleefully informed his audience when he resumed his place in the center of the platform. "And there be more after 'im! Just you wait and see, me fine lords, just you wait and see what Honest John Biddles 'as for you!"

As if on cue, the two men reappeared. They forced their captive up the steps. It was no easy task. Although he was bound securely in chains, he was nearly more than they could handle.

"Upon my soul, he's white!" one of the well-dressed spectators gasped in startlement.

"Where the deuce did you get him?" another demanded of the auctioneer. Others joined in with exclamations of surprise and disbelief, prompting Biddles to raise his hands in an urgent plea for silence.

"Like I told you, me lords, 'e was caught off the north coast!" He curled the whip in his hands and waited until the prisoner had been forced to a halt beside him before announcing, "American, 'e is, and a privateer to boot!"

"The devil you say!" William Stanhope murmured. He and his fellow plantation owners stared at the man standing so tall and proud and forcefully defiant before them in his chains.

He towered above Biddles, towered above his two guards as well, and there was nothing in either his stance or his demeanor to indicate that he could ever be tamed into submission. Half-naked he was, with naught but a fitted pair of dark blue seaman's trousers covering the lean expanse of his lower body. The powerful, bronzed muscles of his chest and arms gave evidence that here was a man who had never been content to lead the soft life favored by so many of his contemporaries. He was a man who knew what it was to work hard, a man who took whatever he wanted from all that life had to offer.

His thick, dark brown hair, cut short and streaked golden by the sun, waved rakishly across his forehead. Eyes of a deep cobalt blue gazed ahead with a piercing intensity, while a pair of firmly chiseled lips tightened beneath a nose that was perfectly suited to the rest of his face. To say that he was striking would have been an understatement—he looked every inch the bold American savage he was.

His rugged, handsome features were impassive at the present moment, but there was no denying the murderous fury contained within the gold-flecked depths of his gaze. And though he had as yet to utter a single word, there were those in the crowd who felt a sudden, involuntary shiver of fear course down their spines.

"What does the military have to say about this?" a recently arrived Colonel Harding demanded of Biddles. His disapproval was apparent. "Blast it, man, if you've taken it upon yourself to cheat His Majesty out of another possible informer, I'll see *you* in irons before the day is through!"

"Well now, me lord, it might please you to know I've been given permission from the lieutenant-general 'imself to 'dispose' of the prisoners!" Biddles assured him with another grin. "It's not against the King's laws to arrange indentures, now, is it? And bless me, it's not against the King's laws for Honest John Biddles to get a little something for 'is own trouble. There be six in all," he revealed, turning back to the crowd. "Six fine, 'ealthy young bucks to work or breed, depending on what it is you've a need for!"

"This is nothing more than white slavery!" Colonel Harding protested angrily. He failed to glimpse the sudden glimmer of respect in the prisoner's eyes.

"It's war, me lord!" Biddles corrected, satisfied when several of the planters nodded their heads in agreement. He gestured toward the man in chains and went on with his business. "This one's the captain—'e be the best of the lot! All you've to do is look at 'im to see he'll be able to do the work of two men! This side of thirty, I'll warrant, and plenty of good years still left in 'im! God strike me dead if I ain't telling the truth! Now let's get on with the bidding! Which of you fine lords is—"

"What is the term of indenture?" someone near the front queried in a deceptively bored manner.

"Seven years, me lord!"

Colonel Harding spun about in disgust and pushed his way back through the crowd. Everyone else remained, either out of curiosity or from a genuine desire to own one of the few white slaves on the island. There was an added attraction, in that the six men being auctioned off by Honest John Biddles were enemies.

Not only that, they were privateers. And privateers were generally acknowledged to be the worst kind of scoundrels, for hadn't they chosen to sneak about like thieves in the night instead of fighting honorably? Men such as these served on *both* sides of the conflict, but the planters were not of a mind to consider anything save their own interests. Yes indeed, the war had brought with it decided benefits.

The bidding began, and quickly intensified. The man whose very future was being sold remained silent and motionless. None could know the white-hot rage simmering within him, nor the fierce resolve to be free at all costs.

Eden, meanwhile, wandered innocently nearer. She had succeeded in bargaining with a local woman

31

over a large sweetgrass hamper from the Carolinas, but now began to regret her success. It certainly wasn't as if she needed another basket, and the blasted thing seemed to become more unwieldy with each passing second.

"I shall never learn," she sighed, frowning at her own impulsiveness.

She grasped the handle, which had already come loose, and hoisted the basket so it rested beneath her arm. Lifting her hat to her head with her other hand, she was surprised to catch sight of Colonel Harding stalking past, obviously disgruntled. She thought about following him to find Jamaica, but wisely decided against it. From the look on his face, it was doubtful Jamaica would be remaining long enough for any conversation.

With a mental shrug, she pivoted about and set a course for the last row of stalls. It was then that she heard Honest John Biddles, in a voice loud enough to wake the dead, extolling the physical superiority of the "strong young animal" being offered for sale on the auction block.

Eden could not say afterward what made her direct her steps toward such loathsome activity, the very activity she had been determined to avoid. Nor could she explain, even to herself, what drew her ever closer to where a handful of men were engaging in a heated frenzy of bidding to determine which one of them would claim ownership of the American for the next seven years.

Fate or free will, she could not say. The only thing that mattered was that she did make her way through the crowd—and in so doing set eyes upon the one man she had prayed never to see again.

She stopped so abruptly that the basket tumbled to the ground. A sharp gasp followed. Her emerald gaze widened in a mixture of shock, incredulity, and something else she refused to acknowledge.

"Roark!"

His name was nothing more than a ragged whisper on her lips. She raised a trembling hand to her breast, where her heart pounded with such violence she was afraid she would faint for the first time in her life.

Two

Roark St. Claire. Dear God, it couldn't be. It couldn't be!

Eden struggled to regain control of her highly erratic breathing. Shaken to the core of her very being, she stood as if rooted to the spot, her face drained of all color and her wide, spellbound gaze riveted upon the magnificent rogue on the auction block.

"Come now, me lords," Honest John Biddles was urging, displaying that yellow-toothed smile of his, "surely you've not lost the stomach for this yet! Why, the captain 'ere's worth twice what you be offering me for 'im!"

"Mayhap you've set his value too high," one of the more skeptical aristocrats opined. Raising his quizzing glass to one eye, he frowned and shook his head. "The fellow looks to be a great deal of trouble to me."

"That's true enough," seconded a portly gentleman only a few steps away from Eden. "Why, how are we to know the wild rascal won't slit our throats the first chance he gets?"

"There are methods by which even the most recalcitrant slaves can be controlled," William Stanhope interjected at this point. With an air of seeming indifference, he lifted a well-manicured hand and upped the bid. "Six hundred."

Eden's eyes flew to her uncle in horror.

Roark St. Claire's gaze flickered briefly downward to rest upon the same target.

"Six hundred!" Biddles repeated, his own eyes virtually leaping into flame with that renewed burst of greed. He flung out an arm toward Roark. "That be more like it, but 'e's still—"

"Six hundred and fifty!" someone else offered.

The bidding intensified once more, but Eden took no notice of it. She looked dazedly back to Roark.

A nightmare, she insisted within the benumbed recesses of her mind. This could be nothing more than a nightmare.

She was scarcely aware of the moment when she began to move again. Her legs, only moments before having threatened to buckle beneath her, seemed to have taken on a will of their own. They carried her forward, through the outer fringes of the crowd and perilously near to her uncle. Like a moth to flame, she was drawn slowly, relentlessly closer to the man who stood so proud and unyielding before his enemies.

How could this have happened? she wondered, her pulses racing with alarming swiftness. Roark St. Claire *here,* here on these distant shores. What had brought him to this cruel moment in time? Merciful heavens, it was beyond belief, seeing him bound in chains and offered up for sale like any other slave. Fate was surely laughing at them both . . . making him pay for the sin of betrayal . . . making her pay for the folly of being so easily deceived. What other explanation could there be?

All the painful memories she had tried her best to forget now came flooding back to haunt her. She was transported back in time, back to the fateful, warm summer night, some ten months ago, when Roark St. Claire had first entered her life—and had forever altered its course.

If she had only known.

He had set out to conquer, and she had surrendered her heart completely. She had never met a man like him before. Truth be told, there *was* no other man like him.

As God is my witness, Eden, I'll not let anyone or anything come between us. Those words, spoken on the occasion of their last few happy moments together, still burned in her ears. She had believed him. Like some foolish, naive young schoolgirl, she had believed him.

"A thousand pounds!" Honest John Biddles appealed. He touched Roark's broad, naked chest with the coiled whip in his hand, then hastily drew it back in wide-eyed apprehension when the other man's steely gaze cut right through him. Retreating to a safer distance, he cleared his throat and cast what he hoped was another encouraging smile at his wealthy patrons. "Which of you fine lords will make it a thousand?"

Eden had approached to within a few feet of the platform by now. She was at present the only woman in the crowd, a vision in white amidst a sea of tall hats and dark tailcoats. Although Roark continued to stare straight ahead in stony defiance, it would have been impossible for him not to catch sight of her eventually.

She was unprepared for what happened when he did.

"Like as not there'll be no others so fine and strong as 'im on these shores!" the auctioneer prompted, beginning to fear that he would not get as much as he wanted. His narrow, expectant gaze returned to the man he considered his best hope. William Stanhope could usually be counted on when it came to slaves as special as this one.

"One thousand pounds," Eden's uncle obliged him by finally offering.

For the second time that day, Roark's gaze sought out the haughty Englishman . . . and seized instead on someone else.

Every muscle in Roark St. Claire's hard body suddenly tensed. A tight expression—perhaps of pain—crossed his rugged features, and his penetrating, deep blue eyes glowed with an almost savage light before meeting the luminous green of Eden's.

An invisible, startlingly powerful current passed between them. Eden suffered a sharp intake of breath and felt hot color washing over her. Her gaze hastily fell beneath the scorching onslaught of Roark's. She could literally feel the way his gaze, bold and warm and full of raw emotion, traveled the entire length of her trembling body. Battling the highly tempting urge to turn coward and run, she forced herself to look up at him again.

It was a mistake. The moment their gazes met and locked, she was trapped for good. Had she but known it, she had just sealed her own fate.

Setting aside, at least for the moment, her vow to hate him, she took a deep breath and found herself wondering how she had ever hoped to be able to forget such a man. Heaven help her, but he was even more handsome than she had remembered. And more splendidly, forcefully masculine—in every sense of the word. His current attire, or rather lack of it, left very little to the imagination.

She swallowed hard, her eyes wandering in irresistible fascination across the bronzed, lithely muscled nakedness of his upper body before drifting downward. She remembered all too well what it had felt like to be crushed against his virile warmth, to have his strong arms wrapped possessively about her slender curves and his firm lips captivating the pliant, completely willing softness of hers.

A sudden tremor shook her, and she was dismayed to feel the familiar yearning, so long repressed, blazing to life once more. With an inward groan, she blushed at the utter wickedness of her thoughts and quickly raised her eyes to Roark's again.

She was shocked to glimpse a spark of devilment lurking within his gaze; she was even more unnerved by the irony in the faint smile playing about his mouth. Her color deepened to a fiery rose. Dear Lord above, it was as though he possessed the ability to read her mind. . . .

"No more, me lords? No more than twelve 'undred?" Biddles pleaded for the third time.

"Damn it, man, we haven't got all day!" William

38

Stanhope complained irascibly. The bidding had already surpassed what he was willing to pay, and he was anything but a good loser. "Sell the thieving bastard and let us see the others!"

There was a quiet roar of general agreement following this suggestion. Biddles, though naturally reluctant to admit defeat in his goal to drive the price even higher, consoled himself with the thought of the money still to come from the other five. He raised his whip in a dramatic gesture of finality and opened his mouth to declare the prisoner sold.

Eden emerged from her daze at last. Her bright emerald gaze shifted to the auctioneer, then swept anxiously across the faces of the men around her. Hidden as she was in the crowd, she could not see her uncle, but she knew he was not far away. She glanced back at Roark. His eyes seemed to bore down into her very soul.

There was no time to think, no time to ponder the wisdom of her actions. As if from a great distance, she heard Honest John Biddles repeat the winning bid.

"Twelve 'undred it be! Twelve 'undred for—"

"Twelve hundred and fifty pounds!"

Eden was startled by the sound of her own voice. She watched, wide-eyed and breathless, as the smile playing about Roark's lips slowly broadened.

Audible gasps of surprise rose in the air. No woman had ever before participated in the slave auction in Bridgetown. No woman had ever dared.

"Twelve 'undred and fifty, mistress?" the auctioneer echoed in almost comical disbelief.

"Twelve hundred and fifty pounds!" she reiterated with as much dignity as she could muster under the circumstances. She found it impossible to keep looking at Roark and maintain any real measure of composure. Spinning abruptly about, she faced the crowd of disapproving males and challenged, "Will any man among you bid higher?"

"*Eden!*"

It was her uncle. He came charging brusquely to the front, his expression thunderous and his voice edged with barely controlled fury. Eden had seldom seen him as angry as he was now. Nevertheless, she faced the brunt of his wrath squarely.

"Yes, Uncle William?" she responded with admirable calm.

"What the devil do you think you're doing?" he demanded in a snarling undertone, furiously conscious of their audience. His face was quite red beneath the wide, curling brim of his hat. And if looks could kill, there was no doubt his beautiful young niece would have breathed her last, there and then.

"I am purchasing this slave, Uncle." She raised her head proudly, then committed the ultimate sin of turning her back on him entirely. "I believe, sir, that the bid stands at twelve hundred and fifty pounds," she coolly reminded Honest John. Still refusing to look at Roark, she was painfully aware of his proximity. She could feel the heat emanating from his body, could feel as well the deadly power waiting to be unleashed.

"That it does, mistress! That it does!" the nervous auctioneer hastened to agree. Anxious to be done with the ticklish matter, he raised his hand again. It mattered not to him where the money came from;

40

Lucifer himself could have offered it for all he cared. "Twelve 'undred and fifty pounds! Twelve 'undred and fifty pounds, and a right fancy bargain the young lady be getting for 'erself! Twelve 'undred and fifty—"

"Eden, I forbid you to do this!" decreed William. He seized her arm in a punishing grip and forced her about to face him again.

Roark's eyes narrowed to mere slits of vengeful rage. Had it not been for the chains binding him, he would gladly have beaten the man to a bloody pulp for his rough treatment of Eden. He forced himself to hold back, but made a silent vow to make certain "Uncle William" learned a few manners at the first available opportunity.

"I have already done it!" Eden declared, angrily jerking her arm free.

"And just how do you propose to pay? You'll get no money from me, damn it, not one blasted farthing!"

"I've my own money and well you know it!" She rounded on Honest John and demanded, "Well? Is it finished? Have I won the bid?"

"Yes, mistress!" To make it official, he hurriedly uncoiled his whip and gave it a good, resounding crack on the stone. "Sold! The best of the lot 'ere be sold to the young lady!"

There was a rumble of disapproval from the crowd, but Eden didn't hear it. She was too overwhelmed by what had just transpired. Her astonished gaze moved from Honest John to her uncle, then finally back up to Roark.

All traces of amusement had vanished from his

41

expression now. His eyes had taken on the look of cold steel, and there was a certain, uncompromising grimness about the set of his mouth. It was as if he had suddenly turned into a stranger.

Eden's eyes grew very round and kindled with something akin to fear. She shuddered involuntarily.

"Do you have any idea what you've done?" raged William, on the verge of apoplexy as a result of his ward's embarrassingly public display of willfulness. "Damn it, girl, do you have any idea at all?"

She did, of course . . . she had a very good idea. And as realization began to sink in, she felt a growing sense of horrified disbelief.

Heaven help her, she had just bought her own husband.

Three

Eden watched as Roark was led down from the auction block. It occurred to her then that he might have suffered some injury as a result of his captivity, but she saw no evidence of it. He appeared to be every bit as hale and hearty as the last time she had seen him—perhaps even more so. These past ten months had apparently been a good deal easier for him than for her, she mused resentfully.

"Rest assured, you insolent scoundrel, that I shall see you paid for this!" William vowed to the auctioneer, treating him to a menacing glare.

"'Tis me own way of thinking, me lord," countered Biddles, grinning unrepentantly. He turned and extended his grimy hand toward Eden. "If it please you, me lady, might I be troubling you for the twelve 'undred and fifty pounds?"

"I . . . I'm afraid I don't have it with me at the moment," she stammered. Her cheeks flaming, she allowed her gaze to fall for a moment before drawing herself proudly erect and telling him, "But I give you my solemn oath that you shall have it before nightfall.''

"Honest John Biddles don't make it a 'abit of granting credit, me lady."

"Then you will simply have to make an exception!"

"Haven't you caused enough of a scene for one day?" William ground out. Furious that so many were witness to his inability to control his wayward niece, he tightened his grip upon the handle of his fancy walking stick until his knuckles turned white beneath the soft leather of his gloves. "I'll give you the money, damn it!" he told Biddles. With stiff, angry movements he reached into his coat pocket and withdrew a small bag of gold coins. He counted out the correct amount, then thrust the payment at the auctioneer. "There! I shall send my manager back for the man this afternoon. See that he's provided with a bath and decent clothing before then!"

"But, Uncle," Eden tried to protest, "surely you—"

"Not one word, do you hear?" he hissed, taking her arm again. He schooled his features into a tight-lipped, unapproachable expression and began propelling her through the crowd.

Eden ventured a hasty glance back at Roark. He gave her the merest ghost of a smile, his deep blue eyes holding a silent promise. The last thing she saw before he disappeared from view was the disturbing sight of his two burly captors shoving him roughly behind the platform. An inexplicable pang of remorse tugged at her heart.

Why hadn't she spoken up? she silently berated herself. Why hadn't she revealed their connection?

44

Perhaps in so doing, she might have spared him further humiliation.

You loathe and despise the man . . . why should you care what happens to him? that inner voice of hers pointed out. It was true. She had vowed never to forgive him, to someday, somehow make him pay for what he had done to her. Indeed, wasn't this the perfect opportunity for revenge?

Her slave. It was still beyond comprehension how it had all come about. But the fact remained—Roark St. Claire was her slave. She *owned* him.

"I hope you're satisfied with yourself," William remarked once they were back at the carriage. His portly, black-clad frame quivered from head to toe with the force of his displeasure. "How dare you defy me in this! Was it not only a short time ago you were spouting that emancipation nonsense of yours? I can scarce believe you had the audacity, the utter *impudence* to stand bold as brass before my colleagues and shame me by offering up a bid for a—"

"Will you not at least allow me the chance to explain?" demanded Eden, though she had no earthly idea how she would go about it.

"Explain? What possible explanation can there be? Damn it, young lady, you have just forced me to spend the ungodly sum of twelve hundred and fifty pounds for a man who will in all likelihood prove to be a thorn in my side for the next seven years!"

"You attempted to purchase him yourself, did you not? And I shall repay you as soon as we get home!"

"That is beside the point!" He practically tossed her up into the carriage, then hoisted his own considerable girth to the other seat.

45

Zach, wistfully eyeing the aromatic bag of conkies in Eden's hand, hastened to close the door. Ezekiel gathered up the reins and set the horses in motion with a gentle flick of his wrists. Eden's hat flew off, but she was not of a mind to care, and her uncle was certainly not of a mind to go back for it. Within seconds, they were heading down Broad Street on their way back to Abbeville Plantation.

"Whatever possessed you to do it?" William continued to rage. He grew increasingly scornful in his attack. "If it's a man you want, you've only to crook your little finger to make young Parkington-Hughes come running. I'll wager he'd be far more suited to your taste than that villain you were so hot to—"

"How dare you!" gasped Eden. Deeply affronted, she turned a blazing look of denial upon him. "Why, I—that isn't the reason at all!"

"Then what, might I inquire, *is?*"

It was a reasonable enough question, and yet Eden could not think of a reasonable enough answer. She didn't know why, but she found herself extremely reluctant to tell him the truth. Although her uncle knew certain "particulars" of her brief, unfortunate marriage, he did not know her husband's name. She suddenly realized that she couldn't bear to reveal Roark's true identity to him. Perhaps it was because she was too ashamed to let him know she had pledged her love to such an unscrupulous rogue. Perhaps it was because she hoped to spare her family any further pain. That her uncle would inform them of this latest development, she had little doubt.

She closed her eyes for a moment and pressed a

hand to her temple. It had all happened so fast. . . .

"You wouldn't understand," she finally murmured. Neither did she, she added to herself. She didn't understand one blasted thing about the events of the past quarter of an hour.

"You're too much of a lady to put a name to it, is that it?" William suggested with a sneer. "I might have known you'd do something like this sooner or later. After all, it was your 'attraction' to an unsuitable member of the opposite sex that brought about your banishment from home, was it not? Whatever the case, I've absolutely no intention of allowing you to own the man. There will be enough talk when word of your disgraceful behavior gets around. By damn, I'm not going to have it said that my niece keeps a healthy young buck like that American for her own personal use!"

"Then what are you planning to do with him?"

"I'm planning to keep him, of course. He'll work in the fields, the same as the other slaves."

Work in the fields? she echoed silently, her troubled gaze widening in surprise again. She couldn't envision a proud man like Roark St. Claire toiling beneath the hot sun from dawn to dusk. Unscrupulous rogue he might be, but no human being alive deserved the cruel fate awaiting him. Hard, backbreaking work it would be, with only one day out of seven in which to rest. His life would be a misery. And she would be on hand to witness it.

Though she tried to convince herself that he had earned this punishment, she failed dismally. No matter what he had done, no matter how much he had hurt her, she could not in all honesty say that she

47

was glad for the misfortune which had befallen him.

She settled back against the leather cushion with a long, pent-up sigh, relieved that her uncle had lapsed into reproachful silence. Once again, her entire world had been turned upside down by Roark St. Claire. Never in her wildest imagination would she have expected to see him here, and most especially not in his present circumstances. The memory of their parting, so fraught with love's betrayal, returned to haunt her anew. Throughout these many long months she had endeavored to forget, only to forget. There was no hope of that now.

Why, oh why had she bought him? she lamented, drawing in a ragged breath and flinging a look of helpless confusion up toward the heavens. Even more important, *what the devil was she going to do now?*

The solution to her dilemma had still not presented itself by the time the plantation's manager returned from Bridgetown with the new slave. It was nearing four o'clock in the afternoon. The sun hung low in the western sky, a windswept tumble of clouds offering the benevolent promise of evening showers. As always, they would provide a welcome respite from the heat.

It would be another full hour yet before the slaves could stop work for the day. There were endless duties to be performed about the plantation, for it was a world unto itself—aside from the sugarcane, livestock had to be cared for, wheat and fruit and vegetables had to be cultivated, buildings and wagons must be kept in good repair. Not even the children were exempt from work; they were charged with simple tasks as soon as they were able to walk. William Stanhope was obsessed with the notion of making his plantation the finest on the island. He would not tolerate idleness among his slaves.

From Eden, however, he expected something entirely different. She was to be the lady of the manor at all times, acting as hostess for dinner parties and other social events, filling her hours with embroidery and music and the like. The role did not suit her in the least. It never had. Even in England, she had never been content to simply sit and let the world pass her by. Her parents, thank God, had always granted her a remarkable amount of freedom to choose the manner in which she lived her life.

And so it was that, in spite of her exalted position as the master's niece, she insisted upon taking an active part in the daily routine at Abbeville Plantation. On frequent occasions, she donned an apron and helped the cook prepare meals, spent an entire morning working on her hands and knees in one of the many gardens, or served as a general angel of mercy to the slaves. Her uncle was forever chiding her for such "woefully common" tendencies, but she disregarded his objections and went her own way.

She had just emerged from the rear garden with Betsy when the manager's wagon rumbled past. Catching sight of Roark shackled to an iron ring in the wagon bed, she came to a sudden halt and nearly dropped the basket of cut flowers she held. She could feel the guilty color flying to her face, and she was dismayed to realize that Betsy was frowning at her in puzzled concern.

"Mistress? There be something wrong?"

"No, Betsy, nothing's wrong!" she hastily denied. She thrust the basket into the other woman's startled hands. "Take these, if you will, and return to the house. I . . . I've some business to take care of."

"Business, my lady?" Betsy, ever curious, eyed her young mistress narrowly. "What kind of business?"

"Never mind, Betsy. Please, just do as I ask!"

Without waiting for a response, Eden gathered up her full skirts and set off across the beautifully kept grounds in front of the great house. She had no idea what she was going to say to Roark or how she was going to say it; she knew only that it was imperative he be cautioned at once against revealing the truth of their relationship. She couldn't run the risk of having him announce to one and all that she was his wife—a wife in name only, but a wife just the same.

Strangely enough, the possibility of *his* exposing her shameful secret hadn't even occurred to her until after she had arrived home from the market. He would gain nothing by imparting such scandalous information, of course, but he might do it just to spite her. Yes, she thought bitterly, she could well believe him capable of further treachery on her behalf.

A sudden knot tightened in her stomach. She quickened her approach, casting a brief, apprehensive glance about her before looking back to where the manager had already climbed down from the wagon seat to unchain Roark. The two men, well-matched in stature but not in strength, stood facing one another when Eden slowed to a stop a short distance away.

Roark's back was toward her. He was clothed now

in a loose, unbleached muslin shirt and trousers of coarsely woven brown cotton—much the same as any other slave—but there was still an undeniable air of authority about him, a certain supremacy which Eden knew owed its origin to something other than outward appearances.

As if sensing her presence, he suddenly tensed. Then, oblivious to the fact that the manager was still in the process of removing his bonds, he turned almost leisurely about.

His eyes darkened when they fell upon the woman he had once pledged to love forever. His handsome face remained inscrutable, but there was a raging inferno of emotion smoldering deep within him. Without uttering a single word, he struck a very real chord of alarm in the heart of his long-lost bride.

She paled beneath his burning gaze. Her courage threatened to desert her entirely. *Sweet Saint Christopher, how am I going to be able to go through with this?*

"Would you be wanting something, Lady Eden?" asked the bemused witness to this strange, silent reunion.

Eden started guiltily. Her eyes flew to Edward Tallant, the plantation's manager. A dark, slender man some fifteen years older than herself, he was frowning at her the same way Betsy had done a few moments earlier.

"Wanting something?" she echoed. A fiery blush crept up to her face, and her gaze fell abruptly toward the ground. "Yes, Edward, I should like to have a word with . . . with the new bondsman."

"A word with him, Lady Eden?" the startled

manager sought confirmation. "Why, he's a dangerous man, and your uncle would—"

"My uncle doesn't have to know!" She smiled
appealingly across at him, unaware that in so doing
she provoked a spark of both wry amusement and
fierce jealousy to kindle in the magnificent blue
depths of Roark's eyes. "Please, Edward, I've my own
reasons, and I promise to summon you without delay
should I need any help. My conversation with him
will not take long." Noting his hesitation, she
stepped forward and laid a hand upon his arm. "Just
this once, will you not do as I ask?"

"I am always eager to please you, Lady Eden,"
Edward capitulated with obvious reluctance, making her a slight bow. He took the precaution of
leaving Roark's hands tied behind his back and
warned him in a low, concise tone, "You will treat
Lady Eden with respect at all times, or else I'll see
that you are well 'rewarded' for your insolence. And
remember what I told you—should you ever be so
foolish as to try to escape, you'll find yourself
dancing with the devil at the end of a rope."

Eden gasped softly at the threat. Roark, however,
appeared not the least bit intimidated by the other
man's promise of retribution. He met Edward's gaze
squarely, allowed a faint, mocking smile to touch his
lips, and then grew solemn again before looking
back to Eden.

"The lady has nothing to fear from me," he
declared.

The dangerous gleam in his eyes completely belied
his words, and his resonant, deep-timbered voice sent
a shiver down Eden's spine. It had been so long since

she had heard that voice. She could well remember the way it had soothed her when—*No, don't think of it!* Mentally cursing her own weakness, she wished for all the world that she had never left the safety of her uncle's carriage that morning.

"Into the barn, if you please," she managed to say with surprising equanimity. Ignoring Edward's frown of disapproval, she led the way toward the nearby building. Roark followed.

Once inside, Eden closed the wide double doors to ensure privacy. She stood with her back to Roark, desperately trying to decide what to say to him while his bold gaze raked hungrily over her beguiling curves. Soft, golden rays of sunlight filtered down through the loft, and the sweet scent of hay filled every corner.

The moment of reckoning had finally come.

She was the first to break the heavy silence between them. "I want something understood between us."

A powerful wave of trepidation washed over her, and she was sorely tempted to forget the whole thing. But she had already come too far for that. Much too far. Casting another dubious glance heavenward—and making a silent promise to obey her uncle for an entire month if only God would give her the strength to endure the next few minutes—she folded her arms tightly beneath her breasts and turned to face her husband.

Her heart leapt in renewed alarm when she glimpsed the mingled desire and determination in his eyes. She knew that look all too well.

"So we meet again at last, my dearest bride," he said, smiling briefly.

Although his hands were bound, Eden eyed him warily and remained close to the only avenue of escape. She would take no chances.

"It was my fervent wish never to set eyes upon you again!" she countered with an angry toss of her head, then was nonplused by his low, vibrant chuckle.

"Still the same wildcat, I see. It seems you've changed little these past nine months, save to grow even more beautiful."

"You can save your breath to cool your porridge, Roark St. Claire! You're wrong, you know. I *have* changed—I've grown to hate you even more!"

"Have you?" It was obvious that he did not believe her.

"Yes, damn you, I have!"

"Then why am I here?" he asked with maddening calm.

"I don't know!" she virtually shouted, her own eyes flashing brilliant green fire. She took a deep steadying breath and allowed her arms to fall stiffly at her sides. "I know not how you came to be auctioned as a slave," she told him in icy, measured tones, "nor do I seek enlightenment. I sought to purchase your contract of indenture merely because . . . because no matter what is in the past, I felt responsible for you. It isn't often I discover a former husband—"

"Former?" he challenged with a frown. He shook his head in a firm denial. "No, Eden. Our marriage was never annulled, else I'd have received notice of it."

"In the event you've forgotten, our countries are at war!" she saw fit to remind him. If she was hoping to

54

steer him away from the truth, however, she was sadly disappointed.

"There has been no annulment. And I've forgotten nothing."

"Nor have I!" Hot, bitter tears stung her eyes at the anguished memories. "You betrayed me, Roark St. Claire!" she charged vehemently. "You *used* me to get to my father, to further your own despicable cause! I should have suspected as much from the very beginning. Why, even your own mother's family wanted little or nothing to do with you when you were in London! And you displayed a highly peculiar interest in my father's connection to the Crown. Had I not been so incredibly, damnably naive, I would have seen you for the low, contemptible American spy you are!"

"I did not use you, Eden," Roark denied quietly. "You were never part of the plan."

"Oh, but I became a very convenient part of it, did I not?"

"No." Again, the ghost of a smile played about his lips. "You were certainly not convenient."

"Then *why?* Why did you—"

"God knows, I tried not to. I'll readily admit that I dealt in my fair share of secrets on behalf of my country, and that I went to England with the intent of gaining vital military information from your father. But you, my love . . . I had not counted on you. The last thing I either wanted or needed was to fall in love with Lord Grayson Parrish's daughter."

"Love?" she echoed with furious disbelief.

"Yes, Eden. Why else would I have married you?" His gaze warmed as it traveled with bold significance over her outraged softness once more. "If I had sought only to seduce you into compliance with my scheme, I could have done so and left you all the wiser for it."

"Why you—" She sputtered indignantly, her cheeks crimsoning. "Faith, sir, you flatter yourself!"

"Perhaps. But the fact remains that you are my wife. And if those two muddleheaded brothers of yours had not interfered, I would have sailed home to Georgia with you and never let you go."

"Thank God my father discovered your treachery in time!" Eden proclaimed with great feeling. "I cannot think whatever possessed me to agree to an elopement in the first place. It was ill luck that saw us wedded before proceeding to the ship that day. Still, I shall be eternally grateful that my brothers arrived on the scene before it was too late! Indeed, if they had not given chase, I—"

"You would have spent the past nine months in my arms," he finished for her, his loins tightening at the thought. He began slowly advancing on her now. "I regret that necessity forced me to leave you behind, Eden—'twas either that, or risk jeopardizing my mission. I would never have left you otherwise. But I vowed to return for you, remember?"

"I remember only your cruel betrayal!" she insisted, backing toward the doors. "You swept an innocent, foolish young woman off her feet and broke her heart, Roark St. Caire! But I am not the same now. You saw to that. Oh yes, I am indeed all the wiser! I am not so easily deceived. You cannot hurt me any longer!"

It was as if she were trying to convince herself as

well as him. She grasped the handle behind her and raised her head in a gesture of proud defiance. Her full young breasts rose and fell rapidly beneath the high-waisted bodice of her gown, while her raven tresses shimmered like black silk in the soft golden sunlight.

Roark's desire for her blazed hotter than ever. He longed to touch her, to crush her against him and kiss her with all the fierce, almost violent passion which had been smoldering deep within him these many months. Moving relentlessly closer, he gazed down into the upturned beauty of her countenance.

"I never wanted to hurt you, Eden. Only to love you," he declared, his eyes suffused with a captivating glow.

"Enough!" she cried hoarsely. She shook her head and fought down the panic rising within her. "It might interest you to know that my father is doing everything in his power to have our so-called marriage dissolved. The war has naturally delayed the process; that, and the small matter of your absence! It seems the courts are not entirely willing to grant an annulment when one of the parties has fled the country. Until you came along, I had never been forced to consider how difficult it is to rid oneself of a husband!"

She paused and drew in another ragged breath. Although Roark's hands were securely bound behind his back, she felt endangered. It was a feeling to which she was not accustomed.

"In the meantime," she continued with as much composure as she could summon, "I must caution you against telling anyone of our . . . our past

57

association. My uncle has decided to keep you. I am quite certain your treatment would be unbearably harsh if he knew your true identity."

"And what of your treatment?" demanded Roark, his features tightening. "Have you suffered at his hands, Eden? If so, then by damn, I'll—"

"You'll do nothing! For heaven's sake, don't you understand? You are his property now!" She finally turned to open the door, but hesitated. She whirled back to meet Roark's burning gaze and asked on sudden impulse, "What *were* you doing here in Barbados?"

"I came to find you."

Her green eyes grew enormous within the delicate oval of her face. For one fleeting moment, she was tempted to believe him. But then common sense prevailed. After all, she told herself, he has lied to me before—how could I expect him to speak the truth about anything now?

Roark watched conflicting emotions play across her face, watched as well the way her emerald gaze sparked with fury and resentment. Although her reaction did not surprise him, he felt a sharp twinge of pain at her willingness to think the worst of him. And yet, he knew he had only himself to blame.

"I sailed to England first," he explained, his body mere inches from hers now. "It did not take me long to discover what had happened. As soon as I learned of your whereabouts, I set sail for Barbados."

"A likely story!" She swallowed hard and struggled to remain unaffected by his nearness. Alas, it was a losing battle she waged.

"A likely story perhaps," conceded Roark. "But a

true one nonetheless." Cursing his bonds, he lowered his head purposefully toward hers. "There is no reason for me to lie, Eden. I told you I would return to claim you one day. It has taken a good deal longer than I would have wished."

Eden's mind screamed at her to flee, but her traitorous flesh refused to obey. She was scarcely aware of the moment when her trembling fingers relinquished their hold upon the door handle.

"I am not afraid of you!" she asserted breathlessly.

"Ah, but you should be, my love," her husband whispered. "You should be."

He kissed her, gently at first. Then, with a low groan sounding deep in his throat, he brought his warm lips crashing down upon the startled softness of hers with an impassioned, ever-deepening thoroughness that demanded a response. She gasped as his body suddenly pressed hers back against the door. Her head spun dizzily beneath the unexpected fury of his assault, and she found herself swaying closer to his hard virile warmth. . . .

Sweet Saint Christopher, what was she doing? This man had already broken her heart once. Was she really so witless and weak-spirited that she would let him do so again?

"No! No, damn you, no!" she seethed, abruptly tearing her lips from his. She pushed at him with all her might, glaring up into the somber, rugged perfection of his features when he stepped back. "Touch me again, Roark St. Claire, and I'll see you hanged!" she vowed, infuriated beyond reason.

She spun about, wrenched open the doors, and made good her escape. Hurrying past both Betsy and

Edward Tallant without a word, she fled across the yard and into the house. Roark stared grimly after her.

Soon, my love, he promised, his determination having just increased tenfold.

He had waited long enough. Hell, some would say he must have been blessed with the patience of a saint. But, like the green-eyed vixen who had stolen his heart, he was no saint. No, by damn, he was all too human.

It was time his beautiful, headstrong bride discovered what it meant to be a wife. *His* wife. If there was one thing he regretted about the past, it was that he had been forced to take flight before claiming her in fact as well as word. He had often cursed his own sense of honor afterward, musing that he should have damned well ravished the very devil out of Lady Eden Parrish and then dragged her off to the altar. At least he'd have had the sweet memory of her passion to console him throughout these past nine months.

But it seemed fate was finally ready to make amends—that is, if one didn't count the misfortune of being captured and sold into slavery, he reflected with an ironic half-smile. A privateer, they had called him. He was that all right, but for different reasons than they had supposed. If it were not for his impatience to find Eden, he would even now be doing his part in tormenting the Royal Navy and seizing the rich cargoes of British merchant ships. Espionage, it so happened, was not his only talent.

His thoughts returned to the situation at hand. He would have to gain his freedom first; that was a small matter to be dealt with at the appropriate time. The five men taken prisoner with him, all members of his crew, would have to be found and liberated as well. He gave silent thanks once more for the fact that his ship had not been captured. When the moment arrived, he and his men would be assured of a swift escape.

Until then, he would keep his eyes and ears open . . . and he would woo his reluctant bride with a vengeance.

Eden. His blue eyes gleaming at the prospect of what lay ahead, he strode from the barn.

Four

"Oh, Eden, is it true?" was Jamaica Harding's highly unorthodox greeting. Without waiting for a reply, she grabbed Eden's hand and pulled her insistently down the corridor to an empty room in the Stewarts' brightly lit mansion. "In here!" she suggested in a conspiratorial whisper.

Eden, after offering only a token protest, allowed herself to be thrust inside. She smiled at the petite blonde in bemusement while lively strains of music drifted out to them from the crowded ballroom.

"Jamaica, what on earth—"

"Is it true?" Jamaica queried again, hurriedly closing the door behind her. She took hold of her friend's shoulders and subjected her to a close, affectionate scrutiny. "Is it true what I've heard? Charlotte and Mary were full of the news when I arrived! Tell me, Eden, did you *really* purchase a bondsman today?"

"I . . . I'm afraid I did," Eden reluctantly admitted. Not the least bit pleased to learn that the gossip had already started to fly, she felt a dull flush stain the creamy smoothness of her cheeks. Her gaze fell before the searching, wide-eyed innocence of Jamaica's. "Or rather, I tried to," she amended with a sigh.

"But, whatever for? Charlotte said the man was an absolute brigand who was, thank heavens, captured before he could do any plundering upon these shores, and Mary said she had it on good authority he was not only American but unbelievably striking as well!"

"It seems the Misses Stewart can always be counted on to provide the necessary details," Eden remarked with more than a hint of sarcasm, then frowned. "I suppose everyone has heard of my 'infamy' by now."

The unbidden vision of Roark's handsome face swam before her eyes—just as it had done with disturbing frequency since her confrontation with him that afternoon. The memory of his treacherous words, and his even more treacherous kiss, still burned deep in her mind, as did the memory of her own brief but completely unforgivable loss of reason. She had shamed herself by dissolving into tears in the privacy of her bedroom afterward, a weakness she was determined never to repeat. No, by heaven, never again would she let Roark St. Claire make her cry.

Mentally consigning both the vision and its damnably flesh-and-blood counterpart to the devil, she turned and wandered over to one of Ambrose Stewart's massive wing chairs. Another sigh escaped her lips.

"They'll probably say this is yet the latest example of willful misconduct by William Stanhope's niece," she murmured, running a hand idly across the top of

63

the chair's smooth leather back. "At the present rate, I daresay I shall be deemed quite incorrigible by summer's end."

"Well, you can rest assured that I shall rise to your defense!" Jamaica avowed loyally. She hastened forward to slip an arm about Eden's shoulders. "Come now, it isn't as if you've done anything all that reprehensible. And you've always been an *original*, have you not? Why, I should like nothing better than to possess your courage and determination and steadfastness of spirit!"

"You make it sound as though I am a paragon of all that is noble," Eden responded with a soft smile of irony. She embraced her friend warmly, then drew away and gazed down at her with a solemn, earnest expression. "I am not half so noble as you, dearest Jamaica. Would that I could be more like you."

"More like me?" the other woman echoed in surprised disbelief. She gave a pleasant trill of laughter and linked arms companionably with Eden, having forgotten all about the scandalous affair of the American rogue. "Stuff and nonsense! Donald Parkington-Hughes would be thoroughly down-trodden if his heart's desire were to change in any way whatsoever, save to fall passionately in love with him, of course."

"You can tease me all you like, Jamaica Harding, but be forewarned that the tables will soon be turned."

"I haven't the faintest notion what you are talking about!" the fair-haired young beauty insisted airily as the two of them strolled from the room.

"Haven't you? Well then, perhaps I should inquire

of Harry Langley if he has any intention of paying his respects to your father in the near future."

"Oh Eden, surely you wouldn't!" gasped Jamaica, blushing fierily.

"No," she affirmed, her mouth curving into a smile of fond amusement. "I would not."

They had reached the doorway to the ballroom by now. With Eden's upswept black tresses and gown of pale blue gossamer silk, and the contrast of Jamaica's blond ringlets and white India muslin, they presented quite an enchanting picture to the assembly. Friends, neighbors, a few mere acquaintances, and several visiting countrymen were in attendance at the Stewarts' plantation that evening.

A waltz had just been struck up, and an audible rustle of silks and satins filled the spacious, elegantly appointed room as the dance's participants took their places beneath a massive crystal chandelier. There were surely more than a hundred ladies and gentlemen present, Eden mused absently.

From her vantage point in the doorway, she was afforded an unobstructed view of the festivities. She saw her uncle talking with their host, a barrel-chested Scotsman with flaming red hair, near the refreshments table. Mrs. Stewart was apparently content to sit with a group of other bejeweled and befeathered matrons along the opposite wall, while both Charlotte and Mary, neither of whom were great beauties, had been fortunate enough to secure partners for the waltz.

Watching everyone, Eden felt a strange restlessness grip her. Her thoughts began drifting with a will of their own . . . back over the startling events of the day . . . back to Roark St. Claire.

Dear God, how was she going to bear his presence at Abbeville Plantation? It was bad enough that he had materialized after so many months of alternate heartache and bitterness; it was beyond the realm of human endurance to think of having to see him day after day. If what had occurred between them in the barn proved to be any indication, the well-ordered structure of her life was about to be transformed into absolute chaos for the second time. And by the same deceitful, wickedly handsome scoundrel who had done it first.

The music's crescendo drew her from her troubling reverie. Her eyes bridled with sudden dismay when she caught sight of the infamous Donald Parkington-Hughes making his way purposefully toward her.

"Dash it all!" she muttered underneath her breath.

"What?" asked Jamaica, her own gaze fastened adoringly upon Harry Langley's attractive features. "What was that you said, Eden?" Her mind following its usual custom of changing course in midstream, she did not wait for an answer before leaning close to recommend, "I do think we should join the others, don't you?"

"I must leave at once!" Eden whispered, whirling to flee before it was too late. Her hopes were dashed when she heard her persistent suitor calling her name. She forced herself to turn and face him like the young lady of refinement and good breeding she was supposed to be. "Good evening, Mr. Parkington-Hughes," she spoke with all politeness.

"You are looking extremely well, Lady Eden," he

offered, beaming rather possessively at her.

He was, as usual, impeccably clad. There was scarcely a crease to be seen in either his dark blue, velvet-collared coat or his tightly fitted fawn breeches. Completing the ensemble were a pair of patterned white stockings and black leather pumps decorated with silver buckles. Of medium height, with sandy-colored hair and eyes that were so pale a blue they were almost transparent, he was the epitome of Anglo-Saxon aristocracy.

Though he would not by any stretch of the imagination be termed handsome, Eden had once remarked to Jamaica, neither would his face serve to frighten young children. If only he were not so . . . so perfectly *ordinary*.

She did not fail to notice the way his admiring gaze lingered upon her décolletage. As was fashionable, a goodly portion of her full breasts swelled above the gown's low, rounded neckline. She impulsively opened her lace-trimmed fan and brought it up level with her bosom, then proceeded to fan herself in a pretense of overexcitement.

"I'm afraid I require some fresh air," she told Donald, giving him a dazzling smile. "Pray, Mr. Parkington-Hughes, please forgive me for my rude abandonment. I won't be away long. You must remain and delight Miss Harding with your company, of course, and—"

"Nonsense," he smoothly cut her off. Making Jamaica a gallant bow, he looked back to Eden and offered her his arm. "I shall be only too happy to accompany you outside, Lady Eden."

She exchanged a quick look with Jamaica, whose

eyes fairly danced with a mixture of sympathy and amusement. There was no escape now.

"Thank you," she murmured, her voice lacking any real conviction. She slipped her hand through the crook of Donald's arm and moved stiffly along with him, across the room to the French doors leading out onto the verandah. Her uncle, taking note of both her destination and her escort, smiled to himself in satisfaction.

A full moon had risen to add its silver-hued brilliance to the congregation of stars twinkling above. The wind, gentle and sweetly scented, caressed the moonlit landscape as the sounds of the sea reached into every corner of the island. Eden breathed deeply of the cool night air, pulling free of her determined suitor to take up a stance beside the stone balcony.

"I am glad we have this opportunity to speak in private," remarked Donald. He joined her at the balcony. "You have no idea how truly exquisite you look at this moment, my dear."

"I am not 'your dear'!" She had no wish to hurt him, and yet she had no intention of engaging in yet another pointless discussion of matrimony. "Please, Donald," she appealed, her green eyes aglow with sincerity as she turned her head to look at him. "Don't let's quarrel. We had quite enough of that this morning."

"We needn't quarrel at all." He placed his hand atop hers and smiled. His gaze was full of such warmth and admiration that she experienced a sharp twinge of guilt. "I can assure you that what happened this morning is all but forgotten." His smile faded when she suddenly drew her hand away.

"I have not forgotten it! And neither should you. I meant what I said, you see. I meant every word!"

"I don't believe you," he insisted stubbornly. "I don't believe you feel nothing beyond friendship for me, not when I have courted you with all patience and reverence these six months or more. You cannot have remained unaffected by my obvious devotion."

"Not completely unaffected, perhaps," she allowed in an effort to spare his feelings, "but—"

"Surely you are aware of the fact that your uncle desires a match between us. He has made his approval known to me on more than one occasion."

"My uncle's approval, or lack of it, has nothing to do with this!" she declared, her emerald gaze sparking with anger now. "I have a perfect right to do as I please in this matter!"

Donald's brow creased into an even deeper frown. Not for the first time, a seed of doubt crept into his mind. He tried to convince himself, just as his mother had done, that a woman who displayed such fire and independence would not make the most suitable of wives. But he had set his heart on Lady Eden Parrish. She was unlike any other woman in Barbados, and he was determined to have her.

He watched as she spun about and marched to the corner of the verandah. Her thick ebony locks were turned a shining blue-black by the moonlight as she stood gazing outward, and he could make out the outline of her detectable curves beneath the clinging silk of her gown. A sudden, incredible thought occurred to him.

"Is there someone else, Eden?" he demanded sharply.

"Yes. I mean, no! *No!*"

Drawing herself rigidly erect, she felt the telltale color rising to her face. It was impossible to tell him the truth. She could never hope to make him understand. *I do beg your pardon, Mr. Parkington-Hughes, but I am at present still married to an American spy.* Oh yes, she could well imagine his reaction to that trifling bit of information.

"Are you quite certain?" persisted Donald.

"Don't be ridiculous!" she snapped.

"Then I must tell you that I intend to announce our betrothal without further delay."

"What?" Eden gasped in shocked amazement. Her eyes grew round as saucers as they flew to the man who, although outwardly normal, must of a certainty be mad as a hatter. She hastened forward to confront him with the possibility. "Have you taken complete and utter leave of your senses?"

"As stated, I already have your uncle's blessings. All that remains is for you to set the date," he decreed calmly. Having decided that she needed only a little more prompting, he was supremely confident of success. Eden, however, was about to set him straight.

"Who the devil do you think you are?" she stormed, balling her hands into fists and planting them on her hips. Righteous indignation only heightened her beauty, but Donald was much too thunderstruck to appreciate it. "I have done everything, every blasted thing, to try to make you understand that I have no earthly intention of marrying you, Donald Parkington-Hughes! Once and for all, will you listen? I am truly sorry, but I do not love you and I will not be your wife!"

"We shall see what your uncle has to say about this," he parried haughtily.

Eden groaned and rolled her eyes in an eloquent gesture of frustration. She was unprepared when Donald suddenly took hold of her shoulders and pressed his lips upon hers. Too shocked at first to resist, she thought dazedly that his firm, controlled kiss was a far cry from the wildly inflamed one Roark had forced upon her earlier that day. Indeed, she went on to conclude in those few, fleeting moments of active comparison, whereas Roark's kiss had threatened to set her afire, Donald's merely left her feeling chagrined.

She cursed her own wickedness and finally pushed her sincere but inadequate conqueror away.

"You forget yourself, sir!" she cried furiously.

"Then I must beg your forgiveness," he replied in a stiff, dutiful manner. He straightened his neckcloth and had the grace to look uncomfortable beneath Eden's fiery regard. But if she had hoped to hear him concede defeat, she was sorely disappointed. "Desperate means call for desperate measures. I will speak to your uncle this very night."

"Surely you cannot still mean to—"

"William Stanhope will not, in all likelihood, be sorry to entrust me with your care," he continued as if she had not spoken. "If there is any truth to the rumors I have heard concerning your behavior, he will face the prospect of our marriage with a great deal of relief."

"There isn't going to be any marriage!" The man is insane . . . truly insane, she thought numbly.

"Oh, and by the way," he added while crossing

71

back to the doors, "there will be no more scenes such as the one you created at the market. Yes, my dear, I know all about it. I simply cannot have it said that my future wife has developed a certain, inexplicable fondness for slaves. If you will not think of your own reputation, then please have the goodness to think of mine."

"I am not your 'future wife'!" she adamantly declared. "And your reputation is the least of my concerns!"

"It will assume greater importance before this night is through." He gave her a curt nod, then disappeared inside.

Eden stared after him in mingled astonishment and outrage. Once again, she could scarcely believe what was happening. The absurdity of the situation was not completely lost on her. Who would have thought it possible that on the very same day her unwanted husband had returned to bedevil her, she was facing betrothal to an unwanted suitor as well? It was really too ludicrous for words.

She was, however, not inclined to laugh.

Muttering a highly unladylike oath, she gathered up her silken skirts and swept into the ballroom. She spied Donald conversing with her uncle, just as he had promised. Her eyes blazed wrathfully, and she was tempted to march forward and tell both men exactly what she thought of their despicable conspiracy. Realizing that a scene would only lend credence to Donald's suit, she settled instead for flinging them a meaningful glare. She then took herself off to find Jamaica.

Jamaica, as she soon discovered, was dancing with

Harry Langley. The pretty blonde's face brightened when she caught sight of Eden, but her brows knitted into a mild frown of worriment when she saw the light of battle in her friend's emerald gaze.

Eden felt a growing need to escape. She managed to exchange pleasantries with several of her acquaintances while she waited for the current dance, a quadrille, to end. Once the music stopped, she was immediately besieged with more than a dozen urgent requests for the next and subsequent dances. She smiled, politely declined them all, and sought out her hostess.

"I beg your pardon, Mrs. Stewart," she apologized, approaching a group of women in the corridor, "but I am afraid I must take my leave of you. I . . . I have developed the most dreadful headache." It was not a complete falsehood.

"I am sorry to hear of it, my dear," the plump, lavender-gowned matron responded. Her gaze was, as usual, devoid of any warmth. Due to her position as the mother of two rather plain and dull-witted daughters, she viewed Eden as decidedly unwelcome competition in the matrimonial arena. "Perhaps you should not have come at all. That is to say, perhaps after this morning's unpleasantness . . ."

Her words trailed away with insulting significance, and she shared a nod of silent understanding with the other ladies. They all stared at Eden, their gazes full of censure and their expressions ill-disposed.

A dull flush of anger set Eden's face aglow. She was determined not to be wounded by their rancor.

"I bid you good evening then, Mrs. Stewart," she

put forth with cool civility. "Would you be so kind as to inform my uncle of my departure? And please tell him I shall send the carriage back for him." She had no wish to face her uncle again that evening. Or Donald.

Moving gracefully away toward the front door, Eden was conscious of the many whispers following her. It was with a feeling of profound relief that she escaped into the welcoming coolness of the night. Ezekiel drove the carriage round at once, and Zach handed her up.

"The master not be coming, mistress?" the young footman questioned in puzzlement.

"No, Zach. You're to take me home and come back for him." She offered no further explanation, for her mind was too preoccupied with other matters.

Ezekiel gave a light flick of the reins, and the horses started forward. The carriage was soon winding its way through the moonlit darkness.

Eden thought of what her uncle's reaction would be when he received news of her flight. That he would be furious, she had little doubt. And Donald . . . well, Donald would probably seize some advantage from her behavior. If only he would listen to reason. If only she could tell him the truth. *If only Roark St. Claire had never been born.*

The trip homeward was of mercifully short duration. Eden stood on the front steps of the great house and watched as the carriage set off again. Her spirits were quite low, and there was a dull ache in her heart. England seemed so very far away at that moment. Her parents had made it painfully clear that they would not, under any circumstances, anticipate her return until the war had ended. It was simply too dangerous to travel by sea, they had insisted, citing numerous examples of English ships being captured by American privateers. Thus, she had no choice but to remain in Barbados for now.

Her troubled gaze was drawn to the slave quarters in the near distance. She knew Roark was imprisoned in one of those thatched roof cabins; she even knew which one. It was customary for any new slave to be kept in the plantation's gaol for the first several weeks, until he was deemed manageable.

Eden's mouth curved into a soft ironic smile at the notion of Roark's "manageability." She was certain such a thing could never be achieved. Her smile abruptly faded when she recalled Edward Tallant's threats.

"Oh, Roark," she whispered. "Why did you come here? Why?"

He had said it was to find her, but she knew better. He was an enemy, a spy, and a rogue. He had come to wreak havoc on these shores, as he had done in England. *A privateer captain.* She could well hate him for that alone.

She turned to go inside, but was detained by a sudden flash of movement near the barn. Curiosity drew her down the steps and across the yard. It never occurred to her that she might be in danger. She feared none of the slaves, and she had yet to be convinced that the bearded elves the Bajans spoke of were real.

"Is anyone there?" she called out softly.

Without warning, a bundle of warm fur came flying at her. A small, breathless cry broke from her lips as she stumbled backward. Her terror turned to wry amusement when she realized that it was not a phantom which had clutched at her skirts before scampering off into the darkness, but a monkey.

Eden smiled to herself and glanced down at the tear in her gown. She knew the mischievous creatures were considered to be nothing more than pests. She had once been horrified to learn there was actually a bounty on their tails. The woods were full of them, yet it wasn't often they ventured so close to civilization.

She released a sigh. A strange uneasiness crept over her once more. Her eyes flew instinctively to the gaol, which was situated at the head of the long, double row of slave cabins. Roark would be asleep by now, she mused. Tomorrow's first light would find him at work in the fields. For seven long years he would have to call another man master . . . for seven years he would face hardship and degradation and the ever-present threat of punishment. The thought, oddly enough, gave her no pleasure.

Wondering how it would ever be possible to gain an annulment if her husband had no rights of his own, she wandered slowly back across the yard. Fate had made a fine mess of things. A fine mess indeed.

Like a flash of lightning, a sudden idea sprang to life in her mind. *Of course!* she told herself, her silken skirts rustling as she came to a halt. Why hadn't she thought of it before? Her gaze shone with triumph and resolution.

Almost before she realized it, her steps were leading her toward the gaol. She hurried along, darting an anxious look back over her shoulder as she went. Her uncle would not be home for at least half an hour or more, and she had told Betsy not to wait up for her. No one need ever know.

She approached the door of the cabin seconds later. Her hand trembled when she reached up to disengage the outer latch. The door was not locked against visitors; there were none foolish enough to brave Edward Tallant's wrath.

Easing the door open, she peered cautiously inside. No lamp burned within, but moonlight spilled into the room from a single high window. The air smelled musty and stale.

Eden wrinkled her nose in distaste while her eyes sought her husband. She could make out a dark form, hopefully Roark's, on the bare planks of the floor in the far corner.

"Roark?" she whispered as loudly as she dared.

"Eden?"

His familiar, deep-timbred voice reached out to her. She quickly slipped inside and closed the door behind her.

"Roark, I must speak to you!"

"What the devil are you doing here?" he startled her by demanding angrily. He had leapt to his feet, wearing only trousers and unable to approach her by virtue of a chain connecting his shackled wrist to the wall. "Damn it, woman, don't you realize the risk you've run in coming?"

"What risk?" she countered, her own temper flaring.

"Suppose you were seen? You claim you want no one to suspect the truth, and yet you are in danger of exposing it this very minute!" In actuality, his annoyance was tempered by pleasure at her nearness, but he forced himself to look severe. He had his own reasons for wanting to keep their marriage a secret. "Go back to your uncle's house, Eden," he commanded tersely. "Go back before it's too late."

Eden bristled at his air of authority. She rapidly crossed the distance between them, her beautiful eyes afire and her body fairly quaking with the force of her anger. The state of Roark's undress was at present unimportant as she fixed him with a hotly reproachful glare.

"It so happens that I have come here to offer you your freedom!"

"Have you indeed?" His mouth twitched with ironic humor. "And how is it you are qualified to make such an offer?"

"My qualification stems from my unfortunate position as your wife!" she retorted, refusing to be intimidated by the fact that he was towering above her.

She abruptly folded her arms beneath her breasts, unaware that in so doing she caused the satiny, rounded flesh to swell even higher above the low neckline of her bodice. Since she was still firmly in the grip of indignation, she failed to notice the sudden tensing of Roark's handsome features. His gaze darkened as it strayed downward to her breasts, and it was with no small amount of effort that he battled a fierce surge of desire.

"What are you talking about?" he demanded quietly, his eyes returning to her face.

"I am talking about freedom—yours and mine!" she answered with a defiant toss of her raven curls. "I will help you escape, if you will in turn promise to see that our marriage is finally annulled!"

Her proposition was met with several long moments of highly charged silence. She was certain Roark would agree. Her mind had already begun racing to formulate a plan. But once again, her husband took her completely by surprise.

"No, Eden." He shook his head. "I want no part of your scheme."

"But whyever not?" She stared up at him in the semidarkness, her own gaze clouded with confusion. "You certainly cannot wish to remain here as my uncle's slave! I can see to it that you are able to get away!"

"Can you?" he challenged, though he had no intention of putting her abilities to the test.

"Of course I can! If you will but promise to—"

He masterfully cut her off. "I will promise nothing, save to make you regret it sorely if you do not get out of here and leave me to my sleep."

It was agony, being this close to her and yet unable to touch her. He would have liked nothing better than to take full advantage of their circumstances, but he knew a stolen kiss would not be the end of it this time. Damn you, Eden, he swore silently. He burned for her with ever-increasing fury.

"How dare you!" she breathed out, blushing fierily. She refused to acknowledge the tremor of fear which shot through her. Uncrossing her arms, she told him in a low, ireful tone, "I should have known you were beyond any measure of reason or integrity! I was fool enough to believe you would look upon my offer with gratitude!"

"Your offer was selfish as well as misguided."

"*Selfish?*"

"Can you honestly say it was prompted by anything other than the simple desire to rid yourself of me?"

"Why, you . . . I owe you no explanation! I owe you nothing!" At that moment, she would have denied all compassion for his plight. "And as for ridding myself of you, rest assured that *that* particular deliverance will soon be forthcoming!"

"You are mistaken," Roark parried softly, his cobalt blue eyes boring down into the luminous green fire of hers. His voice held an undercurrent of smoldering passion when he repeated the promise he had made her so long ago. "I'll not let anyone or anything come between us, Eden. You are my wife. And my wife," he concluded while his features grew forebodingly grim, "you will remain."

"Never!" she repudiated his declaration with great feeling. Then she took an incautious step closer and tilted her head back to fling him a look ablaze with pure, unquenchable spirit, vowing, "I swear by all that is holy, Roark St. Claire—I *shall* be free of you and your treachery before this year is through!"

If she had stopped at that, she would have spared herself the tempestuous scene which followed. But the humiliation and heartache she had suffered at his hands now conspired to make her even more reckless. She suddenly thought of Donald, and decided to use that gentleman's vexatious courtship to add fuel to the fire.

"I intend to make a new life for myself!" she declared loftily. "As a matter of fact, I have received

80

an offer of marriage from a man who is everything you are not! *He* would never treat me as contemptibly as you have done, and I am certain he—"

She broke off with a sharp gasp as Roark's free arm shot out to clamp about her waist. He yanked her roughly against him, his features a tight mask of fury and his gaze smoldering with raw emotion.

"By damn, you little witch, you're mine! No other man shall have you!"

She gasped again and raised her hands to push at his naked chest. Her own gaze was bright with outrage—and more than a touch of very real alarm.

"How dare you!" she raged hotly. "Let go of me!" Her struggles grew more fervent, but his arm merely tightened like a band of steel about her waist. "Let me go, or I . . . I'll scream!" she threatened, painfully conscious of the way her thinly clad curves were pressed against his searing, hard-muscled warmth.

Roark could bear no more. With a low growl of passion's fury, he lowered his head and branded her lips with his own.

A scream of protest rose in Eden's throat. She brought her hands up to his chest again in a desperate attempt to free herself from his grasp, but to no avail. Imprisoned within the bold savagery of his embrace, she was aghast to realize she was tempted to melt against him in surrender. She was even more dismayed to discover that her arms, quite of their own accord, had suddenly crept about his neck.

Dear God, she was doing it again! How was it possible she could let Roark St. Claire, of all men, take such shocking liberties? It was beyond belief. It was completely unforgivable. It was also sheer heaven. . . .

Roark's lips moved upon hers with a fiercely demanding, more than capable, expertise. She trembled and gave a low moan. An audible intake of breath followed when his warm, velvety tongue plunged between her parted lips to explore the sweetness of her mouth. After managing a rather half-hearted protest, she accepted defeat and allowed the sensual invasion, just as she allowed herself to kiss him back with all the long-dormant passions he was awakening within her. It was Roark who had first taught her what passion was; it would be Roark who now tutored that innocent, maidenly passion into a woman's hot-blooded desire.

His hand swept downward. A delicious shiver ran the length of her spine when his fingers curled possessively about her shapely, well-rounded buttocks. He urged her closer. The undeniable evidence of his masculinity provoked a wealth of sensations in her, all of them pleasant. She moaned again and swayed weakly against him as liquid fire raced through her veins.

Roark's mouth relinquished hers, only to scorch a path downward to the creamy flesh which swelled above the lace-trimmed bodice of her gown. His ardent lips roamed hungrily, bestowing a series of bold, provocative kisses upon the exposed curves of breasts while she strained instinctively forward into his moist caresses. Her fingers threaded within the dark, sun-streaked thickness of his hair, and she caught her lower lip between her teeth to stifle a cry that was part ecstasy, part consternation. She was shocked by the utter wantoness of her own actions, and confused by her response to a man she had sworn to hate.

There was, however, no time to think. There was only Roark . . . only this virile, devilishly handsome rogue and his intoxicating kisses.

With a mastery that would not be denied, he bore her downward to the floor with him. He settled back against the wall and cradled her upon his lap, cursing the lack of two free arms with which to hold her. But desire raged so hotly within him that he did not allow the less than ideal circumstances to hinder his lovemaking in any way. While he raised his shackled hand to his wife's enchantingly formed hips, he entwined his other within the long, luxuriant mass of raven curls tumbling down about her shoulders.

"Eden . . . my beautiful Eden," he murmured huskily against her ear, his warm lips teasing at its delicate softness.

"Oh, Roark!" It came out a breathless whisper. She shivered again and feverishly ran her hands along the bronzed powerful hardness of his bare arms. Musing through a swirling haze of passion that he could easily crush the very life from her, she clutched his broad shoulders and squirmed restlessly atop his lean-muscled thighs.

A low groan rumbled up from deep in Roark's chest. He tensed, then swept Eden closer and captured her lips in another fiery kiss. Almost before she knew what was happening, she felt her skirts being tugged impatiently upward, felt a rush of cool air upon her burning skin. Roark's hand trailed upward along the inside of her pale, silken thighs. . . .

Sweet Saint Christopher! she exclaimed inwardly, her eyes flying wide at the first touch of his warm fingers upon the triangle of soft, tiny black curls. She well knew what would follow. No man had ever dared such a shockingly intimate caress, not even *this* man! Horrified to realize just how close to danger her own accursed weakness had taken her, she finally came crashing back to earth.

"No!" she cried out, abruptly stirring within Roark's embrace. "No, I—I will not!" She attempted to fling herself from his lap, but his hand closed about her wrist before she could escape. "Let me go, damn you!" she insisted while hot tears gathered in her eyes.

"Eden, what the devil . . . ?" he demanded, frowning at her in angry bewilderment and near painful frustration.

"No!" With startling violence, she landed a stinging blow to his rugged cheek and staggered to her feet. "I hate you, Roark St. Claire!" she declared tremulously. Her bosom heaved with indignation, and her green eyes were full of murderous intent as she stood glaring down at him. "You are nothing but a . . . a *ravisher!*"

"So help me, Eden, I ought to show you just how much ravishing I can do," he ground out, drawing himself upright as well. The menacing light in his gaze boded ill for her. She whirled and retreated to a safe distance.

"You are entirely deserving of your fate!" she opined haughtily. "If you will not agree to my proposition, then so be it! I promise, however, that

84

you will come to regret your stupid obstinance!"

"And I promise you, my dearest bride, that the next time you come calling in the middle of the night, I will not hesitate to give you what you so richly deserve," he parried with alarming certainty.

Eden paled beneath the savage glint in his eyes. She drew herself proudly erect and spun about to jerk open the door. Roark delivered his parting shot before she had done anything more than cast a quick look outside.

"Remember what I said, Eden. I have no intention of giving you up. I came here to find you, and I'll not leave without you."

"Then you'll not leave at all!" she retorted in a furious whisper.

With that, she made good her escape at last. Her tears threatened to blind her as she flew back across the moonlit grounds. Mortified by what she had done—and by what she had *almost* done—she raced up the steps of the house and soon thereafter flung herself face down across the curtained fourposter in her bedroom.

A deep, restful sleep would elude her that night. And her dreams would be filled with taunting memories of Roark, memories that were both old and painfully recent.

Five

Breakfast the following morning was a dismal affair.

Eden, already not at her best, felt her spirits sink even lower when she saw her uncle's face. Without a word, she took her seat at the opposite end of the carved mahogany table. William immediately subjected her to a blistering reproach concerning her outrageous behavior of the previous evening. His tirade ceased only when Betsy, in a well-intentioned but nevertheless misguided attempt to improve her young mistress' health, brought her a cup of "bush tea" that tasted like brewed tree bark and threatened to destroy what little appetite she possessed.

To make matters worse, she was suddenly informed that her betrothal to Donald Parkington-Hughes would be announced within the week.

That caused her to choke on her tea. Coughing, she raised the fine linen napkin to her lips and turned a look of stunned disbelief upon her uncle.

"Donald and I have agreed upon all the terms," he

revealed with a scowl intended to discomfit her.

"But that . . . that is impossible!" she stammered breathlessly. "I am still married to another!" *And he is only a stone's throw away at this very moment,* an inner voice took delight in adding.

"A trifling matter," said William. As if to emphasize the fact, he leisurely took up a scone and lathered it with a generous portion of sweet cream butter.

Eden, watching him, could think only that he had gone as daft as Donald.

"A trifling matter? For heaven's sake, Uncle, how can you make such a preposterous claim?" she challenged in growing apprehension. "Why, as I reminded you only yesterday, an annulment has not yet been granted! It is not in the least bit fair to give Donald false hopes! Even if I *were* free to marry him, I would never—"

"I have decided to petition the courts in Bridge-town on your behalf," stated William, impassively disregarding her protests. "It was in truth Donald's recommendation that I do so. With his father's legal connections, both here and in England, there is every hope we shall be able to see a solution to your 'problem' without further delay. It is a wonder your father never thought of it before." He did not see fit to make mention of his own oversight.

"You told Donald about my marriage?" Her eyes grew very wide, and she gave an inward groan of dismay.

"I told him only what was necessary. We can, of course, rely upon him to keep the matter entirely confidential. And you need fear no hint of discovery from the courts. It shall be handled with the utmost secrecy and discretion. Lord Parkington-Hughes will see to that."

"And what, pray tell, makes you believe *we* will meet with any more success here than back home?" demanded Eden, furious to learn of all the plotting which had taken place without either her knowledge or her consent.

"Because, my dear," he replied with a faint smile of triumphant satisfaction, "we are going to have your husband declared legally dead."

"*Dead?*" She abruptly rose to her feet. "But he is still very much alive!"

"Sit down." He congratulated himself when she obeyed. "Your husband abandoned you," he pointed out. "Not only that, but your own brothers have testified to the fact that he fled England before the two of you had been wed above half an hour's time. The misfortunate union was never consummated."

Eden's face flamed. She remembered all too vividly how close to consummation the union had come the night before. Dear God, she lamented once more, how could she have been so weak spirited? *Weak fleshed would be a far more appropriate name for it.*

"What does the lack of . . . of 'marital happiness' have to do with what you are proposing to do?" she questioned, returning to the present. "That an annulment is in order, there is little doubt, but how can you possibly seek to pass me off as a widow?"

"It is all quite simple, really." He took another bite of the overly laden scone and followed it with a sip of well-sugared tea. "For whatever reasons, your husband, an American subject, saw fit to return to his homeland without you. We all know what danger lies in wait for those foolhardy enough to cross the Atlantic during a time of war. I intend to suggest that the man perished at sea. If need be, I can even produce witnesses. Well-paid ones, of course," he concluded, looking quite pleased with himself.

Eden stared at him in speechless incredulity. Her head spun as a result of what she had just heard, and it suddenly occurred to her that Roark St. Claire would no doubt be even more surprised than she to learn the details of his "watery demise." She certainly had no intention of telling him. He could rot in hell for all she cared. Still, she mused as her eyes kindled with the light of revenge, it might be enjoyable to watch his reaction to the news of her impending widowhood.

"Now that you are aware of the plan, I would advise you to make your apologies to Donald for your abominable treatment of him," said William, casting her another frown of rebuke. "While it's true he is set upon you as his bride, his affections may very well diminish if you do not mend your troublesome ways."

"For the last time, Uncle, I am *not* going to marry Donald Parkington-Hughes!" She stood and flung her napkin to the table. "If you will please excuse me, I have a good many things to do," she announced coolly. Without waiting for his reply, she swept from the room.

"By damn, I will not allow you to shame me any further!" he called after her in anger. "Do you hear me, girl? I will not allow it!"

Eden could not help but hear him. His words only

prompted her to hasten her flight outside. She paused upon the front steps and tossed a quick glance up at the sky. The promise of rain had not yet been kept; the clouds had been tumbled away by the wind before she and her uncle had left for the Stewarts' the previous night. Morning had brought with it another unrestrained mantle of sunlight, and had brought as well the familiar sounds of the plantation's awakening.

She saw that the grounds were, as usual, bustling with activity. The stable master, Old Sangaree, was giving young Jonah instructions near the barn. Betsy and Zach were stealing a moment of private conversation at the garden gate. Women cleaned and cooked and mended, children were cautioned not to make too much noise for fear of incurring the master's displeasure, and men went about their business with efficiency if not contentment.

The field hands were already hard at work, weeding and fertilizing the ground about the ripening stalks of cane. Harvesting would begin soon—"cropover," it was called by the slaves. Once the cane had been cut by hand, crushed with the aid of windmills, and boiled down into sugar, a great celebration would take place at Abbeville Plantation.

Eden recalled how surprised she had been to discover that her dour uncle allowed such revelry, but she knew his indulgence stemmed from nothing more than the desire to make his workers perform to the best of their abilities. If they had something to look forward to, he reasoned, they would work all the harder. It was their reward. She failed to see how one day of celebration could atone for endless weeks of drudgery.

Her emerald gaze, still simmering over the news of her uncle's scheme, was now drawn to the towering sea of cane some distance away. Roark was there, she told herself. He would be unbound, but under constant surveillance by one of her uncle's carefully chosen supervisors.

"Why the devil wouldn't he listen to reason?" she murmured with a long, uncomplacent sigh. He had vowed never to let her go. But why? He had completed his wretched mission of betrayal and could have no further use of her. She was no longer important. Why then was he determined to remain wed to her?

It struck her that he might yet be planning to take advantage of their relationship, to somehow use it to gain his freedom. But if that was the case, surely he would have made their marriage a matter of public knowledge from the very first. Or at the very least, he would not have turned aside her offer of assistance with such ill-mannered grace. The reasons for his decision, she concluded with another sigh, were entirely beyond her comprehension.

She had ample opportunity to ponder the matter as she busied herself about the plantation. Her uncle, in a stroke of unexpected good fortune, took himself off to church and a parish-wide gathering without her, so that she was left to spend the day in her own pursuits. She did just that, making use of herself in the kitchen and gardens, and even the slave quarters, where her visits were always greeted with genuine warmth and pleasure. The children, in particular, were glad to see her, for she brought them whatever sweets she could spirit away from beneath the cook's nose.

Thoughts of Roark refused to be chased from her mind. A solitary ride in the late afternoon offered her a glimpse of him at last.

He glanced up when her mount cantered past the fields. His gaze darkened when it fell on her, and she could have sworn she saw him smile. She stiffened and hastily averted her face, but not before her cheeks had crimsoned at the sight of his bare, powerful chest and arms. His skin looked all bronzed and gleaming as he toiled beneath the sun's blaze, and the rugged perfection of his features simply would not be denied. There were two other young and attractive bondsmen working beside him—they had been purchased scarcely a month ago—but they were nothing compared to him.

Indeed, how could any man hope to compare? she wondered, then cursed herself for being an over-heated fool.

She urged her horse into a gallop and rode like the very wind back to the house. A short time later, after she had exchanged her riding habit of fine blue Georgian cloth for a simple gown of white muslin, she wandered into the kitchen and found Betsy enjoying a rare moment of leisure.

"There you be, Lady Eden!" the plump house-maid's mouth curved into a broad welcome. She took another drink from her cup while Eden sank into a chair on the opposite side of the flour-dusted work table. "Would you like some of cook's tea?" she offered genially. Her dark eyes twinkled.

"No. Thank you all the same, Betsy, but I have had quite enough of that evil concoction for one day."

"You do be having more color now," said the other woman, directing a critical eye of approval upon her mistress' flushed countenance.

"Yes, well, I daresay my mother would not approve," Eden remarked, a wry smile tugging at her own lips. "It is not at all fashionable, you see, for well-bred English ladies to have color."

"Why so?"

"Because society dictates it. And woe to any who commit the unpardonable sin of choosing defiance over conformity."

"The higher the monkey climb, the more he expose his tail," Betsy recited another of those infamous Bajan proverbs. She shook her head at the strange ways of the English.

Eden's response was to laugh softly. The warm glow of amusement in her gaze, however, soon deepened to a flash of annoyance. Betsy's words of wisdom quite naturally brought to mind thoughts of last night's brief encounter with a woods beast, which led in turn to thoughts of Roark. Blast it all, was she never going to be allowed to forget him?

Apparently not.

"Zach told me the new slave be a big, tall-up man," Betsy suddenly remarked.

Eden's eyes flew wide. It was as if the other woman had read her mind. Her color grew even more unfashionable, and she was forced to look away so that Betsy would not witness her discomposure.

"What prompted you to mention the new slave?" she inquired with deceptive nonchalance. Resting an elbow atop the table, she trailed a finger lightly through the flour, then stole a surreptitious glance at the housemaid from beneath her eyelashes, only to see that Betsy was frowning at her in mild puzzlement. "I mean"—attempting to clarify, she faltered uncomfortably—"I . . . I fail to see why you and Zach should be discussing him at all. He is of little consequence."

"Oh, but there be no other *Americans* here at Abbeville!" pointed out Betsy, her gaze widening in awe. It seemed that, at least to her, Roark's nationality either made him an automatic candidate for damnation to the very depths of hell, or a creature deserving of nearly godlike reverence. "My Zach," she went on to confide, "he heard Mr. Tallant say the new man be causing no trouble, not even a fire-rage over the irons he be made to wear. Mr. Tallant say the American be dangerous and should be watched."

"But why should he think that?" Eden asked in surprise, her bright gaze meeting Betsy's again. "If Ro— If the bondsman is indeed offering no resistance, then why should he be considered dangerous?"

This doesn't sound like Roark at all, she thought, her silken brow creasing. Roark St. Claire was not the sort of man to accept defeat so easily. There had to be a reason for his strange submissiveness. A very good reason . . .

"I disremember exactly how Mr. Tallant put it to Zach," said Betsy. "But what it comes to mean is that Mr. Tallant thinks the new man be full of more tricks than the devil."

She finished the last of her tea and hastened to finish her well-earned "rest off" as well. Rising to her feet, she smiled down at Eden while tucking a few wayward strands of dark, curling hair beneath her white mop cap.

"You know how others act when they first be brought here? Why, they be all caffuffled and grumpus-backed! And touchous, surely touchous. It takes a maulsprigging, maybe two, from Mr. Tallant's whip to make them settle. Well, the American be different, Lady Eden. He be different for sure."

Eden desperately wanted to continue their conversation, to press for further details, but she dared not. She watched in silent disappointment as Betsy straightened her apron and set about tidying the small but expertly stocked kitchen.

"Will you be wanting supper in your room this night?" the housemaid queried while noisily stacking a trio of pots. "The master did say he be coming back late."

"No, thank you, Betsy," murmured Eden. She heaved a faint sigh and drew herself upright. "There is a possibility that Jamaica Harding may pay a call on me this evening. I should like to invite her to remain for supper if she arrives beforehand."

"That young mistress always be a welcome sight. Cook and I will be making a special cohobblepot for the two of you when she gets back from her rest off," declared Betsy, already planning which ingredients to use for the stew.

Eden managed a smile, albeit a preoccupied one, and left the kitchen. She walked past the broad staircase of solid mahogany, her gaze flickering briefly upward. Half a dozen bedrooms opened out of a long gallery on the second floor, each of them with cool balconies and large shuttered windows. The third floor held two additional, exquisitely appointed guest chambers, as well as a large storage room and a cockloft.

This small bedroom, reached by a ladder, was Eden's personal favorite. It was only rarely that any of the servants approached it, and her uncle never ventured above the second floor, so that she was able to conceal herself within its comforting solitude and gaze out upon the whole of the plantation. Sometimes she curled up in an overstuffed wing chair with a volume of Shakespeare's sonnets—or perhaps the more scandalous verses of Byron—while other occasions found her content to take quill in hand and compose a long letter to her parents.

She toyed with the idea of going there now, but decided against it. Feeling strangely restless and out of sorts, she wandered into the drawing room. It was considered by many to be the most magnificent room in the entire mansion, for it was decorated with an array of pictures, engravings, and antiquarian relics. Towering shelves on either side of a marble fireplace contained books, maps, and some rare manuscripts acquired by William Stanhope on his extensive travels throughout Europe. He loved to boast of his fine possessions; never mind how many of his fellow human beings had sweated blood and tears to provide him with the necessary funds to indulge his expensive tastes.

Eden frowned at the portrait of her uncle as she strolled past it. She had just settled onto a velvet-upholstered chaise when she heard the sounds of a carriage drawing up in front of the house. Praying it would be Jamaica, she hurried to the window.

"Thank God!" she breathed, her eyes lighting

with both pleasure and relief when they fell upon Jamaica's fair, delicate features. She spun away from the window and hastened outside.

"Eden! Oh, I do hope I have not arrived too early," said Jamaica, untying the ribbon strings of her bonnet.

"Stuff and nonsense!" Eden retorted with an affectionate smile. She linked arms with the other young woman and began leading her up the steps. "I'm *so* glad you've come. I was quite out of my mind with boredom!"

"What then, am I naught but a cure for your boredom?" teased Jamaica, her blue eyes aglow with an impish sparkle. She looked exceptionally pretty that day, with her blonde curls pinned low upon her neck and her slender figure encased in a gown of primrose cotton. "Actually, I would have been here even sooner, if it were not for the fact that Charlotte and Mary insisted I remain to see their father's newest slaves."

"Newest slaves? Of what possible interest—"

"Did you not know? Mr. Stewart acquired two of the Americans! He bought them from Harry Langley's father only last night. Charlotte and Mary are virtually *beside* themselves with excitement! They think it prodigiously amusing to be able to lay claim to such rascals. I, however, think it a disgrace," she opined with a sudden frown.

"Uncle William told me your father protested their inclusion in the auction," remarked Eden. The memory of Roark's humiliation sent a shadow across her face. Taking a seat on a brocade sofa in the drawing room, she gently urged her friend down beside her. "In truth, I did not approve of it myself, but . . ." But bidding on one's husband is a different matter entirely, she mused with an inward sigh.

"And yet you yourself purchased one of them."

"I . . . I did not intend to. It was an impulsive gesture, and one which, I assure you, I have had cause to regret since."

"They say the other three are in Lord Sandringham's possession," continued Jamaica. "I can only hope they will receive better treatment there than those at the Stewarts'. Ambrose Stewart can be such a harsh man. Why, he had already sent them out to work in the fields." She paused for a moment and colored faintly before telling Eden, "One of the Americans was . . . well, he was quite attractive, not above five and twenty, with hair only a trifle darker than mine and eyes that were more green than blue. He did not appear to be the sort of man one would find among privateers. As a matter of fact, he appeared to have a certain breeding and intelligence. But he was terribly impertinent!"

"Impertinent?"

"Yes!" she reasserted with a nod, her blush deepening. "He looked at me in such a way as to make me feel positively *naked!*"

"Harry Langley would not take delight in hearing of it," Eden offered wryly. Her eyes shone with immediate contrition when she witnessed the other woman's discomfort. "Oh, Jamaica, please forgive me! I should not—"

"It's quite all right," the petite blonde assured her with a rather tremulous smile. "I daresay it was nothing but my imagination. And as far as Harry

Langley is concerned, I'll have you know that *that* gentleman has suffered a considerable fall from grace in my eyes!"

"What on earth has he done now?"

"He danced with me only once last night, and then had the audacity to ignore me altogether," she lamented. "Father still insists that Harry is a cad and a wastrel. At this point, I see little hope in a comeabout of his opinion." Her blue eyes narrowed in sudden recollection of another matter. "Speaking of last night—whatever could have prompted you to leave without saying goodbye? Donald Parkington-Hughes seemed to be quite distressed to learn of your absence, and your uncle made no secret of his own displeasure. But then, I daresay you already know that."

"That, and a good deal more," Eden murmured in annoyance. She saw that Jamaica was eyeing her quizzically. It would be a relief to be able to confide in someone, she thought, and there was none more caring or sympathetic than her young friend. Although she was only two years older than Jamaica, she felt that her own tragic experience with love had gifted her with a superior wisdom. Not that she considered herself far above her friend in any way; it was simply that Jamaica had led such a sheltered life.

"It was because of Donald that you left, wasn't it?" probed Jamaica.

"Yes." Eden nodded and confessed in an angry rush of words, "He and my uncle have conspired together to destroy my chances for future happiness! It seems I am to be married to Donald whether I like it or not—which I most assuredly do *not*—and that our betrothal is to be announced within the week!"

She leapt to her feet and swept across the room to take up a proudly defiant stance at the window. Her eyes, blazing their glorious emerald fire, moved instinctively toward the cane fields.

"Blast it, Jamaica, I cannot bear it! I cannot bear the thought of marrying that . . . that foppish 'mama's boy'! I will not be forced into a union with him, no matter what my uncle says! The two of them can do all the plotting and scheming they like! If I am to be a widow before I am a wife, then—"

"A widow?" Jamaica echoed in wide-eyed startlement. She stood and swiftly crossed the distance between them. "What in heaven's name are you talking about, Eden? How can you possibly be a widow before you're a wife?"

"I . . . I meant only that I would rather be one than the other," Eden stammered uncomfortably, furious with herself for having revealed too much. She quickly sought to make amends for her mistake. "Oh, Jamaica, I do not know what to do! My parents refuse to allow me to return home, and my uncle refuses to listen to reason. I tried discussing things with Donald last night, but he has taken it into his head that we are fated for one another!"

"Are you quite certain that you feel nothing for him?" her friend questioned in an attempt to play devil's advocate. "I have heard it said that a good many marriages lack passion in the beginning. If there is at least a mutual respect and good will, then perhaps—"

"I would never marry without love!" Eden declared with heartfelt vehemence. She remembered all too clearly the dissatisfaction she had felt when Donald kissed her—and the veritable wildfire of emotion when Roark had taken her in his arms. Dismayed to feel the warm, guilty color flooding her face, she fixed Jamaica with a stern look and challenged, "Would you marry a man for whom you felt nothing more than respect and good will? The truth now, Jamaica Harding!"

"Well, I don't . . . that is to say, I suppose I would prefer to follow my heart's wishes, but such a thing is not always possible."

"Why should it not be?"

"Because we are far too civilized to become prisoners to our passions," Jamaica replied dutifully.

"If we have become so civilized that we cannot sanction love," Eden countered with a toss of her raven curls, "then I prefer to become a savage!"

"Oh, Eden, you cannot mean that!" gasped Jamaica, shocked at her friend's outburst. "Would you have us forget all sense of duty and honor and—"

"I would have us *remember* that we, as women, have been put upon this earth to do more than bear children and grace a man's table!" That said, she released a long, ragged sigh and returned to the sofa, sinking down upon it while Jamaica followed suit.

"What is troubling you, Eden?" the younger woman asked softly, her eyes full of genuine concern.

"I don't know," she answered, shaking her head. "I honestly don't know. It's just that, since yesterday morning, my life has become almost painfully complicated!"

"Painfully complicated? Why do you say that?

And what has occurred since yesterday morning to make you—" She broke off as realization dawned. "Good heavens, Eden, you are referring to the slave auction, aren't you? But what has the American got to do with your impending betrothal to Donald Parkington-Hughes?"

"Nothing!" Eden hastened to deny. "Absolutely nothing!"

"I don't believe you. And I think I know why Donald is pressing for an immediate announcement. I think, my dear, that he is jealous."

"Jealous? Of whom?"

"Why, the bondsman, of course!" Jamaica disclosed triumphantly. She was quite pleased to have gotten to the root of the problem. "He was no doubt annoyed with you for having entered a bid at all. But I believe the greater majority of his vexation to have stemmed from the man's physical appearance. Charlotte and Mary did say they had heard he is quite handsome, remember? Donald probably thinks you bought that contract of indenture for no other reason than a sudden, violent attraction for its subject!"

"That is perfectly ridiculous!" Eden pronounced, her cheeks crimsoning.

"Well, I know that! But everyone *was* talking about your mischief—you have yet to tell me what prompted it—and I'm sure Donald could not help but be affected."

"I don't care how 'affected' he was; there is no excuse for his behavior!"

"Perhaps not," allowed Jamaica. Her eyes soon brightened with another idea. "Do you suppose I might see the bondsman while I am here? I must admit, I am curious to know if he is as handsome as

Charlotte and Mary reported.

"No," Eden decreed firmly. The last thing she wanted to do was seek him out.

"Oh, come now, surely it will do no harm," insisted Jamaica.

"Nor will it do any good!"

"He is at work in the fields, is he not?"

"How is it you know that?" Eden asked with a frown.

"I overheard your uncle telling Mr. Stewart," Jamaica admitted, dimpling prettily. She rose to her feet again and pulled on her bonnet. "Very well. I shall go by myself."

"You'll do no such thing, Jamaica Harding!"

"Will I not?" Casting Eden one last mischievous look, she headed blithely for the doorway. "It strikes me that I am in need of some fresh air. A walk about the grounds should prove quite invigorating."

Eden, forced to admit defeat, muttered an oath and gave chase. She was soon strolling with Jamaica beneath the trees, while the afternoon gave way to evening and the clouds offered yet another promise of rain. The long day of work on the plantation would end soon, but the slaves were still in the fields when the two young women paused beside the familiar panorama of sugar cane.

"Which one is he?" whispered Jamaica. Her searching gaze traveled across the half-naked men, many of whom were beginning to show signs of exhaustion.

As it turned out, Jamaica did not have to wait for Eden's answer. Roark's size and bearing set him apart.

"That's the one, isn't it?" Jamaica asked in

103

breathless excitement, nodding toward him. "That's the American!"

"Yes," Eden confirmed reluctantly. She prayed that he would not turn and see them. "Come along now, it's time we returned to the house," she urged her friend. Jamaica, however, would not hear of leaving yet.

"Oh Eden, he is incredibly well-favored!"

"He is incredibly overbearing!"

"What an odd thing to say! Why, one would think you actually knew the rogue!" The fascinated young woman was much too engrossed in her perusal of Roark's masculine charms to notice Eden's sudden tensing. "They say these Americans are completely without scruples when it comes to women. I wonder if it is true?"

"Please, Jamaica, let us go!" said Eden. She cast an anxious glance about them, hoping no one would come riding down the road and catch them ogling the men. It would be even more embarrassing if Roark were the one to catch them. "For heaven's sake, he—*they*—will see us!" she warned in growing apprehension of discovery.

"He is indeed quite handsome, but a trifle too dark for my tastes," mused Jamaica. Her thoughts drifted back to the other bondsman, the one she had seen at the Stewarts'. "I daresay he has made a good many conquests," she murmured, without realizing that she had spoken aloud. Luckily, Eden took no notice of her remark.

"By all that is holy, Jamaica Harding, I am going back without you if you do not . . ."

But it was too late. Roark had seen them.

Eden suffered a sharp intake of breath as she met his gaze. For the second time that day, he sent her a look that burned straight through her. *In such a way as to make me feel positively naked,* as Jamaica had said earlier. It was the same with her. Roark's piercing blue eyes undressed her, then raked over her soft, well-formed curves with such bold intimacy that she felt almost as though he had branded her with his hands.

"Now see what you've done!" she said to Jamaica in a furious whisper, her beautiful face flaming. What the devil must he think of her? she wondered in consternation. He no doubt believed she could not stay away. Oh, how she detested the man!

"What?" the blonde standing beside her asked in all innocence. Jamaica's attention suddenly returned to Roark. "Oh, you mean the fact that he is staring at us? Why, it is rather . . . unsettling, isn't it?"

Eden groaned softly and whirled to take flight. She did not get far.

It occurred to her afterward that fate, once again, had apparently decided to punish her for some real or imagined transgression. Whatever the case, she had traveled only a short distance when Edward Tallant's wagon seemed to come out of nowhere. It rumbled down the tree-lined avenue, the same one she was hurrying along in her haste to get as far away as possible from Roark St. Claire and his damnable ability to provoke her without uttering a single word.

The course of collision was unavoidable. By the time the plantation's manager caught sight of Eden—and she of the wagon—he was unable to stop the racing team of horses.

"Lady Eden!" he yelled, desperately attempting to turn the wagon.

Eden spun about, gasping in alarm. Her eyes filled with sudden terror at the certainty of death. Unable to do anything more than release a small, breathless cry, she was shocked to feel herself being grabbed and flung to the ground, safely out of the path of the wagon's crushing wheels.

Stunned, she lay in an inglorious tumble of white muslin and bare limbs. Her skirts were twisted up about her thighs. Her long black hair streamed wildly about her, and she was scarcely able to draw breath because someone was on top of her.

She blinked up at the man who had saved her. It was Roark. His hard body was pressing the trembling softness of hers down into the grassy earth.

"Dear God, Eden, are you all right?" he demanded in a low, vibrant tone. He raised up a bit, his eyes moving over her in swift, anxious scrutiny. Evidently, he believed her unharmed, for in the very next instant his handsome face grew thunderous. "Damn it, woman, you might have been killed! What the devil were you—"

"Get off of me!" hissed Eden.

His naked skin burned beneath her hands as she pushed frantically at his chest. Her head spun dizzily, but she could not say if her lightheadedness sprang from the rough treatment she had just suffered, or from contact with Roark's powerful, undeniably masculine frame.

"Eden! Oh Eden, I . . . I can scarce believe what happened! Are you all right?" Jamaica exclaimed in a breathless tumble as she came scurrying forward.

106

Her wide, astonished gaze flew rapidly back and forth between the two people entwined with such shocking familiarity upon the ground. *"Eden?"*

Roark finally climbed to his feet and pulled his wife up beside him. She jerked her arm free and shot him a look that was anything but grateful as she hurriedly shook her skirts back down about her legs.

"Lady Eden!" Edward Tallant had succeeded in reining the team to a halt farther down the road, and now arrived on the scene in a horrified rush. "May God strike me dead if I have harmed you in any way!" he uttered dramatically. "Please forgive me, Lady Eden! I could not stop! Would that I had overturned the wagon and killed myself rather than risk doing you injury!"

"I . . . I am fine, Edward," Eden assured him, her voice not quite steady as she raised a trembling hand to smooth the tangled, leaf-strewn mass of hair from her face. She was grateful for Jamaica's arm about her shoulders. "It was through no fault of yours that I was nearly run down," she told the plantation's manager in a calmer tone. "I was quite careless."

Acutely conscious of Roark's lingering presence, she drew herself proudly erect and refused to look at him. He stood silent and motionless, his penetrating blue gaze fastened upon her face.

"Mr. Tallant!" someone called from behind them.

All four turned to see one of the supervisors, a coarse, pockmarked fellow by the name of Fuller, crossing the last bit of distance in their direction. He was out of breath when he reached them.

"Begging your pardon . . . Mr. Tallant, but . . . but Simon here," he said, extending his coiled whip to indicate Roark, "he . . . broke away from the others when I wasn't looking and took off—"

"He saved Lady Eden's life!" Jamaica leapt to Roark's defense. "Why, I daresay she would at this very moment be lying crushed in the road if it were not for him!"

Simon? Eden echoed inwardly. She stole a glance at her husband. Her green eyes kindled with indignation at noting the faint smile touching his lips. She was certain he was secretly laughing at her dishevelment, and at her embarrassment as well. The thought did little to improve her simmering displeasure with him. Not even his heroic action on her behalf could erase the memory of the bold, infuriating behavior he had displayed the night before.

"What Miss Harding says is true." Edward reluctantly conceded the truth of Jamaica's words. He looked to Roark. "You have my gratitude, Simon."

Roark acknowledged the other man's thanks with a curt nod. Jamaica stared at Eden in obvious expectation. It appeared that everyone was waiting for her to speak.

"You have my gratitude as well," she obediently told Roark, though her tone lacked conviction. In truth, she *was* grateful . . . it was just that he was so damnably provoking. And arrogant and insolent and too blasted handsome for his own good.

"It was my pleasure, Lady Eden," Roark surprised her by declaring. His expression was solemn, but his eyes glowed with a disarming mixture of warmth and humor. He made her a slight, gallant bow, which seemed all the more incongruous given the fact that he was half-naked.

"Come, my dear, we must get you back to the house," said Jamaica, urging her solicitously forward.

"Yes, Lady Eden," agreed Edward. "You must rest. If you will allow me, I will carry you there myself."

"Carry me?" Her eyes flew to Roark. She colored and turned back to her uncle's trusted assistant. "No thank you, Edward, I am perfectly capable of walking. Besides, you've the wagon and horses to see to."

"Nonetheless, your suggestion is a splendid one, Mr. Tallant," Jamaica unexpectedly agreed. "It *would* be better if she were to be carried." Her gaze lit with satisfaction as it moved to Roark. "And Simon must be the one to do it."

"No!" gasped Eden.

"Yes," said Jamaica. "I insist. You are much too shaken, dearest Eden, and for all we know your ordeal may have gifted you with hidden injuries. It would be foolhardy indeed to take that risk."

"Simon has work to do," growled Fuller, making no secret of his own unhappiness with the idea.

"That may well be," Jamaica responded with a cool determination that was unusual for her, "but a few minutes away from the fields will exact no hardship on him—or anyone else."

"Miss Harding, surely you must see how unsuitable your suggestion is!" Edward tried reasoning. He frowned and entreated his employer's niece, "Please, Lady Eden, I would consider it an honor if you would let me assist you."

"I do not require any assistance!" Eden proclaimed in growing exasperation.

As if to prove her abilities, she pulled away from Jamaica and set off down the road. She inhaled sharply when a sudden, sharp pain shot through her ankle. It was too much to hope that none of the others had noticed her predicament.

"There is no further use in your being stubborn," said Jamaica. Ignoring the disapproving scowls of Edward and Fuller, she directed Roark, "Simon, carry your mistress to the house at once!"

"No!" Eden furiously objected.

Roark was oblivious to her protests. He strode forward and effortlessly scooped her up in his strong arms. When she muttered a blistering curse for his ears alone, he merely drew his unwilling burden closer and began conveying her toward the house.

Jamaica, meanwhile, lingered to have a word with Edward. Fuller returned to the fields. Eden was alone, at least temporarily, with the very last man she would have chosen to hold her captive in his arms.

"You are no doubt enjoying this greatly!" she accused in an ireful whisper. There was no way she could escape him, at least not without causing herself further embarrassment.

Roark said nothing, which made her all the more angry. She remained stiff and unyielding in his arms. Her senses, however, reeled at this latest contact between them, and she was acutely conscious of the feel of his naked flesh pressing against her.

Even through her clothing, she felt scorched. There was such heat and raw power emanating from his hard-muscled body. His face was mere inches from her own. Her eyes fell, and she was dismayed to discover that the rounded décolletage of her thin muslin gown exposed far too much bosom to his searing gaze. She squirmed in his grasp, but he tightened his relentless hold upon her.

"Be still, Lady Eden," he cautioned, his low, deep-timbred voice sounding close to her ear, "or else I'll give you something to complain about in earnest."

"And what, pray tell, do you mean by *that?*" she demanded, refusing to be intimidated by his threats.

"I could well steal a kiss."

"You . . . you would not dare!" she breathed, shooting a worried glance over his shoulder.

"Would I not?" he challenged. His deep blue gaze raked hungrily over the alluring swell of her breasts before returning to the flushed, stormy beauty of her countenance. "But I want more than a kiss from you, Eden. A damned sight more."

She shivered involuntarily and felt a warmth spreading throughout her entire body. It both frightened and confused her.

"I . . . I don't give a tinker's damn what you want, Roark St. Claire!" she stated defiantly, her own eyes daring him to call her a liar.

"You will, Mrs. St. Claire," he vowed. "You will."

She opened her mouth to offer a scathing retort, but she never got the chance.

"Here I am at last!" Jamaica announced, hastening forward to join them. "How are you feeling, my dear?" she asked her tousled friend.

Eden glimpsed the unholy light of amusement in Roark's eyes. She was seized by a powerful urge to hit him.

"I am perfectly well, thank you," she managed to

reassure Jamaica.

"I am so glad to hear it! A hot bath will be just the thing for you, followed by supper in bed. We must send for the physician to see to your ankle, of course, and then—"

"That will not be necessary," Eden insisted firmly.

Something in her voice must have warned Jamaica she would tolerate no further interference, for the petite blonde smiled and accepted defeat graciously.

"Very well. I'm quite sure Betsy will know what to do." She suddenly transferred her attention to Roark. "I understand you are from America, Simon."

"Yes, Miss Harding," he replied with only the ghost of a smile. "I am indeed."

"I chanced to see two of your fellow countrymen at the Stewarts' only a short time ago," Jamaica casually informed him. She was finding it a bit difficult to keep pace with his long, easy strides, and neither she nor Eden noticed the sudden tensing of his features. "I do not recall their names. In any case, I daresay they would be glad to know you are well."

"This is quite far enough," Eden pronounced as they approached the front steps of the house. "You may put me down now, *Simon*."

He chose not to obey. Carrying her inside, he headed straightaway for the staircase. Jamaica obliged by leading the way up to Eden's bedroom.

"In here, Simon," she directed, opening the second door to the right. She hurried inside to rearrange the bed curtains and position the pillows in readiness for the patient.

Roark crossed the room, which was filled with waning sunlight and decorated in a pleasing combination of cream and rose, and lowered Eden to the embroidered coverlet adorning the plump feather mattress of the fourposter. She refused to meet his gaze as he released her and then straightened to his full, spendidly superior height.

"Thank you, Simon," said Jamaica. As before, she looked to Eden to offer her gratitude as well.

"Yes," murmured Eden, shifting uncomfortably on the bed. "Thank you. You may go now." Go, damn you, and leave me in peace! she raged silently. She glanced up at him.

"As you wish, Lady Eden," he answered with all due respect. His eyes, however, held the promise of such fire and passion that she trembled anew.

Without another word, he turned and left. Eden stared dazedly after him.

"He is decidedly bold," signed Jamaica. "But not at all in an unpleasant way."

Eden closed her eyes and groaned inwardly.

Six

Eden wandered restlessly back to the window. There was a dull ache in her bandaged ankle, and she felt sore and bruised all over as a result of her earlier ordeal, but her physical discomfort was nothing compared to the maelstorm of emotion whirling within her.

She released another sigh and peered outward at the rain-swept landscape. The storm had broken shortly after Jamaica's departure, some two hours ago, and showed distinct signs of worsening before the night was through. Her uncle had sent word that he would be staying over at the Stewarts'. Normally, his absence would have been a source of great relief, but she found herself wishing he had returned.

In spite of Jamaica's endless stream of questions— some of them too near the mark for comfort—she had been sorry to see the other woman go. Anything would have been preferable to being alone with her thoughts. Particularly thoughts of Roark.

A flash of lightning streaked across the sky. It was

followed soon thereafter by a loud, earth-shattering roll of thunder. The storm had certainly come as no surprise to Betsy, who had predicted that the evening's "heat cloud" would give away to a violent downpour before darkness fell. Betsy was right more times than she was wrong, mused Eden.

Pressing a hand to the rain-cooled glass, she stared at her own lamplit reflection. She was tempted to hoist the window all the way upward and delight in the feel of raindrops on her face, but she told herself it would be utter folly to risk catching a chill for those few moments of childish abandonment. Childish or not, she had done it often enough back home.

"Home," she echoed aloud. Strangely enough, memories of her life back in England had become blurred. It was as if some other young woman had once danced and laughed there . . . as if some other young woman had come to Barbados with her heart broken and her reputation in shreds. But no, it was the same Lady Eden Parrish. The same Eden St. Claire, amended the inner voice.

She frowned and turned away from the window at last. Pausing to blow out the lamp, she scrambled beneath the covers on the bed. She had soaked in a tub of hot, lavender-scented water before donning a nightgown of sheer white lawn. Her hair was still slightly damp, and several small, wispy tendrils curled about her face as she lay back upon the pillow.

She chose to leave the bed curtains open. It would have been much too stuffy otherwise, she thought, given the fact that the windows could not be thrown wide. Her gaze traveled up to the ceiling, but there were no shadows dancing there. The moon, so free with its luminscence the night before, had been rendered impotent by thick, rumbling clouds.

"A dark and stormy night," murmured Eden, her mouth curving into a soft smile of irony at the familiar, oft-repeated phrase. Her smile quickly faded. She rolled to her side and punched at the unresisting softness of her pillow, taking perverse pleasure in imagining it was Roark St. Claire's handsome face. Heaven help her, what was she going to do about this impossible situation?

Heaven was about to help her far more than she might have wished.

It happened only a short time later. She had drifted off to sleep with singular ease, only to be startled awake by the sound of the window being raised.

She gasped and came bolt upright in bed, her fingers clutching at the covers while her widened gaze, full of heart-stopping alarm, flew to the window.

"Who . . . who is there?" she demanded in a hoarse, tremulous whisper.

All sorts of terrible possibilities ran together in her mind, but she was taken completely by surprise when Roark's voice reached out to her in the darkness.

"Quiet, Eden," he warned.

He climbed agilely into the room, ducking his handsome head beneath the window's lower edge before straightening to his full height again. He stood, dripping wet, while his open-mouthed bride wavered between relief and outrage.

Eden instinctively pulled the covers all the way up to her chin. Somewhere in the benumbed recesses of her mind, it occurred to her that Roark St. Claire was remarkably adept at climbing into young ladies' bedrooms in the middle of the night.

"Sweet Saint Christopher, what are *you* doing here?" she now demanded. She watched in breathless anticipation as his dark form approached the bed.

"Were you expecting someone else?" Roark parried, a brief, sardonic smile curving his lips.

His amusement vanished in the next instant, to be replaced by a sense of grim determination. He lit the lamp on the table beside the bed, then turned to stare down at Eden.

His fathomless blue eyes traveled swiftly over her alluring dishabille. She was becomingly flushed and wide-eyed, her long raven tresses spilling down about her face and shoulders. Her arms, covered only by the short puffed sleeves of her nightgown, were clasped up against her chest, as if she were seeking to shield her breasts from either his eyes or his touch.

The thought of those sweet, damnably tempting curves beneath the covers made him burn. The seductive scent of lavender drifted up to taunt him. Outside, the storm lashed furiously at the earth, but the room in which he stood was warm and bathed in soft golden light. And the woman he desired above all others was his for the taking.

Roark swore silently. His gaze darkened, and a tiny muscle twitched in the rugged smoothness of his cheek. There were no other outward indications of the white-hot desire blazing within him.

"I've come for some information," he announced.

"Information? Eden echoed blankly. *Information?*

Indignation finally won out over relief. She visibly bristled, her eyes filling with brilliant emerald fire.

117

Her fingers clenched the covers.

"How is it, Roark St. Claire," she fumed, "that you consider it permissible to risk sneaking into my bedroom for *information*, when only last night you threatened me with . . . with bodily harm for seeking you out to discuss—"

"My risk was insignificant compared to yours."

"What do you mean by that?"

"I mean, my dearest vixen, that there was little danger of anyone seeing me this night." He made a negligent gesture toward the window. As if by prior arrangement, raindrops splattered on the sill and danced into the room.

It was then that Eden finally took notice of the soggy condition of her husband. His thick, wet hair fell rakishly across his forehead. His trousers were plastered to his body, revealing every square inch of his hard-muscled leanness. He wore no shirt; she mused dazedly that she should be accustomed to the sight of his powerful naked chest and arms by now.

But she was not. She shifted her hips farther upward in the bed and cursed the wild leaping of her pulses. Taking refuge in her anger, she narrowed her eyes wrathfully at Roark

"How the devil did you manage to escape from the gaol?"

"It seems your Mr. Tallant was so overcome with gratitude for my having saved your infuriating little neck that he ordered me released from my bonds. The fact that some new field hands are expected tomorrow might also have influenced his decision," he added with another faint smile. "I now share more 'comfortable' accommodations with the other two bondsmen."

"But I thought Edward did not trust you!" she exclaimed, recalling what Betsy had told her.

"I do not seek his trust," Roark said with a frown.

Eden grew increasingly alarmed by the look in his eyes. It was beyond belief, she thought, that she should find herself alone with him in her own bedroom. Her mind raced to think of a way to make him leave before . . . before he took it in mind to do a good deal more than simply *look*.

"My uncle will hear you!" she lied, emphasizing the falsehood with a hasty glance toward the door.

"Your uncle is not at home."

"I . . . I shall scream if you do not leave at once!" she tried next.

"You won't scream." His supreme confidence was maddening. "And I'm not leaving until I get what I came for."

"Ah yes, the information," she remarked with biting sarcasm. "Pray, sir, just what is it you wish to know?"

"Miss Harding made mention of the fact that two of my men are at the Stewarts'. I want you to find out where the other three have been taken."

"But I already—" she blurted out, then stopped short and averted her gaze.

"You know where they are?" demanded Roark, his features dangerously solemn.

"No."

"Yes you do. Damn it, woman, where are they?" He took a menacing step closer.

"I will not tell you!" she uttered defiantly, her eyes flashing up at him. "You are an enemy, the captain or a privateer! It so happens that I am a loyal subject of England, and it would be traitorous of me to aid

119

you in any way!"

"You did not hesitate to lay that consideration aside when it suited you," he ungallantly reminded her. "Last night, you offered to trade my freedom for your own."

"That was different!"

"Where are they, Eden?"

"You're plotting an escape, aren't you?" she accused, her eyes growing round with enlightenment. "Do you really think you're going to be able to liberate those five men as well as yourself? For heaven's sake, Roark St. Claire, what you are planning is impossible!"

"For the last time, Eden, *where are they?*" He loomed ominously above her, his steely gaze boring down into the luminous green of hers. She drew in her breath upon a soft gasp and inched farther away to the center of the bed.

"What makes you think I won't tell my uncle what you are planning?" she put to him in a renewed burst of spirit.

"Because you desire nothing more than to be rid of me. Am I not right?"

"Yes, damn you!" Musing resentfully that he would find out sooner or later, she decided to give him the information he sought. Her capitulation, however, was done with ill grace. "They are at Lord Sandringham's. His estate lies just to the south of Ambrose Stewart's.

"An unhoped-for convenience," murmured Roark.

"You're going to get yourself killed!"

"And will you mourn if I do, my love?" he

challenged, only half in jest.

"I shall be the happiest widow in all of Barbados!" she retorted with a proud toss of her head.

Watching her, Roark silently cursed himself for a fool. He had tried to stay away. The need to find his men was not the true reason for his presence there, no matter how much he wanted to believe otherwise. He had come because of her and her alone, because she had set a firestorm of passion to raging within him and he was, after all, every bit as human as the next man.

His heart yearned to make her love him again. His flesh ached to possess hers. Still, he did his damnedest to resist temptation. He had risked enough in coming there. If he were discovered, he could be hanged. He was not a man given to concerns about his own safety, but he had every intention of staying alive long enough—fifty or sixty years should do it—to make his beautiful, headstrong wife pay for the agony she was putting him through. The thought of his revenge, which would be sweet for them both, provoked a sudden, near painful tightening of his loins.

Mustering every ounce of self-control he possessed, he sought a return to reason. There were his men to consider as well; they were his responsibility. No, he told himself sternly, the risk is too great . . .

"Well?" Eden prompted him with angry impatience. "You've gotten what you came for, have you not? Now get out!" she flung one bare arm toward the window in an eloquent gesture of dismissal. "You can leave the same way you came in! And you can *drown* for all I care!"

"You English are a bloodthirsty lot, aren't you?" he countered softly, his mouth curving into a slow, thoroughly devastating smile. Eden swallowed hard and did her best to ignore the warmth contained within those magnificent, gold-flecked blue orbs of his.

"Get out!"

She was satisfied when he moved to the window. He lifted a hand to the sash and turned to face her again.

"Take care, Eden," he warned. "Our positions will soon be reversed."

"Positions?"

"For the moment, you are my mistress. But I will soon be your master."

"It will be a cold day in hell when *that* event takes place, Roark St. Claire!" she shot back, dismayed to feel a tremor of fear course through her.

Her words appeared to have little effect upon Roark. He paused to give her one last scorching look, then made ready to climb out the window. Another flash of lightning streaked across the night sky. The accompanying thunder sounder closer than before. It was almost as if the storm had decided to beckon the lone traveler into its treacherous midst.

Eden did not know what prompted her to speak. She suddenly felt an inexplicable need to detain him. The means by which she accomplished this purpose were neither well considered nor prudent. Impulse can be a dangerous thing indeed.

"It might interest you to know that my uncle intends to have you declared legally dead!" she spoke in a breathless rush.

It worked. Roark pivoted slowly to face her again. A frown creased his damp, sun-kissed brow.

"By what means?" he demanded. His voice was quite low, his tone deceptively even. "As we both well know, there can be no proof of his claim."

"Nevertheless, he intends to petition the courts in Bridgetown! I have never told him—or anyone else—all the contemptible details, but he is firmly convinced that his petition will be granted. Which means I shall be free at last!"

"Why has he suddenly decided upon this course of action? What reason did he give for—"

"That is not important," she murmured. Her eyes fell guilty beneath the penetrating steadiness of his. "I merely thought I should warn you of his intent. It is more imperative than ever that you keep your true identity a secret."

"It is because he hopes to see you wed to another, isn't it?" He had his answer when he viewed the telltale color rising to her face. "And what do you have to say to the prospect?" he asked with deadly calm.

"Why, I . . . I am in favor of it, of course!" she lied unconvincingly. She stood by the ill-advised prevarication, however, and even went so far as to embellish it with, "As I told you last night, Donald Parkington-Hughes is a true gentleman. He cares for me deeply. And I for him. So you see," she concluded, drawing in a deep breath, "there is no reason for you to tarry here any longer. If you are planning to escape, then you might as well be about it! I shall say goodbye to you once and for all, Roark St. Claire. It was an ill twist of fate that brought you to these shores, and I can only pray that—"

She got no further, for at that point Roark suddenly threw all caution to the winds. A loud gasp of alarm broke from her lips as he crossed back to the bed in two long, angry strides.

"You're my wife, Eden, and, *by damn,* no other man shall have you!" he ground out.

Her eyes flew wide, and she blanched at the savage fury in his gaze. She clutched the covers more tightly to her chest again and made a desperate attempt to prevent what had always been inevitable.

"Get out!" she ordered hotly. "Get out before—"

But it was too late. Roark's temper, not to mention his passions, had already flared out of control. He breathed an oath and seized hold of his wife's arms. She gasped when he yanked her roughly up to her knees on the bed.

"You're mine, you green-eyed wildcat," he told her in a voice that was edged with raw emotion. "It's time you faced the truth!"

"I don't know what you're talking about!" she denied, struggling furiously within his grasp.

"I'm the only man for you, Eden. And so help me God, I'm going to make certain you never forget it!" *The risks be damned. . . .*

Without warning, he suddenly blew out the lamp and tumbled her back upon the bed. Imprisoning her body with his own, he grabbed her wrists and held them captive above her head. She opened her mouth to scream, but he brought his lips crashing down upon hers.

The kiss was everything Eden feared it would be— passionate and demanding and so fiercely intoxicating that all thought of resistance threatened to flee. She moaned in protest, then suffered another sharp intake of breath as Roark's tongue stabbed between her parted lips to boldly ravish the moist cavern of her mouth.

He pulled her wrists together and gripped them with one strong hand, so that his other hand could sweep downward to rip the covers away from her thinly clad softness. She twisted and squirmed beneath him, but he would not be denied. In less time than she would have believed possible, he had successfully cast the covers aside, tugged the hem of her nightgown well above her knees, and placed his body atop hers again.

She shuddered in mingled outrage and pleasure when his hand covered one of her breasts. The contact scalded her through the gossamer fabric. His fingers caressed her with both gentleness and wholly masculine impatience. An instant later, he drew the scooped bodice of her nightgown even lower. She trembled violently at the first touch of his hand upon her naked breast.

His lips relinquished hers and began roaming hotly, ardently across the flushed planes and valleys of her face. Her eyes swept closed again, and her senses reeled beneath his delectable assault. She was being swept away by a force more powerful than betrayal or revenge.

"Eden!" he murmured hoarsely. "Dear God, Eden, you've driven me to madness since the first moment I set eyes on you!"

"Damn you, Roark!" she gasped out. "Damn you for . . . for *this!*"

He gave a soft, triumphant laugh and trailed his lips downward along the silken column of her neck. The faint sound of fabric tearing rose in the warm, lamplit air, followed swiftly thereafter by a sharp gasp as his mouth took possession of the breast he had just laid bare. His warm, velvety tongue swirled about the delicate peak, his lips tenderly suckling. Eden arched upward, her head moving restlessly to and fro upon the pillow and her wrists turning within his grasp. She bit at her lower lip to keep from crying out.

He transferred his rapturous attentions to her other breast and released her hands at last. She clutched at his head, her fingers threading almost convulsively within the damp thickness of his hair. His hand swept downward to the junction of her pale, trembling thighs. He tugged the folds of white lawn out of the way.

"Roark!"

She tensed when his warm fingers finally claimed the treasure they sought. Wildfire streaked through her, and she was shocked to feel her legs parting, shocked to feel her hips straining upward into his skillful, wickedly pleasurable caress. She clung weakly to him when he moved back up to capture her lips once more.

The storm outside was nothing compared to the one raging so fierily beneath the fourposter's brocade canopy. Roark set about conquering the last of his bride's defenses. His methods were both sweet and savage, and Eden could not have stopped him even if she had wanted to.

He had not intended to love her with such

126

tempestuous haste, but there was no help for it. Nine long months of waiting had taken their toll—as had these past two days. It had been utter torment, watching her and yet not being able to touch her. And when he *had* touched her, both last night and earlier that same afternoon, he had burned with even more fury. The mere thought of her in another man's arms made his blood boil; *he would never let her go!*

Eden was certain she could bear no more of the exquisite agony Roark was creating within her. Passions built to a fever pitch . . . kisses grew more wildly inflamed . . . every taste and touch added fuel to ecstasy's fire. She was being seduced with such forceful mastery that there was no time to think, no time to remind herself that this was the man who had betrayed her so cruelly. Once, he had held her heart captive. And though she had sworn to hate him always, she could not now find the strength to deny him. Her traitorous flesh, so well loved and well warmed by his caresses, delighted in her surrender.

Roark's own endurance, meanwhile, was perilously near the limit. He waited no longer. With one hand, he unfastened the front flap of his trousers. He slipped his other hand beneath Eden's hips and lifted them in readiness for his final possession.

His hard, throbbing masculinity eased within her honeyed warmth, then plunged all the way to the hilt. Her sharp cry of mingled pain and surprise was lost against his mouth.

She tensed, but could not remain still. Roark's bold thrusts demanded a response. His hands curled about her hips, tutoring her masterfully into the age-old rhythm of love. Pain quickly gave way to a pleasure even more intense than before. Her fingers curled upon his broad shoulders, and she moaned softly when his mouth left hers.

Still, the wild flight of passion did not stop. It was almost as if they were being rewarded for their patience, however forced that patience had been. On and on it went, until at last the very pinnacle of fulfillment was theirs for the taking. They willingly embraced the release it offered.

A small, breathless cry broke from Eden's lips. Roark inhaled sharply, his hot seed flooding her with its potent warmth. The final blending of their bodies sent their very hearts and souls spiraling heavenward, and the victory was so complete that it took several long moments before they drifted back to earth again.

Reluctantly stirring, Roark rolled to his back and swept his bride's flushed, pliant softness against him. His blue eyes gleamed with a combination of love and triumph and satisfaction. She was his at last, he told himself. The risks had been well taken.

Eden was thoroughly stunned by what had just happened . . . and thoroughly contented. Never, *never* would she have believed it possible to feel what he had made her feel. It was beyond comprehension, the way she had reacted to him. Why, she had behaved little better than a wanton. Roark St. Claire had "ravished" her just as he had threatened to do the night before. And she, like some shameless lightskirt who could be tumbled at will, had offered little in the way of resistance.

Sweet Saint Christopher, she belatedly lamented, she must have taken complete and utter leave of her senses to have let him do what he had done. But oh, *what a sweet madness it had been.*

"Eden?" murmured Roark, his deep, resonant voice sounding close to her ear.

She did not answer.

"I must leave you now, my love," he told her. "The hour grows late."

Still, she said nothing. Roark was not surprised by her obstinate silence. His mouth curved into a soft, wryly appreciative smile of amusement, and he ran a possessive hand down along the bare curve of her hip.

"Next time," he promised, "we will not be hurried."

"There will not *be* a next time!" she finally recovered voice enough to declare.

In a flash of renewed spirit, she pushed herself away from him, scrambled to her knees on the bed, and yanked the covers up to her breasts. Her green eyes blazed vengefully down at the man who had stolen her maidenhood with such irresistible skill and ardor. It did not improve her temper any to wonder where the devil he had learned those secrets of seduction.

"I hate you, Roark St. Claire!" Hot tears gathered in her eyes, but she furiously blinked them away. "And I hate myself for having been fool enough to trust you! I could well see you hanged for this, you . . . you black-hearted scoundrel!"

"No court would fault a man for taking what is rightfully his," he replied with maddening equanimity. "You are my wife, Eden. You are mine and mine alone. And after tonight, there is little danger of your forgetting it."

He pulled his tall frame upright from the bed and stood gazing steadily down at her. Eden crimsoned anew as she watched him fasten his trousers. She had no idea what an alluring picture she presented, what with her lustrous black curls tumbling down about her in wild disarray and the silken curve of one shoulder left tantalizingly bare by the ineffectual draping of her nightgown. The last thing Roark wanted to do was to leave, but he told himself it would not be long before he shared a bed with his beautiful spitfire each and every night. The prospect set his eyes aglow.

"I bid you good night, Mrs. St. Claire," he proclaimed quietly.

Before she could guess his intent, he pressed a hard kiss upon her lips and left her. She stared numbly after him, her gaze fastened upon the window through which he had just disappeared into the storm-swept darkness.

And after tonight, there is little danger of your forgetting it. His words, all too true, echoed throughout the fiery turbulence of her mind. Choking back a sob, she flung herself facedown upon the rumpled softness of the bed.

Seven

"You be sleeping too sound to wake, Lady Eden," Betsy explained with a mild frown of bemusement. Telling herself that it wasn't like her young mistress to lie abed until midmorning, she suggested helpfully, "I guess the storm be making too much *bassa-bassa* last night?"

"The storm?" repeated Eden. In truth, she had forgotten all about it. Her memory improved in the next instant. Coloring guiltily, she sailed past Betsy to take her place at the dining table. "Of course, the storm," she murmured, sinking into one of the elegantly carved chairs. "Yes, I'm afraid it kept me awake most of the night."

It is a far better excuse than the truth, she thought, then gave a sudden, inward groan of dismay as she shifted about on the chair. She was plagued by an embarrassing soreness that morning; she ached in places she hadn't even known existed before last night.

"That be the reason I did not disturb you," said

Betsy, her golden brow clearing. "The master be asking for you only a few minutes ago, but I told him—"

"My uncle has returned home?" Eden asked in surprise.

"He be out in the stables," the housemaid confirmed with a nod. She ambled forward to pour Eden a cup of tea. "He said I was to tell you he be waiting."

"Oh, blast," Eden muttered crossly. She was troubled enough without having to listen to one of William Stanhope's bothersome lectures. That he would speak of Donald, she had little doubt. "I think I shall do without breakfast this morning, Betsy," she announced, rising to her feet again. "My appetite has fled."

"You do be looking pale," noticed Betsy. Her eyes shone with renewed concern. "Are you sure there be nothing wrong? Does your ankle pain you still?"

"No. No, my ankle is fine." That, at least, was true. "It scarcely hurts at all anymore. But I must admit, I am feeling a bit out of sorts today," she allowed, managing a brief smile. *How could I hope to be otherwise, given what Roark St. Claire has done to me?* "I shall help you with the baking later if—"

"Oh, but there be a tea at the Stewarts' this afternoon," Betsy reminded her. "Mistress Harding said I was to make sure you be going."

"Very well," sighed Eden, realizing there was no way out of it. She consoled herself with the thought that at least Jamaica would be there.

She took her leave of Betsy and returned upstairs. After changing into her riding habit, she ventured

132

outside to find her uncle. He stood talking with the stable master, who had expressed some misgivings over the recent behavior of his employer's prized stallion.

"We shall discuss the matter later," William told the old man in dismissal, taking note of Eden's approach. The stable master touched his hat respectfully and took himself off.

"Good morning, Uncle," said Eden. There were faint circles under her eyes, and she had a certain air of preoccupation about her, but she looked quite lovely in the blue riding costume and matching befeathered hat. "I trust you enjoyed your visit with the Stewarts?" she inquired politely.

"You are planning a ride?" He eyed her attire with obvious disapproval.

"Do you have any objections?"

"As a matter of fact, I do," he replied with a frown. "Donald will be paying us a call shortly."

"But I have no wish to see him!" she protested.

Indeed, she mused resentfully, that was the very *last* thing she needed. After Roark had left her bed, she had spent the remainder of the night in a tumultuous whirl of confusion, self-recrimination, and righteous anger. This was all tempered by sweet memories of her husband's wild loving, though she would never own up to that. Was she now to spend the next several hours fighting off Donald Parkington-Hughes' highly disagreeable advances?

"You will simply have to inform him that I am not at home!" she told her uncle defiantly, sweeping past him. She was startled when he seized her arm in a punishing grip.

"You listen to me, you little fool!" he growled, his face becoming very red. "I will not see my plans ruined by your continuing obstinance! You *will* be pleasant to Donald, by damn, and you *will* marry him!"

"Why is it so important to you?" demanded Eden. Her own temper flared, and she jerked her arm free. "What difference can it possibly make to you if I do not choose to marry him?"

"Are you totally wanting of sense? Can you not see the advantages of the match?"

"Advantages to whom?" Her eyes filled with sudden understanding as she stared at him. The truth was written plainly on his face, right there for her to see. "Why, you've made some sort of financial arrangement with him, haven't you? Dear God, you've *sold* me to the man!" she accused, horror dawning on her. She felt disgusted by the thought.

"Call it what you like—William did not bother to deny it—"but know that I will not be thwarted in this! The future of Abbeville Plantation rests upon it, my future and yours, and I'll not have you throwing away our best hope for even greater prosperity!"

He calmed himself after that outburst. When he spoke again, it was in an attempt to reason with her.

"Donald's father has been most generous in his offer," he disclosed. "More than generous, considering the fact that his son will be getting a 'tarnished' bride. And you've shown no sign of affection toward anyone else these past eight months. Do you not think it time you finally put your unfortunate past behind you? No hint of scandal can touch you once you are Donald's wife. You will be envied and respected. And your parents can desire nothing more than to see you safely settled with a man of Donald's caliber. They will be overjoyed to hear of your marriage."

"No, Uncle," she disagreed, slowly shaking her head. "I cannot believe they would wish me to marry without love."

"Such sentimental drivel does well enough for the lower classes, but it is far beneath a young lady of your breeding and position. How can it compare with the sort of life Donald is offering you?"

"Life with a man like Donald would be unbearably tedious. But I tell you in all honesty, it would not matter if he were the handsomest, most exciting man on the face of earth—still, I would not marry him!"

You are mine and mine alone, Roark had said. Blast it all, she was no man's!

"You will change your mind," William assured her. His eyes moved past her to where the suitor in question was at that moment approaching them on horseback.

Eden spun about, her own gaze following the direction of her uncle's triumphant one. She watched in dismay as Donald rode down the same tree-lined avenue she and Jamaica had traversed the day before—and with such disastrous results. Sorely tempted to flee, she knew she could not. She was trapped.

"Good day to you, my dearest Lady Eden!" Donald called out, gallantly tipping his hat. He soon drew to a halt and dismounted. His face was wreathed in smiles when he turned to her uncle and said, "It is a

135

pleasure to see you again, sir. My father sends his regards." He looked to Eden again, raising her hand to his lips. "You are an absolute vision this morning. And I see you are ready for our ride."

There was nothing in his behavior to indicate that his affections had undergone a change upon learning of her scandalous entanglement with another man. If anything, Eden thought in exasperation, he appeared to be even more devoted than before.

"*Our* ride?" she echoed meaningfully, casting her uncle a narrow, reproachful look. She disengaged her hand from Donald's grasp and said with a proud lift of her head, "I am sorry, but it seems I completely forgot. I have already ridden." She silently dared both men to call her a liar.

"That's quite all right," Donald spoke like the well-bred English gentleman he was. "But I daresay an additional turn about the grounds will do no harm."

He gave her no opportunity to deny him. Taking possession of her hand again, he pulled it through the crook of his arm and led her away toward the stables.

Eden was soon riding alongside him, wishing for all the world that she had never ventured out of her bedroom that morning. She mentally cursed the fates for having given her not merely one man to bedevil her, but two. But then, she mused in wrathful irony, not every woman could count herself fortunate enough to have both a fiancé *and* a husband.

"I think I should tell you that my father has already set the appropriate judicial wheels in motion," Donald remarked once they were well away from the house.

"What in heaven's name are you talking about?" asked Eden, unable to keep a telltale edge from her voice.

"Why, your annulment, of course," he replied with exaggerated patience. "I rode into Bridgetown first thing this morning. My father assured me that a decision will be forthcoming by the end of the week." He sent her a warm, eagerly possessive look. "We can be married within the month."

"Doesn't the fact that I am a . . . a *tarnished* woman make any difference to you?" she queried, employing her uncle's term for it. He had no idea exactly how tarnished she was.

"Come now, my dear, you do yourself a grave disservice with such talk. Never shall you hear any word of condemnation from my lips. You were undeniably foolish in your judgment, but in the end no real harm was done. Your uncle has told me of the despicable manner in which your husband abandoned you shortly after the elopement."

"Has he also told you that my husband is an American?"

"Was," Donald pointedly corrected. "As far as I am concerned, the villian is every bit as dead as your uncle is willing to claim. But yes, I am aware of the fact that his father was American and his mother English. I must say, I am curious about one thing."

"And what is that?" she was almost afraid to ask. All this talk of Roark was provoking in the extreme.

"The issue of poor judgment aside, I fail to see how you could ever be tempted into an association with such a man in the first place. He was obviously far

137

beneath you."

Her emerald gaze sparked at that. Tempted, she thought bitterly. She had been tempted all right. And the temptation had led her into even more personal calamity than she had bargained for. There was certainly little hope of obliterating all thought of Roark St. Claire now. He had seen to that. And in a highly effective, irreversible way.

Growing warm, she shifted uncomfortably in the saddle and glanced at Donald. The impulse to tell him the truth was great. On the one hand, she reasoned with herself, she should remain silent until after the annulment had gone through. But on the other, she could put a stop to any further discussion of marriage by confessing to him that she was not quite so "kissless" a bride as he believed. It was an awful dilemma, she concluded with a long, ragged sigh.

"I don't understand it myself," she finally admitted in response to Donald's statement of confusion.

Then, before he could introduce the subject of his own undying love and devotion to her again, she touched her whip lightly to her horse's flank and galloped away. Donald flushed in anger at having been left behind with so little attempt at civility. His aristocratic features tightened, and he urged his mount forward to give chase.

Roark caught sight of them when they rode back toward the house. He knew instinctively that Donald was the man who had been paying court to Eden.

His magnificent blue eyes kindled with a savage, near murderous light as jealousy shot through him. In that moment, he would have gladly dragged the fancy Englishman bastard from his horse and thrashed the very devil out of him. His fingers clenched about the shovel he was holding.

Eden could not keep her eyes from straying in his direction as she rode past the fields. Scarcely aware of what she was doing, she tugged on the reins and slowed her mount to a walk.

Embarrassment washed over her when her gaze lit upon Roark's handsome face. She could feel her cheeks burning with guilty color. Musing resentfully that she had half expected him to run off in the night, she was dismayed to realize that her heart was pounding with excitement as well as alarm.

Sweet Saint Christopher, how is it possible that he looks even more wickedly appealing than before? she thought with an inward groan. With shocking and painful clarity, she remembered everything that had occurred between them the past night. Every heated word and kiss and caress . . .

"Eden?" Donald's voice startled her from her reverie. "Who is that insolent fellow?" he demanded, drawing up beside her and flinging a curt nod toward Roark. "I don't like the way he is looking at you."

"That is the American," she murmured. She silently heaped a thousand curses upon his head.

"I might have guessed as much," said Donald. His gaze narrowed as it flickered disdainfully over the tall, broad-shouldered man in the near distance. "He looks to be a common, dangerous rogue. Your uncle was wise to deny you ownership of him."

"Blast it, Donald, you know I do not approve of slavery!" she startled him by proclaiming hotly.

She reined about and took off again. Her bewildered suitor hesitated only a moment before following. Roark stared after them.

Donald's visit was of mercifully short duration. Announcing that he had business to see to at home, he left Eden with the promise of claiming the first three dances with her at the ball Lord Sandringham was giving that evening. She forced herself to bid him a cordial farewell, offered no response whatsoever to his promise, and glared at her uncle's smile of satisfaction before marching angrily inside the house.

Some four hours later found her sitting in the midst of the Stewarts' drawing room. It wasn't often the Misses Stewart invited her to tea; it was even less often that she could be prevailed upon to accept their invitation. Today, however, she had needed the diversion, and Jamaica's presence there was a balm to her sorely tested nerves.

"My father says we are to go home for Christmas," the petite blonde sighed, lowering her white China teacup to its companion saucer. "I endeavored to make him understand that *this* is our home now, but he would hear none of it."

"But you and Colonel Harding have lived here for five years already!" Charlotte pointed out unnecessarily.

She was pale and slender, a pinched-featured young woman whose taste in clothing was far more suited to a girl making her first appearance in society rather than someone who had been "out" for a considerable amount of time. Clad today in a simple, rather childlike gown of cream gauze, she looked virtually colorless.

Her sister, on the other hand, displayed a passion for color—too much color. Mary wore a silk dress of such a vibrant shade of peacock blue that her light brown hair and gray eyes were completely overwhelmed. Neither she nor Charlotte were great beauties, but that might have been overlooked if not for their sour dispositions. They had been frequently waspish to Eden, whom they envied almost as much as they loved themselves.

"I must simply resign myself to the visit," said Jamaica, who could never be melancholy for long. "But I cannot help viewing it with some trepidation. My mother's family . . . well, you see, they are not exactly what one would call warm and welcoming."

"I'm sure our own dear relatives would never behave that way to us," Mary remarked loftily. She transferred her cup and saucer to the double-tiered table beside the sofa and looked to her other guest. "And what do you hear from *your* family, Lady Eden?"

"Only that they are well."

"I suppose your father is quite busy," opined Charlotte, "what with his position in the ministry and this accursed war which drags on and on."

"He is indeed," acknowledged Eden. Her thoughts, however were at present centered on Jamaica and the dangers of a homeward voyage.

"I have never understood why the Americans raised such a veritable hue and cry over the impressment of their sailors into the Royal Navy," Mary saw fit to interject at this point. "Why, we were not asking any more of them then we have asked of our own men. And they do owe us a great deal, do they not? That is to say, if it were not for Britain, America would still be nothing but an uncivilized, godforsaken wasteland inhabited by murdering savages!"

"Perhaps," Jamaica commented thoughtfully. "But my father says impressment was only the last among many reasons the hostilities broke out. Ill feelings, I overheard him remarking to one of our acquaintances only the other day, have existed between the two countries for years. The war with France certainly did not help matters any."

"Well, I say it is those Yankee privateers who are to blame for the majority of the trouble!" This came from Charlotte, who glanced about to make certain she had everyone's attention. She took no notice of Eden's sudden tensing beside her. "Those insolent scoundrels prey upon our ships, steal our goods, and, so it has been reported, are even audacious enough to sail right into British channels and pillage the countryside right under the very noses of our own frigates!"

"We have two American bondsmen in our fields even as we speak," Mary boasted to Eden.

"Yes. Jamaica has told me." Her gaze fell to the half-finished cup of tea she held in her lap. Roark's face swam before her eyes.

"They are themselves privateers! And it so happens they were captured along with the man you saw fit to purchase," said Charlotte, exchanging a smugly superior look with her sister. "He was their captain, you know."

"Was he?" Eden pretended indifference.

"Would you care to see them?" offered Mary.

"No, thank you."

"But we insist! Do we not, Charlotte?"

Jamaica sought to intervene. "I don't think Eden would be interested—"

"Nonsense!" Charlotte cut her off. "Why shouldn't our *dear* Lady Eden see for herself what fine and well-favored men they are. I am quite sure they are even more handsome than the one she has at Abbeville Plantation!"

"Lord Sandringham purchased the other three," Mary took pleasure in reporting. "His own daughters are much too young to suffer any disappointment over the fact, but I have heard it said that his Americans are not nearly so wondrously striking as ours."

"I have a splendid idea!" Charlotte suddenly announced. "After we have taken a turn about our own grounds, we shall journey to Lady Eden's estate so that we may compare the men with even greater—"

"Absolutely not!" pronounced Eden. Rising abruptly to her feet, she set her cup and saucer aside with an accompanying clatter. "What you are suggesting is . . . is positively indecent!"

"How so?" challenged Mary. She and the other two ladies stood as well. "How can you possibly make that charge, Lady Eden Parrish, when you yourself were the one who set the tone of things?"

"Yes!" Charlotte, not surprisingly, threw in with her sister. "You were not too much of a lady to choose one of them at the market yesterday morning!"

"I did not *choose* anyone!"

"Then how did it come about that you offered a bid

for the man?" asked Mary. She cast Eden a knowing smile and said, "Come, my dear, you are among friends here. We do understand, you see."

"And just what the devil is it you think you understand?" Eden demanded, her green eyes flashing.

"There is no need to use such rough language," scolded Charlotte with infuriating calm. "And there is no need to fly off the handle. Donald Parkington-Hughes, while a perfectly delightful gentleman, cannot be nearly so attractive as 'forbidden fruit.'"

"Why, I myself experience a certain trembling whenever one of the rogues casts his eyes upon me," Mary confided with an unbecoming giggle. She directed a mischievous look toward Jamaica. "Even our own Miss Harding seems affected by them."

Poor Jamaica blushed and averted her gaze.

"I'm sure I don't know what you mean," she denied, albeit not too convincingly.

"Come now, Jamaica, we saw you exchange significant glances with the younger of the two when you were here yesterday," teased Charlotte.

"I'll wager Harry Langley never looked at you the way *he* did!" Mary added. "No English gentleman would dare look at a woman that way, unless she were the sort who invited liberties. And even then—"

"Please, may we not change the subject?" Eden recommended in a voice laced with anger, noting her friend's discomfort.

"I say we delay our walk no longer!" decreed Charlotte.

She and her sister linked arms and headed for the doorway. Eden sighed in exasperation. Jamaica looked as if she were battling the urge to take flight in the opposite direction.

"I suppose we must go along," she whispered to Eden.

"Perhaps, with a bit of luck, we can manage to lose them once we are outside."

The pretty young blonde smiled at that. She took Eden's hand and pulled her from the room.

The walk proved invigorating, to say the least. Charlotte and Mary set a brisk pace on the way out to the fields, but the afternoon was pleasantly cooled by the tradewinds, while the air smelled fresh and sweet in the wake of the previous night's storm.

"There they are!" Charlotte was soon declaring. Her eyes shone with excitement as she lifted a hand to rest it atop the white picket fence lining the path. "Are they not every bit as well favored as I said?"

Mary joined her sister at the fence. Eden strolled leisurely forward, but Jamaica hung back.

The two Americans were working together within earshot of the women. One of them spared only a brief, passing glance for the quartet of onlookers, but the other straightened and stared directly at them.

Eden knew right away that he was the man Jamaica had told her about. He was very attractive indeed, she mused to herself. His dark blond hair curled low upon his neck, and his blue-green eyes glowed with an unfathomable light. He was young and strong and nearly as bold as his captain, judging from the way his gaze raked over them. The faint, challenging smile which played about his lips was obviously provoked by one young lady in particular.

Jamaica, standing apart from the others, raised her

eyes at last. She gasped softly when she met the bondsman's gaze. Two bright spots of color stained her cheeks, and she found herself unable to look away.

Something passed between them in that moment, though neither could as yet put a name to it. Whatever it was, they both sensed that, somehow, nothing would ever be the same for them again. . . .

"Well?" demanded Mary, turning to Eden with all confidence of victory. "I defy you to say your new slave is any more pleasing to the eye than ours!"

"For heaven's sake, they are men—not horses!" she admonished in a simmering undertone. She felt decidedly ill at ease, and she chided herself for having been a part of the blasted excursion. Still, she could not help thinking that these men were nothing compared to the likes of Roark St. Claire.

His appearance is masculine perfection . . . as is his lovemaking. Where the devil had that thought come from? she wondered, her face flaming guiltily.

"I suspect that you are jealous," remarked Charlotte in a tone full of spite. "Take a good look at them. Are they not firm and well muscled?"

"Oh, do be quiet!" murmured Eden. She glanced toward Jamaica, only to feel a sharp twinge of concern at the look on the younger woman's face.

"I will not be quiet!" Charlotte replied, much affronted. "Simply because you are too much of a hypocrite to confess an interest in them does not mean that I should be one as well!"

"You know," Mary spoke matter-of-factly, "I should not be at all surprised if my father were to decide to breed them with some of the women—"

146

"Shut up!" Jamaica startled everyone by hissing angrily. "Shut up, you witless girl, they'll hear you!"

Close to tears, she suddenly whirled about and began making her way back through the fragrant greenery. Eden flung both sisters a furious, quelling glare before hurrying after her.

"Jamaica!" she called anxiously. "Jamaica, please wait!"

"Oh Eden, how *could* they?" the younger woman choked out when she finally slowed to a stop. "It was cruel in the extreme!"

"Yes, it was," Eden concurred wholeheartedly. She slipped an arm about her friend's shoulders and smiled archly. "Would it not be vastly amusing to see our own dear Charlotte and Mary put upon the auction block? I daresay *their* breeding capabilities would never be considered." She was rewarded by the pleasant sound of Jamaica's laughter.

"You are a wicked woman indeed, Lady Eden Parrish," Jamaica said tremulously, "and I love you for it!" She bestowed a warm hug upon her friend, then raised a lace-edged handkerchief to her moist eyes. "It isn't so much that I mind their having formed such immodest opinions about the Americans," she sighed, dabbing at her tears. Blushing anew, she went on to confide, "I mean, I myself cannot remain completely . . . well, completely *unmoved* by the sight of him."

"Him?"

"What?"

"You said, 'him,'" Eden reminded her gently.

"Did I?" Jamaica asked in surprise. She appeared quite flustered all of a sudden, and her bright gaze fell

147

hastily beneath Eden's sympathetic one. "I meant 'them,' of course."

"Of course."

Eden smiled and clasped her hand. Happily forgetting about the Misses Stewart, they set off toward the house.

"I . . . I suppose you noticed the younger of the two," Jamaica remarked a few moments later.

"Yes. He is quite handsome. And every bit as bold as I had expected."

"But not nearly so much as Simon."

"No." It was Eden's turn to blush. "None of them can be *that* bold."

"Do you think the war will end soon?" Jamaica queried suddenly.

"We can only pray that it does."

"And what do you suppose will happen to the Americans when it does? I know they are bound into servitude here for seven years, but if England should somehow lose the war, then is it not possible they could be set free?"

"I would not be at all surprised if the Americans are gone from these shores even before the outcome has been decided," Eden remarked with a troubled frown.

Roark would be out of her life soon, she told herself. Although he had vowed never to leave without her, she did not for a moment believe him. He cared nothing for her; he had merely used her for his own selfish purposes—again—with even more disastrous results than before. No matter how desperately she wanted to forget, she knew the memory of his wild, passionate loving would burn in her mind forever.

But he would be gone. He would escape at the first available opportunity. And she would never see him again. . . .

"I daresay Charlotte and Mary would be disappointed in the extreme if that event should occur."

"Event?" she echoed blankly, Jamaica's voice drawing her back to the present.

"If the bondsmen were to leave somehow," Jamaica reiterated. "Though, I must admit, I fail to see how they could do that. There can be no chance of escape. Even if they were to try, they would in all likelihood be apprehended and . . . and punished." There was a noticeable catch in her voice, and a sudden shadow crossed the heart-shaped perfection of her face. "Good heavens, you don't really think they would ever be foolish enough to make such an attempt, do you?"

"It has been my experience thus far that Americans will do as they please—and damn the consequences," Eden pronounced with more than a touch of bitterness.

"Your experience?" It was Jamaica's turn to look baffled. Her brow cleared in the next instant, however, as she said, "Oh, I suppose you are referring to Simon." She would have been astonished to learn just how much truth her words held. "Yes, I can imagine that he would do entirely as he pleased. Under different circumstances, that is."

He has managed quite well under the present ones, Eden disputed silently. Her emerald gaze filled with the light of remembrance once more.

Conscious of Jamaica's scrutiny, she was glad they

had reached the house again. Etiquette made it necessary for them to await their hostesses' return, but Charlotte and Mary were none too pleased when they came bustling into the drawing room a short time later. They pounced, indignant and reproachful, upon their errant guests, accusing them of all manner of jealousies and hypocrisies and sentimentalities.

Eden was only too happy to take her immediate leave. She offered to spirit Jamaica away as well, but it had been arranged that Colonel Harding would come to collect his daughter on his way home from Bridgetown. She had no choice save to abandon her young friend to the two sisters. *Harpies* would be a fitting term for them, she mused with an inward sigh.

Dreading the prospect of the Sandringham's ball that evening, and with her thoughts and emotions in the perpetual, Roark-induced chaos they had suffered the past three days, she returned home. It was her intent to escape into the garden for the remainder of the afternoon, where she would try to sort things out. But in truth, she knew there was little hope of that until Roark St. Claire had vanished from her life again.

Why did the thought of his departure give her no pleasure?

The carriage was drawing up in front of the great house when she spied a crowd of men gathered near the barn. She allowed Zach to hand her down, and was just about to hasten forward to investigate the commotion when Betsy rushed down the steps to enlighten her.

"They be going to whip him, Lady Eden!" the

150

young housemaid reported in obvious agitation.

"Who?" demanded Eden, her eyes flying instinctively toward the barn.

"The American!"

"What?"

"It be because of Jonah!" Betsy explained in a breathless tumble of words. "Mr. Fuller be angry and striking that poor boy, and Simon come running up and grab Mr. Fuller's hand! Mr. Fuller told Mr. Tallant, and then the master be passing by, and now Mr. Tallant be going to whip the American!"

"He most certainly is *not!*" Eden furiously declared.

Outraged by what she had just heard, she spun about and raced across the well-manicured lawn. Her one thought was to prevent the injustice about to be visited upon her husband; she did not pause to ask herself why his welfare should matter so very much. No matter what he had done to her, she could not bear to see him hurt and humiliated so cruelly.

The sound of angry voices drew her onward. She pushed her way through the crowd of men—slaves and supervisors who had been called to watch—and finally broke free into the clearing in front of the barn. Her furious, searching gaze fell upon her uncle. And then upon Roark.

Her heart twisted painfully at the sight of him. He was stripped to the waist, his wrists bound high above his head so that he was imprisoned with his face against the side of the building. He showed no fear, only a grim, smoldering resignation. He was not a man to ask for mercy.

"Eden! By damn girl, this is no place for you!"

William ground out. He stalked forward and grabbed her arm. "Get back to the house at once!"

"I will not allow this . . . this barbarism to take place!" she proclaimed with great feeling, jerking away from his grasp. She looked at Roark again, but would not allow herself to meet his gaze. Her blazing eyes shot to Edward Tallant. He was standing ready, whip in hand, to commence the punishment. "Put that whip down!" she commanded hotly.

"I'm afraid I can't do that, Lady Eden," he replied. His own gaze flickered nervously toward his employer.

"You are not going to whip that man, Edward Tallant!" she decreed, then rounded on her uncle again. "He did nothing more than try to protect Jonah! Betsy told me—"

"I don't give a damn what she told you!" William brusquely cut her off. "No slave can be allowed to lay hands upon his superior!"

"But Jonah is only a boy! It is only natural that Ro—that Simon would seek to protect him!" Her eyes hastily scanned the crowd for Jonah, but there was no sign of him. She did, however, see Fuller. "You had no right to strike Jonah!" she charged. The man's surly expression made her temper flare to an even more perilous level. "But then again, it gives you great satisfaction to intimidate those who are weaker than yourself, doesn't it? Indeed, this is not the first time you have taken advantage of your position!"

"The young whelp got nothing more than what he deserved," rasped Fuller. "I told him to saddle my horse and he gave me some stupid excuse to mask his own laziness!" He flung an arm toward Roark while relating vengefully, "And that Yankee bastard— begging your pardon, Lady Eden—why, he would have gotten his hands about my throat if not for Mr. Tallant's coming along when he did!" He did not see fit to add that it had taken five strong men to subdue the prisoner.

"Enough of this nonsense!" William pronounced in an impatient growl. To Eden he bit out, "Your interference is an insult to yourself as well as to me! Now do as I say and get back to the house!"

"No!" She adamantly shook her head and stood firm. "Tell Edward to put his whip away, Uncle, for I will *not* let this happen!"

"You, my dear, haven't the power to stop it."

He nodded curtly toward his manager, thereby giving a silent command for the whipping to begin at last. Eden's gaze filled with horror. Her mind raced to think of a way to prevent the brutal flogging which had been employed all too often as a means to control the slaves. Dear God, she could not let it happen to Roark. She could not!

Finally, desperation prompted her to fly forward and plant herself squarely in front of her husband. She whirled to face the crowd, folding her arms across her chest and raising her head in a gesture of proud defiance.

"I claim responsibility for this man, and anyone who dares to mistreat him will have to answer to me!" she vowed in clear, ringing tones.

"Get out of the way!" snarled her uncle, his face reddening.

"Please, do as he says, Lady Eden," Edward

entreated in growing alarm.

"Never!" she uttered dramatically. She was startled to hear Roark's deep, authoritative voice sound behind her in the next instant.

"Stay out of this," he ordered in a low tone meant for her ears alone. "I'll not hide behind a woman's skirts."

"You are hardly in a position to choose!" she countered, turning her head to fling him a quelling look.

"Damn it, Eden, get away from the man!" William demanded, his gaze darting anxiously across the faces of the onlookers. Though infuriated and embarrassed by his niece's willful defiance, he was reluctant to make things even worse by dragging her bodily away from the American. "I give you fair warning—"

"Perhaps, sir, we should let Simon's punishment take another form," Edward suggested helpfully.

"There will be no punishment at all!" Eden put forth in a strong-minded manner.

"That is not for you to decide!" said her uncle.

William Stanhope was beaten and he knew it. Once again, his headstrong niece had made him look the fool in front of witnesses. To hell with the little shrew! he swore inwardly, glad that Donald Parkington-Hughes would soon be taking her off his hands. With a silent promise to hold her accountable for this latest impertinence, he signaled to his manager to release the prisoner.

"Get back to work, damn it! All of you!" he angrily instructed the others. He stalked away, soon disappearing inside the house.

154

The crowd quickly dispersed. Eden stepped aside and watched while her husband was untied by two of Edward's men. The plantation's manager stood fingering the whip in his hands as Roark turned to face him.

"Next time, Simon, you'll not be so lucky," Edward warned in a voice full of ill will.

A faint, mocking smile touched Roark's lips, but he offered no response to the other man. His fathomless blue gaze moved to fasten upon his wife.

"You should not have troubled yourself on my account, Lady Eden. But my thanks to you all the same," he told her quietly.

His eyes strayed boldly downward, lingering first upon the sweet mouth he had ravished with his own . . . and then upon the full young breasts he had branded so completely with his lips and hands. His desire for her burned hotter than ever; that first tempestuous union had only succeeded in stoking the blaze of passion's fire.

His thoughts were all too clear to Eden. Hot color flew to her cheeks, but she did her best to maintain a semblance of composure.

"I would have done the same for any man," she insisted with admirable calm, then groaned inwardly. She had little doubt he would attach a different meaning to her words. Now that the ordeal had passed, she was feeling both awkward and defensive. "I . . . I consider Jonah a friend. I am grateful for your intervention on his behalf."

"Back to the fields with you," Edward directed Roark, giving him an impatient jab with the whipstock.

Eden stared after him as he was led away. She unconsciously raised a hand to her lips, which tingled anew with the memory of his kisses. Watching him stride away with that easy, masculine grace of his, she could not help but be reminded of the way his body had possessed hers.

"You are no better than Charlotte and Mary!" she muttered to herself.

Eager to postpone the inevitable encounter with her uncle, she heaved a ragged sigh and turned her steps toward the garden. Each day of late brought new troubles, she reflected unhappily. And each night brought a passion she was too weak to resist.

Damn you, Roark St. Claire. Something had to happen soon, else she'd begin to welcome the darkness with open arms.

Eight

Twilight crept over the lush tropical splendor of the island, bringing with it the promise of a deep, starlit night. There were no storm clouds looming on the seaswept horizon, and nothing else to give even a symbolic warning of what lay ahead.

Eden stood alone in her bedroom. She had dressed with particular care, for she was determined to look her best when she faced everyone at Lord Sandringham's ball. There was, after all, something to be said for putting on a brave front when facing one's social adversaries.

"Oh, mistress, you do be looking fine!" Betsy pronounced as she materialized in the doorway. She bustled amiably across the elegant Persian carpet to stand before the gilded mirror with Eden. "Why, even your uncle be pleased when he sees you!"

Eden smiled wryly at that. She subjected her appearance to a critical scrutiny while Betsy looked on. The gown she had chosen to wear was a new one. Fashioned of a gossamer satin in a color termed "celestial blue," it featured a low-cut square neck-line, a lace tippet edged with a border of Vandyke lace, and a very narrow banding of black velvet on the gently gathered skirt. She had arranged her thick black tresses into a pearl-enclosed knot high on the back of her head, but had left a profusion of soft curls to tumble delightfully about her face.

With accessories that included a double necklace of pearls, a square cornelian brooch set in gold, delicate pearl drop earrings, and a pair of long white kid gloves, she looked every inch the beautiful, well-bred young Englishwoman she was. Slippers of blue kid with small pink bugle rosettes completed the ensemble.

Beneath the high-waisted gown, she wore only a thin white lawn chemise and single cotton petticoat. Even during the summer, she had never been tempted to follow the example of some of the older ladies and dispense with undergarments altogether. She was far too modest for that, though she did make the concession of laying aside the lace-bordered drawers which Jamaica had assured her were quickly gaining in popularity among the higher classes. They were not entirely comfortable; too warm and restricting, she had decided.

"The master be waiting for you downstairs," announced Betsy. Her thick brows drew together in a frown when she predicted, "Like as not, he be planning to scold you again if you don't hurry."

"His anger does not frighten me, Betsy."

"Maybe not. But you'd best be hurrying all the same."

Eden released a faint sigh and turned away from

the mirror. Snatching up her bead-embroidered reticule from the bed, she swept gracefully from the room and down the stairs. Her uncle was pacing in the front entrance foyer.

"High time you put in an appearance!" he snapped.

"It is early yet," she replied unconcernedly.

"If it were not for the fact that Donald will be expecting you, I would damned well lock you in your room until morning!" Still fuming over that afternoon's incident, he fixed her with a highly spleenful glare that would have made any other woman quake with fear. Eden, however, merely affected an air of wide-eyed innocence.

"I will gladly stay behind, Uncle," she offered.

"No, by damn, you will not!" He lifted his hat to his balding head and flung open the door. "Outside and into the carriage!" he ordered tersely, then followed her from the house.

Reaching their destination less than half an hour later, they discovered that they were among the first guests to arrive. The towering stone mansion, even more splendid than the one at Abbeville Plantation, was aglow with the light of a dozen crystal chandeliers. Carriages wound their way up a long, tree-lined drive, pulling up before the great house to spew forth their richly dressed occupants. Lord and Lady Sandringham, whose proud demeanor belied their humble beginnings, stood ready just within the doorway to welcome everyone.

Eden smiled to herself as she approached her middle-aged hosts. It was well known that Lord Sandringham's father had purchased the title for him. Of course, no one would dare make mention of his family's involvement in trade, nor would they ever think to suggest he was anything but high-born such as themselves. He and his wife were cold and haughty in the extreme, as if they hoped to make amends for having blood that was not quite blue.

"Good evening,"· Lady Eden." Lord Sandringham greeted her with stiff civility. His manner held a bit more warmth when he nodded to her uncle. "William."

"How lovely you look, my dear," Lady Sandringham told Eden, though her gaze was anything but commendatory. She was an attractive woman, or would have been, if not for the excessive amount of paint and powder she used in a vain attempt to look younger.

"Thank you, Lady Sandringham," said Eden politely. Her own eyes twinkled in secret amusement at the sight of the large, heart-shaped beauty patch on the woman's heavily rouged cheek.

Looping the satin strings of her reticule over her arm, she clutched her fan and drifted away to find Jamaica. She was disappointed to learn that Colonel Harding and his daughter had not yet arrived. Disappointment turned to annoyance when Charlotte and Mary suddenly bore down upon her.

"I was not at all certain we would see you here tonight," Charlotte remarked with what could only be called a catty smile..

"Yes indeed," seconded Mary, "I feared the 'excitement' of the afternoon would have proven too much for you."

"Not at all," Eden assured them, searching for a

means to escape. Her emerald gaze made a quick sweep of the ornate, music-filled ballroom, but there was no sign of an ally.

"In the event you are looking for Donald Parkington-Hughes," Charlotte obligingly informed her, "he is at present closeted with some of the other men in Lord Sandringham's library."

"Thank you, but I was *not* looking for him."

"Have you heard the latest news of the war?" asked Mary. Before Eden could answer, she disclosed in a burst of patriotic zeal, "We have another victory! Our own dear Royal Navy has successfully laid siege to the Americans' capital. Washington is in flames!"

"And they say we are planning to mount attacks on other cities as well!" Charlotte added triumphantly. "Perhaps we can finally put an end to this tedious conflict. I should like to return to England for a visit. Why, it has been two whole years since we have been to London!"

"I wonder what our bondsmen would say if they knew," Mary remarked with a frown, then immediately brightened. "I know. We shall tell them! I should like to see their faces when they learn of their country's defeat!"

"The war has not yet ended," Eden pointed out. Her thoughts, as usual, were drawn to Roark. What would his reaction be?

"Nevertheless," said Charlotte, "I am quite certain we shall soon be able to resume a more normal routine. It has been vexing beyond belief, hearing about the war day in and day out. That is all the men ever talk about. And I daresay that once . . ."

It was at this opportune moment that Jamaica

161

finally chose to put in an appearance. Catching sight of her friend, Eden inwardly heaved a sigh of relief and hastily excused herself. She could hear the Stewart sisters gasping at her abrupt departure, but she did not care.

"Jamaica!" She hurried forward to embrace the petite blonde, who was resplendent in a gown of white piña cloth. "You have rescued me from a fate worse than death!"

"Have I truly?" Jamaica replied with a soft laugh. "Had I known that you were in peril, I would have come sooner!"

The ballroom was beginning to get crowded by now, and it was necessary for the two young women to move toward the elaborately furnished buffet table in order to have a few moments of private conversation. A waltz was struck up as soon as they began talking, so that they had to put their heads close together in order to be heard.

"Have you seen Donald yet?" queried Jamaica.

"No, thank heavens. But I know an encounter is unavoidable."

"It so happens I spied your uncle talking with him as I came in. I must say, they appeared quite pleased with themselves about something."

"And I am afraid I know what that particular 'something' is," Eden remarked with a frown of dissatisfaction. She hastened to change the subject. "Jamaica, do you suppose you might return to Abbeville Plantation with me after the ball tonight?"

"Why do you ask?" responded the younger woman, studying her closely. "Is something wrong, Eden?"

"No. No, of course not." She lent credence to her words with a brief smile. "It is simply that . . . well, that I could use the company. My uncle is angry with me, you see, and I fear that tonight will bring only further evidence of his displeasure."

"What has happened this time?"

"Nothing of importance," she lied.

The reason she had given for her invitation was also a falsehood. It wasn't her uncle's wrath she feared—it was the night. The possibility that Roark might see fit to sneak into her bedroom again set her heart to pounding fiercely. Desperate to throw as many obstacles as she could in his path, she waited anxiously for Jamaica's answer.

"I'm sorry, but it has already been arranged for me to spend the next several days with the Stewarts," the blonde confided with sincere regret. "My father is planning to sail for Cuba at first light. I would much rather come with *you*, dearest Eden, but—"

"That's quite all right," Eden insisted, concealing her disappointment with another smile. "It was terribly impulsive of me, after all, and I should have asked you before now." She turned her head and saw that a certain, unquestionably dashing young gentleman was coming their way. "It seems you are to have the first dance with the gallant Mr. Langley," she remarked to Jamaica on a teasing note.

"Yes. It does, doesn't it?" Jamaica murmured with a surprising lack of interest. Strangely enough, she found that she was no longer enthralled by Harry Langley's aristocratic good looks. Perhaps, she told herself, it was because the vision of a rugged, golden-haired man kept insinuating itself into her mind.

Eden watched as Jamaica, reluctantly granting Harry's rather smug request for a dance, was spun away into the graceful movements of the waltz. The lilting strains of music filled the room, along with the sounds of small talk and flirtatious laughter. She could find no pleasure in any of it. Soon, she was surrounded by her usual bevy of admirers, all of whom were willing to risk their mama's disfavor for the chance of securing a dance with the beautiful, yet slightly scandalous, Lady Eden Parrish.

She had already suffered through two dances and the requisite light conversation when Donald came forward to pay his respects to her. Her uncle, she quickly noted, was watching them from the door-way.

"I would not have thought it possible, but you look even more ravishing than ever," pronounced Donald, lifting her gloved hand to his lips.

"I suppose you and Uncle William have been plotting again," she charged accusingly. She freed her hand from his possessive grasp and raised her head to a defiant angle. "It will do you no good, you know."

"You are mistaken, my dearest Lady Eden." He smiled, but there was an unsettling gleam in his pale blue eyes. "I apologize for not making my presence known to you before now, but there were certain 'business' matters which required my attention."

"Yes, I can well understand that the purchase of a wife might be termed a business transaction!" she remarked, her color heightening angrily. "Pray, sir, do you intend to make public the amount my uncle has exacted from you?" Before he could respond, she declared in a low, furious tone, "Your father's money has been ill spent, Mr. Parkington-Hughes. I am not for sale!"

"Everything, and *everyone*, has a price," Donald insisted with maddening superiority. "It would be entirely useless to deny it."

"Neither you nor my uncle can force me into a marriage I do not desire!"

Once again, she found herself battling the urge to tell him that she was already wed, and that, by damn, her husband had seen to it that she was no longer a wife in name only. *No other man shall have you,* Roark had vowed. Why did those words continue to burn in her mind?

"Let us speak of it no further for the moment," Donald suggested with a patronizing air. "I believe this next dance is mine."

Although still angry, she did not resist when he claimed her hand again and led her out to join the others in the center of the room. She knew she could not hope to escape the inevitability of his presence throughout the evening. But she was somewhat consoled by the prospect of being spared his odious company for the next three dances, which she had fortunately promised elsewhere.

The endless whirl of dancing and socializing continued as the night wore on. Eden did not have another opportunity to speak with Jamaica for quite some time, until the two of them were momentarily abandoned by their current partners near the buffet table.

"So, we are here again at last!" Jamaica remarked with a breathless laugh. Fanning herself, she nodded in Donald's direction as he danced with Charlotte. "What on earth do you suppose the two of them can find to talk about?"

"I've no idea," sighed Eden, "but she is far more suited to him than I am." She opened her own lace-edged fan and stole a look back over her shoulder at the young man who had just hurried off to fetch her a glass of punch. "I swear, if Henry Wilkes trods upon my feet one more time . . ."

Roark St. Claire is an excellent dancer, that inner voice complacently reminded her. It was true. Her silken brow creased into a sharp, sudden frown at the recollection of the many dances they had shared back in London. Why the devil couldn't she forget the man for even one single, blasted evening?

"Eden, what is it?" Jamaica asked, missing little.

"I wish I could prevail upon my uncle to leave."

"I should think there's little hope of that. Judging from the way he has been paying such close attention to the Widow Hamilton all night, I doubt if he would consider an early departure."

"Perhaps I shall have an aunt at last," Eden murmured with a faint smile of irony. She sobered again when she saw that both Donald's father and mother were moving purposefully toward her. "Dash it all, they're headed this way!"

"Who?" demanded Jamaica. Following the direction of Eden's troubled gaze, she inhaled sharply and said, "Good heavens, I expect they mean to discuss their son's intentions with you! I'm afraid, dearest Eden, they've made no secret of their disapproval. His courtship of you has been mentioned with great frequency, you know."

"If that is truly their intent, then I shall set them straight!"

"Would you like me to stay?"

"No. Thank you all the same, but I would rather you intercepted Henry Wilkes. The discussion may very well take an unpleasant turn."

Jamaica nodded in silent agreement, then whirled away to do her part. Eden steeled herself for the impending confrontation.

"Good evening, Lady Eden," Donald's father greeted her in his usual brusque manner. Although not a particularly large man, he possessed the innate ability to intimidate those around him.

"What an interesting gown," his wife opined, her gaze flickering disdainfully over Eden. She did not hesitate before getting right to the point. "Tell me, my dear, is it true you have had the unmitigated *impudence* to express displeasure with my son's attentions?"

"If you are asking whether or not I intend to marry him, then the answer is no," Eden stated calmly.

"Foolish girl!" growled Lord Parkington-Hughes. "Do you not realize the dangers of playing loose with him? Why, he has already persuaded me to use my influence with the courts on your behalf. I don't mind telling you that I was quite reluctant, quite reluctant indeed, to involve myself in this distasteful affair, but it seems he will not be deterred!"

"Are you really so lost to shame," Lady Parkington-Hughes demanded angrily, "that you cannot see he is far above you? I, too, would much rather he had settled his determination on a more suitable young woman. Your past conduct has been reprehensible! However, since he has made it perfectly clear he means to have *you* and no other, I am prepared to overlook your misdeeds. He is, after all, my only son, and his happiness is worth—"

"Whatever you paid my uncle," Eden finished for her. She was doing her best to control her rising temper, but the mutual and highly vocal condemnation of Donald's parents was too much to bear—particularly since she had no intention of marrying their precious son. Her eyes blazed their brilliant emerald fire as she declared in a voice laced with simmering indignation, "I am well aware of the fact that a settlement of money is involved. But the decision is mine and mine alone. And the truth is, I do not love Donald."

"Love?" Lord Parkington-Hughes gave an ungentlemanly snort of disgust. "Damn it, girl, what the bloody hell does love have to do with anything?"

"I always knew you were exceedingly common!" pronounced his wife. She subjected Eden to a hot, venomous glare. "My son is offering you the sort of life about which most young ladies can only dream. You are naught but an ungrateful little baggage!"

"Call me what you will," Eden countered proudly, "but nothing could ever prevail upon me to marry your son!"

No sooner were these words out of her mouth, than the infamous Donald himself took up a stance in the center of the ballroom and requested everyone's attention. The music stopped, and the talk slowly died away.

"I have an announcement to make," he began. His

gaze traveled significantly across the room to where Eden stood with his parents. "I should like to announce my betrothal to Lady Eden Parrish."

Eden felt as though she had been struck. A loud gasp broke from her lips, while the color drained from her face. She stared at Donald in stunned, wide-eyed disbelief. Sweet Saint Christopher, she thought, numbly, it isn't possible . . . surely I didn't hear him correctly.

But it was all too true. His announcement, although greeted with silence at first, elicited a polite round of applause. Eden found herself surrounded by well-wishers, while Lord and Lady Parkington-Hughes stood looking almost as incredulous as she was. She watched as Donald made his way through the crowd. He was smiling at her.

"I can see you are surprised, my dearest Eden," he offered with fond indulgence. Taking her hand, he stood beside her and drew it firmly through the crook of his arm.

Eden's mind was still reeling. Her horror-stricken gaze moved across the faces before her, and she was only dimly aware of the congratulations the "happy couple" was receiving. Finally, when her uncle stepped forward to brush her cheek with a kiss and shake hands with Donald, she emerged from the benumbing haze with a vengeance.

"*No!*" she cried, shaking her head in furious denial. "No, by damn, you shall not bend me to your will so easily!"

"Eden, please," Donald cautioned tightly, forcing a smile to his lips. "Do not create a scene."

"I don't give a hang what everyone thinks, Donald

Parkington-Hughes!" she retorted. Jerking away from him, she rounded on her uncle. "You knew what he was planning, didn't you?" she demanded in a seething undertone.

"As did you," William replied evenly. "You were aware of the fact that an announcement was forthcoming."

"But not such a . . . a *premature* one!"

Sudden tears gathered in her eyes. Furiously blinking them back, she looked up and saw Jamaica's face in the midst of the crowd. She broke away from the two men who were determined to make her life a misery, and hastened toward her friend.

"Oh Jamaica, please," she whispered shakily, "do let's get out of here!"

"Of course!"

With Jamaica's arm about her shoulders, she made her way out of the room and into the relative privacy of the corridor. The evening, which had never been enjoyable to begin with, was now completely ruined.

Eden's uncle followed shortly thereafter. His expression was oddly impassive as he approached her, and she was surprised to discern no anger in his gaze—only a strange glint of determination. Donald, thank God, was nowhere to be seen.

"I think it would be best if you returned home, my dear," William suggested quietly.

"You do?" replied Eden, much surprised. She exchanged a quick glance with Jamaica. "Very well, Uncle." Leaving was exactly what she'd wanted to do.

"I have arranged transportation for you."

"Transportation?" she echoed in bemusement, but had no time to ask him what he meant. She was scarcely able to bid Jamaica goodbye before he took her arm and propelled her outside. "Are you coming as well?" she inquired as they moved down the front steps.

"No."

"Then should I send the carriage back for you?"

"No, thank you. That will not be necessary."

They had reached the drive. Eden noticed that the carriage which had just drawn up before the house was not their own. She turned to her uncle with a mild frown of puzzlement.

"What—"

"Get in," he ordered as the footman hurried around to open the door.

"But, Uncle, this is not—"

"*Get in,*" he reiterated in a tone that was both cold and furious.

Eden had no further opportunity to protest, for she was suddenly thrust inside the enclosed warmth of the carriage. She cried out softly as she tumbled forward onto the leather seat. The door slammed shut behind her.

"I am sorry for the deception, dearest Eden, but it was entirely necessary."

Her eyes flew wide at the sound of Donald's voice. She righted herself on the seat just as the carriage set off down the drive.

"How dare you!" she stormed, her fiery emerald gaze seeking him out in the darkness. "Stop this carriage at once!"

"I have your uncle's permission to see you home,"

he informed her smoothly. "If you will but calm yourself so that we may talk—"

"The only thing I can think of to say to you at the moment, Mr. Parkington-Hughes, would be unfit for your *gentlemanly* ears!" she declared with biting sarcasm.

"Silence will do just as well."

And silence it was, for the duration of the half-hour's journey. Eden sat fuming over Donald's unforgivable conduct, and his even more unforgivable announcement of a marriage that would never take place. He, sitting opposite, contemplated what was to come. His eyes gleamed with secret pleasure, a pleasure that was insured by his assurance of William Stanhope's blessings for his plans.

When the carriage pulled up before the great house at Abbeville Plantation, Eden flung open the door and took flight. Donald gave leisurely chase, following her up the steps. She spun about to confront him when she realized he meant to come inside.

"Good night to you, sir!" she ground out.

"I promised your uncle I would remain until he saw fit to return."

"Then you may stay and rot for all I care!"

She flounced inside and headed for the staircase. Donald surprised her by following again. He took hold of her arm and pulled her to a halt.

"Please, Eden, will you not grant me a few moments in which to explain?" he appealed, seemingly contrite.

"Explain? What can there possibly be to explain? You humiliated me in front of everyone!" she charged, her eyes ablaze. "How could you *do* such a thing to me? You had no right to announce our betrothal without giving me fair warning—you had no right to announce it at all!"

"I know. And I am truly sorry for it. If you will but come into the drawing room with me, I shall endeavor to make you understand the reasoning behind my actions.

Peering narrowly up at him, Eden wavered between anger and uncertainty. If she was ever to have peace, she reasoned with herself, she had to put a stop to Donald's ill-conceived courtship once and for all. She certainly couldn't go on fighting him off at every turn. It was, as he had said, a time for understanding. *It was time to tell him the truth.* There was no other way.

"Very well," she finally acquiesced, then stipulated, "But before you offer me any explanations, you must hear what I have to say. I am afraid you will not like it in the least."

Donald nodded in silent agreement. She led the way into the drawing room, sinking down upon the chaise while her overconfident, soon-to-be erstwhile suitor chose the wing chair opposite.

"My uncle has given you false hopes," she began coolly. "Whatever arrangement the two of you have made is for naught. For the last time, Donald Parkington-Hughes, I do not love you, and I will not marry you."

"You are only saying that because your sense of honor forbids you to care for me," insisted Donald. "It is because you are still wed to another."

"No." She frowned and shook her head. "That is not the reason, at least not in the way you believe."

173

"Have my parents sought to influence you?" he demanded. His eyes narrowed in suspicion.

"Yes, of course they have, but that has nothing to do with—"

"They shall not dissuade me! I am determined to have you for my own, dearest Eden, and I shall not allow them to interfere. I have every confidence they will accept you once—"

"*Will* you be quiet!" she cried in exasperation, rising abruptly to her feet. Her hands doubled into fists at her sides, while her eyes flashed across at Donald. "Blast it all, you obstinate man, haven't you heard a word I've said? For months now, I have done my absolute best to discourage you, and yet you have stubbornly ignored all but your own wishes! If I *did* care for you, neither your parents nor my uncle nor anyone else would be able to keep me from marrying you! But the fact remains that I do *not!* And what's more, I am not at all what you believe me to be!"

"What are you talking about?" he asked with an obviously wounded air.

Standing before her in the lamplight, he looked even stiffer and more haughtily superior than ever. Nevertheless, she would have been filled with remorse, were it not for the certainty that he did not truly love her. To a man like Donald, she could never hope to be an equal. She would be nothing more than a possession, someone to grace his home and bear his children and—heaven forbid—warm his bed at night. Never could he make her feel what Roark had. . . .

"Eden," Donald prompted impatiently, "what the deuce did you mean by that peculiar remark? How could you not be what I believe? Why, I have known you for quite a number of months now, and since your past has been revealed—"

"I am not a kissless bride!" she blurted out at last. She watched as mingled shock and incredulity spread across Donald's finely chiseled countenance.

"What did you say?" he demanded in a low, even tone.

"You heard me! My husband did not abandon me quite soon enough!" It was a sort of roundabout truth, she told herself, but it would do well enough. There was no reason to disclose anything more, she certainly had no intention of confiding that the blasted consummation had taken place a scant twenty-four hours ago. "For heaven's sake, Donald, don't you understand? I am neither maid nor widow, and I cannot marry you!"

A long, highly charged silence greeted her confession. Donald's face grew flushed, and a dull glint shone in his pale blue eyes. Eden waited for him to speak. When he did, his words struck a sudden cord of alarm deep within her.

"Well then. It seems, my dear, that I have indeed been misled. But it changes nothing." His expression was forebodingly grave as he closed the distance between them in a few unhurried steps. "Since this appears to be the appointed hour for divulging secrets, it might interest you to know that your uncle encouraged me to be alone with you tonight. It was more than that, actually. He suggested that I take matters into my own hands, in order to make you agree to our marriage."

He paused here, leaving Eden to stare up at him in

mingled bafflement and annoyance. She could tell that he was making an effort to keep his emotions under a tight control. Her alarm increased tenfold in the next moment.

"And that, dearest Eden," he went on to acknowledge, "was the true reason I brought you home—I had planned to compromise you beyond repair and thereby force you into compliance. Ironic, is it not?" he remarked with a faint humorless smile.

"*What?*" breathed Eden. As his words sunk in, outrage conquered fear. "You have the audacity to stand there and tell me you were planning to . . . to take me against my will?"

"Seduction would be the polite term for it, I believe," offered Donald, his tone deceptively casual. The look in his eyes grew dangerous. "I wasn't at all certain I could go through with it, in spite of my desperation to make you care for me. But now I see my qualms were unjustified. It turns out that you are no blushing virgin after all."

"Virgin or not, there can be no excuse for your intended treachery!"

Not only had *he* meant to commit what amounted to an act of criminal violation, she seethed inwardly, but her own uncle had been a co-conspirator in the whole despicable scheme. She would never have believed it possible that William's greed could take such a turn. Pained by the discovery of his cruel betrayal, she glared murderously up at the man who had been prepared to force himself upon her.

"I thought you a gentleman, but I can see that I was very much mistaken!" Infuriated nearly beyond reason, she lifted a trembling hand and pointed

176

toward the doorway. "You will leave at once, do you hear? I never want to see you again! Get out, damn you, before I—"

She broke off with a sharp gasp as Donald's arms suddenly wrapped about her and tightened like a vise.

"I'll get out all right," he told her in a voice edged with both anger and lust, "but only after I've proven to you that I am not a man to be trifled with! Though you've been possessed by another, I still want you—perhaps more than ever!" His gaze bored relentlessly down into hers. Disregarding her struggles, he clenched his teeth and said, "You can hide behind your innocence no longer, my *dearest* Eden!"

"Stop it! Let go of me!" she cried hotly, pushing and twisting within his grasp.

"No other man will want you after tonight!" he proclaimed with smug satisfaction. "You'll have no choice but to marry me once I've finished with you!"

"No."

Her heart leapt in terror, but she told herself she would die before she let him take her. Managing to free one arm, she did not hesitate before doubling her hand into a fist and smashing it against Donald's face. He muttered an oath and momentarily relaxed his hold. She jerked away from him and raced toward the doorway.

"Our 'discussion' is not yet over, Lady Eden!" Donald snarled contemptuously, fingering his reddened jaw.

He was upon her in an instant, his fingers closing about her wrists with bruising force. She cried out in pain as he roughly spun her about and twisted her

177

arm behind her back.

"No, damn you, let me go!" she demanded breathlessly, then watched in dismay when he reached out to turn the key in the lock.

Tempted to scream for help, she decided it was not yet time to resort to such drastic means. She had no wish to involve Betsy or any of the others in the humiliating situation. And, after all, Donald Parkington-Hughes was a gentleman. He had momentarily lost his head, that was all. She had always been able to reason with him before; surely she could reason with him now.

"Please, Donald," she implored with as much composure as she could muster, "you . . . you must not do this!"

"Oh, but I must," he parried, completely unrepentant. "You will thank me for it in the end."

"Thank you?" she gasped, her eyes widening.

"Surely you realize that I am your only hope of making a respectable marriage. Any other man, upon discovery of your blemished past, would only see fit to offer you a clandestine 'arrangement.' In spite of your family's connections, you are quite ruined."

"As God is my witness, I shall never forgive you if you do not release me at once and—"

"Resign yourself to your fate, my dear. It will go much easier if you do."

He was done with talking. With a strength that surprised his furiously struggling captive, he bore her back across the room and flung her down upon the chaise. She opened her mouth to give a belated

178

scream, but he silenced her with a hard, punishing kiss. His body lowered atop hers, and his hands began roaming feverishly up and down her writhing curves.

Dear God, please don't let this happen! she prayed in rising panic. Too late, she realized her mistake in believing her attacker capable of rational thought. He was lost to all reason . . . he had become a sinister, cold-hearted stranger.

She pushed against him with all her might, kicking and squirming while his brutal assault intensified. He raked up her silken skirts and tore at the bodice of her gown. Battling a sudden wave of nausea, she finally managed to tear her lips away from the ruthless possession of his.

"By damn, I—I'll kill you if you do this!" she threatened in a hoarse, choking voice.

Again, she tired to scream, but his mouth ground down upon hers with such force that she tasted blood. Hot tears of defeat scalded her eyes.

Suddenly, a loud, splintering *crash* filled the room.

Before Eden knew what was happening, she was free. The crushing weight of Donald's body was gone.

Dizzy with relief, she blinked up through her tears to watch as her elegantly clad assailant was sent hurtling against the wall. Her sparkling emerald gaze flew to the man who had just rescued her.

"*Roark!*" she breathed in stunned disbelief.

His attention, however, was not focused upon her at the moment. He laid hands upon Donald again, spun him about, and brought his fist smashing up against the other man's unguarded chin.

Eden clutched at the torn edges of her bodice and hastily sat up. The look on Roark's face frightened her, and she realized that he might very well kill Donald. Judging from the savage gleam in his eyes, he meant to do just that.

"Roark, no!" she cried out.

She did not pause to consider if her plea for mercy stemmed from concern for Donald, who deserved punishment but not death, or for Roark, who would of a certainty be hanged if he murdered the Englishman. In any case, it did not matter. Her husband was impervious to everything but his intent to exact revenge upon her would-be violator.

Filled with a smoldering, white-hot rage at the memory of the man's hands upon Eden, Roark hit him again and again. Donald could not hope to defend himself, though he did make an attempt to flee. He broke free and staggered toward what was left of the door, only to be caught and given a beating he would never forget—if he survived.

"Roark! In heaven's name, stop it!" Eden implored desperately. She sprung to her feet and raced across the room. Grasping his arm, she cried, "He isn't worth it! Don't you see? He isn't worth it!"

Roark finally listened. With one last burning glare at the unconscious man sprawled at his feet, he straightened and turned to Eden.

"Are you all right?" he asked quietly. His gaze darkened anew when he viewed the tattered condition of her gown and the tangled mass of hair streaming down about her shoulders. "By damn, if he hurt you—"

"No!" she hastened to assure him. "No, I am all right." Glancing down at Donald's prone body, she shuddered involuntarily. "I . . . he was going to . . ."

"I know," Roark ground out.

"What are you doing here?" she suddenly thought to ask. Her brow knitted into a puzzled frown. "How did you know what was hap—"

"I was coming for you."

"Coming for me?" She blushed fierily when it occurred to her that he must have been planning a repetition of last night's madness. "Whatever your reasons for being here, you've got to get out before someone sees you!"

"My thoughts exactly." He longed to take her in his arms, to give her comfort and love her with tenderness. But now was not the time for that. Later, he promised himself, his eyes aglow at the prospect.

"Well then, I . . . I suppose I should thank you for your assistance," she murmured. Though she would never admit it, she felt a sharp pang of disappointment for the fact that he had given up so easily.

"I will exact my own brand of reward from you before this night is through," he vowed. A faint smile touched his lips when her eyes flew back up to his face.

"What do you mean by that?"

"It's time we were away."

Eden frowned again, then watched in surprise as he quickly stripped off his white cotton shirt.

"What—"

"I'll have a blasted mutiny on my hands if my men see you like that," he remarked wryly, his gaze shifting to where she still attempted to cover her breasts with the remnants of her low-cut bodice. The sight of her pale, satiny flesh made him groan inwardly.

Before she could ask him what men he was referring to, he had pulled the shirt down over her head. She accepted his gift for the sake of modesty.

"Come, my love," he suddenly decreed, seizing her arm in a firm but gentle grasp.

"Why, I . . . I'm not going anywhere with you!" she stammered in confusion.

"Ah, but you are indeed, Mrs. St. Claire."

"Blast it, Roark, what *are* you talking about?"

"I am leaving Barbados this very night. And you are coming with me."

"What?" Her eyes grew enormous within the flushed, delicate oval of her face. "Do you mean to say you are *escaping?*" She had known this moment would come. Her heart twisted painfully now that it had. But what was it he had said about her coming with him? Surely she hadn't heard him correctly! "Roark, I—"

"We shall have a lifetime in which to talk. Right now," he commanded, leading her toward the doorway, "you are to remain quiet and do as I say."

"I am not coming with you!" she insisted, still unable to believe he actually planned to take her along. She tried to pull free, but he held fast and propelled her swiftly to the front door of the house. "No! Damn you, Roark St. Claire, I will *not* go with you!"

She gasped at feeling herself being swept upward and then flung facedown across his broad shoulder.

"Roark! Roark, put me down!" She kicked and beat at the naked, hard-muscled expanse of his back with her fists, but he would not be deterred.

"I'll caution you once again to remain quiet," he told her in a low, vibrant tone. "You hold the fate of myself and a dozen other men in your hands. While I recall you having expressed a desire to see *me* hang, I doubt you'll want their blood on your conscience."

His words threw her into a quandary, for they were all too true. She lapsed into a turbulent silence as he carried her down the steps and into the welcoming darkness. Almost before she knew it, they were well away from the house and beyond the fields of cane. He lifted her onto a horse and swung easily up behind her. Her wide, luminous gaze swept about to see that there were eight or nine other men on horseback, all eagerly waiting to do their leader's bidding.

"Are we going to ride for Colfax and Farrell now, Captain?"

"We are," Roark confirmed with a nod. "They're being held only a short distance from here."

"What about Thurley and Swain?"

"And Rhodes?"

"All three are together," said Roark. "We'll collect them last, on our way to the ship."

"Ship?" gasped Eden. Sweet Saint Christopher, he really *did* mean to set sail that very night. And with her as his prisoner. . . .

His strong arm slipped about her waist and pulled her back against his hardness. She stiffened, but he merely laughed softly in her ear.

"Let's go!" he ordered his men, his authoritative voice ringing out in the starlit darkness.

Eden had no choice but to hold onto him as he urged the horse into a gallop. They thundered away across the night-cloaked landscape, and into the adventure of a lifetime.

Nine

Eden knew that she would never forget the wild ride that followed.

They had reached the Stewarts' estate within minutes. Roark left his wife in the care of two of his men, then set off on foot with the others to free his first mate, Seth Colfax, and the ship's boatswain, Benjamin Farrell. They made their way quietly and efficiently across the grounds, heading toward the slave cabins situated only a short distance from the imposing grandeur of the mansion.

It was at this inopportune moment that Jamaica Harding decided to seek the cooling freshness of the night air. The decision, had she but known it, was to seal her fate.

She and her hosts for the next several days had only just returned from the Sandringham's ball. The elder Stewarts had immediately taken themselves up to bed, leaving their beloved daughters to entertain Jamaica. Jamaica, as it turned out, did not wish to be entertained, and neither Charlotte nor Mary was in the mood for a late-night stroll about the grounds.

"Go on then," Charlotte instructed their guest crossly. "Have your tedious little walk. I am quite sure Mary and I shall find something to talk about amongst ourselves, shall we not, Mary?"

"Indeed we shall," her sister declared with a lofty, emphatic nod. "After all, we have not yet discussed Lady Eden Parrish's shockingly outrageous behavior. And then, of course, there is the matter of Donald Parkington-Hughes' announcement of their so-called betrothal!"

"*I* say she must have forced him into it somehow," opined Charlotte.

"She is without a doubt the boldest creature I have ever known," Mary then offered, warming to the task.

Jamaica released a long sigh of discontentment and was only too glad to escape from the drawing room. She had no wish to hear any further insults hurled at her absent and very dearest friend. Silently lamenting the fact that she could not have accompanied Eden back to Abbeville Plantation, she wandered out onto the lower verandah and drew her shawl more closely about her.

The clear, fragrant summer night beckoned her farther. She glanced back toward the house, only to see that Charlotte and Mary were still engaged in steady conversation. A strange restlessness suddenly crept over her. With a will of their own, her eyes traveled to where she knew the handsome young American was sleeping. She blushed at the wicked turn of her thoughts.

Harry Langley had paid court to her quite

devotedly throughout the evening, but to no avail. She chided herself for her fickleness. Why, only three days ago she had considered herself almost in love with the gallant Mr. Langley. What on earth was happening to her?

Sighing again, she trailed a hand along the stone balustrade and ventured down the steps. She had no particular destination in mind; she would simply allow impulse to lead her.

Roark, meanwhile, returned to the horses with his men. Their mission had been a success. Eden recognized the two newest members of their entourage as the same men she had seen working in the fields earlier that day. She watched them hasten toward the mounts which had been brought along for their use.

"It's time we split up," Roark decreed, swinging up behind Eden again. "Seth, you take four of the men and head northward. The rest of us will make for Lord Sandringham's estate."

"Aye, Captain," the first mate replied solemnly.

"We'll have to hurry if we hope to make the tide," one of the crew members warned, tossing a quick glance up toward the sky.

Roark pulled his wife securely back against him once more. For a moment, she was tempted to resist. She could put a stop to things there and then if only she had the courage to scream and rouse Ambrose Stewart's men. But it wasn't for lack of courage that she remained silent, and well she knew it. No matter how much it galled her to admit the truth, even to herself, she knew she could not bear to see Roark St. Claire caught and hanged.

Perhaps later she would be able to slip away and make good her escape. Yes, she thought, her green eyes sparkling, she could take flight and conceal herself somewhere in the darkness. Roark would have no choice but to leave without her. . . .

"One more stop, lads, and we're homeward bound!" he proclaimed. His own gaze was alight with both determination and excitement.

Eden could hear the pleasure in his deep voice, and she realized that he could not help but be pleased at the prospect of going home. *Home.* Apprehension filled her heart at the uncertainty of what lay ahead.

They were off again, this time setting a course for Lord Sandringham's plantation. Seth Colfax and the four men in his group were just about to follow their captain's orders and head northward, when they caught sight of Jamaica.

At first, it seemed she was nothing more than an apparition, a ghostly vision in white who had come to haunt them. She floated gracefully across the starlit grounds, her countenance pensive and her gaze drifting repeatedly toward the nearby row of cabins.

As Seth's eyes gleamed with recognition, he felt his pulse quicken. His heart came alive as it had never done before, and he knew in that moment that he could not leave her behind. They had never spoken a single word to one another, and yet he knew she belonged to him.

There would be hell to pay—most of it from the captain. And what the devil would his family have to say about it? She was English, after all. Damn the consequences, he told himself defiantly, she is mine!

"Why, 'tis the young beauty!" Farrell murmured beside him. "Jamaica Harding, them other squint-eyed English cats did call her."

"Take the men and go," Seth instructed.

"What about you?"

"I'll catch up. Now go on!"

Although obviously reluctant to obey, Farrell nonetheless did so. He rode away with the others, leaving the young first mate to dismount and slip through the gently rustling greenery to where the pretty, unsuspecting object of his affections had paused to adjust her shawl.

Jamaica tensed. Certain she heard the muffled sound of hoofbeats, she suddenly whirled about and found herself face to face with the young bondsman. She gasped in startlement, her eyes widening while she colored rosily.

"What . . . what are *you* doing out here?" she demanded breathlessly.

"My name is Seth Colfax."

"Seth Colfax?" she echoed, the sound of his low, mellow voice sending a delicious shiver down her spine. She hastily sought to conceal her response behind an attitude of stern propriety. "I am afraid, Mr. Colfax, that you are in danger of severe punishment if you are found—"

"I haven't the time to woo you properly, Jamaica Harding," he cut her off with a brief, splendidly disarming smile, "so I'll just tell you that I knew the first time I saw you that you were the woman for me."

Jamaica's fine, china doll blue eyes grew round as saucers. Her mouth formed an incredulous *O*, but no sound issued forth.

"I hope you won't take it in mind to scream, for I'll have to stop you if you do," warned Seth.

Without another word, he caught her up in his strong manly arms. She gasped at feeling her feet leave the ground. Too shocked to do anything more than wind her own arms instinctively about his neck, she was borne swiftly away to where his horse was waiting. He tossed her up to the animal's sleek back, then mounted behind her.

"I'm sorry it has to be this way. As soon as I can, I'll send word back to your family that you're safe," he promised. Taking hold of the reins, he clamped an arm across her waist and pulled her close.

Jamaica trembled as her hips were pressed into shockingly intimate contact with the lean hardness of his thighs. She came to life at last.

"What in heaven's name do you think you are *doing?*" she demanded indignantly. "Where are you taking me?"

"To paradise!"

With that, he urged the horse to action. Jamaica cried out softly and grasped her handsome young captor's arm. It had all happened so fast; she could not yet comprehend the truth of her circumstances. A merciful numbness descended upon her as Seth Colfax spirited her away . . . right under the very noses of the Misses Stewart.

It was some two hours later before Eden caught her first glimpse of Roark's ship.

He had encountered a bit of difficulty in collecting his last three crewmen. Lord Sandringham, it turned out, was a good deal more cautious than his neighbors. His slaves were kept under lock and key at night, and there were guards posted at each end of the row of cabins. Eden recalled having once heard him confess that he feared a rebellion.

"Want me and Boyd to take care of the two bastards standing guard, Captain?" one of his men offered.

They had drawn rein beneath the lofty, heavily branched spread of a tamarind tree. Eden could not help but be reminded of the old legend about its seed bearing a marked resemblance to an innocent man who had long ago been hanged from just such a tree. She shuddered at the horrible thought of it.

"I do," answered Roark, smiling faintly at the other man's eagerness. "The rest of you stay close behind me and wait for the signal. I'll find out where Swain and the others are being kept." He swung down while the two volunteers hastened away to silence the guards.

"You'll get shot!" Eden predicted, her voice sharp with reproach as well as apprehension. "Lord Sandringham's men are always armed and—"

"It gives me great comfort to know you fear for my safety, my love." His eyes gleamed with a rougish light. "But I have no intention of getting killed." He left her glaring after him in simmering resentment when he turned and disappeared into the darkness.

She waited for what seemed an eternity. It did not occur to her that she might seize advantage of the moment to make good her own escape. In any case, Roark had once again wisely stationed a man on either side of her. She could do nothing but remain still and quiet and listen for the dreaded sound of gunfire.

Finally, her eyes detected movement in the clearing

ahead. She felt lightheaded with relief when she saw the men returning. They moved swiftly toward her. But Roark, she soon realized, was not with them. *Dear God, where was he?* Her throat constricted with alarm.

"What about the captain?" the man to Eden's left whispered, his brow creasing into a worried frown.

"He's gone after Rhodes!" It was Thurley who answered. He and the man called Swain were fortunate enough to have been imprisoned in the same building. "He told us to wait for him here!"

"And where the hell is Rhodes?" Eden's other caretaker queried in a gruff undertone.

"In the gaol!" replied Swain. He muttered an oath and disclosed wrathfully, "The poor son of a bitch was flogged for making the mistake of raising his eyes to the lordship's ugly English face!"

"Surely you're not all going to stand about and do nothing while Roark is in danger?" demanded Eden. Her emerald gaze flashed with accusatory disbelief. "Why, there could easily be other guards—"

"It wouldn't do to go against the captain's orders, my lady," said Thurley. His shipmates had already warned him that the captain's lady—a highborn Englishwoman, no less—was coming with them.

"Who the devil cares about *orders* at a time like this?" Eden retorted angrily. "Blast it all, he may very well get killed!"

"Begging your pardon, my lady," another of the Americans told her in a respectful albeit patronizing manner, "but you can be sure the captain knows what he's about. I've seen him get out of scrapes that would have made any other man give up."

"That may well be, but—"

She broke off with a sharp gasp when a gunshot rang out in the jasmine-scented night air. *No!* her mind screamed.

In the very next instant, Roark came into view. He was half-dragging Rhodes, whose back had been cut to pieces by the manager's whip. Eden watched as he hurried forward with the injured man and relinquished him into the care of the others.

"Get him on his horse!" Roark directed curtly. He mounted behind a speechless, wide-eyed Eden and gathered up the reins. "Ride like the devil, lads!"

Eden suffered a sharp intake of breath when his arm tightened forcefully about her waist. Then they were off like a shot, the horse beneath them flying across the darkened countryside as the others quickly followed their captain's lead.

Shouts filled the air behind them. Lord Sandringham himself dashed from the house when the alarm was raised. Upon learning of the bondsmen's escape, he ordered that they be hunted down and brought back to justice. His men hastened to obey.

Roark set a northwesterly course, which would take them across a rolling, densely wooded portion of the island and thence on to where his ship lay anchored off the rugged Atlantic coast. Eden clutched at the horse's flowing mane and knew with a certainty that they would be pursued. She was only dimly aware of her surroundings; the landscape was naught but a blur as Roark held her tightly against him and urged the horse ever onward.

The ride was both long and difficult, but none dared to lessen the headlong pace. The darkness made the journey even more perilous, so that it was necessary for them to exercise great caution as well as haste. Eden closed her eyes and prayed for the wild, jarring flight to end soon.

Finally, they reached the cliffs. The horses would do them little good now. All eight riders reined to an abrupt halt on the very edge of a green-mantled terrace, a hundred feet above the crashing roar of the ocean's waves. Roark dismounted and swung Eden down beside him.

"This way, Captain!" one of the men exclaimed as he hurried to lead the way. "The path is over here!"

Eden's gaze was drawn instinctively toward the sea, where she spied the ship's sails gleaming pale and almost dreamlike in the starlit darkness. Roark captured her hand with the strong warmth of his and began pulling her along with him to where the others were making their way as swiftly as possible down the cliff.

It was now or never, she told herself. This was her only chance for escape. Why did she feel so torn?

"No!" she choked out. Holding back, she jerked her hand from her husband's grasp. She shook her head in an adamant denial, while her eyes filled with sudden, inexplicable tears. "I am staying here! You have used me for the last time, Roark St. Claire! Your freedom is before you. Now go!"

"Damn it, Eden, we haven't the time—"

"I am not going with you, I say! You betrayed me once. I will not allow you to do so again!" She drew in a ragged breath and proclaimed hoarsely, "Dear God, how I wish I had never met you! I hate you, do you hear? I hate you! Go back where you belong! Go, damn you, before . . . before they catch you!"

She spun about and stumbled blindly toward the horses. A strangled cry broke from her lips as Roark caught her.

"You're my wife!" he ground out. "I came here to find you, and by damn, I'll not leave without you!"

"No!" she screamed, fighting him like a veritable tigress now. "Let me go! I shall never—"

Her struggles abruptly ceased when the sound of gunshots split the night air. Eden jerked her head about to watch in speechless horror as a group of horsemen, at least twenty in number, thundered vengefully down upon them.

Roark muttered an oath and swept Eden close. Without further preamble, he flung her over his broad shoulder again and raced for the path. His footing was swift and sure as he made his way down the rocky trail to the shoreline below. His men were waiting in readiness at the longboat.

Seth Colfax and his group had arrived only a short time earlier. They had already taken passage out to the ship in another boat, leaving Benjamin Farrell behind to assure Roark of their presence on board.

"All be waiting, Captain!" he shouted above the ocean's roar.

Eden found herself thrust unceremoniously into the longboat. She made a final, desperate attempt to escape, only to be yanked back hard against Roark as he lowered his tall frame to the bench behind her. His arms enveloped her with their sinewy warmth, holding her captive while his deep-timbred voice raised in a command to shove off.

"Give the devil his due!"

His crewmen apparently understood this enigmatic remark, for they nodded in accord and hastened to obey.

Four of them pushed the longboat clear of the sand, then clambered inside to join the others at the oars. On the edge of the cliffs above, the pursuers halted their mounts and sprang forward to take aim. Bullets whizzed past the heads of Roark and his men, embedding, with a strange muffled *hiss*, within the thick, wet sand. Benjamin Farrell growled a curse when a bullet tore a jagged path across his arm, but he did not falter in his efforts.

It was hard work, rowing against the swelling waves, but the Americans were well accustomed to it and reached the ship in a matter of minutes. Roark hauled Eden upright and lifted her to the rope ladder which had been flung over the side. Though tempted to cast herself into the black waters and swim back to shore, she instead listened to the voice of reason and took hold of the ladder.

Her long skirts tangled about her legs, but modesty prevented her from catching them up to make the going easier. She gasped in outrage when Roark's hand pressed familiarly against her derrière to give her a compelling boost.

"Welcome my bride aboard, Mr. Colfax!" he called out to his first mate.

Seth reached down to grasp Eden's hands. He steadied her progress up the ladder, then swung her onto the deck. She opened her mouth to thank him, but then mused it was hardly suitable to offer gratitude to one's abductors.

Roark followed close on her heels. Looking every

inch the handsome, dashing pirate Eden believed him to be, he seized her arm and propelled her masterfully across the deck while his men cheered his return.

"Make ready to sail!" his authoritative voice rang out above the din.

The deck became a flurry of activity as each crewman scrambled to take up his assigned post. Eden glanced back over her shoulder, only to tense. Her widened gaze traveled over the men who were spilling down onto the beach a short distance away. Their guns would do them little good now.

Roark turned his head to look as well. He smiled at what his eyes beheld.

"You English are not only bloodthirsty, but also incredibly behindhand."

"Indeed?" Bristling at the sardonic amusement in his voice, she challenged, "Then how is it you came to be captured?"

She was pleased to see that her remark had struck home. Roark's smile quickly faded, and his eyes glinted like cold steel at the memory her words evoked.

"For no other reason than carelessness—my own and no other's," he recalled grimly. "In my haste to find you, sweet vixen, I invited disaster."

"You are issuing the same invitation once more! Do you really believe my uncle will let you go so easily? And what about your abduction of *me?* My father and mother charged him with my guardianship, and—"

"And there is little love lost between you. No, Eden, I myself saw how he treated you. Kinsman or

197

not, he'll spend few sleepless nights on your account. Nor will he waste a great deal of time and effort in order to have you brought back." His eyes darkened at the thought of William Stanhope. He regretted never having gotten the chance to beat the bloody hell out of the bastard.

Eden wanted to deny all that he said, but she could not. In any event, it soon became apparent that her infuriating husband considered their discussion at an end. He seized her arm once more and led her firmly toward the gangway.

"You're to go below and remain there until we're well away," he commanded. "I don't expect trouble; there hasn't been enough time for the garrison to be notified. But I've work to do and can't be bothered with you anymore at present."

"Bothered with—" Eden sputtered indignantly. She rounded on him, the light of battle in her fiery emerald gaze. "I did not ask to be brought along, and I am not now asking to be *bothered with* by you or anyone else! Pray, sir," she challenged with resentful sarcasm, "why don't you simply cast me overboard and be done with me altogether?"

"Don't tempt me."

Her eyes hurled invisible daggers at his head, but he was completely unscathed by them. He pulled her down below, flung open a door, and thrust her inside a darkened cabin.

"The quarters will seem a bit cramped after what you're used to, but you'll be sharing them with me. Compensation enough, wouldn't you say, Mrs. St. Claire?" he asked with a faint, ironic smile.

Eden opened her mouth to offer him a blistering

retort, but he slammed the door shut before she could speak. She was dismayed to hear the lock being turned in the next instant. A long, heavy sigh escaped her lips as she stood glaring after her betrayer/seducer/abductor in the darkness. He was all these things and more, she mused irefully.

"Eden?" a frightened whisper sounded behind her.

With an almost violent start of alarm, she whirled about.

"Who's there?" she demanded tremulously, her heart pounding in her ears. Good heavens, she realized, it was a woman's voice she had heard!

The mystery woman struck a match and lit the same lamp she had hastily blown out at the sound of Roark's approach only moments earlier. Eden's gaze grew wide with shocked amazement when she saw that it was none other than Jamaica Harding who peered back at her in the dim light of the cabin.

"*Jamaica?*" she breathed, unable to believe the evidence of her own eyes.

"Oh, Eden!" A wretched sob broke from Jamaica's lips as she suddenly hurled herself upon her startled friend's bosom and began to cry as though she would never stop.

Eden was too stunned to do anything more than put her arms about Jamaica and wait for the storm of weeping to run its course. Exactly how the other woman had come to be there, she could not imagine; nor could she imagine what Roark would say when he discovered her presence aboard.

For a moment, it occurred to her that perhaps Roark was responsible for Jamaica's presence. Yes, she mused while her eyes blazed even more wrathfully, the arrogant rogue might very very well have planned to have two women at his disposal—*in his bed*. Her heart, however, told her this was impossible. Somehow, she knew he would not play her false, at least not in that way.

"I . . . I have been abducted!" Jamaica announced when she could finally speak again. She allowed Eden to lead her over to the three-quarter bed in the corner. A single porthole offered a glimpse of the island's dark outline, but neither woman's gaze was drawn outward as they sank down upon the bed and traded explanations that were equally astonishing.

"Who brought you here?" demanded Eden.

"Seth . . . Colfax!" She gratefully accepted Eden's proffered handkerchief, dried her tears, and sought to bring her ragged breathing under control. "He is . . . the young man from the Stewarts, the one who . . . who was so bold!"

"But why should he bring *you* along? And how on earth did it happen he was able to carry you off without—"

"I was taking a turn about the grounds . . . alone. Oh Eden, it all happened so quickly! Truly, I hadn't time to scream or offer much resistance! He told me . . ." Her voice trailed away for a moment, and she blushed from head to toe before confiding, "He told me he knew the first time he set eyes upon me that I was . . . his woman." She swallowed hard and met Eden's gaze again. "Never, *ever*, would I have believed it possible that I would be carried off by an American!"

"The scoundrel shall be made to pay for his mistreatment of you!" vowed Eden. Her eyes kindled

200

with green fire once more. "And by damn, Roark St. Claire shall be forced to pay as well!"

"Roark St. Claire?" Jamaica echoed in bewilderment. "Who is he? And was that not Simon who locked you in here with me?"

"Yes . . . and no."

"Why did he call you 'Mrs. St. Claire'?"

Eden sighed heavily and rose to her feet. She wandered to the porthole. Her eyes clouded with both pain and confusion, and no small amount of anger, as she lifted a hand to the salt-spotted circle of glass.

"I am indeed Mrs. St. Claire," she confessed, reluctant to do so but realizing there was little help for it. "Though it is a name I would as soon forget!"

"You mean you are *married?*" Jamaica asked in disbelief.

"For the space of more than eight months now." She released another long, discontented sigh before adding, "It happened back in England."

"And that was the reason you were sent to Barbados?"

"Yes. I was very foolish, Jamaica, and the man was . . . well, he was not what he appeared to be. Perhaps someday I shall tell you the whole truth, but for now it is only important that you know my husband is the captain of this ship."

"Simon," Jamaica guessed at last. She smiled gently as Eden turned to face her. "I sensed there was something between the two of you."

"There is all too much between us!" murmured Eden. She returned to the bed and sat down beside her friend. Her gaze twinkled with an irrepressible spark of humor as it traveled over Jamaica's dishevelment. "I suppose I look even worse than you."

"Much worse!" the petite blonde confirmed, smiling again through the remnants of her tears. She dropped her eyes significantly to Roark's shirt. "Why are you wearing—"

"That is also something to be explained at a later time," said Eden. A shadow of remembrance crossed her face, and she could not help but wonder if Donald would recover from the beating he had suffered at Roark's hands. Determinedly pushing such thoughts to the back of her mind, she told Jamaica, "We must think of a way to escape!"

"Yes, of course we must, but how?"

"I don't know. The ship will be underway soon. If only . . ." A pensive frown creased her brow while her mind raced to think of a plan. Her gaze drifted back to the porthole, only to light with sudden triumph. "We can get out through *there!*" she decreed with a nod toward the window.

"Oh no, Eden, I don't think we can!" Jamaica protested, her own eyes widening in dismay. "Why, it is much too small, and I . . . I am not at all certain I would be able to swim so far!"

"I'll help you!"

Eden sprang to her feet and flew to the porthole. It opened easily enough, and she thrust her head outside to survey the watery depths below. The shore appeared a good deal farther away than she would have liked, but she would not allow her courage to fail her now.

"Eden, no!" pleaded Jamaica, apprehension filling her heart. Standing beside the bed, she cast a worried look toward the door. "What if we are discovered?"

"How the devil can we be any worse off than we are at present?" Eden responded with a touch of impatience.

Spying a map chest, she quickly tugged it beneath the porthole. She then gathered her skirts high above her knees and stepped up. Behind her, Jamaica grew more and more nervous.

"Are you sure there is no other way?"

"None which comes to mind!"

She pushed herself headfirst through the small circular opening, testing to make certain her plan was even feasible. It was a perilously tight fit about her hips, but not an impossible one.

"You see?" she challenged Jamaica, ducking back inside the cabin. "It can be done! Now do come along, we've no time to waste!"

"I can't!" Jamaica insisted breathlessly.

"You certainly cannot mean to remain here! For heaven's sake, Jamaica Harding, we are being held prisoner by the *enemy!*"

"But the captain is your own husband, is he not? Perhaps, if you talked to him—"

"It would avail me nothing!" Eden declared with an angry toss of her head. "He would never willingly set me free!" Furious with herself as she recalled how disgustingly easy it had been for him to spirit her away, she demanded of Jamaica, "Surely you don't wish to place yourself at the mercy of that villain who abducted you?!"

"*No!*" The younger woman denied it a bit too adamantly. "I most certainly do not!"

"Well then, there's nothing for us but to flee while we have the chance!" She moved to take Jamaica's arm in a firm, no-nonsense grasp. "I'm sorry, but there is simply no other way open to us!"

"Very well," Jamaica finally capitulated. She did her best to look brave. "But you must go first!"

Eden disagreed. "No, I shall follow you. To be honest, that is the only way I can be sure you will not lose courage!" She pulled her friend toward the open porthole. "Up you go, quickly now!"

Jamaica drew in a deep, unsteady breath and pushed her head outward. The cool, salt-scented ocean breeze swept tauntingly across her, while the noise on the deck above threatened to paralyze her with fear. She knew a moment's panic before hoisting herself all the way out. A scream broke from her lips the instant before she hit the water.

Eden hurried to fling herself into the sea as well. She managed to get the upper half of her body through the opening without any difficulty, but her hips, more rounded than Jamaica's, stubbornly refused to budge, in spite of the fact that they had given every indication of doing so only a few moments ago.

"Blast!" she muttered. She could scarcely make out her friend thrashing about in the water below, and dread struck her as she realized the other woman might very well drown if she did not help her soon. "I'm coming, Jamaica!" she called out softly.

"Hurry!" Jamaica spluttered back.

Eden tried again. Stifling a cry of pain, she squirmed and kicked in a desperate attempt to push free.

"What the—" Roark suddenly ground out behind her.

She inhaled upon a sharp gasp, her eyes flying wide. No! she cried silently. Cursing her ill fortune, she glanced down at Jamaica again and gestured toward the island. "Go!" she whispered. "Go on!"

"Damn it, woman, what do you think you're doing?" Roark demanded in a low, tight voice.

He crossed the room in two long strides and seized her forcefully about the hips. Hot, bitter tears of defeat stung her eyelids as she was yanked back inside the cabin. Once on her feet, she pushed away from her husband and rounded on him with vengeance.

"I *think*, Roark St. Claire, that I was doing what any woman with half a mind would want to do—and that is get away from you!"

"How? By drowning yourself?" he charged, his blue eyes glinting dangerously.

"I wouldn't have drowned!"

"You little fool, the current is treacherous this far out! No matter how strong a swimmer you believe yourself to be, you'd never have made it back to shore!" His gaze narrowed in sudden suspicion as he watched the color drain from her face. "What is it, Eden?"

"Jamaica!" she gasped. Her eyes, full of dawning horror, shot back to the porthole. "Jamaica is out there!" She hastily scrambled back on top of the map chest and ducked her head outward again. "Jamaica! Dear God, Jamaica, are you all right?"

With a savage oath, Roark jerked her away, lifted her bodily, and flung her atop the bed.

"Stay there!" His deep voice, whipcord sharp,

filled the lamplit cabin with its authority.

Eden lay sprawled, in a wild tumble of skirts, on the bed. Sitting up, she watched in wide-eyed breathlessness as Roark strode purposefully from the room. Her thoughts returned to Jamaica. Sweet Saint Christopher, she thought, what if that poor girl panics before help arrives? Fear, combined with a sharp twinge of guilt, burned within her. In complete disregard of her husband's orders, she rolled from the bed and scurried up on deck.

She arrived just in time to see Roark diving overboard. Several men, none of them yet aware of what was happening, gathered at the ship's rail to watch their captain stroke expertly through the water. Seth Colfax was among them.

Eden hurried forward. Her eyes quickly adjusted to the darkness as she made her way to the rail. She could not see Roark or Jamaica, and her alarm increased with each passing second.

Please, God, please keep them safe! she prayed, closing her eyes briefly. Opening them again, she glanced at the man standing to her right. The young first mate had just leaned far out over the rail when Eden stiffened beside him. Recognition was immediately followed by vengeful fury

"If she has suffered any harm, Mr. Colfax, I shall see you hanged!" she promised him vengefully. He jerked his head about to look at her. She was surprised to watch him pale as his startled gaze then flew to where Jamaica, coughing loudly now, battled to keep her head above water.

"Miss Harding is—" he started to say, then broke off abruptly as the awful truth hit him. Without another word, he leapt overboard to join Roark in saving Jamaica.

In no time at all, the unfortunate escapee was aboard and being borne swiftly across the deck by the very man who had brought her there only a short time earlier. Seth returned her to the dubious safety of Roark's cabin and placed her upon the bed. Eden was close behind, her eyes bright with unshed tears as she gazed upon her friend's pale countenance.

Roark, meanwhile, remained above to give the order to weigh anchor. All had been made ready. The sails had been hoisted, the rigging secured. And, as it turned out, none too soon.

A cannon suddenly boomed in the near distance. Roark cursed when he caught sight of the British ship bearing down upon them. It was the same coastal patrol which had captured him several days earlier. He was determined to avoid a repetition of that fiasco at all costs.

"Hold steady, lads!" he thundered. His exhortation was followed by the twelve-pounder's second roar.

The cannonball struck just off the starboard bow, sending up a massive spray of water but causing no damage. The enemy's ship, a three-masted schooner similar to the vessel she pursued, was closing in fast; it was only a matter of time before her guns would be able to fire with more deadly accuracy.

Roark stood tall and resolute on the quarter-deck. His commanding presence was, as always, an encouragement to his men. They would gladly follow him in to hell if he asked them to. Their loyalty had been hard won, but could not now be lost.

With the wind filling her sails and the stars to guide her, the aptly named *Hornet* was away at last. She had been built for speed, and now gave evidence of that fact, gliding through the dark waters with swift and graceful ease. The land grew ever smaller behind them, and the British found themselves increasingly hard pressed to keep up.

At the first sound of the guns, Seth had taken himself above and left the two women alone in the cabin. They gazed at one another in mingled surprise and alarm when they realized their countrymen were giving chase.

"Oh, Eden, what will happen if the Americans are caught?" asked Jamaica. She pulled the blanket more tightly about her drenched form and glanced toward the ceiling. "They'll be hanged, won't they?"

"I'm sure that's what the recommendation would be," Eden reluctantly conceded. A sharp pain touched her heart. "But I . . . I don't think they *will* be caught!"

As if to lend credence to her prediction, the cannons ceased their firing. It could only be supposed that the chase had ended almost as quickly as it had begun. Eden breathed a sigh of relief.

"Safe, thank God," she murmured, without even realizing that she had spoken aloud.

"Why, you sound as though you actually want them to escape!" remarked Jamaica in surprise.

"I don't wish to see them killed," she replied evasively, looking away.

"Nor do I," the pretty blonde admitted with a sigh. She shivered and pushed a wet lock of hair back from her face. Eden's gaze filled with remorse again.

"Forgive me, dearest friend," she implored, "for being so damnably stupid! I should never have forced you to—"

"It's all right, Eden, truly it is!" Jamaica hastened to assure her. She smiled wryly and confided, "I was a terrible coward about it, you know, and I doubt I'd have been able to get a stone's throw away before screaming like a banshee. Thank heavens Mr. Colfax came along when he did. He saved my life. And Simon, too, of course," she added as an afterthought.

"Roark," Eden impulsively corrected.

"What? Oh yes, Roark. I suppose I shall have to get used to calling him Captain St. Claire." She paused and studied Eden closely for a moment. "You aren't still in love with him, are you?"

"In love with *him?* Don't be silly! How could I possibly be in love with a man who—" She broke off, realizing that she had been on the verge of telling Jamaica the whole despicable truth. She wasn't ready for that . . . not yet. "Roark St. Claire and I," she explained more calmly, "are from two different worlds. Our relationship, or rather *former* relationship, was fated for disaster from the very beginning."

"Still, you do look at him in a strange way," Jamaica persisted. "And it is perfectly clear to anyone with eyes that he adores you."

"It is no such thing!" denied Eden. Dismayed to feel the warm, telltale color staining her cheeks, she quickly sought to change the subject. "We should get you out of those wet clothes before you catch a chill. Surely we can find something for you to wear."

Her searching gaze traveled about the room, then lit with satisfaction when it fell upon the large, leather-banded sea chest resting beside Roark's desk. She moved to open it, only to discover that it was locked. And the key, she knew without being told, was in Roark's possession.

Just then, a knock sounded at the door. The two women exchanged a quick, wide-eyed glance. Eden lifted her head proudly and then swept forward to open it. Seth Colfax stood before her in the dim light of the passageway.

"I'm sorry to bother you, Mrs. St. Claire, but I've come to see how Ja—how Miss Harding is faring," he proclaimed earnestly.

"We are in the clear?" Eden asked, tossing a meaningful look up toward the main deck.

"Yes," he confirmed with a nod. "The British have fallen back." He cleared his throat softly and asked, "Miss Harding is well?"

In spite of his unforgivable conduct, Eden could not help warming to him a bit. His concern for Jamaica, she sensed, was genuine. And after all, she reasoned with herself, who was she to judge someone for the folly of letting his heart rule the head? She had once committed that same crime.

Still, she decided, he had abducted Jamaica and should now be made to suffer the consequences.

"Miss Harding is well enough, sir, considering the ordeal this night has offered her!" Eden told him severely. "She has been torn away from all she holds dear, she has endured God only knows how much pain and terror, and now she has very nearly drowned!"

"I did not intend that she should suffer—"

"What the devil *did* you intend?"

"Please, Mrs. St. Claire, may I not talk to her?" he requested somberly. His blue-green eyes sought Jamaica, but Eden blocked his view.

"No, Mr. Colfax, you may not! When my husband hears of your misdeed, he will—"

"He will what?" Roark's low, splendidly resonant voice cut her off.

Ten

Eden suffered a sharp intake of breath. Catching her lower lip between her teeth, she watched as the master of the *Hornet* sauntered forward to stand beside his first mate.

"Come inside, Mr. Colfax," he directed grimly. "We've a matter of grave importance to discuss."

"No!" Eden denied them entry. "Not until Jamaica has changed into dry clothing! Unless, of course, you wish to have her death on your hands?" She was about to demand the key from Roark, but he anticipated her words.

"You'll find all you need in the larger of the two chests. The key is in the middle drawer of the desk." He directed a faint, sardonic smile at her, and his penetrating blue gaze provoked a wealth of emotion—not all of it unpleasant—deep within her. "You and I have matters to discuss as well, my love," he added softly.

"*You*, Roark St. Claire, may go to the devil!" she retorted, then closed the door with a good deal more force than was necessary.

She crossed angrily to the desk, found the key, and knelt to open the sea chest. Her eyes grew round with surprise when she viewed its contents.

"Can you find something suitable?" asked Jamaica, rising from the bed.

"There should be no difficulty in that!" Eden replied in obvious displeasure. Her gaze kindled with a green fire that had nothing to do with the color of her eyes. "The blasted thing is full of ladies' clothing!"

Wondering why Roark's cabin should be so well equipped with feminine fripperies, she rummaged furiously through the dresses, undergarments, stockings, and slippers. Each item she discovered only served to heighten her indignation.

"Please, Eden, do hurry!" Jamaica prompted with an anxious look toward the door. "They are waiting!"

"They may stand cooling their heels until doomsday for all I care!"

Shortly after that startling outburst, she finally settled upon a simple, pale rose muslin gown, a delicate white chemise and petticoat, a pair of black kid slippers, and white cotton stockings. She climbed to her feet and thrust the fine garments at Jamaica, who accepted them gratefully and hastened to strip off her wet clothing.

"I do hope the gown is not too ill fitting!" the petite blonde said as she shivered again.

"What difference does it make? For heaven's sake, we are about to face our captors, not some gentlemanly admirers calling on us in the safety of our own

213

drawing rooms!"

"Are you not going to change as well?" inquired Jamaica, undaunted.

Eden released an audible sigh. She had completely forgotten about her own appearance. Dropping her gaze to Roark's shirt, she battled the temptation to follow Jamaica's example and change. *No,* she told herself firmly, *I'll not wear what was clearly intended for another woman!*

When Jamaica was properly attired once more—the gown was a surprisingly good fit—she tied her damp blond tresses back with a ribbon and suggested that her friend at least do something with her own hair.

"I think we should look our most presentable," she opined reasonably. "Since we are indeed among the enemy, we are representatives, in a way, of the Crown. My father would of a certainty wish me to comport myself with pride and dignity."

"I wonder if he yet knows of your disappearance," Eden remarked with a troubled frown. Colonel Harding adored his daughter and would stop at nothing to get her back; William Stanhope, as Roark had so bluntly pointed out, would consider himself well rid of his headstrong niece.

"Papa will be sick with worry when he finds out," Jamaica murmured, tears starting to flood her eyes. "But Mr. Colfax has promised to send word to him."

"I would hesitate to believe the word of a privateer."

"Well, *I* believe him!"

"Oh, Jamaica," sighed Eden, shaking her head. She did, however, take the other woman's advice on

214

one matter. Snatching up another ribbon from the accursed chest, she soon managed to bring at least some semblance of order to her own riotous curls.

Roark and Seth were waiting in the passageway when she swung open the door. Seth's expression was one of sober contrition, but his captain's handsome face gave no evidence of remorse. As a matter of fact, Eden noted with a flash of resentment, Roark appeared to be in remarkably high spirits.

"You may come in now," she granted coolly. Lifting her head to a proudly defiant angle, she stepped aside as her husband's tall, muscular frame filled the doorway. Seth followed him into the cabin, which seemed even more cramped than ever as the two men joined their feminine counterparts within its small lamp-lit confines.

"Mr. Colfax, I believe, has something to say first," pronounced Roark.

Eden moved to Jamaica's side and placed her arm protectively about the younger woman's shoulders. She flung Roark a scathing glare before turning her reproachful gaze upon the first mate. Jamaica, however, blushed prettily and shyly raised her eyes to Seth's attractive features.

"I . . . I have come to offer you my apologies, Miss Harding," he began, obediently enough. But he shot Roark a rebellious look in the next instant and declared, "Although I regret my methods, I do not regret bringing you along. For me to say so would be a lie. And I've no wish to be branded a liar in your eyes."

"Why, of all the—" Eden was visibly bristling. "Better a liar, sir, than an unrepentant scoundrel!"

She looked to Roark and demanded, "Are you both so lost to reason that you cannot understand what it is you've done? You have carried us off against our will! You have no right, no right at all, to—"

"I have every right," Roark disputed with infuriating calm. His blue eyes twinkled roguishly when he added, "And Mr. Colfax seems to think his victim was not all that unwilling."

"*What?*" gasped Eden. She turned to Jamaica, only to watch in dismay as the fair-haired beauty colored guiltily. "Good heavens, Jamaica, surely you must deny this insult!"

"I do!" Jamaica hastened to comply. "Why, of . . . of course I deny it!" She could not, however, force herself to meet Seth's gaze again.

"There you have it!" Eden told Roark in truimph. "You must take Miss Harding back to Barbados at once! If you've even one shred of decency, you'll see that she is returned home!"

"I'm afraid that is impossible."

"Why?"

"Because, madam wife," he answered, his deep voice tinged with ironic amusement, "we have just escaped the clutches of your navy. I'll not risk the lives of my men by going back. However, I give you my word that Miss Harding will be put ashore at the first available opportunity, and thereby be able to book passage homeward on another ship."

"And just when do you expect this 'opportunity' to become available?"

"Soon" was all he would say. Disregarding his wife's icy stare, he turned to Seth and directed, "Show Miss Harding to her quarters. She is no doubt exhausted by now. Any further discussion can wait until morning."

"Jamaica and I will be sharing *these* quarters!" Eden insisted. Her gaze met and locked with his in silent combat. Neither wavered.

"Do as I say, Mr. Colfax," he reiterated evenly.

"No!" Eden's arm tensed about Jamaica's shoulders. "By all that is holy, Roark St. Claire, you cannot expect her to sleep alone and unprotected aboard a ship full of . . . of rogues and rascals!"

"She will be perfectly safe," he assured her. "No passenger aboard this vessel has ever been in the kind of danger you imply. The men know their lives are in peril if they dare to break the rules."

He gave his mate a curt nod, and Seth moved forward to take Jamaica's arm in a firm but gentle grasp. She trembled at the touch of his hand, but she offered no resistance as he led her toward the doorway. Once there, she paused and looked back at Eden.

"Don't worry, dearest Eden. I . . . I am not frightened, truly I am not."

"And where will Mr. Colfax be sleeping?" Eden suddenly demanded of her husband, furious at having to admit defeat.

"Miss Harding will occupy his cabin. He will bunk in with the other officers."

Jamaica gave Eden one last tremulous smile, then allowed Seth to escort her down the passageway to a cabin only a few steps away. Eden fumed in silence as she watched the couple leave. Alone now with Roark, she folded her arms tightly across her breasts and angrily tossed her beautiful head.

"I shall bid you good night, *Captain* St. Claire!"

His only response was to close the door, leisurely cross the room, and saunter past Eden without a word.

"Did you not hear me?" she stormed. "I, too, am exhausted! Now take what you will need and get out!"

"I'm not going anywhere," he proclaimed quietly. He stopped at the washstand secured to the wall in the corner opposite the bed. Pouring water from a pitcher into a porcelain bowl, he spared only a passing glance for his wife. "But I will indeed take what I need." He bent and splashed water on his face.

His words threw Eden into a quandary. She stared at the broad, hard-muscled expanse of his naked back. Until this moment, she hadn't really thought about what would happen to her once she was aboard Roark's ship. She had been too preoccupied with other matters—first the wild flight across the island, then Jamaica and that foolish attempt at escape. *Her own fate was upon her now.*

Growing warm all over, she swallowed a sudden lump in her throat and pushed the long sleeves of Roark's shirt above her elbows once more.

"I . . . I can share Jamaica's cabin." She set off to do just that, but Roark intercepted her before she had reached the door.

"No, Eden," he decreed, slowly shaking his head. "You'll not be leaving. You see, it is customary for the captain's lady to share the captain's quarters."

"Is it indeed?" she challenged haughtily. Her eyes flashed up at him in renewed anger. "Perhaps that explains why you keep a trunkful of women's clothing in your chest! Precisely how many other 'ladies' have shared the captain's quarters?"

Roark's mouth curved into a slow, thoroughly devastating smile. Eden was dismayed to feel her knees weaken.

"Do I detect a note of jealousy in your voice, sweet vixen?"

"Jealousy?" she echoed in furious disbelief. "Why, what a perfectly asinine notion!"

She stiffened in alarm as he reached over her shoulder to draw the inside bolt. He did not touch her—not yet.

"It so happens I've brought none but you into this cabin. But if it pleases you to believe otherwise, so be it."

"Then how the devil do you account for those gowns and petticoats and the various other accoutrements?" she could not refrain from asking.

For some inexplicable reason, she wanted desperately to hear him explain them away. It pained her more than she cared to admit to think that another woman—or perhaps, heaven forbid, *several* women—had enjoyed Roark St. Claire's attentions.

"Suffice it to say, my love, that I have had no need of them since I first set eyes upon you that night in London," he told her in all honesty.

He strode unhurriedly past her to the bed now. Eden spun about to watch as he flung back the covers. Her eyes grew enormous when his hands moved to the front closure of his trousers.

"What are you doing?"

"Exactly what it looks like." He began unfastening the row of buttons. "I'll have to be up at first light. It's time we were abed."

"We?"

"Yes, Eden," he confirmed with only the ghost of a smile. "We are no longer on your uncle's plantation. There is no one to prevent us from sharing what other husbands and wives share. I told you our positions would soon be reversed. It seems I am *your* master now."

"No!" Her eyes flew to the door, but she knew he would never let her go. And then, of course, there was no place to run.

She blushed crimson and averted her gaze as he stripped the trousers from the lean hardness of his lower body. He stood before her, naked and unashamed, in all his masculine glory, but she refused to look.

"I have waited long enough," he said. His low, vibrant tone held an undercurrent of passion. "Too long. Damn it, woman, I have been through hell these past eight months! But no more. You will learn what it is to be mine, completely and without restraint. I mean to love you well, Mrs. St. Claire. Well . . . and often. In other words," he clarified while his smoldering, possessive gaze hungrily raked over her, "we are going to make up for lost time."

"You do realize, of course, that I shall never forgive you for what you have done this night?" she countered with an outward show of bravado that belied the mingled alarm and excitement coursing through her. She tried, unsuccessfully, to ignore the wild beating of her heart as she fixed her wide, luminous gaze on the uncooperative porthole.

"It isn't your forgiveness I seek," Roark declared. He advanced on her at last.

She started to ask what he did seek, only to break off with a sharp gasp when his arms suddenly enveloped her with their strong, sinewy warmth. She jerked her head about to face him, green eyes ablaze and pulses racing fierily. "Let go of me!"

"It's your love I want, Eden," he told her softly, though his deep-timbred voice was laced with steel. "It's all of you, body and soul. I'll not settle for less."

"You shall have nothing at all!"

Her voice rose on a shrill note, and she grew perilously lightheaded as Roark's arms tightened about her. She struggled against him, yet knew all the while that she fought a losing battle. This moment was inevitable . . . heaven help her, she had always known it.

"I love you, Eden." His gaze, full of captivating warmth and tenderness and desire, seared down into the stormy emerald depths of hers. "I married you for that reason and no other. You loved me once. And by damn, I'm going to make you love me again!"

"Never!"

She gave a breathless cry of protest as he swept her up in his arms and carried her to the bed. Instead of lowering her to its welcoming softness, as she had expected him to do, he set her on her feet and masterfully yanked the borrowed shirt from her body.

"*Roark!*" she gasped in shocked disbelief. She lifted her hands to her torn bodice, but he seized her wrists and forced them behind her back.

"I mean to see all of you, my wildcat bride," he

221

vowed, an exultant smile playing about his lips. "The time for maidenly modesty has passed. I am damned well going to fill my eyes with the sight of your sweet body, and then I'm going to kiss you until you beg for mercy!"

"No! No, blast you, I will not—" Once again, her words ended on a sharp intake of breath, for he suddenly lowered his head and pressed his warm lips to her nearly naked breasts.

Eden stifled a moan as wildfire streaked through her. She made a feeble attempt to squirm free, but her efforts only served to bring the delectable roundness even farther upward into Roark's bold possession. His lips wandered across her pale, silken flesh, then abruptly relinquished their prize when he raised his head.

She blinked up at him in surprise and no small amount of disappointment, but her abandonment was mercifully brief. In the next moment, he brought a hand up to the back of her bodice and began liberating the tiny pearl buttons. With his other hand still imprisoning her wrists, he captured her lips in a deep, gloriously intoxicating kiss. At the same time, he began unfastening her gown. It all happened with such dizzying swiftness, she was startled when the cool air swept across her scantily clad flesh.

Her dress lay in a heap about her ankles; her petticoat soon followed. She stood clad only in her chemise and stockings now, her senses reeling and her resistance all but forgotten. Kissed into submission, her conscience chided in reproach and disgust. But she did not care. Nothing mattered save Roark and the sweet madness he was creating within her.

Her husband, as she soon discovered, was a man of his word. Raising his head again, he released her wrists and went down on one knee before her. She glanced down at him in bewilderment, her green eyes full of passion's glow when they fell upon his manhood. Embarrassed color washed over her, but she could not draw her fascinated gaze away from the sight of the rigid, pulsing hardness which sprang from a cluster of tight black curls between his thighs. Though she lacked the means of comparison, she knew without a doubt that he was endowed with a truly magnificent instrument of passion. The thought made her blush all the more.

"Roark?" she whispered, then gasped when he pressed a light, tantalizing kiss to the skin just above her gartered stocking.

Her eyes swept closed again as his fingers slipped into the top of the stocking and slowly eased the delicate cotton downward. A delicious shiver ran the length of her spine. After baring the other leg as well, he stood and lifted the hemline of her chemise.

Eden crimsoned anew. She instinctively protested, clutching at the thin garment in a last, futile attempt to save herself from Roark's determined mastery of her body. A soft smile touched his lips, and his blue eyes gleamed with loving amusement.

"I will see all of you, Mrs. St. Claire," he reiterated.

She shook her head numbly, but he would not be forestalled. He tugged the chemise from her trembling form, then seized her arms to prevent her from shielding any portion of her lush, womanly curves from his scorching gaze.

His eyes darkened as they traveled over her with

bold intimacy. They lingered, in wholly masculine appreciation, upon the satiny, rose-tipped fullness of her breasts and the downy triangle of raven curls at the apex of her slender thighs.

"You're even more beautiful than I imagined," he pronounced, his voice tinged with a splendid huskiness.

"Please . . . let me go!" she murmured brokenly. She didn't know which frightened her more—his passion, or her own.

"No, Eden." The slow, disarming smile which spread across his handsome face quite literally took her breath away. "You're mine. We both knew it the first time our eyes met. What we felt then hasn't been destroyed. It's only grown stronger."

"That isn't true!" she exclaimed, her eyes bright with sudden tears as she gazed up at him in the lamplight. "I . . . I foolishly believed myself to be in love with you all those months ago, but I will not make that mistake again! You may be able to possess my body, Roark St. Claire, but you'll never possess my heart! I shall never freely give you my love!"

"Ah, but you will, sweet vixen. And sooner than you think."

With that, he scooped her up in his arms and bore her relentlessly backward to the bed. She fought him with a renewed vengeance, but he held her arms above her head and lowered his body atop hers. Her eyes flew wide as the entire length of his virile, hard-muscled frame came into contact with her struggling softness. The shocking sensation of naked flesh meeting naked flesh sent a powerful tremor of half-fear, half-pleasure through her.

MORE PASSION AND ADVENTURE AWAIT... YOUR TRIP TO A BIG ADVENTUROUS WORLD BEGINS WHEN YOU ACCEPT YOUR FIRST 4 NOVELS ABSOLUTELY *FREE*
(AN $18.00 VALUE)

Accept your Free gift and start to experience more of the passion and adventure you like in a historical romance novel. Each Zebra novel is filled with proud men, spirited women and tempetuous love that you'll remember long after you turn the last page

Zebra Historical Romances are the finest novels of their kind. They are written by authors who really know how to weave tales of romance and adventure in the historical settings you love. You'll feel like you've actually gone back in time with the thrilling stories that each Zebra novel offers.

GET YOUR FREE GIFT WITH THE START OF YOUR HOME SUBSCRIPTION
Our readers tell us that these books sell out very fast in book stores and often they miss the newest titles. So Zebra has made arrangements for you to receive the four newest novels published each month.

You'll be guaranteed that you'll never miss a title, and home delivery is so convenient. And to show you just how easy it is to get Zebra Historical Romances, we'll send you your first 4 books absolutely FREE! Our gift to you just for trying our home subscription service.

BIG SAVINGS AND FREE HOME DELIVERY

Each month, you'll receive the four newest titles as soon as they are published. You'll probably receive them even before the bookstores do. What's more, you may preview these exciting novels free for 10 days. If you like them as much as we think you will, just pay the low preferred subscriber's price of just $3.75 each. *You'll save $3.00 each month off the publisher's price.* AND, your savings are even greater because there are never any shipping, handling or other hidden charges—FREE Home Delivery. Of course you can return any shipment within 10 days for full credit, no questions asked. There is no minimum number of books you must buy.

4 FREE BOOKS

TO GET YOUR 4 FREE BOOKS WORTH $18.00 — MAIL IN THE FREE BOOK CERTIFICATE T O D A Y

Fill in the Free Book Certificate below, and we'll send your FREE BOOKS to you as soon as we receive it.

If the certificate is missing below, write to: Zebra Home Subscription Service, Inc., P.O. Box 5214, 120 Brighton Road, Clifton, New Jersey 07015-5214.

FREE BOOK CERTIFICATE

4 FREE BOOKS

ZEBRA HOME SUBSCRIPTION SERVICE, INC.

YES! Please start my subscription to Zebra Historical Romances and send me my first 4 books absolutely FREE. I understand that each month I may preview four new Zebra Historical Romances free for 10 days. If I'm not satisfied with them, I may return the four books within 10 days and owe nothing. Otherwise, I will pay the low preferred subscriber's price of just $3.75 each; a total of $15.00, *a savings off the publisher's price of $3.00.* I may return any shipment and I may cancel this subscription at any time. There is no obligation to buy any shipment and there are no shipping, handling or other hidden charges. Regardless of what I decide, the four free books are mine to keep.

NAME

ADDRESS _____ APT _____

CITY _____ STATE _____ ZIP _____

TELEPHONE ( )

SIGNATURE _____ (if under 18, parent or guardian must sign)

Terms, offer and prices subject to change without notice. Subscription subject to acceptance by Zebra Books. Zebra Books reserves the right to reject any order or cancel any subscription.

019102

GET
FOUR
FREE
BOOKS
(AN $18.00 VALUE)

"I shall always hate you!" she cried hotly.

"Hate me if you will for now," he replied, his gaze smoldering with desire, "But know that I will soon tame your wild heart and hear you beg me to take you!"

She opened her mouth to deny it, but he silenced her with a kiss that was even more fiercely demanding than the one before it. His tongue thrust between her parted lips to ravish the moist sweetness of her mouth, stabbing and exploring so provocatively that she moaned in helpless surrender. He released his iron grip on her wrists. His hands swept downward over her supple curves, molding her to his will, searching out every inch of her smooth, silken body and making her gasp repeatedly against his mouth with the sweet savagery of his caresses.

It soon became apparent to her that this time would be different from the first. While there was an equal amount of passion—in truth, even more—this time held none of the tempestuous haste of their first union. This time, Roark was making love to her with a leisurely perfection that kindled a flame deep within her, and then nurtured that flame until it blazed higher and higher. He was determined that her desire should burn as white-hot as his own; he would show her in the most effective way known to man that, while woman may have been created for a multitude of purposes, it was this one particular purpose that could bring an earthly pleasure like no other.

Eden's arms entwined about the corded muscles of his neck. She kissed him back with an increasing boldness that delighted him, and at the same time threatened to send his own passions out of control. With a low groan, he tore his lips from hers and trailed a searing path downward along her neck to the beckoning fullness of her breasts. His mouth closed about one of the delicate peaks. His warm, velvety tongue flicked with light, sensuous strokes across the nipple while his lips gently suckled.

"Oh, Roark!" Eden breathed raggedly. Her hands clutched at his head, her fingers threading within the bronzed thickness of his hair. Arching her back instinctively upward, she thrilled to his ardent possession of her breasts.

Minutes later, he raised up and rolled her to her stomach on the bed. She glanced back at him in mingled surprise and bemusement, but her unspoken question was soon answered in a most satisfying manner.

Roark tugged the ribbon from her hair, smoothed the thick, luxuriant mass of raven tresses aside, and pressed his lips to the back of her neck. He followed the graceful curve of her spine, his warm mouth trailing downward until he reached her hips.

She blushed rosily when he dropped a kiss upon her bare bottom. He followed that kiss with several others, his teeth as well as his lips teasing playfully, erotically at the alluring roundness of her flesh. Her hips moved restlessly beneath his wicked but highly pleasurable tribute, her eyes sweeping closed as her arms tightened about the pillow.

Then, she was being turned upon her back again. Roark's head remained level with her hips as he knelt straddling her legs. She met his gaze. Another faint, unfathomable smile tugged at his lips, and there was something in his eyes that filled her with sudden apprehension. Without a word, he bent toward the triangle of soft, delicate black curls.

"Roark, no!" Eden protested, thoroughly shocked at his intent. She stiffened and gasped out, "Surely you cannot mean to—"

He not only meant to; he did. She cried out softly at the first touch of his lips. True to his word, he soon had her begging for release. Her hands clutched weakly at his broad shoulders, and her head tossed upon the pillow as the rapturous longing built to a fever pitch within her.

"Roark . . . *please!*"

"Please what?"

"Please, stop! Sweet Saint Christopher, I . . . I can bear no more!"

He finally raised his head and slid his body upward upon hers. His skillful fingers, however, continued the exquisite torment, making her gasp and squirm as she tried desperately to hold onto her pride.

"Say it, Eden," he commanded. His gaze bored down into the fiery, passion-drugged virescence of hers. *"Say it!"*

"All . . . all right, damn you!" she gasped out at last. "I . . . I want you to . . . take me!"

She knew she would hate herself for it afterward, but there was nothing else she could do. Heaven help her, she would go mad if he did not put an end to this sweet, near-painful agony!

Roark's blue eyes gleamed triumphantly. He was only too happy to oblige.

"With pleasure, Mrs. St. Claire!" he murmured with a soft laugh.

Slipping a hand beneath her hips, he lifted her and positioned himself in readiness. He plunged into her well-honeyed passage, his manhood sheathing with perfection.

Eden shuddered with passion and clung tightly to him. Her hips instinctively matched the rhythm of his slow yet demanding thrusts. She rode the crest of passion with him, soaring higher and higher, until she had reached the shattering fulfillment only the truest of lovers can ever know.

A scream of pure pleasure broke from her lips when it came. She collapsed, out of breath and completely drained, back against the pillow. Roark stiffened an instant later, spilling his hot, life-giving seed into her fertile softness. Nature would take its own course now.

In the soft afterglow of their loving, Roark stretched out on his back and drew his wife's pliant curves against him. Neither of them spoke; there was no need for words at the moment. They could certainly never hope to express themselves any better than their bodies just had.

The *Hornet* continued her swift journey through the waters of the Caribbean while the night deepened. The ship's gentle rocking motion soon lulled Eden and Roark to sleep. It had been a long, decidedly adventurous day. Tomorrow would come soon enough.

Eleven

Eden stretched contentedly in the bed. Still lingering in blissful half-consciousness, she did not come fully awake until the rumbling of a man's voice on the deck above forced her to abandon sleep once and for all. Her eyelids fluttered open, and she knew a moment's panic before gaining recognition of her surroundings. *So, it wasn't a dream after all.*

She came bolt upright in the bed, only to groan as her head spun dizzily. Her eyes widened in dismay when they fell upon her naked breasts. She colored hotly and snatched the covers up to her chin. Her gaze then flew to the empty space beside her, which still bore the faint indentation of her husband's tall, undeniably masculine frame.

"Dash it all," she murmured with a heavy sigh, "what have I done?"

The memory of last night's wild, sweet ecstasy came flooding back. She recalled, with mortifying clarity, the way she had surrendered to the handsome scoundrel who was her husband. And now, just as she had known she would, she despised herself for her weakness.

She glanced toward the single porthole, where the morning sun warmed the glass before filling the cabin with its soft radiance. Idly wondering what time it was, she shifted her troubled gaze to the door. She had not heard Roark leave; she only remembered falling asleep in his arms. Truth be told she had never felt so warm and secure. And loved.

"Fool!" she muttered in furious self-recrimination. Roark St. Claire did not love her. He took what he pleased and spared little regard for the pain he caused in so doing. No one had ever hurt her as much as he had done. She had wanted to die when she had discovered his betrayal.

Her green eyes clouded with the sudden recollection of that day when her whole world had come crashing down about her. Forgiveness was something her husband would never get from her. No matter how long it took for her to escape, no matter how irresistible she found his lovemaking—heaven help her, she felt wickedly aflame at the mere thought of it—she must take care to keep her heart hardened against him.

It would be difficult, she mused with another sigh. Very, very difficult . . .

She flung back the covers and tumbled from the bed at last. Snatching up the sheet, she wrapped it about her nakedness and padded barefoot across to the washstand. She poured water into the bowl, found a cake of soap and a sponge, and allowed the sheet to fall to the floor. Hurriedly bathing, she scrubbed at her skin until it was pink and glowing. It was almost as though she hoped to erase all memory of Roark's captivating "affections."

Her hair, she decided with a dissatisfied frown at the long, riotously streaming tresses, would have to wait. She drew the sheet up about her again and wandered back to stand beside the bed. Another frown creased the silken perfection of her brow as she stared down at the various articles of clothing strewn about her feet. Her gown, she knew, was beyond repair. She couldn't very well face anyone clad in nothing but her chemise and petticoat. And Roark's shirt—well, she would just as soon go naked before she'd wear it again!

As if on cue, the door swung open behind her. She started in alarm and whirled about, only to find herself facing the man she had just mentally consigned to the devil.

"I believed you still abed, Mrs. St. Claire," drawled Roark. His eyes gleamed warmly at the sight of her adorable dishabille.

"You did not wake me!" she retorted, her voice holding a distinct note of wifely reproach.

She clutched the sheet up about her breasts and raised her head proudly, which made Roark smile. He closed the door behind him.

"I thought it better to let you sleep." He did not add that he had also thought it better to let her remain in bed for another reason entirely. "Miss Harding, by the way, asked me to reassure you of her safety."

Good heavens, Jamaica! A sharp twinge of guilt struck her, for she had forgotten all about her friend.

"Where is she?" she demanded of Roark.

"Above. Mr. Colfax is playing host to her at present."

She could not help being aware of the fact that he looked more rakishly handsome than ever. Clad in his seaman's attire of tightly fitted blue trousers, a thick leather belt, a white cotton shirt, a pair of black knee boots, and a double-breasted, dark blue coat with brass buttons, he was the epitome of all the roguish American privateer captains she had heard so much about. It was no easy task for her to return to the subject of Jamaica, but she determinedly did so.

"I expect you to honor your promise to ensure Miss Harding's safe return to Barbados!"

"I honor all my promises." He negligently tossed his hat so it landed atop the desk. "Surely, my love, you have realized that by now."

"I have realized a great many things about you, Roark St. Claire, foremost of which is the fact that I cannot trust you!"

"You can trust me," he told her with his usual, thoroughly maddening equanimity.

Sauntering forward, he shrugged out of his coat and flung it across the chair. Eden's heart leapt in renewed alarm.

"What are you doing?"

"My presence is not required on deck at the moment." This was his bemusing reply.

"Well, mine is!" Eden insisted with a defiant toss of her head. "Miss Harding is no doubt quite concerned about me by now! I must join her without further delay, so if you will be so kind as to get out and allow me to dress—"

"Miss Harding will do very well without you for

another hour or so," decreed Roark. He bent his tall frame into the chair and tugged off his boots.

"Another hour or so?" Her eyes grew round as saucers. "Surely you cannot mean to—" She broke off, blushing fierily as her suspicions were confirmed by his actions.

Setting his boots aside, he stood and began unbuckling his belt. His wife's shocked gaze flew to the porthole.

"Why, it . . . it is broad daylight!" she protested in a small, breathless voice.

"So it is," he agreed with a soft, ironic smile. He pulled off his shirt and cast it into the chair. Eden's pulses took to racing wildly, and she was dismayed to feel a tingling warmth spreading outward from the vicinity of her lower abdomen. .

"What you have in mind is . . . why, it's positively *indecent!*"

"What I have in mind," parried Roark, his fingers liberating the buttons of his trousers now, "is to simply keep one of the promises I made. As I said only last night, sweet vixen, we are going to make up for lost time."

"And is it your intent, then, to keep me a prisoner in this cabin for the entire voyage?" she demanded indignantly. "Am I to be naught but a captive for your pleasure?"

"A highly tempting prospect, wouldn't you say?" His blue eyes danced with unholy amusement. His trousers were unfastened now, but he did not yet choose to remove them.

"I would say you . . . you American savage," Eden seethed as her emerald gaze kindled with fire, "are without question the most outrageously arrogant, overbearing, infuriating man it has ever been my extreme displeasure to encounter!"

"I may be all those things and more, but know this, Eden," he warned, all trace of humor vanished now. "I will have your obedience aboard this ship, or else you'll suffer the consequences. You may storm at me all you like whenever we are alone, but I'll not allow you to do so in front of my men."

"Pray, sir, what consequences would I suffer?" she countered with biting sarcasm. "Your anger does not frighten me, nor does—"

"Unless you want to feel the flat of my hand upon that pretty bottom of yours, you'll do as I say."

"Damn you, Roark, I am not a child!" Tears of outrage, and no small amount of fear, sparkled in her eyes.

"Then don't force me to treat you like one," he warned grimly. He closed the distance between them with slow, measured strides. Towering above the beautiful, raven-haired spitfire he loved more than life itself, he gazed deeply into her eyes and challenged in a tone that was splendidly low and vibrant, "Don't you think it's time you forgot about the past? I can't change what happened, Eden. I did what I had to do. We've a new life ahead of us now."

Eden swallowed hard. Feeling small and vulnerable and incredibly feminine with Roark standing so tall and virile before her, she could not deny that there was at least some truth to his words. She was tempted to give in, God knew she was tempted, but she would not allow herself to do so. The possibility that he would betray her again refused to leave her mind.

"I have no intention of spending the rest of my life with you," she declared stubbornly. Her eyes flashed up into his. "And the very moment an opportunity presents itself, I shall escape!"

"That is your pride talking, my love," he responded with a disarming half-smile, "not your heart."

"Will you never understand that I cannot love you?" Seized by a sudden and inexplicable desire to fling herself upon his broad, naked chest and burst into tears, she cursed herself for a fool.

"You can and will, Eden."

He reached for her at last. She found it difficult to resist him—only one reason being that she risked dropping the sheet—but she did her best. Squirming within his warm, possessive grasp, she found herself easily imprisoned. A sharp gasp escaped her lips when the sheet was suddenly yanked from her body.

"No!"

Crimsoning from head to toe, she sought to fold her arms across her naked breasts, but Roark swiftly pressed her back upon the bed and molded her softness against him once more. She was startled when he rolled so that she was atop him.

"Roark! Roark, what—"

"You've the most beautiful breasts, Mrs. St. Claire," he murmured, then proceeded to emphasize the bold compliment by tugging her upward and capturing one of the full, rose-tipped globes with his mouth.

Eden gave a breathless cry of pleasure. Though tempted to demand how the devil he had become such an authority on women's physical charms, she was much too preoccupied at the moment to do so. Roark's hands swept down her back to curl about her hips, his fingers kneading the firmly rounded flesh while his warm lips and velvety tongue drove her to near madness.

He did not neglect her other breast, nor did he neglect the soft pink treasure between her thighs. In no time at all, he had inflamed her passions to such an extent that she feared she could once again have to beg him for release from the exquisite torment.

This time, however, he proved merciful—and wickedly, delightfully inventive.

Eden was bewildered when he placed her facedown upon the bed. She attempted to turn over, but his hand pressed firmly upon the small of her back.

"Roark?" she gasped out.

He seized her about the hips and urged her purposefully up to her knees in the bed, then pushed his trousers down over his own hips and pulled them all the way off. Eden blushed at the shocking position in which she found herself.

"Roark?"

Still, her husband did not answer. Positioning himself on his knees behind her, he gave a soft, truimphant laugh and pulled her back into his masterful embrace. Eden cried out in mingled pleasure and surprise when his throbbing hardness eased within her feminine warmth.

She strained back against him, thrilling to his slow, pulsing thrusts. His hands moved to her breasts. Her breath became nothing but a series of soft gasps as her shapely white bottom curved against the lean hardness of his thighs. His thrusts grew more fiercely demanding. Soon, the earth-shattering sweetness was upon them both. They welcomed it in almost perfect unison, their passion completely sated and their bodies remaining entwined as they lay in the bed for several long moments afterward.

Roark was the first to break the spell. Though he would have liked nothing better than to stay and make love to his bewitching young bride the whole day long, he had detected the sound of some minor trouble on the deck above. He consoled himself with the thought of what he would do to Eden—and she to him—when the night came.

"You've my permission to come above if it suits you," he told her once he had quickly dressed. He stood beside the bed, his gaze burning down into hers. "Or perhaps you are in need of sleep in order to regain your strength," he teased roguishly.

By damn, he mused to himself with pleasure, his little Englishwoman was even more passionate a bed partner than he had dreamt she would be. That they were well mated, there was certainly no doubt. His loins tightened anew at the memory of how she had met each kiss and caress with an answering fire of her own.

Eden bristled beneath the loving amusement in his gaze. Careful to keep the covers over her nakedness— Roark's blue eyes gleamed all the more roguishly at her belated attempt at modesty—she sat up and lifted her head in that gesture of proud defiance he knew so well.

"What I am in need of, Roark St. Claire, is privacy!" she retorted with spirit.

"You may have it," he generously conceded, then added, "For now."

Before she could prevent it, he leaned down and pressed a hard, decidedly breathtaking kiss upon her lips. She was left to stare after him in flushed and stormy silence as his long, easy strides carried him from the room.

It was soon afterward that she ventured up on deck. She had reluctantly attired herself in one of the gowns from the sea chest; there had been no other choice open to her. The high-waisted, white gauze dress fit her much too tightly, exposing a scandalous portion of her bosom and clinging to the well-rounded curve of her hips. Fortunately, she had also found a tucker of cream-colored lace and had thereby managed to diminish the décolletage to some extent. All of the clothing had clearly been intended for someone of Jamaica's petite stature. She frowned and wondered once again about its intended wearer.

"Eden!" Jamaica called out when she caught sight of her. The fair-haired young beauty made her way carefully across the rolling, sunlit deck to where Eden stood waiting at the top of the narrow stairway. "Oh, Eden, I am so very glad to see you!"

"I . . . I am sorry I have not been in contact with you before now, dearest Jamaica!" she apologized with genuine remorse, embracing the other woman warmly. She drew back and searched her face. "Are you truly all right? No one has dared to offer you insult?"

"No!" Jamaica hastened to assure her. "Not at all. And I am quite all right!"

She certainly *looked* well enough, thought Eden.

Her eyes were shining brightly, and there was a becoming color to her cheeks. Abduction seemed to agree with her.

"Captain St. Claire told me you might be hungry," said Jamaica. "Why don't you come along to the galley with me? I have already had my breakfast, but—"

"I beg your pardon, Jamaica, but where *is* Captain St. Claire?" Eden demanded, her fiery gaze searching for any sign of him.

"He and Seth—I mean, Mr. Colfax," Jamaica amended with a guilty blush, "are up on the quarter-deck." She nodded to indicate their whereabouts.

Following the direction of her friend's gaze, Eden looked to where Roark was discussing a change in the ship's course with his first mate. Neither of the two men spared so much as a passing glance at their beautiful young captives, a fact which provoked an unaccountable twinge of irritation within Eden's breast.

"Very well," she told Jamaica, heaving a sigh. "I suppose I could do with a little something to eat."

"Of course you could. And what's more, I have so much to tell you!"

They went below to the galley. Jamaica had already made the acquaintance of the ship's cook, a kindly older man by the name of Smith. His bearded face was wreathed in smiles when Jamaica led Eden inside the galley's aromatic warmth.

"Pleased to be making your acquaintance, Mrs. St. Claire," he told Eden sincerely. "I've known the captain since he was no taller than a cypress stump. Mighty bullheaded he was, even as a boy."

"He has not changed," murmured Eden. She could not help returning the man's smile. "It is a pleasure to meet you, Mr. Smith."

"Call me Smitty if you will, ma'am. No one stands on formality down here in the belly of the ship, leastways not in my galley!"

Leaving Smitty to make good on his promise to prepare her a breakfast fit for a queen, Eden next allowed Jamaica to lead her into the adjacent officers' mess. It was small but comfortable, with a carved, rectangular table and enough chairs to seat eight.

"This is where Captain St. Claire and his officers eat," explained Jamaica. "Of course, you and I shall be taking our meals here as well. The men are really quite nice, you know. They are not at all what I expected!"

"Meaning, I suppose, that they do not fall upon their food and devour it like wild beasts?" Eden queried wryly. She grew serious again in the next instant. "You must remember, Jamaica, that no matter how nice they appear to be, they are our captors as well as our enemies."

"But they do not seem like enemies," the other woman insisted. "Not in the least. And as for being our captors, I could almost forget that in the face of their unfailing kindness to me thus far."

"Kindness?" Her green eyes widened in disbelief. "For heaven's sake, Jamaica Harding, what sort of *kindness* is it that sees you carried off in the middle of the night, by a man who is nothing but a stranger? Why, he may very well be a cold-blooded murderer for all we know, or have a wife and six children—"

"Seth Colfax is a gentleman!"

"He is an American privateer!"

"And your husband is his captain!" Jamaica pointed out. "A circumstance which you have yet to explain to me!"

"It . . . I am afraid it is a long story," Eden stammered with another sigh.

"We have an abundance of time." The persistent blonde took a seat and pulled Eden down beside her. "Start at the beginning, if you please, for I wish to know everything!"

Eden visibly hesitated. Jamaica, she told herself, was quite naive and had always led such a sheltered life. How could the dear girl possibly understand what had happened? What did Colonel Harding's sweet young daughter know about love and betrayal, and the irresistible force of passion?

Colonel Harding's daughter, as she soon discovered, understood a good deal more than she had given her credit for. A *suprisingly* good deal more.

It was time, of course, thought Eden. Her sister in misfortune deserved to hear the truth. So, she told her everything—or at least, very nearly everything, She left out several embarrassingly intimate details, all of which pertained to the most recent past. Jamaica listened with rapt attention, never once interrupting.

"And so you see," Eden concluded at the end of her startling tale, "I am every bit as much a prisoner as you, dearest Jamaica. Yet my determination to escape grows with each passing hour!"

"You are right about one thing, you know," Jamaica remarked thoughtfully. "Captain St. Claire will never let you go."

"Because he intends to use me to his own advantage," muttered Eden. Then she flushed guiltily at the memory of Roark's latest *husbandry*.

"No." Jamaica shook her head. "It is because he loves you."

"You . . . you are mistaken! Roark St. Claire does not love me!"

"Oh, but he does, Eden. Why else would he have risked his very life to find you? And did he not jeopardize his mission back in England by eloping with you? Indeed, I fail to see what good it can have done him to marry you," she put forth with a pensive frown.

"I was only a pawn in his nefarious scheme!" insisted Eden, though her voice lacked its usual tone of conviction.

Ever since Roark had come back into her life, she had found herself plagued by doubts and confusion about the past. Part of her wanted to believe he had once truly loved her, for that would have given her some small measure of consolation. But still another part of her argued that there must have been another reason entirely. He was a master of lies and deception. And he had done his job well. . . .

"Then why should he come all the way to Barbados in search of you?" Jamaica's voice broke in on her unpleasant reverie.

"I do not believe him on that score, either! It was an odd coincidence, nothing more." Was it truly? the inner voice challenged archly. Eden bridled with anger. "He has no doubt spent these past eight months wreaking complete and utter havoc throughout the Caribbean. Why should he not be doing more of the same in Barbados?"

"Very well," Jamaica conceded, deeming it wisest not to press farther on that subject. She did, however, raise yet another question. "But for what reason did he abduct you? His business in England is long since finished, so what use can there be in his holding you captive?"

"I don't know," admitted Eden. She absently lifted a hand to smooth a wayward strand of hair from her forehead. "I have nevertheless resolved to seek my freedom at the first available opportunity. The arrogant rogue cannot hold me forever!"

"Perhaps not. But, I must say, Captain St. Claire appears to be the sort of man who does not accept defeat easily. And anyway, I am not at all certain that an attempt at escape would be well advised."

"How the devil could it *not* be?"

"Oh, Eden, even if we were able to escape somehow, what then? We should be all alone in the world, far from home with no resources at our disposal. Why, we might very well be placing ourselves in even greater jeopardy! At least now, we are assured of favorable treatment. Mr. Colfax has given me his word that—"

"No matter what he has told you, Jamaica, you cannot believe him," Eden cautioned severely. "I'll grant you that he cuts a dashing and highly romantic figure, but his intentions are not honorable!"

"How can you say that?" the petite blonde leapt to his defense. Her blue eyes sparkled with an uncharacteristic fire. "It's true that he should not have carried me off, but he has been nothing but kind and respectful ever since I came aboard!"

Eden realized it would serve no purpose to try to reason with her. It was painfully clear that Jamaica had formed some sort of attachment to Roark's first mate. She could only hope that the innocent girl did not lose her heart to the man. His association with Roark St. Claire was certainly cause enough for concern.

Smitty entered the room soon thereafter, bearing a tray laden with ham and eggs, hot coffee, and freshly baked biscuits with sweet butter. Eden, much to her own surprise, suddenly discovered that she was famished. She thanked the ship's cook for his thoughtfulness, offered polite praise for his culinary achievements, then set about consuming such a generous amount of the food that Jamaica gazed upon her with faint startlement.

By the time they returned topside, the sun was blazing almost directly overhead. Jamaica was disappointed to see that her gallant young captor was taking a turn at the ship's wheel and was thus unable to converse with her. Eden's gaze was drawn immediately to Roark, who, upon catching sight of his wife, descended from the quarter-deck. He strode toward her with sure, unhurried steps that left little doubt he was well accustomed to the feel of a ship's rolling deck.

"I take it you've had your breakfast?" he queried with a soft, devilishly provoking smile. His gaze strayed downward to where her full young breasts swelled enticingly above the borrowed gown's lace-tuckered bodice. The smile vanished, to be replaced by a frown of stern disapproval. "By damn, woman, you'll start a mutiny yet!"

"Good!" she retorted saucily, though she blushed beneath his intimate, possessive scrutiny. She was glad Jamaica had wandered away to the rail. "Were it not for the fact that your former *paramour* was such a small woman, I should not now be forced to endure your insults!"

"Another spark of jealousy, sweet vixen?" His blue eyes virtually danced with loving amusement when he explained, "It so happens I took those fancy trappings off a British merchantman. I'd no idea they belonged to someone of lesser 'endowment' than yourself."

"Pray, sir, it is either these blasted trappings or nothing at all!"

"Another tempting dilemma. Naturally, I choose the latter—but not until we are below. For now, I'll thank you to refrain from breathing too deeply." His wryly gleaming gaze then dropped to her hips, whose shapeliness was outlined by the thin, clinging fabric. "And try not to parade yourself too closely to the men. God knows, the poor bastards will find it difficult enough to concentrate on their duties with women aboard."

"A circumstance for which I am entirely blameless!" she saw fit to remind him. "And I have no intention of 'parading myself' at all!"

She shivered ever so slightly as his strong hand closed about the bare flesh of her arm. It was impossible not to be reminded of the wicked pleasures they had shared only that morning. Sweet Saint Christopher, she was set afire every time he touched her!

Oblivious to the effect he was having upon his

wife, Roark led her across the deck to join Jamaica at the rail.

"If there is anything you require, Miss Harding," he offered with all politeness, "you've only to ask."

"Thank you, Captain St. Claire." In spite of all that Eden had told her, Jamaica could not help liking him. "I require nothing at present."

"Well, *I* require something at present!" Eden avowed pointedly. She tried to pull her arm free, but Roark held fast.

"And what is that?" he asked, his lips twitching.

"I want to know where we are going!"

"Home."

"Whose home?" Her eyes flashed in growing impatience.

"Mine. And yours." His own eyes lit with pleasure and anticipation at the thought of what lay ahead.

"Mr. Colfax has told me you live in Georgia, Captain," Jamaica wisely interjected.

"Mr. Colfax had told you the right of it, Miss Harding," he replied with a smile. "St. Simons Island has been home to my family for a number of years now."

"And I . . . I understand Mr. Colfax lives there as well?"

"He does. His father and mine were friends long before we were born."

"So your father is an American?" Jamaica next inquired. She recalled Eden's having told her that his late mother had been English.

"Was," Roark corrected. "He was killed ten years ago; he and a good many others. For all its charm and beauty, the island has had its fair share of storms."

246

Eden, listening to this exchange, felt her heart stir with sudden compassion. A prayer of silent thanks rose in her mind, for her own mother and father still lived. She had scarcely given them a thought of late. What would they say when they found out she had been carried off by one of her uncle's escaped bondsmen? She sighed inwardly, musing that they would be even more shocked if they knew of her abductor's true identity.

"What do you and Mr. Colfax do there? I mean . . . that is . . . when you are not at sea?" Jamaica colored faintly.

"We grow cotton." Another smile tugged at his lips, and his eyes twinkled with ironic humor. "The finest in the world, Miss Harding. The Colfax plantation is but a short distance from my own."

"And I suppose your fields are tended by slaves?" Eden finally spoke up. Her voice held a sharp note of accusation.

Roark's hand released her arm at last. His handsome face grew solemn, and his eyes glinted dully now.

"Yes, Eden," he acknowledged. "But they are not treated the same as your uncle's."

"Indeed, Roark St. Claire, it is no surprise to me that you should make that claim!"

"What do you mean by that?" he demanded with a frown.

"Only that you cannot expect me to believe slavery in any form is tolerable! My uncle offered his own excuses, of course, but to no avail. He was well aware of my feelings on the matter, for I made no secret of them!"

"That is certainly true," sighed Jamaica.

"I despise you all the more now that I have discovered this!" Eden proclaimed with great feeling to her husband. "Why, you are no better than my uncle!"

"Damn it, woman, lower your voice," he warned grimly. "Take me to task if you will, but not here and not now."

"I shall do whatever I please!" she continued in angry defiance. "It is bad enough that you should rape and pillage and plunder your way across—"

"I've never found it necessary to do any raping," he ground out. A fiery blush rose to Eden's face.

"Please, dearest Eden," implored Jamaica, "do calm yourself. In truth, Captain St. Claire cannot be held accountable for the institution of slavery. It existed long before his birth."

"As did all manner of treachery!" parried Eden. She rounded on her husband again. Her eyes shot emerald sparks up at him, while her breasts rose and fell rapidly beneath the gown's low-cut bodice. "The more I learn about you, *Captain*, the more I am convinced I was wrong to save you from the whip! It would have been no more than you deserve!"

"And the more I learn about you, my love, the more I am convinced you are in dire need of a strong hand," he told her with deceptive calm. "It's a good thing I came along when I did. You've become a hellcat these past eight months. Rest assured that I am the man to tame you."

With a curt nod at Jamaica, he seized his wife's arm once more and pulled her firmly away from the rail. Eden, however, would have none of his manhan-

248

dling. She jerked free, raised her other arm, and dealt him a stinging blow across the bronzed ruggedness of his cheek.

Jamaica gasped in stunned disbelief. Eden was more than a little surprised herself. Her wide, luminous gaze traveled swiftly about the deck, only to see that the men were staring at their captain and his lady in eager expectation. She looked back at Roark. His handsome face was dangerously impassive.

It was not Roark's intent that there should be witnesses to his forceful wooing of the beautiful, headstrong vixen he had taken to wife. But a man must be master of his own ship. He therefore slipped an arm about Eden's waist, yanked her close, and kissed her with such fierce, sweetly compelling passion that she was afraid her legs would give way beneath her. The crewmen smiled and exchanged laughing remarks with one another at the sight of her "chastisement."

Eden was left becomingly flushed and breathless when the kiss ended. Her head was spinning as she gazed up at Roark, and she was dismayed to realize that everyone, including Jamaica, was looking at her with indulgent humor. Her anger returned to hit her full force.

"Damn you!" she hissed at Roark. She pushed herself away from him with a vengeance. Two bright spots of color rode high on her cheeks, and she was made all the more furious by the unrepentant light of amusement in her husband's gaze. "Touch me again, you conceited scoundrel," she threatened rashly, "and I'll make you rue the day you were born!"

"Get below," was his only response.

"I . . . I most certainly will not!" she sputtered in wrathful indignation.

"Ah, but you will, madam wife," he insisted in a tone that let her know he would brook no further defiance. "And what's more, you'll stay there until you've learned the proper respect for your lord and master."

"Lord and master?"

"Miss Harding, you may remain above if you like," he told Jamaica, then promised Eden, "We'll continue this discussion at a later time."

"You, sir, may go to the devil!"

She spun about and marched angrily back across the deck. Roark's gaze darkened as it fastened upon the seductive sway of her hips. He cursed the fire in his blood, and cursed Eden as well. She was making it too blasted difficult to keep his mind on his duties.

"You love her very much, don't you, Captain St. Claire?"

He smiled ruefully at Jamaica's observation.

"That I do, Miss Harding."

"Unless I am very much mistaken," the petite blonde ventured with a shy, tentative smile, "she is still in love with you."

"You are a very astute young woman."

"I am not at all certain of that, but Eden is my dearest friend in all the world and I . . . well, I should not like to see her hurt." She drew a deep, steadying breath and cautioned with rare severity, "Treat her with kindness and patience, Captain St. Claire. Her life has not been an easy one since the two of you parted. She has told me of the circumstances

250

surrounding your marriage, you see, and I think you should know that she has suffered a great deal as a result of your betrayal—intended or not."

"I have shared her pain," murmured Roark, a sudden shadow crossing the rugged perfection of his features. His brow cleared in the next moment, and his blue eyes filled with warmth as he assured Jamaica, "You have my word, Miss Harding, that I will do everything in my power to make her happy. Patience, however, is not always easy for a man to come by."

"I am well aware of that, Captain," she replied with a faint sigh. Her eyes moved instinctively to Seth, who gazed back at her from his position atop the quarter-deck. "I am indeed."

Roark smiled to himself. Although musing that there was too damned much courtship taking place aboard what was supposed to be a wartime vessel, he nonetheless relieved his first mate at the wheel and charged him to assume the duty of looking after the *Hornet*'s unmarried female passenger. Seth, visibly delighted with his orders, hastened to obey.

It was some two hours later before Eden finally dragged herself from the bed. She had flung herself upon the quilt and wept tears of mingled fury and confusion. Sleep had overtaken her at last; a deep and dreamless sleep that gave her renewed courage but left her feeling a trifle drowsy.

She now stood, heaved a slightly uneven sigh, and wandered across to the washstand. The long folds of white gauze had crept up about her thighs while she slept. She cursed the too-tight gown anew and tugged the hemline back down into place. Then, catching a welcome breath of fresh sea air as she passed the open porthole, she poured water into the bowl and bent over to splash some on her face.

Roark, meanwhile, had decided it was time to pay a visit to his recalcitrant bride. She had not been out of his thoughts since storming below, and he recalled Jamaica's naive but perceptive advice as he moved down the stairs.

"Patience, he repeated silently. His lips curved into the merest suggestion of a smile. He would try. Hell, he would be as patient as Job if it meant Eden's heart would be his again.

His timing was either perfect or disastrous, depending on whose opinion was sought. He opened the door quietly, took one look at his wife's curvaceous, temptingly poised derrière, and knew that he would not be returning to his post above for a while yet.

Still unaware of his presence, Eden remained bent to her task. She was taken completely by surprise when Roark's hands suddenly closed about the firm roundness of her bottom.

A sharp gasp of alarm broke from her lips. Abruptly straightening, she whirled to face her bold caresser. She saw that it was Roark who stood smiling down at her, his eyes full of both amusement and the undeniable promise of passion. Hot color washed over her.

"I should have known it was you!" she blurted out in reproach, then gave an inward groan at the utter stupidity of her words.

"Were you expecting someone else, my love?"

"Would that I *had* been! You've no right to . . . to

accost me in such an ungentlemanly manner!" She felt lightheaded at his nearness, and it was so blasted hard to remain angry with him when he persisted in looking at her that way.

"But I am no gentleman, remember?" He leisurely enfolded her with his strong arms. "We American 'savages' go about accosting our women whenever it suits us."

"Is that how you came to be born?" she retorted caustically.

"Of course." He cast her a smile of such warmth and affectionate good humor that she melted inside. "You've a wicked tongue, Mrs. St. Claire. I suppose I'll get used to it in time. But God help me if our children inherit your spirit of defiance."

"Children?" she echoed, her eyes growing very round. Good heavens, she had not even considered the possibility of children!

"An even dozen, if it suits you," teased Roark. "The house at Liberty Point is large enough to quarter a small army."

"Liberty Point?"

"You've a habit of repeating everything I say," he pointed out in mock exasperation. "Liberty Point is the name of the St. Claire plantation."

"Paid for with the spoils of war, no doubt!" She squirmed rebelliously within his embrace, but he merely tightened his arms about her.

"My father purchased it some thirty years ago," he told her in all seriousness. "And it might interest you to know that, other than what I allow to be divided among my crew, I keep none of what the *Hornet* seizes."

"I find that difficult to believe! You are, after all, a privateer, and it has always been my understanding that privateers are interested only in what profit they can make—"

"A popular misconception. While there are some who are prompted by greed, there are others of us who are driven by something else entirely."

"And what is that?" she demanded skeptically.

"A love for our country. A desire to see all men granted the freedom to govern the courses of their destinies." His eyes glinted like cold steel now. "You English have never understood what it is that makes us fight."

"And I suppose you would employ that same nonsensical excuse for your actions back in England?" Eden challenged, lifting her head to a proud, unforgiving angle. "You hurt not only me, but my family as well! It was all my father could do to conceal your treachery. And I doubt my mother shall ever recover from the shock of seeing her only daughter wed to an enemy spy!"

"Perhaps, when the war has ended, we'll return to England," said Roark. His eyes glowed with wry amusement once more. "I wouldn't want it said that the son-in-law of Lord Grayson Parrish is completely lacking in the social graces." He pulled her closer, his gaze darkening. "But enough talk for now, sweet vixen.

"No, Roark! Let—let go of me!" Her protests sounded ridiculously weak, even to her own ears. She gasped as the lace tucker was suddenly yanked from her bodice.

"I've been wanting to do that ever since you came

above in this damned dress," murmured Roark. Urging her farther upward, he bent his head and pressed his warm lips to her half-naked breasts. His hands swept downward to close upon her buttocks.

Eden moaned low in her throat and swayed against him. There was no help for it. She was conquered again . . . but oh, *what a sweet surrender it was*.

Twelve

"No, Eden, I am quite certain I heard him correctly!" insisted Jamaica. "He said we are to be putting in at Cuba this very afternoon!"

"Cuba? Why, that's where your father was bound, is it not?"

Blast it all, Eden swore silently as she stood upon the ship's deck with her friend. Roark had refused to tell her anything. As a matter of fact, he had done very little talking these past several days. But, Sweet Saint Christopher, she mused with a fiery blush of remembrance, she had suffered no shortage of his *attentions*.

"Yes, it is!" Jamaica confirmed with a nod, then declared worriedly, "Oh, I do hope Papa isn't waiting there when we arrive! He is very likely to shoot Mr. Colfax before I have the chance to offer any explanations!"

"What explanations could possibly satisfy him?" Eden asked with a frown. "Your father has every right to seek revenge. Now, pray, dearest Jamaica, don't look at me like that! I do not wish to see Mr. Colfax murdered at your father's hands any more than you do, but it is only natural that the possibility should exist."

"I know," the pretty blone allowed reluctantly. She smoothed her hands along the top of the sun-warmed rail and heaved a sigh. "You will think me incredibly foolish, no doubt, but I cannot help wishing that Captain St. Claire was not so intent upon sending me home. I should like to stay with you, Eden, and . . . well, to be truthful," she confessed while telltale color flew to her cheeks, "I should also like to stay near Mr. Colfax. I have never experienced anything like this before, and I am not at all sure what to make of my own feelings."

"You have gone and fallen in love with him, haven't you?" Eden probed gently.

"Yes. I think I have." Sudden tears glistened in her blue eyes, and her voice held such a wistful note that Eden's heart stirred with compassion. "But, I have known him only a few short days, and I cannot yet be sure. . . ."

"This is a fine muddle," murmured Eden. A faint smile, an ironical one, touched her lips. Her emerald gaze was drawn to where Roark and Seth were talking together at the ship's wheel. A fine muddle indeed, she told herself.

"You aren't still thinking of escaping, are you?" Jamaica asked at a sudden thought.

"Escaping?" she echoed in surprise. Of course, she then recalled, she had vowed to escape at the first opportunity. Why in heaven's name did the prospect give her no pleasure? Her eyes clouded with perplexity—and pain, if she would but admit it—as she acknowledged in a small voice, "I suppose Cuba is as good a place as any."

'Perhaps, if I truly must go back, we can book passage on the same ship." Like Eden, she sounded less than enthusiastic about gaining her freedom.

"Perhaps."

They lapsed into silence after that, each of them lost in their own troubled thoughts. It was difficult to believe they had left Barbados only a few days ago. In some ways, it seemed they had been aboard the *Hornet* for a good deal longer. And now, now to think of returning to their orderly, uneventful lives back home . . . the future awaiting them was anything but bright.

Even Jamaica could find no joy in thoughts of home. For, although she was assured of her father's continued love and devotion, she had lost her heart to a handsome, golden-haired stranger. Her life had been forever altered the very first time their eyes had met.

Eden, on the other hand, could not bear the thought of seeing her uncle again. And, to make matters worse, she was certain he would make her life a veritable hell on earth because she had dared to thwart Donald Parkington-Hughes' advances. No, she could never return to Barbados. She would have to make for England instead. Strangely enough, that thought filled her with even more dread. How could she hope to settle into her old life after all that had happened to her? *How could she hope to forget Roark St. Claire?*

"Well, at least I've nothing to pack," Jamaica

finally spoke again.

"Nor I," said Eden.

Her gaze lit with an uneasy determination when she spied the outline of an island on the sea-swept horizon ahead. She looked at Roark again—and battled the sudden, inexplicable urge to call his name.

The *Hornet* slipped gracefully through the deep blue waters of Cumberland Bay later that same day. The harbor was crowded with ships from around the world, for the town was a neutral port. Neutral or not, however, experience had taught Roark to exercise great caution when encountering enemy vessels.

Today proved to be no exception. A squadron of three British warships, bound for the eastern coast of America to join in the blockade, was sighted just off the starboard bow as Roark expertly guided his three-masted schooner into port. His eyes glinted with a savage light while traveling swiftly in turn over the brig, the frigate, and the massive gunship of the line.

"I count over a hundred guns in all, Captain," Seth reported grimly.

"We'll take no chances," decreed Roark. "Tell the men to stand at full watch."

"Full watch, Captain?"

"Yes, Mr. Colfax," he affirmed with a faint, sardonic smile. "After we've taken our turn at the wharf, we'll keep the *Hornet* in waters too shallow for those fat-bottomed barges to follow."

"Are you anticipating an attack then?" Seth asked, his brows knitted into a troubled frown.

"I am. To their eyes, we'll present an easy target. I doubt they'll pass up the opportunity. But I'm damned well going to make them work at it."

"Aye, Captain."

Eden and Jamaica stood together at the rail when the anchor was finally dropped. Seth came toward them. His manner was one of quiet resignation, but his blue-green eyes were full of unhappiness.

"The captain has instructed me to see you ashore, Miss Harding," he announced. His heart twisted at the sight of her pale, tear-streaked face. She looked every bit as miserable as he felt.

"Am I to go ashore as well?" demanded Eden.

"No, Mrs. St. Claire, I'm afraid not," Seth told her. "Your husband has given orders that none save myself and Miss Harding, and the men who have been charged with the duty of securing water and supplies, are to leave the ship."

"Then I . . . I suppose we must say goodbye now, dearest Eden," faltered Jamaica. There was a noticeable catch in her voice, and her eyes sparkled with a fresh onslaught of tears. "I hope you'll send me word of your whereabouts as soon as possible!" She hugged Eden tight and whispered close to her ear, "I don't know how you're going to get away! I wish you were coming with me!"

"I cannot!" Eden whispered back. "But rest assured I will send you word!"

"From England?"

"God willing!"

They drew apart, embraced warmly once more, and managed a brief, tremulous smile for one another. Roark approached in the next moment. He tugged the hat from his head and faced Jamaica.

"Again, Miss Harding, you have my apologies for the inconvenience Mr. Colfax has caused you. He is under the strictest orders to see that you are put aboard a ship bound for Barbados."

"I . . . I thank you, Captain St. Claire." She knew it was useless to argue with him, for she had already tried to convince him to let her stay. He was adamant that she should go. And he was equally adamant that Eden should remain. "I wish you well," she added, her voice quavering.

"And I you, Miss Harding." He gave a curt nod to Seth. "I am counting on you to remember your duties, Mr. Colfax," he reiterated in a dangerously low and level tone.

"It is not in my nature to forget, Captain," replied Seth.

His eyes were suffused with barely suppressed anger. He and Roark had been friends their whole lives, and he had never once questioned the other man's authority. This was the first time he had ever been tempted to disobey. God help him, how was he going to carry out his captain's orders when the only woman he had ever loved was his for the taking? How could he give her up?

But Roark had given his word. And no matter what his personal feelings were in the matter, he had no choice but to do as Roark said.

"This way, Miss Harding," Seth pronounced at last, his hand curling firmly about Jamaica's elbow. He led her toward the lowered gangplank.

Eden's throat constricted painfully. She was only scarcely aware of Roark standing beside her as she watched Jamaica being escorted ashore. The petite blonde soon disappeared into the midst of the bustling crowd along the wharf, but not before turning and giving her friend one last wave.

"I'm sorry, Eden," Roark said quietly. He frowned at the sight of the tears glistening in her eyes.

"Are you?" she shot back. "Damn it, Roark, couldn't you see how desperately in love she is with Seth? And he with her?"

"She said nothing of—"

"How could you expect her to? Jamaica Harding is a sweet, innocent girl who knows nothing of such things!" Her eyes flashed resentfully up at him. "You men are all the same! You force us to care for you, and then you expect us to be able to stop caring when it pleases you!"

"And have I forced you to care for me?" he challenged with only a ghost of a smile.

"I was talking about Jamaica!"

"Were you?"

"Yes!"

"What would you have had me do, Eden?" he put to her, sobering again. "You know as well as I do that her father will never rest until she is found. It would not have been fair to her, nor to Seth, to wait until we had reached Georgia. The parting would only have been that much more painful."

"That does not change the fact that they are already in love!" She blamed herself, too, of course. If only she had gone to Roark and told him of Jamaica's regard for his first mate, he might possibly have been persuaded to relent. As it was now, Jamaica was miserable, Seth was miserable, and she

262

was feeling as guilty as hell.

"If they truly love another, nothing will change it," allowed Roark. "But Seth knew better than to take her. And he must now face the consequences of his impulsive actions."

"And what about your own 'impulsive actions'? You took me against my will and—"

"We are legally wed. No one can deny me the right to take you any place and any *way* I see fit."

"You forfeited that right the day you fled England!" Eden proclaimed hotly.

"Damn it, woman, are we to have this same quarrel for the rest of our lives?" he demanded in a voice that cut straight through her.

"I can only hope you'll soon tire of me altogether and let me go!"

"Never that, sweet vixen." His gaze burned down into the stormy depths of hers. And though he did not touch her, she nevertheless felt branded as his own. "Like it or not, I mean to grow old with you. If you don't kill me with that tongue of yours first," he added softly.

Eden stared after him as he turned and strode away. It was several long moments later before she forced her gaze back to the wharf in the near distance. Her thoughts returned to Jamaica, and she offered up a silent prayer for her friend's well-being.

It was only a short time later that Seth led his reluctant charge toward the ship that would take her home. A British merchantman, it carried a number of other female passengers, and in its hold were all manner of luxuries to delight the well-heeled, highborn inhabitants of Barbados.

"From all accounts, the voyage should be a comfortable one," Seth told Jamaica when they emerged from the small, cluttered office at the end of the dock. She had waited by the door while he made all the necessary arrangements with the ship's agent. "I'm sorry I was unable to book you a private cabin, but at least you'll be sharing quarters with a respectable widow."

"And what if she should turn out to be unrespectable?" teased Jamaica. The playful amusement in her eyes quickly vanished. She drew in a shuddering breath and lamented, "Oh, Seth, what are we to do?"

"Exactly what we are doing, Jamaica." His eyes reflected all the love in his heart when he pulled her to a stop and gazed down into the delicate beauty of her upturned features. "I'll come back for you. I give you my word—*I'll come back for you!*"

"But how?"

"I'll think of a way," he declared with the supreme confidence of a man in love.

"I shall wait for you!" vowed Jamaica. Her own gaze was sweetly adoring. "I shall wait for as long as it takes!"

"Come on," Seth directed, his self-control tested to the very limit. He took her arm again. "We'd better get you aboard."

"No!" Jamaica suddenly held back and shook her head. "No, I won't go! I know I said I would, but I can't! I can't bear to leave you so soon after . . . after . . . oh, Seth, I love you!" she proclaimed. All the tender feelings he had aroused within her joined together to give her the courage to defy him now. Oblivious to the curious stares of the many passersby, she flung her arms about his neck and tilted her head back to gaze deeply into his eyes. "I love you, Seth Colfax, and I shall never leave you!"

"By heaven, Jamaica, I love you, too!" Seth murmured hoarsely.

He lowered his head and captured her lips with his own. Although they had shared a number of stolen kisses aboard the *Hornet*, this was the first to be so boldly impassioned. Jamaica swayed against him, while Seth delighted in her sweet response. The kiss deepened.

But Seth's conscience finally got the best of him. He forced himself to put an end to the delectable torment. Raising his head, he firmly drew Jamaica's arms from about his neck and set her away from him.

"A man can only bear so much!" he ground out, though not in anger.

"I . . . I did not mean to shock you," stammered Jamaica, blushing rosily.

"Shock me?" He smiled tenderly down at her. "It was not that, Jamaica. It's just that I want you so blasted much, and—" He broke off and drew in a deep, steadying breath. "I've got to get back to the ship. And you've got to go home."

He determindly led her up the gangplank, presented the required documents to the officer on duty, and turned back to her with a look of such warmth and longing that she feared she would cast herself upon his chest again and shamelessly beg him not to leave her. Eden would no doubt caution her against forgetting her pride. But Eden wasn't the one being torn away from the man she loved.

Seth reminded Jamaica of her promise. "You'll

265

write to me?" He cursed the fates for having allowed him a taste of happiness and then cruelly denying him more.

"Yes. And . . . you must do the same." She battled yet another wave of tears. "I'll be waiting for you, my dearest Seth!"

His eyes were full of helpless pain and frustration as she suddenly whirled and fled across the deck. She disappeared below, leaving him feeling more wretchedly alone than he had ever felt before. Muttering an oath, he strode back down the gangplank and turned his angry steps toward the spot where the *Hornet* lay anchored.

He made his way swiftly through the crowd of sailors and vendors, women in brightly colored dresses, English aristocrats, American privateersmen, and all other manner of humanity, food, drink, merchandise, and entertainment. The port had always been a busy one, but it was particularly so now that the war had escalated. Neutral territories were enjoying a boom such as they had never before experienced; they also faced an increasing danger of being drawn into the conflict.

Upon reaching the ship, Seth brushed past Roark without a word and climbed to the quarter-deck. He stood gazing out to sea, his conscience still doing battle with his heart. Jamaica's face swam before his eyes.

Roark could not help but be aware of his friend's turmoil. The seed of doubt Eden had planted in his own mind had by now grown into a rare, full-fledged uncertainty about the wisdom of his decision. He smiled to himself as he faced the truth. By damn, he mused wryly, his green-eyed spitfire was making him soft.

"Mr. Colfax!" his deep voice rumbled across the deck. Seth turned to face him with a stoic expression.

"Yes, Captain?"

"I trust Miss Harding is safely aboard the other ship?"

"Yes, Captain," the first mate ground out, his eyes glinting dully.

"Then what the bloody hell are you waiting for?"

"Waiting for, Captain?"

"Blast it, man, go and fetch her back!" His gaze twinkled at the sight of the other man's incredulity. "And be quick about it! I've no wish to let those limey bastards find us tied up here come nightfall!"

"Aye, Captain!"

Seth was off the ship and flying back along the wharf in a matter of seconds. His heart soared higher and higher as he neared the British merchant vessel again, and his mind raced with thoughts of what he would say—and do—to Jamaica once they were alone.

He headed up the gangplank, only to stop dead in his tracks when he saw that Jamaica was heading down it.

"Seth!" she breathed in stunned astonishment. Her face lit with the joy of realization. "Oh, Seth, you've come to take me back!"

"That I have, Miss Harding!" He closed the distance between them, caught her up against him, and kissed her right there on the gangplank, in front of God and anyone else who cast an indulgent eye upon them.

When Seth finally raised his head again, his beloved was flushed and breathless and more suprememly happy than she had ever been in the entirety of her eighteen years upon this earth.

"I . . . I had decided not to go!" she confessed, thrilling to the strength of his arms about her. "I didn't care what you or Captain St. Claire or anyone else said! I don't even care what my father will say! I only know I've got to be with you, Seth Colfax!"

"I'll never let you go!" he vowed huskily. "And it was the captain who sent me to fetch you back! So you see, my dearest Jamaica, you'll soon find yourself wed to a man who's far from perfect, but who loves you with all his heart!"

"Indeed, sir, that is all I ever wanted!"

He kissed her again for good measure, then finally led her down the gangplank.

"We must send word to your father," he said, drawing her toward the shipping office. A sudden frown creased his brow. "He may very well follow us to Georgia."

"That is true," Jamaica agreed with a sigh. "But once he sees how happy we are, he will not think of parting us."

"You'll be my wife," Seth reminded her firmly. "He'll not be able to part us."

"Mrs. Seth Colfax. Oh, I do like the sound of that name! Are you *quite* certain you've no other wife waiting for you in Georgia?" she challenged on an affectionately teasing note.

"Perhaps."

"Perhaps?" Her eyes grew round as saucers. Seth laughed softly and dropped a light kiss on the end of her nose.

"If I had, you adorable little minx, do you think I'd risk bringing you home with me? I'd be taking my life in my hands and well I know it!"

Jamaica beamed a perfectly captivating smile up at him. With a bright future stretching before them, they stepped inside the shipping office.

Long after night had fallen, Eden stood alone at the ship's rail and glanced overhead at the starlit sky. A quarter moon cast its silvery light upon the waters of the bay, and outlined the dark figures of the men standing watch aboard the *Hornet*.

Roark stood with his feet planted apart on the quarter-deck above, his hands clasped behind his back as he kept a vigilant eye on the surrounding darkness. Every so often his piercing blue gaze strayed to his wife. They'd had only a brief moment's conversation since that afternoon, and even then about purely impersonal matters. He longed to take her below. But his duties took priority at present. If his suspicions proved correct, there would be trouble before the night was through.

A faint sigh escaped Eden's lips. She thought of Jamaica again, and her eyes sparkled with affection. Her friend had been a beautiful, radiant bride. And Seth had never looked more handsome. Roark, with the authority granted him as captain of the ship, had married them less than an hour after Jamaica's return. It was still beyond belief . . . Jamaica Harding of all people, wed to an American. Of course, she herself was in much the same position, but, somehow, that did not seem quite so shocking.

The newlyweds were happily ensconced within Seth's cabin. They had been there for several hours now. Eden colored anew as she recalled the toast Roark had made them. *May all your nights be long, and all your days, God willing, short.* No one else appeared to have found his words impertinent, but she had bristled when his eyes, smoldering with both passion and unholy amusement, sought her out immediately afterward.

So, she now mused with another sigh, Jamaica was coming to Georgia. They would be neighbors. Or would have been, she amended, if not for the fact that she had no intention of remaining there. She had spent all afternoon trying to think of a way to escape, but Roark had watched her like a hawk. And she had little doubt that he would continue to do so.

"Dash it all," she muttered to herself, "he'll have to let his guard down eventually!"

She pushed away from the rail and spun about. Her eyes flew toward Roark. He looked so damnably irresistible, standing up there like some dashing buccaneer of old. Only he *was* a pirate, and she, God help her, could not find it in her heart to hate him any longer.

Not that she loved him, either, she hastened to deny to herself—no indeed. How could she possibly love him after all he had done to her? It was simply that she no longer despised him. She had come to this startling realization only a short while ago, when he had escorted her above, following supper. He had taken her completely off-guard with an admission of guilt concerning his treatment of Seth and Jamaica.

And what he had done for the two young lovers that afternoon made him seem all the more human.

Human, she repeated silently, her eyes aglow. Oh, he was that, all right. He was no paragon, but a real, flesh-and-blood man who possessed the unnerving ability to make her forget all else save him. The whole world receded whenever she was in his arms . . . nowhere else did she feel so incredibly safe and secure . . . nor so wickedly wanton. He took her to dizzying new heights of passion every day, drawing her gently but masterfully along with him into their own world of earthly pleasure and heavenly delight. She could not imagine sharing such intimacy with any other man.

Though he had betrayed her once, she could not now summon the will to seek revenge. Something had happened to her since he had brought her aboard the *Hornet*. It seemed she had fallen under Roark St. Claire's spell once again. But it was different this time. This time, she thought as her heart gave a strange leap within her breast, she had fallen completely.

"It's time you were below, Eden!" Roark suddenly called out to her.

"Are you not coming as well?"

She regretted the question as soon as it rolled off her tongue. Groaning inwardly, she cast a quick, anxious glance about at the crewmen standing watch. She could well imagine how they would interpret her words. It required little imagination to gauge her husband's reaction. A slow, thoroughly devastating smile spread across his handsome face, while his blue eyes filled with warm amusement.

"My apologies, madam wife, but duty prevents me from obliging. I'm afraid I'll not be along before morning."

"Morning?" Disregarding his raillery, she frowned in puzzlement and asked, "Are you perhaps anticipating some kind of trouble? Is that why all the men—"

"Any captain worth his salt anticipates trouble," was all he would say. "Good night, Mrs. St. Claire. And stay below. That's an order."

Eden, finding herself summarily dismissed, narrowed her eyes in mingled suspicion and resentment. Wondering why the devil Roark was so intent upon getting rid of her, she was sorely tempted toward defiance. But she had no desire to create a scene in front of the men, and she could remember all too clearly what had happened the last time she had dared to defy him before witnesses.

"Good night!" she replied at last, her voice holding a discernible edge. She swept proudly across the deck and down the stairway. Roark's penetrating gaze followed her until she was out of sight.

"Do you think they'll make their move soon, Captain?" one of the men asked as soon as Eden was gone.

"They may not make a move at all, Hawkins," answered Roark. "But I've a feeling they will."

"The captain's instincts are usually in the right of it," a man named O'Connell remarked from his post in the stern. He absently scrutinized the grapeshot-loaded cannon before him while adding, "Leastways, when it comes to the British they are."

"Shut your trap!" growled Hawkins. "Have you

forgotten the captain's lady is one of them?"

"Not anymore she isn't," said O'Connell. He flashed a broad, meaningful grin in Roark's direction. "She's been educated."

"Stow the talk, damn it!" Roark commanded tersely.

He had glimpsed sudden movement out of the corner of his eyes. His gaze traveled swiftly across the dimly lit waters, only to confirm his suspicion. Four launches, carrying more than a hundred and fifty of the enemy, were closing in fast on the *Hornet*.

"Make ready to fire!" he ordered, his eyes gleaming at the prospect of battle.

The men obeyed without hesitation. Since the guns were already loaded, they had only to take up their positions and wait for the order to fire. They watched, tensed for action, as the enemy approached.

"Hold steady, lads!" Roark exhorted them. "Let them make the first move!"

They had not long to wait.

"Surrender your vessel, Captain St. Claire!" a British officer demanded, his voice ringing out in the highly charged silence. Roark's ship was well known to his enemies.

"I'll remind you that we're in a neutral port!" countered Roark. "And I'll give you one warning and one warning only—fall back before I blow you out of the water!"

"In the name of his majesty, King George of England, I place you and all your men under arrest!"

"Your king be damned!" Roark pronounced in disgust. "Fall back, man, or else you'll leave me no choice but to fire!"

"That is your final word?"

"It is!"

There was no hope for it. The British took aim immediately thereafter, their guns setting up a deafening roar while they drew closer and prepared to board. If their bullets had found any human targets, there was no way of knowing, for everything happened quickly after that first ill-advised barrage.

"Fire!" thundered Roark.

Bloodcurdling screams filled the air as a murderous broadside of grapeshot cut across the enemy boats. More than a dozen attackers fell. Enraged by the stinging repulse, yet forced to admit a momentary defeat, the British finally fell back. The launches retreated into the darkness while the men of the *Hornet* cheered their own victory.

"I guess we taught those bastards a thing or two, didn't we, Captain?" boasted one of the men.

"Perhaps," Roark allowed with only the ghost of a smile. "But you can be certain they've not finished with us yet."

"You think they'll come back tonight then?"

"I do." He caught sight of his first mate, who had come above at the first sounds of trouble. "Sorry to disturb you, Mr. Colfax!" he quipped dryly.

"Why the devil didn't you tell me what you were about?" complained Seth, striding forward with cutlass in hand.

"Your presence was not yet required," said Roark. His gaze moved significantly toward the passageway. "The women?"

"Safely below," Seth reassured him, then smiled crookedly. "Though it was all I could do to make

274

them stay there! My bride quite naturally feared for my safety. And yours, Captain—well, she nearly took my head off before I 'convinced' her to remain in her cabin. I'm afraid it was necessary for me to lock the door."

"A wise move, Mr. Colfax." In truth, his heart twisted painfully at the thought of Eden in danger. If a full-fledged battle ensued, she could very well be hurt . . . *or even killed*. His gaze filled with a savage light. "Tell the men to reload. I doubt we'll find it so easy to drive them off next time."

"Aye, Captain."

The second assault came less than an hour later. It was soon apparent that the enemy's resolve had only been strengthened by their first humiliating defeat, for they now sent twelve boats filled with men and armed with swivel-mounted carronades against the *Hornet*.

"Make ready to fire!" came Roark's order once more. He had no intention of showing the British mercy. As soon as they were within proper distance, he gave the order to fire and the cannons were put to flame.

A series of ear-shattering *booms* split the night air. The Americans' broadsides were instantly answered by the enemy's carronades and small arms. Two of the boats were sunk. Roark's ship miraculously sustained only minor damage; none of her masts were toppled. But it was not the enemy's intent, after all, to sink the *Hornet*. No, they wanted both her and her crew alive. Captain Roark St. Claire had been a thorn in the Royal Navy's flesh for too long.

The cannons soon stilled their terrible roar as the

British closed in. In less time than seemed possible, they had managed to gain the ship's bow and starboard quarter.

"Board!" the young commanding officer shouted above the din. He leapt into the fray, his heart pounding in his ears and his mind filled with thoughts of glory.

The Americans fought like the demons they had been reputed to be. They fired muskets into the faces of their attackers and cut at them with pikes and cutlasses. Men fell left and right. Still, the British gained the deck and began pressing aft.

"Hold steady!" commanded Roark. "Remember the *Chesapeake*!"

With that popular rallying cry, he led his men into the very heat of the battle and with their help began to drive the British back. Eden's face flashed across his mind. If he had lacked courage, the thought of her would have given him plenty.

He wielded his cutlass with both skill and accuracy, never once wavering as he fought to keep his ship from falling into enemy hands. The Americans were, to a man, prepared to die for their freedom. And by damn, they would take as many British with them as they could.

But it soon became apparent that the tide had turned in their favor. Reeling beneath the almost maniacal defense mounted by the Americans, their attackers were forced farther and farther back. Finally, with certain defeat looming over them, the British could no longer hold steady.

The survivors, including the young commanding officer, leapt over the side. There were still men waiting in the boats below, ready to take their turn at boarding, but they were thankfully spared that peril when the order was given to retreat.

Once again, a victorious cheer rose up from the men of the *Hornet*. They had saved their ship. Watching as the British rowed away into the darkness for the last time, they grew silent. The victory was a bittersweet one; they turned away to see to their dead and wounded.

Roark had suffered a deep cut across his arm, but he impatiently shrugged off his first mate's concern.

"See to the men, Mr. Colfax," he directed, his eyes glinting dully as he gazed upon the devastation wrought by the British. By all accounts thus far, there were more than a dozen casualties among the men, but only a day or two's worth of repairs to be made to the ship. He would rather it had been the other way around.

"I'll be back shortly," he told Seth.

"You're going below?" asked the other man. His own thoughts had been on Jamaica.

"Yes." A faint smile played about his lips, but there was no humor in his gaze. "I'll tell that bride of yours she's not yet a widow."

He strode across the deck and down the stairs. He found Jamaica standing in the passageway. She hastened forward when she saw him.

"Oh, Captain, is it . . . has it ended?" she stammered in worriment. At his nod, she then demanded anxiously, "And Seth? Is he—"

"He is safe."

"I must go to him at once!" She swallowed hard and gazed up at Roark through her tears. "Are the

277

others all right?"

"Most are. But we've several wounded." He did not make mention of the dead.

"Perhaps I can be of help!"

Roark did not try to stop her as she flew past him. He told himself the men would be glad of her presence.

Unlocking the door to his cabin, he swung it open and stepped inside. Eden was across the room in an instant.

"Roark!" she breathed in profound relief. It occurred to her that she had never in her whole life been so glad to see someone as she was to see him now. Her heart soared at the confirmation of his safety. "Dear God, Roark, what has been happening?" Her gaze fell upon his injured arm. "Why, you . . . you are bleeding!"

"It's nothing," he insisted quietly. He slipped his good arm about her and drew her close. His gaze burned down into hers when he demanded, "Are you all right?"

"Yes, of course!" Though tempted to sway against him, she was determined to see to his injury. "Come! Your wound must be cleaned and bandaged!" She tried to pull him toward the lamp, but he held back.

"No, Eden. I can't stay."

"But your arm—"

"Will still be there when I have finished my duties above." He pulled her to him again and pressed a quick, hard kiss upon her lips. "You might be interested in knowing we've repelled an attack by your countrymen. We'll have to remain in port a couple of days longer."

"Oh, Roark, is Jamaica safe? And Seth? And what about the men?"

"Seth and Jamaica are both above at present. As for the men," he said, a sudden shadow crossing his features, "they fought bravely. Some were not so fortunate as others."

"Then I must do what I can for them!" She flew across to the sea chest, opened it, and hastily sorted out an armful of petticoats and chemises. "We'll need these for bandages! Have you any iodine on board?"

"Smitty has some in the galley." Already, the horrors of battle were subsiding now that he was with her again. His heart swelled with both love and pride for her willingness to help, and he could not resist giving her another kiss before leading her above.

Roark sent someone to fetch the iodine, then left Eden and Jamaica with their care of the wounded. He and Seth made their rounds of the ship, inspecting the damage and performing the sad but necessary task of arranging burial for those who had been killed—British as well as American.

The long night wore on. Finally, half the crewmen were sent below to fall, exhausted, into their bunks. Roark stood watch with the others. Although he had been persuaded to let Eden bandage his arm, he refused to comply with her orders that he get some sleep. There would be plenty of time for sleep later, he decreed with all the infuriating stubbornness she had come to expect from him. She left him and returned to the loneliness of her bed, while Seth and Jamaica returned to their newly married bliss.

When the first rays of dawn crept over the horizon, Roark, after supervising the exchange of the watches, finally allowed himself to go below.

Eden was still abed when he came in. She awakened to the feel of her husband's strong arms slipping about her. Sighing contentedly, she snuggled against him and drifted back to sleep. The soft, steady sounds of their breathing mingled, and their hearts, though they did not know it, beat as one.

Thirteen

"What the devil *is* it?" Eden queried with a frown of complete bafflement.

"Why, it is a bathtub, of course!" Jamaica supplied, laughing.

"Where did it come from?" She continued to eye the object dubiously, for she had never quite seen the likes of it before.

"Seth told me that Captain St. Claire instructed him to purchase it in town yesterday afternoon, when he went ashore to fetch the wood and other things for repairs. It seems your husband meant to surprise you." She heaved a dramatic sigh. "I do hope he won't be too angry with me for having spoiled the surprise."

"How could he be?" Eden pointed out, an ironic smile tugging at her lips. "It was certainly through no fault of yours that the ridiculous-looking thing was discovered sitting in the very midst of the galley. I suppose our dear friend Mr. Smith was under the strictest orders to conceal it." The thought of Roark's having gone to so much trouble on her account sent a warm sparkle to her eyes.

They had sailed from Cuba only that morning. The way had finally been cleared by virtue of the timely departure of the enemy squadron; the three warships had sailed the day before. Since the British had been guilty of violating the laws of neutral territory, the town fathers of Caimanera had made it perfectly clear that they were no longer welcome.

True to Roark's estimation, the repairs to the *Hornet* had required a full day's time and no longer. The Americans had left behind five of their dead and two of the more seriously wounded, promising to return for their injured comrades as soon as possible. A north-northwesterly course was set now, and home lay only a few days farther.

"It would be so nice to have a bath again," Jamaica remarked wistfully. She heaved a sigh for effect as her gaze fastened upon what had once been a whiskey barrel but now passed for a bathtub.

"You are welcome to use it any time you please," Eden offered with another smile.

It was good to feel lighthearted once more, she reflected. The past two days had been full of so much sadness. There were still wounded to be seen to, but the six men were already well on the road to recovery and needed little in the way of actual nursing. The routine aboard the ship was returning to normal.

And Roark, thank God, was beginning to act more like himself again. Although, now that she thought about it, she wasn't at all certain *that* was something to be thankful for. He would no doubt behave as arrogantly and overbearing as ever—and she would no doubt melt in his arms the very instant he laid hands upon her. In truth, she admitted to herself while a becoming flush crept up to her face, the prospect was not at all an unpleasant one. *Not at all.*

"Seth told me we've plenty of water now," said Jamaica, "so I suppose it would do no harm to try it out this very evening."

"You and Seth are very happy together, aren't you?" There was really no need to ask, she mused, for anyone with eyes could see that the newlyweds were perfectly suited to one another. Still, she regretted the fact that she and Jamaica had had so little time to talk since the wedding.

"Yes, Eden, we are very happy indeed," the other woman confirmed, glowing anew at the thought of her handsome young spouse. She blushed and dropped her eyes in an unconscious gesture of modesty. "Seth is the most gentle and considerate of husbands. And he is a truly remarkable—" She broke off and colored even more rosily. "Well, you . . . you know what I mean."

"Of course," Eden murmured softly. If Seth Colfax was anything at all like the captain, then she could well understand Jamaica's claims of his "remarkableness."

Sweet Saint Christopher, she thought with an inward groan, would she never escape this sweet madness? It was positively wicked to enjoy Roark's lovemaking the way she did. What had happened to the prim and proper Lady Eden? In actuality, she had never existed. A fire had always burned deep within the real Lady Eden, a passion for life and all it had to offer. It had only been waiting for the right man to come along and coax it to the surface. And Roark St. Claire, though she was loathe to admit it, was the right man.

"Come," said Jamaica, taking her hand. "Let's find Smitty and have him fetch it up to your cabin. I know I am anxious to see if it leaks!"

"You may have the honor of the first bath," laughed Eden. "But I fear you are more in danger of the ship's pitching the water clean out of it!"

They had soon located the ship's cook, followed after him as he pulled and tugged the brightly painted half-barrel up to Jamaica's cabin, and offered to help him carry the several buckets of water it would take to fill the tub. Waving away their offer of assistance, he returned to the galley with the stated intention of heating water and finding two of the men to do the carrying.

In no time at all, Jamaica was lowering herself blissfully into the water's soothing warmth. The makeshift tub did not leak, but Eden's prediction about the water being pitched over the top proved correct. Still, the new bride enjoyed her bath immensely and, when she was done, recommended it with all enthusiasm to her friend.

The tub was thereupon emptied and dragged across the passageway into Eden's cabin. After being filled again, it beckoned her toward its lightly steaming contents. She hastened to close the door, draw the inner bolt, and peel off every stitch of her clothing. The tub was soon obliging her with the same benevolence it had recently shown Jamaica. Water splashed out to soak the floor with each roll of the ship, but she did not care.

After luxuriating in the all-over warmth of the bath for quite some time, she decided to seize advantage of the opportunity to wash her hair. She and Jamaica had always found it necessary to help one another perform this task, which had been anything but easy with only a pitcher and bowl at their disposal.

She drew herself upright and stepped from the bathtub. Wrapping a length of toweling about her glistening softness, she knelt upon the damp floor, tugged the ribbon from her hair, and bent over to lower the long, silken black tresses into the water.

"Eden?"

The sound of Roark's deep voice startled her. She inhaled sharply and peered through a thick curtain of dripping wet hair toward the door.

"Eden, open the door!" commanded Roark. He knocked insistently.

"I . . . I am occupied at present!" she called out. "Please, go away!"

"Occupied or not, you will open this door at once!"

"I most certainly will not!" She bent over the tub again and blithely continued soaping her hair. "It will do you no harm to wait until I am finished."

"Damn it, woman, open the blasted door!" He was obviously in no mood to be defied. *"Now!"*

"No!" she shot back wrathfully. Just when she had begun softening toward the man, he had to come along and act like a perfect barbarian. She had intended to thank him properly for the gift of the bathtub, but she'd now be hanged if she would. "For heaven's sake, can I not have so much as an hour's privacy aboard this ship?"

"I told you once there would be no locked doors between us," he reminded her in a dangerously low and level tone. "Open the door, or else I'll break it down."

His threat, though uttered with surprising calm, was not to be taken lightly. Eden's temper, however, had flared in the face of his unreasonable behavior, and her anger made her reckless. Without pausing to consider what might have occurred to put him in such an ill humor, she decided it was high time Roark St. Claire realized she had not been set upon this earth for his pleasure alone.

"Go away!" she reiterated.

Her defiant words were greeted with several long moments of silence. She smoothed the wet hair from her face and stared expectantly at the door. Just when she was beginning to think Roark had finally seen the error of his infuriating, dictatorial ways, he made good on his threat.

The door suddenly crashed open. Eden gasped in alarm and scrambled to her feet, clutching the towel about her body. Her wide, startled emerald gaze met and locked with the smoldering blue fury of Roark's. He closed the door behind him.

"Are you never going to learn to obey me, Eden?" he asked in a tone laced with steel. His eyes traveled swiftly over her, darkening at the sight of her towel-clad loveliness. The long raven curls were streaming wetly down about her face and shoulders, and her beauty was only heightened by the indignation which set her green eyes to blazing. A faint, sardonic smile touched his lips as he glanced toward the bathtub. "So, I see you've discovered my little surprise."

"Yes! And I would offer you my gratitude, save you have just spoiled whatever enjoyment I might have taken from the blasted thing!"

"You made me angry," he replied matter-of-factly, and without even a spark of contrition. His anger was now quickly evaporating, to be replaced by a desire that would not be denied. He had sadly neglected his headstrong bride these past two days, but he would make up for it now. He burned to possess her again, to bury himself so deep inside her that the both of them were to the point of begging for mercy.

Eden recognized the look in her husband's eyes. She grew flushed, and was quite dismayed to realize that she wanted him every bit as much as he wanted her. It would do her no good to say it was not so; besides, she was tired of hypocrisy and all the obligations that went with it.

"It strikes me, madam wife, that I could do with a bath myself," said Roark.

Eden watched as he began taking off his clothes. She asked herself what manner of man she had married. He was practically ready to beat her at one moment and ready to make love to her the next. How the devil was she ever to learn his many moods?

"It . . . it was good of you to purchase the tub," she stammered breathlessly, not knowing what else to say.

A delicious warmth crept over her when he flung his clothing aside and stood naked before her. Good heavens, she thought as her eyes traveled the whole, unabashedly masculine length of his body, simply looking at him was enough to send liquid fire coursing through her veins.

"Perhaps next time, we could share the bath," he suggested, bending his tall, hard-muscled frame down into the tub. He muttered an oath at the water's soap-clouded coolness.

Eden's own anger had by now gone the way of his. Suppressing a laugh when he scowled darkly, she was not inclined toward humor an instant later when he commanded her—much the same as he thundered out orders above—to come hither and scrub his back.

"Scrub it yourself!" she retorted saucily, her eyes flashing at his arrogance. She took up another length of toweling and began to dry her hair.

"I can see you are in need of another lesson in wifely obedience," pronounced Roark.

His gaze was full of a warm, predatory light as he stood. Heedless of the fact that he was sending water everywhere, he stepped from the tub and began advancing purposefully on Eden. She drew in her breath upon a sharp gasp while color flew to her cheeks.

"What are you doing? Why, you—you've not yet finished your bath!"

"It occurs to me, sweet vixen," he told her, "that it's time your defiance was rewarded with the punishment it so richly deserves."

"*Punishment?* Eden repeated silently, frowning. It was difficult for her to tell if he was being serious or merely playful. A twinge of fear tempered the desire already blazing within her. She clutched the towel to her breasts and hastily retreated behind the desk.

"I am no child!" she saw fit to remind him.

"I know that better than anyone." He kept coming, prompting her to move again and thereby keeping the desk between them. "But a wife must submit to her husband's will—in everything." His eyes fairly danced with roguish amusement. "Even in England, it is the tradition for a man to be master of all he surveys."

"No!" She shook her head in vehement denial. Sensing his determination, she grew increasingly alarmed. "We are no longer in the dark ages, when a woman was little more than a slave to a man's desires! I am no slave, Roark St. Claire, and I shall *not* be treated as such!"

"It isn't a slave I seek, Eden," he disputed with a faint unfathomable smile that served to make her pulse race all the more.

"Then what is it?"

Her eyes flew to the door. Roark, noting the direction of her gaze, laughed softly. She lifted her head to a proud, spirited angle and made the mistake of moving too far toward the corner of the desk. A breathless cry escaped her lips when Roark's hand shot out to seize her arm. He pulled her along with him to the bed, while she struggled to keep the towel securely about her nakedness.

"Roark! Roark, let go of me!" she demanded, twisting within his grasp. "What are you doing?"

"I am but teaching you a lesson, my love," he responded in a low, vibrant tone that sent a shiver down her spine. Before Eden could guess his intent, he lifted a foot to the edge of the bed and sent her flying facedown across his bent knee.

"Stop it!" Her efforts to escape were considerably hampered by her reluctance to lose the towel. She gasped anew to feel the folds of thick, softly looped fabric being raised above her hips. "Roark!" She crimsoned at having her bottom bared to him. "Damn you, Roark, let me go!"

"Not until you've learned to conform instantly and without question to your husband's will." His arm was clamped like a vise across her waist, holding her captive for what she feared would be an effective punishment indeed.

"Roark!" His name was a strangled cry upon her lips as his hand descended with one light smack upon her bottom. The blow was more tingling than painful, but she took great exception to it just the same. "Stop it, you . . . you lout!"

She flung a blistering curse at his handsome head, but he was not in the least bit deterred. His large hand found its wriggling target once more.

"It appears, Mrs. St. Claire, that you've still a great deal to learn," he decreed, his blue eyes gleaming. He was of a mind to taunt her a bit, to offer a fitting retaliation for her defiance. But as he soon discovered, his thoughts of husbandly chastisement were taking a far different turn. The sight of his wife's naked, adorably shaped backside was certainly enough to make him want to tumble her to the bed and love her like the very devil.

As he did just that, Eden suddenly found herself lying on her back atop the quilt. Roark imprisoned her with his strong arms in the next instant, stretching out beside her and laughing at her furious struggles as he pulled her up hard against him.

"By damn, those sweet curves of yours would tempt a saint," he murmured, his voice tinged with a splendid, disarming vibrancy.

"I shall *never* forgive you!" Eden declared with great feeling. Her bottom felt as though it were on fire, and her eyes were shooting emerald sparks at the memory of the playful but highly energetic spanking she had just endured at her husband's hands. She cried out in protest as he suddenly yanked the towel free.

"You'll forgive me all right," he insisted with maddening confidence. Smoothing a hand down along the curve of her hip, he gave another quiet chuckle and rolled so that she was atop him. "And what's more, my wildcat bride, you'll love every minute of it."

"I most certainly will—" She had started to deny it, but the sentence was left unfinished as Roark's hands closed about her buttocks and urged her upward so that her full, rose-tipped breasts were on a level with his mouth. Ever resourceful, he proceeded to take full advantage of this convenient position.

Eden, straddling his lean hips, moaned low in her throat and closed her eyes. Her damp locks tumbled down about her like a shimmering black curtain. The room was filled with the pleasant scent of soap and the warm glow of fading sunlight, but she was oblivious to her surroundings. Resistance, of course, was entirely out of the question. As always, Roark conquered and she surrendered. *But the victory belonged to them both.*

She clutched weakly at his shoulders, her fingers curling about their bronzed hardness while his warm lips and tongue teased provocatively at her breasts. Nor were his hands idle. They swept over her trembling, satiny curves with bold possessiveness, making her gasp repeatedly as his knowing fingers brought her to a point of ecstasy and yearning that was near painful in its intensity.

"Oh, Roark!" she said in a breathless whisper. "Dear God, Roark, wha—what are you doing to me?"

"Only what I've longed to do from the first moment I saw you," he murmured hoarsely. He pulled her back down and wrapped his arms about her waist. His gaze burned into hers. "I love you, Eden, I'll never stop loving you."

His words struck a sharp, powerful chord of response deep within her. She knew in that moment that he spoke the truth. Sweet Saint Christopher, she thought dazedly, he truly loved her. *Roark St. Claire loved her.*

The realization threw her into even further confusion about her own feelings. After all, she told herself, it was difficult to hold the past against him now that she knew it had been love and not treachery which had prompted him to marry her. Still, after all these months . . . heaven help her, she didn't know what to think! And anyway, how on earth could she hope to consider the matter in a calm and rational manner while in his arms?

Taking note of her dilemma, Roark smiled softly and smoothed his hands back along the curve of her spine to seize her well-rounded buttocks in a sweetly masterful grip. She could not help be aware of his arousal beneath her, and she grew warm all over.

"Someday soon, my love," he proclaimed, "you'll say the words I long to hear. Until then, I'll settle for what you are willing to give."

"You . . . you mean what *you* . . . are willing to *take!*" she retorted, though it was hard to sound convincing when one of his hands crept purposefully toward the delicate bud of femininity between her thighs. She stifled a moan as his warm, strong fingers found their mark.

"Give and take," he told her, his voice tinged with a thrilling huskiness. "That's what it's all about, sweet vixen." He cast her another heart-melting smile before repeating, "Give and take."

With that, he finally captured her lips with his own. She wound her arms tightly about his neck and kissed him back with all the fiery passion he had unleashed the night—was it possible it was only days ago?—he had climbed through her bedroom window. He had been delighted to find her such a quick learner; in truth, she had taught him a thing or two as well.

Desire flared hotter than ever between them. Soon, Roark rolled so that she was beneath him again, then plunged inside her. His throbbing hardness was sheathed to perfection within her moist, soft warmth. She shivered and met his almost violent thrusts, her hips following the age-old rhythm of his as she clung to him. When the moment of fulfillment was upon them, he claimed her lips again and swallowed her breathless cry of pleasure. Their own sweet paradise had been sought and found once more . . . and the journey would only get better.

Long after Roark had left her to return to his duties

above, Eden lay in the bed and thought of all that had happened throughout the past several, unbelievably adventurous days. She might well have remained there until her husband returned, were it not for Jamaica. The new Mrs. Colfax knocked at the door and called her name softly.

"Eden?"

"Just a moment, please!" she replied, her gaze widening in dismay. She could well imagine what Jamaica must be thinking.

Coloring guiltily, she scrambled from the bed, flung a rose silk dressing gown about her shoulders, and slipped her arms into the sleeves. The garment, like all the others, was woefully snug, but there was no help for it. Roark had promised to commission a dressmaker to fashion an entire wardrobe for her as soon as they reached Georgia.

Belting the robe, she opened the door at last. Her face was flushed, her hair a wild tangle of ebony curls, and her green eyes suspiciously bright as she smiled across at the petite blonde.

"I . . . I am afraid I was resting," she stammered by way of explanation.

"Oh, Eden," said Jamaica, "I am sorry to disturb you, but Seth just told me we are facing severe weather ahead!" She stepped inside and turned back to Eden, a worried look on her face. "I thought you should know!"

"I am sure there is no need to concern ourselves too much," Eden gently reassured her. "Why, we've encountered a few storms before, and—"

"This is much more serious. Captain St. Claire has given the order to batten down the hatches and lower the sails. I don't mean to be such a coward, but I . . . I cannot bear the thought of anything happening just now. Seth and I have been together such a short time!" Her blue eyes were full of dread, and there was a pitiable catch in her voice.

"Your fears are perfectly understandable, dearest Jamaica. But they are as yet unfounded." Seeing that her friend was still far from convinced, Eden closed the door and hurried to dress. "We shall go above and investigate the situation ourselves."

"But Seth told me to stay—"

"I'm quite sure he did," Eden cut her off with a mock frown of exasperation. She smiled in the next instant. "As you will soon learn, it can benefit a man a great deal to learn he is not so all-powerful a lord and master as he would like to believe. And, I might add, it can benefit his wife as well!" Her eyes sparkled at the memory of the *education* of her own husband.

"Very well," Jamaica reluctantly agreed. She heaved a ragged sigh. "I must admit, I am anxious to see what we are facing. I pray it is nothing more than what we have faced already."

Minutes later, they were climbing the stairs to the ship's deck. The seas beneath the *Hornet* were still rolling gently, but the height of the waves was steadily increasing with each passing minute. Jamaica and Eden made their way to the rail on the starboard bow and turned their gazes northward.

Although the sky immediately overhead was clear, the heavens in the near distance were choked with dark, foreboding clouds. Twilight was fast approaching, which made the prospect of a storm all the more dangerous.

"It always looks much worse than it is," remarked Eden, though in truth a certain uneasiness had crept over her.

She was conscious of the fact that the wind was getting stronger. It whipped her long skirts about her legs and tugged at her upswept hair. The fresh, unmistakable scent of rain filled the rapidly cooling air. And those clouds . . . they were virtually boiling. She had seen a sky like that only once before, less than a week after she arrived in Barbados. She could well remember the devastation the ensuing storm had wrought, both upon the island and its terrified inhabitants. A sudden, involuntary tremor shook her.

"I hope you're right," Jamaica murmured beside her. "But it does appear that we—"

"*Jamaica!*"

It was Seth's voice. He came striding across the deck to confront his errant bride. Nodding politely at Eden, he then frowned down at Jamaica. Guilty color rose on her smooth cheeks, and her gaze fell before the reproachful anger of his.

"I thought I made it clear you were to stay below," he reminded her.

"Yes. You did." Jamaica sighed. She raised her eyes to his and suddenly recalled Eden's words about teaching him a lesson in humility. Giving a defiant toss of her blond curls, she bravely asked, "Would you deny me the right to know the perils I am to endure?"

"Damn it, Jamaica, what's gotten into you?" demanded Seth, surprised by her uncharacteristic behavior. He glanced toward Eden, who had the

296

grace to look a trifle penitent. A faint smile touched his lips as realization dawned on him. "No, don't tell me," he said. "I think I know the answer already."

"Please, my love," Jamaica now implored, "do not be angry with me!" No matter how hard she tried, she could never be as courageous as Eden. "We wanted only to see what lay ahead. From what you told me earlier, I . . . I feared the worst!"

"It was not my intent to frighten you," he replied, his gaze softening. He gave her a warmly indulgent smile and drew her arm through the crook of his. "I'm certain we'll weather the storm easily. But you must do as I say and remain below. The deck will become treacherous once the storm breaks. I could not bear it if you were washed overboard."

"But what about *you?*"

"I know what to do. And so do the others." He turned to Eden. "You should go below as well, Mrs. St. Claire. The captain would skin me alive if he knew I hadn't taken steps to ensure your safety when I had the chance."

"While I appreciate your fears, Mr. Colfax," she said, a twinkle in her green eyes, "I am nonetheless determined to speak to my husband first."

"As you wish." With another nod, he led a submissive Jamaica away.

Eden went in search of Roark. It did not take her long to find him, for he was exactly where she had expected him to be. She climbed up to the quarter-deck and was greeted with a disarmingly crooked smile. Her husband stood at the wheel, his blue eyes alight with wry amusement.

"I take it Mr. Colfax was unable to persuade you to

accept the honor of his escort?'' he queried.

"He tried,'' answered Eden, lifting her head proudly.

"I'm sure he did.'' Roark's quiet chuckle made her pulse race anew. "No one knows better than I how damnably stubborn you can be.''

Disregarding his ungallant remark, she moved to stand beside him. Her troubled gaze fastened on the darkening horizon.

"Roark, are we to have a bad night of it?'' she asked in all seriousness now. "Those clouds look quite dangerous.''

"They are,'' he replied honestly. "It's no mere storm you're looking at, Eden. By all signs, it's a full-fledged hurricane.''

"A hurricane?'' she gasped. Her eyes clouded with alarm. "Dear Lord, how are we going to—''

"Do I detect a lack of confidence in my abilities, madam wife?'' he asked with a mock scowl. His brow cleared when he explained, "We've set a course that should take us clear of the worst part of it. Even then, there's no denying we're in for a rough time.'' He turned and gave her a hard, stern look. This time, it was evident he meant business. "I want you to stay below. No matter what happens, no matter what you hear, stay below. Is that understood?''

"Perfectly!'' Bristling at his authoritative manner, she saw fit to remind him, "I am not one of your men to be ordered about, Roark St. Claire!''

"Indeed you are not,'' he concurred with surprising equanimity. "But I care for you a great deal more than I do for any of them. And I'll be damned if I'll let anything happen to you.''

Knowing that his concern was genuine, she felt a sharp twinge of remorse. It was harder than ever to know how to deal with him now that she was certain of his love. She had long ago convinced herself of his betrayal, and had carried within her the desire for vengeance these many months. Though she told herself he was still guilty of other crimes, she could accuse him of nothing more at present than being on the wrong side of a conflict that was giving neither country any real victory.

She sighed inwardly. Each day with the man she had married brought new complications—and new pleasures.

"I shall stay below," she finally consented, then hastened to add, "But I have no intention of going to a watery grave while shut away in that blasted cabin!"

"There's little likelihood of that," he insisted. His handsome features wore a look of grim determination. "The *Hornet* is not yet ready to give up the ghost. And neither am I." His mouth curved into a faint, ironic smile. "It's true what they say about a woman making a man cautious. Before I met you, I'd have gone up against Satan himself and never spared a moment's thought for the dangers."

"Well, *I* don't think you've changed at all," opined Eden, frowning.

"Ah, but I have, madam wife. I've been giving more and more thought of late to settling down and becoming a gentleman planter like my father before me."

"You mean you are actually planning to give up command of your ship?" she asked in disbelief.

299

"I am. But not until the war has ended."

"I thought as much!" Her eyes flashed angrily. "I daresay you expect me to sit at home with my knitting while you are off playing the 'Scourge of the Seven Seas'!"

"It comforts me to know you've given some thought to it yourself. To living at Liberty Point, that is," he clarified, his own eyes glowing warmly.

"What makes you so certain I won't return to England?" she challenged. "Indeed, if you are not there to keep me prisoner, then how can you be sure I—"

"You'll not leave."

It was on the tip of her tongue to demand what made him so blasted sure of himself, but she never got the chance. A sudden flash of lightning ripped across the sky, signalling the end of their conversation and the beginning of the long night's troubles.

"Get below," Roark commanded her. His tone was one of steadfast calm.

Eden wisely chose not to argue. She tossed another glance overhead toward the threatening rumble of the sky, then moved down the stairs and back across the deck. Pausing at the top of the companionway, she turned and looked at Roark. Her throat constricted at the sight of him standing so tall and indomitable in the gathering fury. It was only with a great effort that she forced herself to go below. She would much rather have remained at his side and faced the danger with him.

Jamaica was waiting for her in Roark's cabin. Glad for the other woman's comforting presence, she suggested that the two of them try and occupy their minds by reading aloud from a volume of Shakespeare's sonnets she had found in the desk a few days ago. That they would get little sleep that night, there was no doubt. Jamaica was in complete agreement, and offered to start things off. She opened the book, cast a quick glance upward, then began reading in a sweet, clear voice that belied the knot of anxiety tightening in her stomach.

The seas grew increasingly rougher, the sky darker and more ominous. Soon, the *Hornet* was being mercilessly pitched and tossed about by the white-capped swells. Most of the ship's crew had been ordered below to the safety of their quarters, to rest while they could. A storm watch, however, had remained stationed on deck should the need arise for the bilge pumps to be set into action—or, if worse came to worse, for the half-dozen lifeboats to be lowered. It had never yet been necessary for Roark to give the order for the latter; he was determined that it never should.

Both Eden and Jamaica were plagued by tormenting visions of their husbands being struck down in the midst of the steadily worsening storm. They perched atop the bed, their legs curled up underneath their long skirts. Clinging to one another with one hand, they held tight to the edge of the wooden, three-quarter bunk with the other while the ship rocked violently to and fro. Although they made a brave attempt to press onward with their reading, they had no choice but to abandon their efforts when the towering waves began to loom up over the sides of the ship to crash with a roar upon the deck. Water tore at the legs of the men above and poured down the stairs, filling the passageway.

"Eden, *look!*" Jamaica gasped in horror.

Eden's gaze widened at the sight of the water seeping in from beneath the door to spread rapidly across the floor. In a matter of seconds, the cabin stood several inches deep.

"We . . . we must have courage, Jamaica!" she exhorted, feeling perilously near cowardice herself.

She glanced toward the ceiling and repeated a silent prayer for deliverance from the "watery grave" she had earlier mentioned, half in jest, to Roark. Her husband's face swam before her eyes. *Please, God, don't let anything happen to him!* she beseeched earnestly. The thought of losing the man she had once sworn to hate forever sent a sudden, sharp pain slicing through her heart.

"Oh, Eden, I am so very frightened!" Jamaica choked out.

"So am I!" she confessed, slipping an arm about the other woman's trembling shoulders. "But it is absolutely imperative that we keep our wits about us!"

"I . . . I could not bear . . . to die without seeing my beloved Seth again!"

"Come now, you mustn't talk like that! We are not going to die!" She closed her eyes for a moment and willed herself to remain strong. Forcing a smile to her lips, she predicted, "Why, I daresay the storm will seem like naught but a bad dream come morning!"

No sooner were the words out of her mouth than the ship suddenly listed far to the port side. The swirling mass of water on the cabin floor streamed back under the door, while everything that was not bolted down or attached to the wall went crashing forward along with it. Jamaica screamed and would have tumbled from the bed if not for Eden's firm grip upon her arm.

"Good heavens, Eden, *we are sinking!*"

"No!" Eden denied adamantly, as much for herself as for the other woman. Calling upon every ounce of self-will she possessed, she pulled Jamaica back with her toward the upper corner of the bed and grabbed hold of a brass candlestick fastened directly above her head. Her fingers clenched tightly about it as she observed, "No, we . . . we have simply run into a patch of rougher seas! It will not last long! I recall having encountered much the same on my voyage to Barbados!"

Every muscle in her body was tensed, and her heart was pounding in her ears. She tried to ignore the awful sounds of the storm raging above. *Roark!* she silently called out.

"What about Seth and the men on deck?" Jamaica asked in rising panic. Shuddering uncontrollably, she clung to Eden and shifted her bright, terror-filled gaze to the ceiling. "Dear God, do you suppose they—"

"I am sure they are safe! As Seth told you, they are well accustomed to such storms!" Her outward show of bravado was in direct contrast to the alarm racing through her, and were it not for Jamaica, she might very well have surrendered to the faintness which threatened to overcome her. "Hold on!" she exhorted breathlessly, feeling another treacherous surge of the waves beneath them.

A second hoarse, strangled cry tore from Jamaica's

lips when the ship suddenly heaved to and began listing to the starboard side. Water gushed into the cabin again with such force that the door was hurtled open. Chests, books, maps, and other articles were picked up and slammed against the opposite wall. Relentlessly, the crashing seas tumbled over the sides of the ship and down the stairs. The level of water in the cabin rose higher and higher.

"I cannot bear it!" screamed Jamaica, her voice shrill and unsteady. Great, heaving sobs wracked her body. Eden tried to comfort her, but it was no use. She jerked free and, without warning, flung herself from the bed and into the midst of the water. "I must go to Seth!"

"No, Jamaica! *No!*" cried Eden in dismay. "Come back! It's too dangerous!"

But Jamaica would not listen. She waded and stumbled to the doorway, her long, sodden skirts weighting her down as she pulled herself determinedly toward the stairs. Her one thought was to get to her husband, for she was convinced they would all soon be dead.

"Jamaica, please, listen to me! You must come back!"

"No, Eden! I'm sorry, but I must go! Stay here if you wish, but I . . . I am going above!"

Eden watched as her friend disappeared into the passageway. Her emerald gaze clouded with uncertainty as well as trepidation. Telling herself that someone had to look after Jamaica, she knew what she must do. She hastily scrambled from the bed to give chase.

Roark was at the wheel, employing almost

superhuman strength in his efforts to keep the vessel steady throughout the storm's lashing fury. Seth was at his side, ready to lend a hand should it be needed. It was he who caught sight of his wife when she staggered to the top of the stairs.

"*Jamaica!*" he breathed in horrified disbelief.

"Take the wheel, damn it!" thundered Roark, following the direction of his first mate's gaze.

Seth started to argue, but in the end was given little choice but to obey. He grabbed the wheel and watched as Roark swiftly made his way down from the quarter-deck and toward the spot where Jamaica stood reeling beneath the wave's roar.

Rain and salt water pelted her without mercy. She was already soaked from head to toe, and it was all she could do to hold onto the stairway's railing while the wind ripped at her hair and skirts. The deck was rolling violently, causing her to stagger to and fro.

Roark, however, kept his balance and his footing as he closed the distance between them. It had crossed his mind that if Jamaica was fool enough to come above, then there was every likelihood that his own bride would follow. He knew her better than she might have wished.

Eden, meanwhile, had reached the passageway at last. She was just about to start up the narrow stairway when the ship rocked the other way again. Water poured down upon her from the deck, and a sharp cry escaped her lips as she was sent tumbling forcefully against the wall. The breath was knocked from her. She seized hold of the door frame for support and gathered courage again. Righting herself with some difficulty, she headed up the stairs.

"Jamaica!" she called out, raising her voice to a shout in order to be heard. "Jamaica, come down!"

She narrowed her eyes against the water's cold sting and saw the other woman at the top of the stairway. Emerging upon the deck herself, she clutched at Jamaica with one hand and at the rail with the other. The wind whipped the rain into a frenzy about her, and she found it virtually impossible to draw breath enough to speak.

"Please!" she gasped out. "Let us . . . go below!"

"No!" In spite of the obvious dangers, Jamaica remained adamant. "I . . . I want to find Seth!"

"You cannot!" Eden shook her head. "Not in this!"

The seas loomed menacingly higher as they spoke, and soon broke upon the deck with foreboding intensity. Eden's grip weakened. She found it necessary to let go of her friend and grasp the rail with both hands.

"We'll be . . . washed overboard if . . . we stay up here any longer!" she cried. It was all too true. She was already growing weary, yet she was determined not to go below without Jamaica. "Come on!"

"No!"

They bent their heads beneath the terrible onslaught and fought to keep from being ripped away from the rail. The rain and wind, darkness and motion combined to make it seem they had been cast into a wet, earthly hell from which there was no escape. Eden prayed for guidance and for strength; it was apparent she would need a good deal of both if she hoped to make Jamaica choose wisdom over fear.

A short distance away, Roark ground out a savage

oath. He had expected to see his wife join the other woman on deck, but that did not prevent his blood from boiling at the sight of her. His handsome face was quite grim, and his eyes glinted harshly as he advanced upon them.

Something made Eden look up. Her gaze widened when it fell upon her husband. Relief and alarm warred together within her breast. Relief won out, at least temporarily, as she told herself that Roark would of a certainty be able to force Jamaica to return to the safety of the cabin.

But the seas chose that precise moment to make their superiority known. When the wall of water crashed upon the deck this time, it was with such gleeful vengeance that Jamaica lost her battle to hold on to the rail. She had no time to scream before being flung roughly to the deck.

"Jamaica!" yelled Eden.

She could not remember afterward exactly how it all came about, but she managed to grab Jamaica's ankle just in time and pull her back toward the companionway. Tugging with all her might, she fell to her knees at the top of the stairs and literally shoved the other woman down them. She staggered to her feet again, intending to follow Jamaica, but it was not to be.

Yet another enormous, black tower of water engulfed the *Hornet*. Eden was tossed about so violently that she was flung quite some distance before the deck finally came up to meet her.

Strangely enough, she could have sworn she heard Roark call her name the instant before she lost consciousness. . . .

Fourteen

"So help me woman, if you weren't lying there with a bump the size of an egg on your pretty, stubborn little head . . ." Roark's voice trailed off huskily. His deep, cobalt blue gaze was full of such tenderness and warmth that a rosy blush stained her cheeks.

"Pray, sir, I suppose I should be grateful for having been injured!" she retorted. Carefully easing herself farther upward in the bed, she winced at the pain in her head. "Are you quite certain Jamaica is all right?" she demanded once more.

"She is. A bit bruised and battered, perhaps, but she'll soon recover." A roguish smile tugged at his lips when he added, "If her husband doesn't wring her neck, that is."

"The poor girl could not help it," sighed Eden. Her eyes darkened at the memory. "She was terribly frightened, as was I. In truth, it *did* seem that we were going to sink."

"Well, we've come through it now, and only a

little worse for wear," said Roark. "No lives were lost, thank God, and the *Hornet* is as rock-ribbed as ever. It would take more than a mere storm to make her cry uncle."

"A mere storm?" she echoed in wide-eyed disbelief. A frown creased the silken smoothness of her brow. "It was far worse than any I have ever seen." At least while at sea, she amended in silence.

Roark took a seat on the edge of the bed and smiled softly down at her. She looked more beautiful to him than ever, in spite of the fact that her hair was a tangled, salt-sticky mass and a thick bandage had been wound about her head. Her damp clothing was plastered to her lush curves, so that there was very little left to the imagination. His heart stirred at the sight of her, and desire burned within him, but he forced himself to refrain from showing her just how glad he was that her life had been spared.

"How fortunate for me that you were on hand," she remarked in a small voice, almost as though she had read his mind. She met his gaze, and he saw that her eyes were glistening with sudden tears. "You saved my life, Roark. I . . . I can never repay you for that."

"I don't want payment." His tone was splendidly low and vibrant, while his eyes held the promise of a passion that would never wane. He took her hand and clasped it within the strong warmth of his. "I love you, Eden. You're the only thing in this world that truly matters to me. If I had lost you, I'd have lost everything."

A sudden lump rose in her throat, and she was unable to keep the tears from spilling over to course down her face. All her life, she had dreamt of being the recipient of such a love. And when it had finally presented itself, she had refused to believe in it. But no longer. Roark loved her—of that, she was certain.

And she loved him as well. It was true. Sweet Saint Christopher, it was true! She still loved him . . . she had never stopped. How could she have been so blind?

She saw everything clearly now. No matter how much she had tried to hate Roark, no matter how often and how vehemently she had vowed never to forgive him, she had still loved him. From the very first moment their eyes had met, she had been his. She had fallen in love with him then; she had remained in love with him throughout these many long months of exile in Barbados. Deep in her heart, she had always known it.

He was still an enemy, of course. Their countries were yet at war, and her loyalties lay with England alone. Enemy, yes, she told herself, but a beloved one. *A beloved one.*

Gazing up at him, she felt her whole body come alive with joy. He could read the truth in her eyes.

"Say it, Eden," he commanded in a voice that was scarcely more than a whisper. "I want to hear you say it."

"I love you." The moment the words left her lips, she felt as though a terrible weight had been lifted from her shoulders. Drawing in a deep, uneven breath, she smiled tremulously before declaring, "I love you with all my heart, Roark St. Claire. You are without a doubt the most arrogant, obstinate, perfectly infuriating man I have ever known, and yet

I love you still!"

She trembled at the sound of his quiet chuckle. His hand tightened about hers, and she grew serious.

"I don't know that I can ever understand what happened in England," she told him, "but it no longer matters. I love you as much as I did then—no, even more. And I shall keep on loving you until the day I die."

Roark's patience had finally been rewarded. His eyes glowed with triumph and exulatation. Without a word, he tenderly enfolded his wife within the loving circle of his arms and held her close. She was his!

Eden released a sigh of utter contentment and rested against his broad, hard-muscled chest. Her eyes swept closed. She was home at last . . . home in his arms where she belonged. Although he had once brought her heartache and the pain of betrayal, he now brought her the most complete happiness she had ever known. Love had set her free from the bonds of the past, and she knew that love would see her through whatever lay ahead. With Roark St. Claire at her side, she could endure anything.

They remained entwined like that for quite some time, both of them silently marveling at the caprice of fate. It was with great reluctance that Roark finally set her away from him.

"You must rest," he decreed. He pressed her gently back to the pillow and gave her a smile that quite literally took her breath away. "I'll be back come morning, Mrs. St. Claire. The best thing for you now is sleep."

"And what makes you so certain of that, Captain

St. Claire?" she challenged. Her eyes twinkled delightfully up at him. With an inward groan, he forced himself to stand.

"By damn, you're driving me to distraction," he growled in mock displeasure, then smiled crookedly down at her again. "But I'll have my revenge as soon as you're well. It will be a sweet revenge indeed."

"And just what the devil do you mean by *that?*" she demanded archly.

"I mean, you green-eyed vixen," he explained, "that I'll make you forget what it was like before you were mine."

He bent and brushed her forehead with his warm lips, then turned and strode from the water-logged cabin. Eden stared after him, her lips curving into a slow, thoroughly satisfied smile. She sighed again in the next moment and lay back down.

There was still so much to learn, so much to forgive, and yet they would seek enlightenment together. Half the joy would be in the learning. Her green eyes sparkled with ironic amusement. Jamaica would be pleased, she told herself, for it seemed she would be living in Georgia after all.

Closing her eyes, she pulled the covers up over her weary, storm-tossed body. It wasn't long before she had drifted off into a slumber filled with dreams of Roark, and of her own plans for their future.

She awoke shortly after dawn the following morning. Though she had slept only a few hours, she felt considerably refreshed. Her muscles were still a bit stiff and sore, but at least her head no longer ached. Sitting up, she tugged the bandage free and surveyed her dimly lit surroundings.

Water had soaked into every corner and crack and crevice, and she knew a complete drying out was the only solution. She and Jamaica could take the clothing and bedding up on deck and spread it out beneath the sun's warmth, but the only way to remove the musty smell from the cabin was by filling it with as much fresh air as possible.

She swung her legs over the edge of the bed and pulled herself upright. Ignoring any discomfort she suffered as a result of her actions, she crossed to the porthole and opened it. The sun's rays were just beginning to set the water afire.

Peeling off her clothes, she quickly performed her morning toilette and, promising herself the luxury of a bath later in the day, dressed in a gown and petticoat which were only slightly damp. She brushed as many tangles from her hair as she could, then twisted it into a coil and pinned it securely atop her head. That done, she swung open the door, left it ajar to aid in the circulation of fresh air, and hastened up the stairs to the deck.

Her heart soared with the knowledge of her love for Roark. She knew that she would never forget last night's storm, for it had given her the gift of freedom. Her green eyes shone at the prospect of seeing her beloved again.

"What the devil are you doing up here?" was his peculiar way of greeting her. A frown of disapproval creasing his handsome, sun-kissed brow, he strode forward to take her arm in a firm grip. "You should be in bed."

"But I am feeling perfectly well!" she insisted. Her lips curved into a thoroughly captivating smile. "As a matter of fact, I have never enjoyed better health!"

If appearances counted for anything, she was certainly speaking the truth. She looked more beautiful, more radiantly aglow, than ever. It was all Roark could do to refrain from catching her up in his arms and kissing her until they were both lightheaded. His features relaxed, and his gaze filled with a warm light as he reluctantly capitulated. He released her arm, but kept a possessive hand at her waist.

"All right, Eden. But you're not to overdo it, is that understood?" he cautioned sternly.

"Absolutely." It was now her turn to play caretaker. Studying her husband closely, she pronounced in a no-nonsense manner, "You, sir, are in obvious need of sleep yourself. It seems *you* must be the one to go below at once." Her eyes danced anew when she added, "And do not think I have forgotten your vow of revenge, my dearest captain. Indeed, I shall hold you to it once you are yourself again!"

She was rewarded for her wifely impertinence with a playful swat upon her backside. Blushing, she scolded Roark for daring such familiarity in front of witnesses. He laughed softly and planted a quick, hard kiss upon her parted lips.

"It so happens I was about to relinquish command to that unusually lazy first mate of mine. His bride has no doubt persuaded him to neglect his duties and remain abed."

"It isn't fair to blame Jamaica!" Eden rushed to her friend's defense. In a pretense of righteous indignation, she lifted her head proudly and remarked, "I daresay it is far more likely Seth's fault. Heaven knows how overbearing you men can be when it comes to such things."

"Guilty as charged, sweet vixen. I readily confess to doing my best to keep you abed." Had he not gone without sleep these past twenty-four hours, he would gladly have demonstrated his *overbearingness* once again. "Now, go and get some breakfast. Good health or not, you look as if you could do with a bit of food."

Effectively silencing her protests with another disarming kiss, he took himself below. Eden shook her head and smiled after him.

Later that same day, she learned from Roark that they would be putting in at Savannah first. She expressed puzzlement as to why they did not sail directly to his home on St. Simons Island.

"I've some business to take care of," he replied evasively. He led her to the rail and tossed a negligent glance overhead toward the brilliant blue of the sky. "If the weather holds, we'll reach Savannah by the end of the week."

"I had heard we—the British, that is—had blockaded your eastern seaboard. How can it be possible for you to make it past our ships?"

"First off, Mrs. St. Claire, you're going to have to start thinking of yourself as an American from here on out," he decreed, his gaze burning down into hers. The merest ghost of a smile touched his lips. "And getting past the enemy has never been a problem yet."

"Very well. Providing we make it to Savannah, how long do you plan for us to remain there?"

"A few days, no more. I am anxious to see how Liberty Point has fared during my absence."

"Do you have family living there?" Realizing that she still knew so little about the man she had married, Eden sighed inwardly and promised herself that she would remedy that condition soon enough. *If* she could somehow dissuade him from sailing away again.

"Not at present," answered Roark. "I've a grandmother in Charleston, and a few other relatives scattered throughout Georgia. But no one at home." He frowned and gripped the rail with both hands. "I left someone in charge of the plantation, a man by the name of Handley. To be honest, I doubted his conviction to our cause. But I had little choice."

"How long have you been away?"

"Nearly six months." He turned his head and gave her a look that was at once tender and fiercely passionate. "I had to find you, my love. I'd have taken a lifetime if necessary."

"So you . . . you really did come to Barbados because of me," she murmured, her heart filling with immense pleasure at the thought.

"And to England," he added pointedly.

"To England!" Her eyes grew very wide. "But you might have been caught! Sweet Saint Christopher, they would have hanged you as a spy!"

"And they'd have been correct in doing so," he parried with a brief smile filled with irony. He sobered in the next instant, and his gaze darkened with sudden anger. "I had no way of knowing that you had been packed off to Barbados. By damn, why did your father see fit to punish you for my transgressions?"

"It wasn't meant to be a punishment," she replied,

her own gaze clouding. There was a discernible catch in her voice when she told him, "He thought only to save what was left of my reputation. He and my mother both. Their plan failed dismally, of course, for the scandal—or at least a hint of it—followed me to Barbados. That's why my uncle was so anxious to see me wed to Donald. That and the prospect of lining his own pockets," she concluded sadly. The memory of William's treachery had not yet completely dimmed.

"I may yet take it in mind to go back and make the bastard pay for his cruel treatment of you," Roark said in a low tone edged with vengeful fury.

"No!" Eden cried breathlessly. "Please, Roark, it . . . it is best forgotten. I want to think of it no more."

He could not remain unmoved by the entreaty in her wide, luminous green eyes. Slipping an arm about her waist, he pulled her close to his side and gazed warmly down into her upturned countenance.

"No one will ever hurt you again, Eden," he vowed. "I'll do whatever it takes to ensure your happiness."

"I need only you," she declared, meaning every word of it. "Only you, my dearest captain."

She soon found herself encircled by both of his strong arms, and she was not the least bit inclined to protest when he kissed her right there in front of the crew. Much later, well after night had fallen, he finally made good on his threat of "sweet revenge." His words had been aptly chosen.

317

Fifteen

Savannah! Eden's gaze lit with excitement as it swept across the city which lay perched on the river's bluff just ahead. She recalled what Roark had told her about its history—about how it had been founded as a small English colony nearly a hundred years ago and had quickly flourished, how it had met with defeat and then a stunning victory during the last war, and how it had enjoyed even greater prosperity afterward as the surrounding tobacco, rice, and cotton plantations had transformed it into an important shipping center.

She had also been made aware of the fact that, during the present conflict thus far, Savannah's five thousand residents had successfully deterred attack by the British naval vessels lurking constantly off the coast—the same vessels the *Hornet* had managed to slip past without having once found it necessary to engage in battle. It seemed that one of the enemy's warships had actually been captured not too long ago and brought into the harbor, where it had been relieved of more than ten thousand dollars in gold.

A soft, indulgent smile tugged at Eden's lips as she remembered the pride in her husband's voice when he had spoken of his fellow Georgian's accomplishments. Heaven help her, but it was impossible to think of him as the enemy.

"Why, it looks perfectly charming!" Jamaica, who was standing beside Eden, remarked. "Those church spires appear to be reaching toward heaven, do they not? And I have never seen such neat and orderly wharves!"

"Perhaps the Americans are noted for their unfailing tidiness," her friend quipped dryly.

"Seth is anything but." Jamaica sighed dramatically. Then her delicate, heart-shaped features immediately brightened. "I do not care, of course, since he makes amends for it with his generous nature and sweet temperament."

"It seems to me, Jamaica Harding Colfax, that you fall more deeply in love with your husband every day," teased Eden, her green eyes aglow with affection.

"'Tis true, I fear," laughed Jamaica. "But then, if I may be so bold, Mrs. St. Claire, you have made no secret of your own affections!" She turned her attention back to the city spread out upon the flat of the hill above the steep banks of the Savannah River. "I must admit, I am quite anxious to feel the land beneath my feet again. Seth told me we are to spend the night at his brother's house. I did not even know he had a brother until this morning. Oh Eden, I *do* hope his family can find it in their hearts to accept me!"

"How can they possibly help it?" Eden reassured her, smiling warmly. "Aside from being English, you are everything they could hope for. And even that will not matter once they become acquainted with you."

"At least I shall have the comfort of your friendship once we reach St. Simons Island. You cannot know what it means to me, your living such a short distance away. My father will be glad to hear of it as well." She heaved a sigh, and her eyebrows drew together into a thoughtful frown. "I suppose he is already on his way here."

"I should think so. But there is no need to worry about that just yet. You and Seth will be well settled into your new life before he arrives." Providing, of course, that Roark does not sail away and take Seth with him, she added silently. She had not as yet broached the matter with her husband, but she fully intended to do so before they left Savannah.

It wasn't long before the *Hornet* had dropped anchor. Roark, after making certain the ship was secure, led Eden down the lowered gangplank to the wharf. Seth and Jamaica followed close behind.

"Unless you receive instructions to the contrary, I'll expect to see you back here tomorrow," Roark told his first mate.

"Aye, Captain," agreed Seth. "And you can count on my bringing the info—" He broke off at a sharply quelling look from the other man. A dull, guilty flush rose to his face as he took Jamaica's arm again. The pair bid goodbye to Roark and Eden before climbing the wide stone steps which led to the top of the bluff.

"What was that all about?" demanded Eden, rounding on her husband.

"I'd say the first order of business, sweet vixen, is to get you some decent clothing," he pronounced, ignoring her question altogether. His gaze flickered briefly downward over her clinging, low-cut muslin gown, and he made no secret of his displeasure. "Hell, I can't very well turn you loose on the streets of Savannah dressed like that. You'll cause a riot."

"I most certainly will not!" she hastened to deny. Giving a spirited toss of her ebony curls, she saw fit to remind him, "I wore this gown aboard your ship, did I not? Well then, what possible difference—"

He masterfully cut her off. "The difference is that I can control my own men, but I can't go about thrashing every blasted man in the city, which is exactly what I'll have to do if I don't take care to keep those beguiling charms of yours for my eyes alone."

Her emerald gaze kindled at that, but she did not protest when he drew her hand through the crook of his arm and compelled her along with him to the steps. In no time at all, the two of them were seated beside one another in an elegant, brightly painted carriage that rolled down Bay Street.

The city's inhabitants, attired in all manner of clothing—some of it even more revealing than hers, thought Eden with an inward smile—could be seen strolling leisurely about, hurrying to conduct their affairs, or simply perching upon one of the wrought-iron benches situated at frequent intervals along the way. There was a feeling of vitality in the fragrant, flower-scented air, as though the city were aware of its own enchantment and thus determined to make everyone else acknowledge it as well.

Eden was intrigued by the rhythmic pattern of the wide, unpaved streets, the beautiful, two- and three-storied houses built in Greek revival or Regency style, the handsome squares with the tall, moss-draped live oak trees thriving in their midst, the many gardens and shops and churches. The whole effect was, indeed, one of absolute enchantment.

"Perhaps you were expecting a collection of mud huts and half-naked savages," suggested Roark, his blue eyes filled with a challenging, roguish light as he took note of her fascination. "I'm sorry if we have disappointed you in any way."

"That's quite all right," she countered loftily. She smiled and confided, "It *is* all a bit surprising, you know. Nothing I have ever heard about America prepared me for what I see. Is all of it like this?"

"No, not all of it. But, with the possible exception of the Carolinas, you'll not find anything to compare with Georgia's beauty—or its hospitality."

"I fear, Captain St. Claire, that your opinion is a trifle biased."

"It is extremely biased," he admitted with a broad grin. "And yours will be every bit as much so once you've lived here a while."

The carriage pulled up before the townhouse a few minutes later. Although Roark had told her his father had purchased the "cottage" many years earlier and that it was far from the luxury she was used to, Eden was delighted by what her eyes beheld. The white clapboard house, trimmed in blue, stood three stories high and featured a charming gambrel roof. Shaded by live oak, dogwood, and magnolia trees, and surrounded by a variety of flowering shrubs, it was reached by a flagstone path leading through a beautiful wrought-iron gate and up to the steps of a covered front porch.

"Oh, Roark, this is far more than a cottage!" exclaimed Eden.

"Come along then, and you can tell me what you think of the inside."

The interior, as Eden soon discovered, was every bit as captivating. There was fine woodwork and paneling throughout, set off by polished pine floors, massive, black-green marble fireplace fronts, and exquisite furnishings, the likes of which rivaled anything she had seen at Abbeville Plantation.

An attractive, dark-haired woman of perhaps forty years of age had met them at the door. Roark had introduced her as Bertha McManus, the housekeeper. She had welcomed Eden warmly, and now led the way up the narrow, curving staircase to the bedrooms above.

"Your husband is in town so seldom, Mrs. St. Claire," said Bertha, "that I'm afraid the house tends to get a bit dusty. The girls employed to clean do not take as much care as they should during his absence. Had he warned us of his return, we might have taken greater care to have everything ready."

She paused at the top of the stairs and turned to cast Roark a look full of mingled reproach and affection. It was obvious she adored him, though only as an employee of long standing. She always kept the lines between master and servant clearly drawn.

"Don't let her words deceive you," he cautioned Eden, smiling unrepentantly. "I have never yet been here when the floor wasn't clean enough to serve as a dining table. She rules the household with an iron hand, she does, and woe to the poor fool who makes the mistake of crossing her."

"Come now, sir, you'll have your bride thinking I am some kind of ogre!" chided Bertha. Her brown eyes twinkled at Eden. "If there's anything you need, Mrs. St. Claire, anything at all, you've only to let me know."

"I should like it very much if you would call me Eden," the younger woman declared, responding to the older one's friendliness.

"Oh, that wouldn't do at all, I'm afraid. But perhaps we can settle for Mistress Eden. And I am never more than just plain Bertha." Smiling again, she opened a door at the end of a bright, rose-papered hallway and stepped aside. "This will be your room. Your husband's, of course, adjoins this one. There is a connecting bathroom. And your windows look down on the garden below, so you should not find yourself bothered by the noise of the city."

Eden's gaze shone with pleasure as she entered the room. Decorated in pastel shades of cream and blue and gold, it was airy and spacious. A canopied bed stood against the far wall, and a huge, carved wardrobe nestled in one corner. The other furniture was equally well fashioned, though not at all overwhelming.

"Thank you, Bertha," Eden told her sincerely. "It is quite lovely."

"Well then," said the housekeeper, "I'll leave the two of you alone. Supper will not be served until nine o'clock so you've plenty of time to rest." With that, she glided away, her silken skirts rustling gently as she moved back down the stairs.

Roark followed his wife into the bedroom and closed the door. His gaze softened as he looked at her, for she was set aglow by the sunlight streaming in through the lace-curtained window.

"Do you have it in mind to rest?" he asked.

"No."

"*No?*"

The gleam in his eyes would have been indication enough of his meaning, but it was fortified by the way his gaze traveled with bold significance toward the bed. Eden colored faintly and set him straight.

"I have it in mind to bathe, you impossible rogue! Far be it for me to complain about the facilities aboard your beloved ship, but I should like nothing better at the moment than to immerse myself in a tubful of water that does not dance about at will!"

"Have it your way then," he replied, closing the distance between them. He lifted his hands to her shoulders. "I'll be away for an hour or two, so you can soak to your heart's content. You should be well satisfied by the time I return."

"Where are you going?" she demanded, eyeing him narrowly. "Does it have anything to do with what Seth said—or rather, what he *tried* to say?"

"Perhaps," was all Roark would tell her. He took her in his arms and kissed her thoroughly, then set her away from him and smiled again. "Rest well, my love. I'll be back in plenty of time for supper."

"I think I have a right to know just what this 'business' of yours is," she insisted. "Indeed, was it not you yourself who said there shoud be no secrets between us?''

"It escapes my memory," he lied complacently. He sauntered to the door and opened it. "Bertha is as good as her word. She'll look after you while I'm gone." He was already out the door when he said this last.

"I don't need looking after!" Eden called after him.

She flew to the doorway and watched his handsome head disappearing down the staircase. Tempted to fling him yet another reminder of her capabilities, she thought better of it. After all, she told herself, it wouldn't do to go about screaming like a banshee at one's husband in front of the servants. The thought made her eyes sparkle with amusement.

She luxuriated in a long, lavender-scented bath, washed her hair and dried it while seated at the window, enjoyed the tea Bertha brought up to her, spent a restful hour in bed afterward—and *still* Roark had not returned. Irritation soon gave way to worry.

Asking herself what could possibly be keeping him so long, she sat down before the mirrored dressing table and frowned at her reflection. The gown she wore was the same, pale pink muslin, which Bertha had obligingly pressed for her while she bathed. She paid little heed to her actions as she wound her long raven tresses into a chignon and pinned it low upon the nape of her neck. Her troubled thoughts were centered on Roark.

"What on earth can he be doing?" she murmured, then heaved a sigh.

A knock sounded at her door, causing her to start in surprise. She sprang to her feet and hastened to answer it.

"Roark? I—" she began, but broke off when she saw that it was Bertha, not Roark, who stood smiling across at her.

"I'm sorry to disappoint you, Mistress Eden, but I've just received word from your husband. He sends his apologies, and says that he will not be home until quite late."

"But where is he?"

"I'm afraid I don't know. Perhaps we could ask the boy who brought the message. He is waiting in case there should be a reply."

"Yes, of course," agreed Eden. "An excellent idea, Bertha!"

She was down the stairs in a matter of seconds. Her eyes lit purposefully when they fell upon the slender, straw-haired adolescent, no more than fourteen or fifteen, who stood obediently within the entrance foyer.

"I am Mrs. St. Claire," Eden declared while approaching him. "I understand you have brought a message from my husband." Receiving a speechless nod of confirmation, she asked, "Where is my husband?"

"I . . . I don't think he'd want me to tell you that," the boy stammered indecisively. Dressed in a dark blue coat and trousers, he fidgeted with the sailor's cap in his hands.

"Why should he not?"

"Well, I . . . there's not many men want their wives and mothers to know they're 'meeting the grog' down at The Pirates' House." The truth slipped out before he realized it. He dropped his eyes guiltily and shuffled his feet a bit on the gleaming pine floor.

"Is that where he is?" demanded Eden. "The Pirates' House?" Again, her inquiry was met with a nod. "Where is this place? And how do I get there?"

"But you can't be meaning to go there yourself!" the lad protested, visibly alarmed. "It's a tavern down on the riverfront, a place for seamen and the like! No decent woman would—"

"Never mind!" Eden cut him off, then softened her words with a brief smile. "I shall simply instruct the coachman to take me there. I am sure he'll know the way."

"The boy is right, Mistress Eden!" Bertha's face wore a look of apprehension as she came forward to intervene. "The Pirates' House is no place for a woman such as yourself! If it is so important that you speak with your husband, why not simply send the request to him via the boy? I'm quite certain he will return at once if he knows his presence is required."

"No, I am determined to seek him out myself," Eden proclaimed firmly.

Her green eyes kindled with fire at a sudden vision of Roark sitting in a dark, smoke-filled tavern with a painted strumpet on his lap and a tankard of ale in his hand. Business indeed! she mused in ireful resentment. Hot tears started to her eyes, but she furiously blinked them back and tried to ignore the painful twisting of her heart.

"Please, Mistress Eden!" implored Bertha. "You must not do this!"

"I am afraid I must!" She turned back to the boy. "Will you take me there?"

"Well, I guess since you're going anyway . . ." He

consented reluctantly, then cautioned with all the superiority of his youthful manhood, "But once we get there, you can't go inside 'til I've cleared it with the captain."

"Agreed!" She started out the door with him.

"Wait!" Bertha called out. "If I cannot dissuade you from going, I can at least make certain you get there safely. I'll have the carriage brought round." Telling herself she'd be no kind of housekeeper at all if she let anything happen to Roark St. Claire's new bride, she hurried toward the small carriage house out back.

Eden and her gallant escort, whose name she soon learned was Tom Shea, were soon on their way to the riverfront. Night had recently fallen, but the city's streets were illuminated by tall, beautifully scrolled iron lamps. The carriage rolled back along Bay Street until reaching the corner of East Broad Street, where the infamous old seamen's inn had stood for a very long time—the present structure having been built some thirty years ago on the site of an earlier tavern of the same name.

New or old, The Pirates' House had always been a flourishing haven for sailors from all corners of the world. Though once a rendezvous for bloodthirsty pirates, it had now settled into an easy existence as a place where seamen came to drink and trade discourses on their exciting—and sometimes real—adventures.

"The Pirates' House, Mrs. St. Claire," the coachman announced when he had pulled the horses to a halt.

"Thank you," said Eden. Quickly alighting, she

knew a moment's uncertainty when she caught sight of the rough-looking men gathered in front of the tavern. Music and laughter drifted outside.

She told herself that what she was doing was madness, that Roark loved her and would never leave her to wait and worry so that he could indulge in a night of drunken revelry. And yet, no matter how much her brain cautioned her against proceeding, her heart encouraged her to go ahead. She unwisely chose to follow her heart.

"Stay here," Tom Shea ordered as if born to command.

"I most certainly will not!"

"But you gave me your word—"

"I know I did," she admitted, looking a trifle shamefaced, "and I am sorry for having found it necessary to deceive you. But I have no intention of allowing you to warn my husband that discovery is upon him!"

Squaring her shoulders, she drew her borrowed shawl more closely about her and swept forward in a proud, regal manner that belied the pain and anger burning within her. Tom Shea muttered a curse before giving chase.

Eden blithely ignored the lewd comments and would-be advances of the tavern's colorful patrons as she stepped inside. The smell of strong spirits, smoke, and unwashed bodies came up to hit her full force, prompting her to cough and narrow her stinging eyes. She knew in that moment that she had done the wrong thing in coming. She knew it, and yet she would not allow herself to turn back.

"Your husband is in the Captain's Room!" Tom

said behind her. He was forced to shout to be heard. "Come on!"

Frowning in exasperation, he led the way across the noisy, crowded front room. Eden had little choice but to follow him through what seemed to be a mysterious maze of rooms, all filled to overflowing with sailors and wharfmen, and others whose professions could only be guessed at. There were also more than a few women of easy virtue; *their* profession required no conjecture on Eden's part.

She was feeling perilously close to nausea when Tom finally paused before a door and rapped loudly upon it. A voice on the other side bellowed out permission to enter. Tom opened the door and stepped aside to let Eden go first. She paused for a brief moment, gathering her courage about her, then preceded him into the room.

It was quite dark and foreboding inside. The only light came from a single lamp hanging above, where massive, hand-hewn ceiling beams were joined together with wooden pegs. Eden's searching gaze traveled swiftly about the room, and her heart sank when she saw that Roark was not among the half-dozen men seated around the table.

"What is it you've brought us, Young Tom?" asked a brawny, black-bearded man.

He eyed Eden lustfully, his gaze moving with slow insolence over her beautiful face and alluring curves. His companions treated her to the same bold scrutiny. She shivered, her pulses leaping in alarm.

"I . . . I am afraid I have made a mistake," she faltered, instinctively tugging the shawl across her breasts. *Dear God, where is Roark?*

"Have you now, my sweet?" the dark giant challenged with a broad, yellow-toothed grin. He looked to the boy at her side and remarked, "Your powers of selection have improved, young Tom. I'll see you well rewarded for bringing me such a tasty morsel."

"He has not brought you a *morsel* at all—tasty or otherwise!" Eden declared with a flash of spirit. "I have come here in search of my husband! His name is Roark St. Claire, and I—"

"St. Claire?" one of the other men growled, scowling darkly. His narrowed gaze shot to Tom. "Does she speak the truth, boy? Is she St. Claire's woman?"

"His *wife*, if you please!" Eden corrected while drawing herself proudly erect. She refused to be intimidated by these ill-mannered ruffians, in spite of the fact that a warning bell had sounded in her brain.

"She's his wife, all right," confirmed Tom, though it apparently gave him little pleasure to do so. "She wouldn't listen when I told her not to come!"

"Where is my husband?" Eden demanded of the black-bearded fellow. Her eyes made another hasty, encompassing sweep of the dimly lit room. "It was my understanding that he was here."

"Well now, it looks like your 'understanding' is a wee bit off its timing. St. Claire's come and gone."

"Gone?" she echoed in growing dismay.

"Aye, madam, but I'll be glad to warm you in his place!" the youngest one of the six offered. The others laughed heartily and seconded the offer. Eden's face flamed, and her emerald gaze turned fiery.

"Would you be so kind as to tell me *where* my husband has gone?" she queried in a tone simmering with fury and indignation.

"Through there," yet another man answered. He gave a jerk of his head to indicate what appeared to be a solid wall behind him. "He always goes out that way once we've completed our business."

"Business?" Eden repeated, her brow creasing into a thoughtful frown.

So, she told herself, it was true. Roark had indeed come to the tavern for a reason other than the contemptible one she had suspected him of. How could she have been so blasted foolish? She suddenly felt very ashamed—and very uneasy.

"But . . . there is no door," she remarked in bafflement, peering closely at the wall.

"It's there." To prove it, the swarthy giant stood, brought his hand back, and slammed it against the dingy oak paneling. A hidden door opened. "The stairs lead down to the old rum cellar and then outside."

"Oh, I . . . I see." She swallowed hard and forced a smile to her lips as she turned back to Tom. "May I rely upon your escort once more, Mr. Shea?"

"Aye, lad, give her your 'escort'!" one of the men sneered.

"Never call upon a boy to do a man's job," someone else remarked, while indulging in a leisurely, audacious perusal of Eden's charms.

To Tom's credit, he did make an attempt to lead Eden out through the secret passageway. But he was thrust aside by the apparent leader of the coarse group.

"Save your strength, Young Tom." Of the six, he was the one Eden feared most—and not because of his size alone. "I'll see the lady gets home all right."

"I thank you for your generous offer, sir," Eden told him with only a hint of sarcasm, "but that will not be necessary. My carriage is waiting."

"Then I'll take you to it," he insisted. Before she could try to prevent it, he seized her arm and propelled her across to the hidden door.

"No!" she protested, struggling in his relentless grasp. "Please, let go of me!" Her wide, apprehensive gaze sought out Tom Shea, but the boy dared not interfere.

"Watch out for that husband of hers!" one of the men called out gleefully. "He's a dangerous one, he is! It strikes me he'd not take kindly to having his pretty little bride in your clutches, you hot-blooded son of a bitch!"

"I can handle St. Claire."

"Aye, and we've no doubt you'll 'handle' his wife before the night is through!"

Their raucous laughter burned in Eden's ears as she was led through the doorway and down the narrow wooden staircase. Three sets of torches blazed on the walls of the cool, musty-smelling rum cellar. The door above creaked shut, leaving her alone with her self-appointed guardian.

"There was a time when many an unwary bastard found himself shanghaied and carried down these same steps," he told her. The sound of his deep, rumbling chuckle struck fear in her heart.

"I can find my way alone from here," she proclaimed with remarkable composure.

Inwardly, she was fighting down a surge of panic. She cursed herself once more for ever having been fool enough to come in the first place. Jealousy and anger had prompted her to cast aside trust. She vowed never to make that mistake again.

They had reached the last step now. Eden forced another smile to her lips and looked up at the man who, although surprisingly behaving as a gentleman thus far, had the light of deviltry in his dark eyes.

"Please, sir, will you not take your hand from my arm and allow me to continue on my own?" she requested coolly. It was all she could do to refrain from screaming at him.

"You're a polite one, I'll give you that!" said the bearded giant, chuckling again. He suddenly drew to a halt and eyed her closely in the flickering torchlight. "Strike me dead if you aren't English! Well I'll be a horn-footed swabbie," he murmured to himself in wonderment. "I'd never have thought Roark St. Claire would take himself a bride from among the enemy!"

"Have you . . . have you known my husband long?" she asked, still trying desperately not to lose courage.

"Long enough. He pays me well for my services. But not well enough to keep me honest."

Before she could ask him what he meant by that enigmatic remark, he urged her along with him to a tunnel which led outside to the rear of the building. He grabbed up one of the torches before starting through the dirt-floored shaft, and Eden offered up a quick, silent prayer as she found herself being pulled into it as well. She felt almost giddy with relief when they emerged into the fresh air outside.

It was quite dark behind the tavern, and overgrown with a tangle of shrubbery and weeds. There was no one about. Eden, mistakenly believing that her fears had been for naught, began to relax. She released a long pent-up sigh when her burly escort finally let go of her arm.

"Thank you," she offered, raising her eyes to his face.

His features appeared more darkly menacing than ever as he stood looming over her with the torch held high in one hand, but she reminded herself that appearances can be deceiving. After all, he'd had the opportunity to accost her back in the rum cellar and had chosen not to do so. Though he certainly looked the worst of the lot, he had proven himself to be a decent fellow. A rough-looking one, perhaps, but decent just the same.

"I shall return to my carriage now," she announced. "I daresay my husband has returned home by this time."

"He left only a short while ago. Maybe he's taken it in mind to pay a visit elsewhere," the man suggested.

There was something in the way he said it that provoked a sharp, renewed twinge of uneasiness within Eden. She swallowed hard and tightened her grip on the shawl draped about her shoulders.

"Well then, I shall bid you good night."

She turned to leave, but a startled gasp broke from her lips when the man's hand shot out to detain her.

"Not so fast, you little English bitch!" he growled with terrifying ferocity. His fingers clenched her wrist so tightly she feared it would break.

"Let go of me!" she cried, hot tears of pain starting to her eyes as she tried to pull free. She gasped again when he roughly yanked her to him.

"I might have resisted temptation, had you not been what you are!" Holding her captive with one arm, he laughed scornfully at her furious yet ineffectual struggles to escape. "I hate the English, I do, and all they stand for! Why, it will give me no end of pleasure to do what I can for the 'cause.' No end of pleasure," he repeated, his eyes narrowing into mere slits of rancorous lust.

"No!" she choked out. Her own gaze was filled with horror. She opened her mouth to scream, but her captor flung the torch back into the tunnel and wound both arms about her, crushing her to him as his mouth descended with brutal force upon hers.

Bile rose in Eden's throat. Sickened by the stale, sour taste of rum and tobacco on his lips, and repulsed by the overwhelming odor of smoke and sweat, she battled a sudden wave of nausea. Her hands came up to push at his chest, but to no avail. Alarmed to feel herself growing faint, she attempted to tear her lips away from the punishing fury of his. He merely clamped a hand to the back of her head, his coarse fingers threading within the upswept thickness of her hair while his hot, seeking tongue stabbed into her mouth.

Dear God, this cannot be happening! She could not bear the thought of this man forcing himself upon her. He would take what belonged to Roark alone . . . what they had shared in love would now be violated in the cruelest way possible.

The prospect of suffering such a fate gave her a

renewed burst of strength. Screaming low in her throat, she curled her hands into talons and raked her fingernails down both of her assailant's swarthy cheeks. He thrust her violently away and rasped out a blistering oath. She staggered backward, crashing up against the building so hard that the breath was knocked from her body.

"You've torn the skin off me, you English whore!" the black-bearded giant charged, his fingers wet with his own blood. Though it was dark, Eden knew that his eyes burned with murderous rage. "I'll make you pay for this!" he ground out vengefully. "I'll damned well take it out of your hide, and then I'll—"

The remainder of his threat was lost to Eden, for she finally recovered breath enough to whirl about and flee. The man lunged for her, but she was too quick for him. She ran as fast as her legs would carry her, back around to the front of the building and the safety of the waiting carriage. Oblivious to the shouts and curious stares of the men who spied her racing past, she stumbled up into the carriage before the coachman could open the door for her.

"Mrs. St. Claire? Mrs. St. Claire, are you all right?" he asked with genuine compassion. He, too, had tried cautioning her against coming to such a place, but he correctly sensed this was no time to be reminding her of it. "Mrs. St. Claire?"

"Yes, I . . . I am all right!" she assured him in a breathless, quavering voice. "Please, just take me home!"

She would not have thought it possible that she could feel any more wretched than she did at that moment, but matters only worsened when she got home.

Roark was on his way out of the townhouse again when the carriage pulled up before it. His long, furious strides led him down the walk to confront his wife, and his eyes were smoldering as he wrenched open the door and virtually yanked her out of the equipage.

"Damn it, woman, what the hell were you thinking of to go—"

He broke off when he saw her face. She stood, gazing up at him through her tears, her whole body trembling while the lamplight revealed her alarming dishevelment. Her hair was streaming wildly down about her face and shoulders, and the bodice of her muslin gown was stained with several, telltale drops of her attacker's blood.

Roark's anger with her immediately vanished. His heart twisted painfully at the sight of her distress, and his blood boiled as he vowed there and then to exact revenge upon the person responsible for it. He gently took hold of her shoulders, his fathomless blue gaze boring down into the glistening depths of hers.

"What happened?" he demanded quietly. The steadying calm of his low, deep-timbred voice belied the raw emotion blazing within him.

"Oh, Roark, I . . . I made a terrible mistake!" she confessed in a broken whisper. "I thought you . . . had treated me unfairly, and I . . . I went to The Pirates' House to find you!"

"What happened, Eden?" he demanded once more. Torn between the desire to scoop her up in his arms and let her spill her tears on his chest, and the urge to be off on his search for her tormentor, he forced himself to keep a clear head. "Tell me, my love."

"I tried to leave when I discovered you were not there, but . . . but one of the men in the Captain's Room insisted upon escorting me out through the rum cellar!" She paused for a moment and drew in a deep, ragged breath before disclosing with a shudder of remembrance, "He offered me no insult until we were outside. But then he said something about hating all the English, and . . . and the next thing I knew, he was trying to force himself upon me!"

"What was his name?" asked Roark. His eyes filled with a savage gleam, and his handsome features tensed in white-hot fury.

"I don't know! He was quite large, with a black beard, and—" She inhaled upon a sharp gasp as it suddenly dawned on her why he sought the man's identity. "No, Roark, no!" she pleaded, her hands clutching at his powerful arms. "You can't be meaning to go back there! Why, you could get killed! Those men are—"

"Those men are well known to me," he told her. "And the one who dared to attack you has never been anything but trouble. I've overlooked difficulties he's created in the past. Tonight, however, he has gone too far."

He turned and gave a curt, wordless nod toward his first mate, who had been waiting on the front porch. Seth came forward to stand beside him. Eden's wide, sparkling gaze moved anxiously from one man to the other.

"Please, you must not do this! I am not harmed!" she tried to reason with them. Her heart leapt in alarm at the thought of the danger they would be facing. On their faces were grimly determined looks

340

that boded ill for her assailant. *Sweet Saint Christopher, what have I done?*

"He has to be dealt with, Eden," decreed Roark. He motioned to the coachman and instructed him, "Take my wife inside, Patterson, and see that she is placed in Bertha's care."

"Yes, Mr. St. Claire," the older man replied dutifully.

"Roark, please listen to me!" cried Eden. Holding fast to his arms, she refused to leave him. "I am partially to blame for what happened, don't you see? Everyone tried to warn me against going there, and it was because of my own foolishness that I sought you out! Surely it will serve no purpose to place your life in peril!"

"You are my wife. I'll not let any man lay hands upon you."

Disregarding her protests, he set her firmly away from him and moved to gather up the reins of the horse he had left tied in front of the house. He swung up into the saddle without another word. Seth met Eden's fearful gaze and gave her a solemn, polite nod before mounting his own horse.

"Roark!" she called after her husband. But it was too late. She could only stand and watch as he and Seth rode away into the darkness.

"Come inside now, Mrs. St. Claire," said Patterson, his voice full of kindness. "You've nothing to worry about, nothing at all. Why, Mr. St. Claire knows how to take care of himself. And he's always had the devil's own luck when it comes to such things."

"I can only pray his luck holds," she murmured disconsolately. With a knot of dread tightening in her stomach, she finally allowed the coachman to lead her into the house.

It was approaching midnight when Roark returned. Eden lay beneath the covers of her bed, where the housekeeper had insisted upon bundling her after another hot, soothing bath. The waiting had been almost unbearable. She had envisioned all sorts of terrible things happening to her beloved, and had cursed herself again and again for being the cause of his endangerment. Heaven help her, but she had learned her lesson well. Never again would she doubt him. *Never.*

The minutes had stretched into hours, and the hours had seemed like days. She was just about to defy Bertha and leave the bed, when she glanced up and saw that her husband stood framed in the doorway. He was smiling softly as he stepped inside and closed the door.

"Roark!" she breathed. Profound joy and relief mingled within her breast, and her whole body was flooded with warmth. "Thank God you're safe!"

Flinging back the covers, she sprang from the bed and flew across the room to cast herself upon his broad chest. His strong, welcoming arms came up about her, pulling her close.

"I'd have been back sooner, but Seth took it into his head to get his shoulder hurt. I had the devil of a time explaining it all to his wife."

"Oh, Roark, is he going to be all right?" asked Eden, tilting her head back to look up at him.

She noticed for the first time that his own handsome face bore the marks of battle. The rugged, clean-shaven smoothness of his left cheek was a bit bloodied and bruised, and there was a small cut above his lip.

"But . . . look at you!" she exclaimed. Her eyes filled with loving concern. "You've been hurt as well!"

"My injuries are little more than nothing. The same cannot be said for the man who inflicted them." All traces of amusement were gone when he told her, "He'll not bother you again, my love."

"What happened?" She'd almost been afraid to ask. She could well imagine the fellow lying dead behind the tavern; she was relieved to learn otherwise.

"He has shipped out."

"Shipped out?"

"A fitting punishment indeed, since he'll be spending the next several years aboard one of our own navy's vessels. Perhaps they'll be able to teach him better manners."

"You mean you didn't—"

"He can count himself fortunate Seth was on hand to remind me that vengeance is best served upon the living." His gaze darkened anew at the thought of what Eden had suffered. He would gladly have killed the bastard with his bare hands. "It's done," he said, drawing her close again. "And since I think you've been punished enough, I'll not scold you for running off to that blasted hellhole like you did. But I trust you won't ever do anything so foolhardy again."

"I certainly won't!" she hastened to assure him. She sighed and snuggled closer to his hard-muscled warmth. The long, voluminous nightdress she wore was one of Bertha's. "I am truly sorry for doubting you, Roark. If only you had not kept your whereabouts or the manner of your business such a secret, I might never have been tempted toward mistrust."

"I suppose I should have told you the truth," he admitted. "Those men at The Pirates' House were in my employ, at least on an occasional basis. In other words, I pay them to help me gather information about the enemy's plans and strategies." A faint smile of irony played about his lips. "We are all of us spies, sweet vixen."

"I suspected as much." She drew away a bit so that she could meet his gaze once more. "And Seth is in on it as well, isn't he?"

"Yes."

"Does Jamaica know?"

"She does now." His eyes sparked with wry amusement. "It was necessary to tell her the truth, else she'd never have believed Seth was at the tavern on a matter unrelated to pleasure. She, too, was inclined to doubt her husband. But not to the same extent as you. No, by damn, I've a wife who risks life and limb just for the satisfaction of telling me I'm wrong!"

"Well, you need *someone* to tell you, Roark St. Claire!" she retorted saucily. "And who better than I?"

"Who better indeed," he concurred. Finally allowing himself the luxury of scooping her up in his arms, he carried her toward the bed.

"But, what about your supper?" Eden felt obliged to protest. Her voice, however, was woefully lacking in conviction. "I doubt you have spared the time to eat throughout this whole disastrous evening, and—"

"What I hunger for, madam wife, is you."

"Oh, Roark," she murmured, blushing delightfully. "Will you always be so . . . well, so hungry for me?"

"No."

"No?" Her beautiful eyes grew very wide, and a frown of disappointment creased her silken brow.

"I give you fair warning, Mrs. St. Claire—I fully expect my appetite to increase. By the time we have been married fifty or sixty years, you'll be heartily sick of me," he teased.

"Never!" she emphatically denied.

He lowered her to the bed. But when he would have joined her there, she was bold enough to insist that he allow her to tend to his injuries before things progressed any further. He capitulated, though with an ill grace, and soon paid her back for making him wait. . . .

Sixteen

"I simply cannot credit it," sighed Jamaica, her brows knitting into a mild frown of perplexity as she stood with Eden in the entrance foyer of the St. Claire townhouse. She stepped to the gilt-framed mirror near the door and affected a quick readjustment to her blond curls. "Seth admitted to me that he had been much more than a privateer all this time, but I never would have thought it possible he could turn spy! I questioned him as much as I dared after Captain St. Claire brought him home last night. Alas, he revealed little."

"My husband was equally reticent," Eden confided with a faint smile. She pulled on her gloves and added thoughtfully, "Of course, I daresay they do not want us involved."

"But, why should they not?"

"Because we are women. And because we are English. That alone is reason enough—to their 'superior,' entirely masculine way of thinking, anyway—for them to want to keep us in the dark

346

about their activities. In truth, after having made the acquaintance of those men at the tavern, I can well understand why our husbands should be so reluctant to grant us enlightenment." She experienced a sudden, involuntary shudder of remembrance.

"I suppose you are right," conceded Jamaica, sighing again. "The doctor pronounced that Seth's arm should heal completely within the space of a week or two, thank God, but I know I shall never forget what happened." Her frown deepened when she moved on to another subject. "I . . . I should not speak ill of my new family, to be sure, but Seth's brother has been far less than civil to me. Neither he nor his wife, who is not so very much above my own age, will even acknowledge my presence unless Seth is there to force them into it. I . . . I was so in hopes of their acceptance."

"Of course you were," murmured Eden. Her eyes were full of sympathy, and more than a hint of anger directed toward those who had mistreated her friend. She smiled warmly as she linked arms with the petite blonde. "Never fear, my dearest Jamaica. They will accept you in time. They are simply not yet accustomed to the idea of Seth's being married, that's all. And it must have been something of a shock for them to discover that he had taken it upon himself to find a bride during his many travels."

"They do not know the entire truth, of course. I should feel quite humiliated if they were ever to learn of the shocking ease with which Seth carried me off," Jamaica declared, blushing at the thought. She allowed herself to be led outside, where the carriage awaited in front of the house.

"There is always the chance they might deem it wonderfully romantic," suggested Eden, trying to make light of the situation and thereby lift the other woman's spirits. "However, I propose we put all thought of family and spies—*and* husbands—behind us for the day, and get on with the belated task of accumulating our trousseaus. I own I am more than eager to follow Roark's instructions in that regard. He has given me leave to purchase whatever I wish, so long as I do not choose anything too revealing." Her emerald gaze sparkled at the memory of his stern, cautionary remarks.

"I cannot put all thought of Seth from my mind," insisted Jamaica. "'Tis impossible."

"Nevertheless, I am determined that you should try!"

The rest of the morning, and part of the afternoon, was spent in a pleasurable whirl of shopping and sightseeing. Roark had warned Eden that he and Seth would be occupied with other matters—entirely legitimate, he had assured her—until evening. Though she would rather he had been on hand to provide an escort about the city, she enjoyed the excursion with Jamaica immensely.

Both young women marveled at the numerous old cemeteries and mansions, and gazed with dubious interest upon a pair of brass cannons displayed proudly on Bay Street. The "Washington Guns," so called because they had been presented to the local Chatham Artillery by President Washington himself some twenty-odd years ago, had been captured from the British at Yorktown during the last war. Since they knew very little about the history of their newly adopted homeland, neither Eden nor Jamaica realized the true significance of the monuments to freedom scattered throughout Savannah. They would learn in time, of course, and would one day feel the same pride and affection for this beautiful, fiercely independent country as their husbands did.

They returned to the townhouse shortly after three o'clock, their arms laden with the fruits of their efforts and their hearts considerably lighter than before. Jamaica tarried only a short while longer before taking her leave. Eden hurried to bathe and dress in one of her new gowns before Roark came home. Anxious that her appearance should meet with his approval, she chose carefully, finally settling upon a gown of purest white satin.

It had required only a minimal adjustment by the dressmaker, and now fit her slender, beguiling curves to perfection. Trimmed with varicolored bead embroidery, it also featured a scarf of sheer white gauze with an embroidered leaf border. The neckline was square and low-cut, but not immodestly so, while the skirt, falling from a high waist, flared softly outward over her hips.

"I defy you to find fault with *this* ensemble, Roark St. Claire!" she remarked aloud as she stood facing the mirror.

"Your defiance comes as no surprise to me."

She started guiltily at the sound of her husband's deep voice. Whirling about, she saw that he was leaning negligently against the door frame, his arms folded across his chest. He flashed her a wayward grin.

"Since I hold little hope of persuading you to wear

clothes that hide your charms," he drawled, "I suppose I'll have to relent and grant you permission to look as beautiful as you do now."

"How perfectly magnanimous of you!" Pleased at the compliment, even if it had been offered in a rather left-handed manner, she watched as he closed the door and sauntered toward the connecting bathroom.

"We're to dine with Seth and Jamaica tonight," he told her, unbuttoning his shirt.

"Are we? Jamaica said nothing of it."

"Nor should she have. It was decided upon only a short while ago."

"And was it also decided upon that we are still to leave Savannah tomorrow?" she challenged archly.

"It was." The merest suggestion of a smile touched his lips. "We'll spend tomorrow night at Liberty Point."

"Providing the *Hornet* is able to slip past the Royal Navy once more."

"She will," he decreed with confidence.

Eden moved to stand in the doorway, watching while he drew off his shirt and bent over the washstand to splash water on his face. The bronzed, hard-muscled expanse of his back and arms looked even more powerful in the waning sunlight which filled the small room. Her eyes traveled appreciatively downward over his buttocks and thighs, their leanness molded by the tight-fitting blue trousers. She grew warm, and chided herself, albeit only halfheartedly, for behaving like an absolute wanton. Heaven help her, she thought with an inward sigh, but it seemed that she would never tire of looking at her husband's magnificent, undeniably virile body. *Never.*

350

"Roark?"

"Yes?"

"We . . . we haven't really had an opportunity to discuss it of late, but I should like to do so now."

"Discuss what?" Snatching up a towel, he dried his face and turned to give her a quizzical half-smile.

"Your plans, of course. Or rather, *our* plans."

"You've an active mind, Mrs. St. Claire, but I fear I cannot yet read it," he admitted, his eyes twinkling roguishly across at her. "What the devil are you talking about?"

"Our future!" she clarified in exasperation, then demanded to know, "Are you still planning that I should remain at your plantation while you return to the war?"

"I've little choice, Eden." He had grown quite serious now. "I can't sit at home while my country needs every able-bodied man to do his part. Even you could not ask that of me."

"I most certainly could! Sweet Saint Christopher, what difference will one man make? There must be others who would take command of your ship and—"

"I am the only master the *Hornet* will ever know," he vowed in a low tone edged with steel.

"And so you would leave me alone? After all the pain and heartache we have endured, after so many long months of waiting to be together, you would jeopardize our every chance for happiness?" she asked, unable to keep the bitterness from her own voice. "I thought you loved me more than that!"

"I love you more than life itself." Breathing an oath, he flung the towel aside and swiftly closed the distance between them. He took hold of her shoulders,

351

his gaze burning down into the stormy emerald depths of hers while she tried in vain to turn away. "Damn it, Eden, I cannot be less than what I am! Don't you understand? I mean to do everything I can to ensure that the future *is* a happy one—for us and for our children as well."

"No!" she replied, shaking her head in vehement denial. "I do not understand at all! You expect me to wait for God only knows how long, while you are off waging war against my countrymen and . . . and endangering your life at every turn! The prospect is a dismal one at best, and one I shall not willingly embrace!"

"I am sorry for that," he said. His eyes glinted dully, and there was a look of grim determination on his handsome face. "But, until the war is over, we'll simply have to do what must be done. By damn, I like the idea of our separation no more than you, and yet—"

"And yet you will do nothing to prevent it!"

She knew she was being irrational, but her emotions were in utter turmoil at the thought of being without him for several months—or perhaps even years. How in heaven's name was she going to bear it?

It was a woman's place to wait, her mother had once advised her. And indeed, throughout the ages, women had remained at home to wait and worry while their men marched off to war. But Eden was determined not to do the same. Somehow, she would think of a way to be with Roark. Her eyes kindled with a determination that was the equal of her husband's. Yes, she mused, even if she had to stow away aboard the *Hornet*, she would not let herself be left behind by Roark St. Claire!

"I'll remain at Liberty Point long enough to see you settled," he told her quietly.

"What a comfort that shall be," she murmured with more than a hint of sarcasm. She met his gaze squarely again and queried, "If it was your intent all along to bring me to America and then *abandon* me, why did you see fit to carry me off at all?"

"Because, you little green-eyed witch," he ground out, "I hold what's mine!"

Alarmed by the almost savage gleam in his eyes, she gasped to feel his strong arms sweeping her up roughly against him. She opened her mouth to speak, only to find herself silenced by the fierce, demanding pressure of his lips upon hers. He kissed her as though he would brand her very soul, as though he would teach her who was the true master of their sweetly tempestuous relationship. But the gesture failed to achieve that purpose; it only made her more determined never to be parted from him again.

The kiss might well have led to a late arrival for supper, save for the timely intervention of the housekeeper. Bertha knocked on Roark's bedroom door and delivered the news that there was a visitor awaiting him downstairs.

Reluctantly letting go of his flushed and breathless bride, Roark hastened to put on his shirt again and open the door. He frowned down at Bertha.

"A visitor, you say? Who is it?"

"I don't know, Mr. St. Claire," she answered. "He said only that I was to fetch you at once. He is an older gentleman, and quite distinguished looking, but I have never seen him before."

Nodding silently at Bertha, Roark finished buttoning his shirt and then went downstairs to confront the mysterious caller. The housekeeper followed close behind. Eden, her own curiosity aroused by what she had overheard, quickly readjusted her scarf and tidied her hair. She was soon on her way downstairs as well.

Roark's voice drifted out to her from the open doorway of the drawing room as she paused in the entrance foyer. At hearing the other man's voice, she stopped dead in her tracks. Her eyes grew round with incredulity.

"Colonel Harding!" she whispered. Good heavens, Jamaica's father had found them already!

Coming to life again, Eden swept into the drawing room. Roark and the older man stood facing one another like two adversaries, which in truth they were. Colonel Harding's expression revealed barely suppressed fury, while Roark's was coldly distant.

"I . . . I am surprised to see you here, Colonel Harding!" proclaimed Eden. She moved to her husband's side. "Of course, we expected that you would come eventually, but—"

"Where the bloody hell is my daughter?" the Englishman growled at her, his face reddening, and his eyes full of rancor.

"Speak to my wife like that again, sir, and you'll find yourself meeting the hard dirt of the street," Roark cautioned with dangerous calm. It was no idle threat.

"You do not frighten me, you thieving bastard!"

Harding's gaze sliced back to Eden as he declared, "This is all your fault!"

"My fault?" she echoed weakly.

"I made inquiries! I discovered the truth of your connection to this . . . this scoundrel!" he said, jerking his head toward Roark. "Once I reached Cuba and got that blasted message informing me that I could reach my daughter through Captain and *Mrs.* Roark St. Claire, it did not take long for me to realize that you were to blame for her disappearance! No doubt you were plotting with your husband and his friends all along. I suppose Donald Parkington-Hughes should count himself fortunate to be alive after the beating he suffered! Yes, I went to Abbeville Plantation in the vain hope of finding my daughter," he added bitterly, taking note of her surprise. "What I want to know is why you saw fit to involve Jamaica!"

"You are mistaken," interjected Roark, his own gaze darkening. "Eden had no part in any of it. Your daughter's abduction was not planned. It was an impulsive action—"

"Impulsive? Yes, by damn, it was that!" roared the other man. He rounded on Eden again. "And to think that we all feared for your safety! The whole island will be shocked once they learn of your treachery! I know not how Lady Eden Parrish came to be wed to an American, and a privateer at that, nor do I care! I only want to know that my daughter is safe and then to take her home where she belongs!"

"She is safe," Eden assured him. She swallowed a sudden lump in her throat. Her heart was pounding with alarm, for she knew that Colonel Harding was all too capable of violence when it came to protecting

355

his beloved only child.

"Then where is she? And what was that nonsense I heard about her being involved with a man by the name of Seth Colfax? Is he the bondsman who abducted her?" Though he'd had the devil of a time booking passage on a ship bound for Georgia, it had not been difficult for him to find the captain of the *Hornet* upon his arrival in Savannah. But he was in no mood to tolerate any more lies. "Tell me, blast your eyes!" he snarled, glowering at Roark now.

Eden cast a helpless look up at her husband. He gave her a faint, bolstering smile and slipped an arm about her shoulders.

"Your daughter is married to Seth Colfax, Colonel Harding," he revealed.

"Married?" The older man's expression grew even more thunderous. "The hell you say!"

"It is true!" Eden exclaimed breathlessly. "She and my husband's first mate were married aboard ship before we left Cuba!"

"Enough!" bellowed the Englishman. To Eden he said, "Where is she, damn it? Is she here? If so, I demand that she be produced at once!"

"Your daughter isn't here." This came from Roark, whose own rugged features displayed an increasing proclivity toward violence. "She is with her husband."

"I . . . I know you have worried a great deal, Colonel Harding, but, truly, Jamaica is safe and happy!" Eden hastened to inform him.

"Where is she?"

"It so happens," said Roark, "that my wife and I were planning to dine with the Colfaxes this very

356

evening." Reminding himself that the man had every right to be angry, he battled his own flaring temper and offered impassively, "We'll take you there."

"And do you expect me to thank you for it?" snapped the older man, his eyes narrowing. "By thunder, St. Claire, you've a lot to answer for yourself! And don't think I will not see you are made to do so!"

"We are in America now, Colonel Harding. Freedom is the password here—*not tyranny*."

He took Eden's arm and led her from the drawing room. Colonel Harding jammed his high-crowned beaver hat atop his head before stalking after them.

The confrontation which followed was every bit as unpleasant as Eden had feared it would be.

Jamaica burst into tears at seeing her father. She flung herself on his chest, pleading with him to forgive her and spare the life of the husband she passionately loved. Seth's brother and sister-in-law fled the dining room, leaving Eden and Roark to stand guard just outside the closed double doors as Jamaica struggled to prevent her father from beating her abductor-husband to within an inch of his life.

"I offer you my sincere apologies for the manner in which I deprived you of your daughter," Seth declared stiffly. His attractive features betrayed no fear. Standing tall and proud, with his left arm in a sling, he told his new father-in-law, "For Jamaica's sake, I hope that we can put the unfortunate matter behind us. I love your daughter very much, Colonel Harding, and I give you my word that she'll always be well provided for."

"Your word isn't worth a tinker's damn, you

unscrupulous young savage!" snarled the older man.

"Papa, please!" Jamaica cried brokenly, glimpsing the murder in his eyes. She refused to relinquish her desperate grip upon the front of his coat. "Seth is right! What's done is done, and I . . . I could not bear it if the two men I love most in the world did not make peace with one another!"

"There is little chance of that!" her father parried. He seized her arm in a firm, commanding grip. "But I have no wish to prolong this travesty any longer. Since I doubt I should be able to lay so much as a finger on Mr. Colfax without that St. Claire bastard throwing himself into the fight, I shall leave punishment to the proper authorities. You may rest assured that Mr. Colfax will be made to pay for his crimes! Come, Jamaica. We are going home!"

"No!" She shook her head, while her wide, glistening blue eyes flew to Seth. "I am married now, Papa! I will not leave my husband!"

"Husband or not, you *shall* come with me!" her father decreed. He hauled her unceremoniously along with him toward the doorway, but Seth moved to block his path.

"No," he insisted, his voice deceptively low and level. "Jamaica is my wife now. She'll be staying with me. Take your hands off her, Colonel Harding."

"No daughter of mine will remain wed to an enemy and a pirate! I'll damned well have the marriage, if it was ever legal to begin with, *dissolved!*"

"It's legal. Now take your hands off her," Seth reiterated. His eyes were filled with a dangerously foreboding light.

358

"Please, Papa, let go of me!" implored Jamaica, trying to pull free. "It's too late, don't you see? I cannot go back to Barbados with you!"

"And what will happen to you if you stay here?" he demanded, his voice raw with pain and fury. "He'll tire of you soon enough, Jamaica—his kind always do! What will you do when he leaves you here all alone in a strange country, without friends or family?"

"Roark and Eden are my friends," she pointed out. "But he will not leave me! He loves me, Papa, he truly loves me!"

"How can you know what love is? You are so very young, and innocent in the ways of the world." Harding glared menacingly at Seth. "But I suppose you've taken care of *that*, haven't you, you hot-blooded son of a bitch?"

"Papa!" Jamaica breathed in horror.

"I've done no less than any other husband would do," stated Seth.

His words only added fuel to the fire. Colonel Harding grew visibly enraged. Without warning, he flung Jamaica aside with one hand and brought his other fist smashing up against his son-in-law's unguarded chin.

"Seth!" screamed Jamaica.

On the other side of the door, the commotion was all too noticeable. Eden's eyes widened with concern, and she turned expectantly to Roark.

"Aren't you going to put a stop to it?"

"No."

"But, why not?"

"Because, sweet vixen," he replied with a brief,

359

mocking smile, "it has occurred to me that we might have a daughter someday." His blue eyes gleamed with a touch of wry humor while Eden frowned up at him in bafflement.

"What the devil does that have to do with—"

"I would be every bit as entitled as Jamaica's father," he coolly stated, "to exact my pound of flesh from any man who dared to touch her."

"Why, that is absolutely barbaric!" Eden protested, her gaze sparking with indignation. "How will it help matters any if Colonel Harding kills him?"

"He won't kill him."

And indeed, he did not. But only because Seth Colfax was wise beyond his years. He took his "medicine" like the man he was, putting up only a token resistance as Colonel Harding thrashed him soundly. In the end, when he had slumped half-conscious to the floor and Jamaica ran to kneel beside him, he was only dimly aware of his surroundings yet filled with the satisfaction that he had done his part to ensure a reconciliation of the past with the future.

Jamaica lovingly cradled her husband's golden head in her lap. She subjected her father, who was visibly tired and gasping for breath, to a reproachful look.

"Now see what you've done!" she charged angrily. "So help me, Papa, if . . . if you have gone and made me a widow, I shall never forgive you!"

Colonel Harding offered no response. He stared down at the younger man and frowned. Having done his duty as a father, he did not know which course of action to choose next. Jamaica, after all, had made it clear she would not leave. He had not counted on that. God knew, he loved her dearly, but at this particular moment he was glad he had only the one daughter.

The evening, as it turned out, was not yet in complete ruins. Miraculously enough, Jamaica secured her father's begrudging agreement to spend the night under the Colfaxes' roof. He went one step farther and consented to sail to St. Simons Island with them the next morning, though he did not fail to make mention of his reluctance to set foot aboard a ship that had been responsible for the worst piracy on the seas. However, since he could not persuade his daughter to return to Barbados with him, he decided he could at least make certain she would not be living in abject poverty.

Seth, having recovered very nicely from the beating he had suffered at the older man's hands, expressed his solemn gratitude for the chance to prove himself worthy.

"You'll never be that, Mr. Colfax," declared Colonel Harding with his usual gruffness. "My daughter is far above you and shall always be so. But her happiness matters a great deal to me." He relented with a heavy sigh. "And since it appears she is determined to throw her life away on an ill-mannered rogue such as yourself, I have little choice but to declare a truce. For the time being, that is."

"Well spoken," Roark quipped dryly. Standing, he raised his glass of wine and encompassed the other six diners with his fathomless blue gaze. "I should like to propose a toast to the newlyweds." He disregarded the quelling look his wife shot him. "To

361

Seth and Jamaica," he said simply. A smile tugged at his lips when Eden released a soft sigh of relief beside him.

"To Seth and Jamaica. And to freedom!" Seth's brother saw fit to add, his eyes moving significantly toward the only Englishman at the table.

"Long live His Majesty, King George!" countered the loyal Colonel Harding. He quickly downed every drop of his wine.

This signaled the end of the meal. Afterward, the sexes followed the time-honored custom of separating, with the gentlemen repairing to the library for brandy and cigars, and the ladies settling themselves in the drawing room with their tea and gossip. In some respects, mused Eden, life in America was not so very different from that in England or Barbados after all.

Later that night, as she lay stretched contentedly beside her husband in his massive, brocade-canopied bed, she was surprised to hear him admit to doubting the wisdom of a return to Liberty Point.

"But, what is it you fear?" she asked.

"It's more of a misgiving than a fear," he corrected with a faint smile. His hand trailed lightly downward over the curve of her naked hip, sending a delicious tremor through her. "I've received some news that, if it proves reliable, could mean a danger I had not counted on."

"What sort of danger?" There was something in his voice that gave her pause. It was not like him to be uncertain of anything.

"The British may well be planning to invade the island." His handsome, sun-kissed brow creased into a frown, and his eyes became suffused with a dull glow. "I've always followed my instincts before. Hell, I've lived by them since I was old enough to walk. But I confess to being torn in my decision now. I want to see you settled at Liberty Point before I must leave again, and yet I can't help but think it might be better for you to remain here in Savannah."

"The dilemma could be easily solved if you would but listen to reason," she sighed, her own hand smoothing across his broad, softly matted chest. "Take me with you, Roark. Take me with you when you sail."

"No."

"But I sailed with you all the way from Barbados, did I not? What difference can there be in—"

"No, Eden. There would be a difference. When my men and I sail this time, it will be to a return of our maneuvers against the enemy. I'd not be able to do my job if you were aboard; your presence would make me too cautious. A wartime vessel is no place for a woman."

"And why is it not?" she demanded with a touch of feminine outrage.

"This discussion is pointless. You will not be going with me." His voice was low and authoritative, and it was clear he would not be pushed any further.

Eden bristled at his dictatorial attitude. Pushing herself away from him, she rolled abruptly to her side. She pulled the covers up over her supple curves, then lay stiff and unyielding in the darkness.

Roark's brow cleared. His gaze filled with a warm, tenderly predatory light, he turned upon his side and, lifting the sheet, brought the length of his hard-muscled nakedness into intimate contact with his wife's angry softness. His arm slipped about her waist.

"We've only a few days left to us before I leave," he murmured close to her ear. His vibrant, splendidly deep-timbred voice made it necessary for her to battle the temptation to surrender there and then. "Come now, sweet vixen, let's not waste time by quarreling."

"The quarrel is of your choosing, Roark St. Claire!" she retorted. It was impossible for her not to be aware of his manhood pressing against her hips, but she stubbornly refused to acknowledge his obvious desire.

"Then the resolution will be of my choosing as well."

Before she could ask him what he meant by that remark, he lifted the covers again and trailed a slow, fiery path downward with his lips. Eden tried in vain to remain impervious to his skillful, highly inflaming efforts at seduction. She bit at her lower lip to suppress a moan and closed her eyes against the waves of pleasure he set in motion.

"*Roark!*" Her eyes flew wide when his teeth gently nipped at the roundness of her buttocks. A bold kiss followed.

"You've the sauciest bottom, Mrs. St. Claire," he murmured, giving a soft laugh of triumph while she colored rosily.

"Roark, stop . . . it!" she gasped out. She was not yet ready to let go of her anger, an anger which she had convinced herself was entirely righteous. "No!"

He was taken off-guard when she suddenly flung herself from the bed. She snatched up her dressing gown and fled across the room toward the relative safety of her own bedchamber. Muttering a curse, Roark gave chase.

"Damn it, Eden, come back here!"

"Go to the devil!"

She made it as far as the bathroom. A breathless cry escaped her lips when Roark's hand captured her wrist. He yanked the dressing gown from her hand and brought her up hard against him, but she would not admit defeat so easily. Struggling and twisting within his grasp, she finally succeeded in making him relax his grip.

But escape was not to be hers. No sooner had she pulled free entirely, than she lost her balance and went toppling backward into the huge, claw-footed bathtub. Roark caught her before she hit the bottom.

"What the hell do you think you're doing, you little fool?" he demanded in a quiet, furious tone. He hauled her upright and imprisoned her with his arms. "You're behaving like a child!"

"And you're behaving like an idiot!" she countered hotly.

"Then I'd say we're well-matched, wouldn't you?"

"No, I most certainly would *not!*"

She suffered a sharp intake of breath when he propelled her none too gently back into his bedroom. Pausing to light the lamp, he bent his tall, naked frame down into the velvet-upholstered wing chair beside the bed. He pulled Eden onto his lap, holding her captive in spite of her wrathful protests.

"Once and for all, Eden, I cannot take you with me," he told her. His tone, though steady and commanding as ever, held such undeniable regret that she could not help feeling a sharp twinge of remorse. "I've tried to explain my reasons to you. But, whether you understand or not, I must go."

She did not say anything for the longest time. He waited patiently, his arms holding her tight while he searched her face for any sign of surrender. When she finally turned to meet his gaze in the soft lamplight, he saw that her beauftiul eyes were full of contrition.

"I . . . I am sorry Roark," she declared tremulously.

Her anger had vanished, leaving behind a fierce desire to make amends. No matter what happened, no matter how much his decision to leave was hurting her, she could not bear being at cross purposes with him. Her determination to find a way to be with him was as strong as ever, and yet she knew that he was right—it was foolish to waste one moment of their time together.

"I love you," she whispered, lowering her head so that it rested upon his shoulder. She released a long, uneven sigh. "I never expected to love you this much."

"And why the devil not?" he demanded in mock reproach. His lips curved into a soft, crooked smile, and he swept her even closer to his hard warmth. "I love you as well, sweet vixen. I pray the war will end soon."

"Oh Roark, do you . . . do you think it will?"

"By all indications, it should. But there's no way of knowing. The British have intensified their efforts. And we have responded in kind."

He had learned earlier that day of a rumored plan involving the enemy forces up in Canada. Frowning at the other things he had heard, he firmly pushed all thought of them to the back of his mind. He was holding the woman he loved in his arms, and he'd be damned if he'd allow anything to interfere with their few remaining hours together.

"Be forewarned, you green-eyed wildcat," he teased, "that the next time you take it in mind to run away from me, I'll see you well chastised for your troubles."

"Will you indeed?" she challenged. She lifted her head and gave him a smile that sent wildfire coursing through him. "I know of a fitting punishment, my dearest captain."

"And what is that?"

"Ah, but I think you know already."

Emboldened by love and passion, she threaded her fingers through the sun-bronzed thickness of his hair and drew his head purposefully downward. A soft, mellow laugh rumbled up from deep within his chest.

"I love the way your mind works, madam wife."

"Then pray, sir, follow its example!" Her words ended on a gasp of pleasure as his mouth closed about one of her breasts.

She squirmed atop the lean-muscled hardness of his thighs, her naked hips provoking a wealth of hot, delectable sensations within him. He reciprocated by loving her breasts well with his lips and tongue, and by caressing her silken flesh with such sure and gentle strokes that she was soon gasping for breath— and pleading oh so sweetly for mercy.

Roark, ever the master of invention, moved her about so that she was still atop his thighs but facing him. She blushed at the shocking position in which she found herself, for her legs were parted wide and straddling his. However, she had long since learned to question him not; in truth, he had never yet disappointed her.

She moaned and closed her eyes, her head falling back as he returned to his wickedly pleasurable conquest of her body. Her hands curled upon his broad shoulders. She arched her back, and in so doing allowed him even greater access to her moist, highly appreciative charms.

"Sweet . . . Sweet Saint Christopher," she gasped out, "you . . . will drive me to . . . to madness!"

"And a fine madness it will be," he murmured huskily.

He pulled her head down to his and captured her mouth with his own, his tongue plunging between her parted lips. She gave herself up to the betwitching call of desire, and was soon rewarded for her compliance in the most satisfying way possible.

A cry of sheer ecstasy broke from her lips when Roark lifted her hips slightly and brought her down upon his fully aroused manhood. She felt as though he touched her very womb.

"Dear God, how I love you!" he whispered hoarsely. His hands gripped her hips while they matched the slow, rapturous movements of his.

"Oh, Roark!" She clutched weakly at his shoulders again, her face flushed and her long raven tresses streaming down her back as her beloved conqueror's mouth returned to her full, rose-tipped breasts.

Their mutual fulfillment was both sweet and savage, flinging them both heavenward before

368

allowing them to drift back to earth once more. Roark would not allow his well-loved bride to move for quite some time; they remained as one until he finally, reluctantly, forced himself to stir. He scooped her up in his arms and carried her to the bed, lowering her to the plump feather mattress. Stretching out beside her, he pulled her close.

"I've decided to take you to the island after all," he told her a short time later.

"I am glad. I would much rather wait for you there." She consoled herself with the thought that it was only half a lie.

"Then off to sleep with you, Mrs. St. Claire. I've a great deal to do tomorrow. Tempt me no more this night," he commanded, his voice tinged with loving amusement.

"As you wish," Eden replied obediently. She smiled to herself and closed her eyes, then released a soft, contented sigh. "As you wish, oh lord and master."

Seventeen

Eden knew that she would never forget the way her heart swelled with pride and pleasure when she saw St. Simons Island for the first time. *She was home.*

"Liberty Point's not far from the lighthouse," Roark informed her, nodding toward the well-known guardian of the island's coast.

Her fascinated gaze traveled the length of the seventy-five-foot tall tower, which had been constructed of tabby—a mixture of sand, lime, water, and oyster shell—some six years earlier. She looked to the top, where an iron frame equipped with oil lamps hung suspended by chains.

"You can see nearly all of the island from up there," said Roark.

"You mean you have actually been to the top of it?" she asked, her eyes growing very round.

"Why do you sound so surprised?" he challenged, his lips curving in a brief, disarming grin. His hands, however, maintained a steady grip upon the ship's wheel, and he kept a vigilant eye on the *Hornet*'s progress through the glistening blue waters of the Sound. "I suppose I've done a lot of things that would surprise you, my love. But none I care to reveal."

She was too preoccupied to take any notice of his attempts to bait her at the moment. Although she was tired after a long day of travel, during which time she had constantly feared a confrontation with the numerous British ships they had sighted—and had easily outdistanced—she was excited at the prospect of seeing her husband's plantation.

The island itself, she had already decided, was quite beautiful. Roark had told her that, though it was one of Georgia's largest barrier islands, it was only twelve miles long and three miles across at its widest point. Its forests were largely composed of great live oaks. From their twisted branches hung shrouds of gray Spanish moss, vines of jasmine and coral brightened the shadows, while myrtle bushes and palmettoes joined together to form a thick undergrowth. The air, fresh and buoyant with the salt-tinged sea breeze, was filled with the rustling of palm fronds and the high-pitched cries of the gulls.

So heavily wooded was the landscape that Eden saw very little evidence of civilization. The whole effect was one of almost eerie enchantment, and she was thoroughly captivated. She smiled at the sight of the dazzling white beach ahead, and listened to the thundering crash of the waves as the ship neared the wharf.

"Everything is so green," she observed. "I had not expected that."

"The island has more than its fair share of water.

Marshes, creeks, rivers—and enough sunshine to turn you as brown as our friend Betsy," he added with a touch of wry amusement.

"Have you a great many neighbors here as well?" she asked, peering toward the small collection of buildings she now sighted in the distance. A store, a tavern, and a few charming, shuttered cottages were all that remained of the once thriving settlement. War and the ravages of nature had combined to diminish its prosperity.

"Not any longer," answered Roark. His gaze suddenly darkened. "There are, in fact, more than a dozen plantations on the island, but I've heard that most of the planters and their families have fled inland. The threat of a British invasion has disrupted life more than I would have thought possible. Still, I cannot blame them. I can only hope that things at Liberty Point have not changed." His voice sounded grim.

Eden's heart twisted at the thought of his disquietude. She lifted a hand to his arm and sighed, her eyes traveling to where Jamaica and Colonel Harding stood together below at the rail.

"Does Seth have family awaiting him at his plantation?"

"No. He has only the one brother."

"Well then, at least Jamaica will not have to worry about gaining acceptance here."

And neither would she, of course. If the island proved to be as deserted as Roark had been led to believe, she would be spared the mistrust and hostility she had expected to face. She was well aware that, until the war ended, her every word and action would be suspect. Strangely enough, however, she no longer thought of herself as an Englishwoman . . . she was only Mrs. Roark St. Claire now. She would always love England, would always love her family there, but Roark had become everything to her. His country was hers.

The *Hornet* soon lay anchored at the wharf. Jamaica and Eden said their temporary farewells, while Roark gave instructions to his men regarding the ship's watch and the division of the goods they had relieved the enemy of throughout these past six months. As he had once told Eden, his own share would be donated to the cause. Seth would do the same.

Determined that they should not be taken unawares by the British, he ordered that the ship be kept ready to sail at all times. There would be no other way to escape.

Eden glimpsed only a handful of men and women in the area, all of whom called out a greeting to Roark as he led her toward a waiting carriage. His impatience to set eyes upon Liberty Point after so long an absence was obvious. He wasted little time in handing his wife up into the carriage and taking a seat beside her.

Wondering how the driver could have known that his services would be required, Eden quickly settled her skirts about her and turned her head to meet her husband's gaze.

"How long until we reach home?" she asked him.

His blue eyes lit with warmth, and a slow, completely devastating smile spread across the rugged perfection of his countenance.

"Home," he repeated. "The sound of it is sweet upon your lips, my love." At a nod from him, the driver cracked the whip above the horses' heads and the carriage rolled forward. "We'll be there in less than half an hour's time."

Eden tossed a glance overhead at the sapphire sky, where a few white clouds sought to chase away the last, lingering rays of sunlight. Night was fast approaching.

"Oh, Roark, I do hope I can prove myself worthy!" she remarked in growing apprehension. Now that the moment was upon her, she could not help but feel nervous at the prospect of being presented as the new mistress of the plantation. "How many people live at Liberty Point?"

"When I left, there were more than a hundred."

"And are . . . are all of them slaves?" A sudden shadow crossed her face. Although Roark had told her that things were different from what she had known in Barbados, she still doubted her own ability to embrace a system founded on the domination of one human being over another.

"No. About half are freemen." He smiled again at her expression of surprise. "And by damn, now that I have gone and married a woman who is so adamantly in favor of emancipation, I wouldn't be at all surprised if the other half find themselves freed before the year's end."

"You would actually do that for me?" she asked in stunned disbelief, her eyes growing even rounder.

"Yes, Eden," he replied solemnly. "And for myself as well. I might well have done it before now, save for the fact that I honestly wanted nothing to change.

But changes are sometimes forced upon us. After the cruelty I witnessed in Barbados, I can well understand why you find our way of life so despicable." He clasped her hand within the strong warmth of his and gazed deeply into her eyes. "Mind you, I'm not saying the transformation will come about over-night. These things take time."

"We have a whole lifetime," she pointed out. Tears of love and gratitude sparkled in her eyes now, and she smiled tremulously up at him. "You are truly master of your own fate and mine, Roark St. Claire, and I shall never doubt it again."

"Perhaps not," he allowed dryly. "But I'll warrant you'll never stop trying to master *me*."

He silenced her retort with the intoxicating pressure of his lips upon hers. She melted against him and willingly gave herself up to the sweetness of the moment.

The carriage wound its way along the road beneath an endless canopy of trees, until at last heading down a long drive flanked by a magnificent burst of color. Here, the air was even more redolent with the mingling perfumes of the sea and the orchards and the late-summer flowers.

"My father purchased the land from a Scotsman who served in Oglethorpe's regiment," said Roark. "During the last war, a Loyalist friend of his sent the first seeds of Anguilla cotton here to the island. We still grow that same cotton, though it's termed Sea Island cotton now"

"Is it very profitable?" asked Eden, straining outward a bit in an attempt to see what lay ahead.

"Very," he confirmed with a soft laugh. He pulled

her back into place beside him. "In other words, Mrs. St. Claire, you'll have plenty of pin money. *If* the plantation has managed to survive my absence, that is."

"I should not care if we were poor," she assured him in earnest, then smiled mischievously and added her own stipulation. *"If* I were granted the compensation of your presence, that is."

Her wifely impertinence earned her another long, deliciously provoking kiss. By the time her husband let her go, the house was well in sight.

"Oh, Roark!" breathed Eden, her eyes aglow with delight at what they beheld. "Why, it's . . . it's lovely!"

And indeed, it was. Although it was a simple, whitewashed frame house of sturdy English design, it looked to be quite spacious. Built of handhewn timbers, with a shuttered verandah and a gabled roof, it appeared to have materialized from the pages of a childhood storybook. Formal gardens, ablaze with almost every flower and shrub known to the region, stretched out in every direction, while shell walks led through a delightful maze of arboretum. And the view from the charming, three-storied structure was all that could be hoped for, since it faced the beach and the Sound and another, smaller island beyond. Liberty Point's location there on the south end of St. Simons offered the convenience of a nearby town, as well as the closest route to the mainland.

"It's much the same as General Oglethorpe's place at Frederica," Roark told her as the driver reined the horses to a halt. "My father hoped that, like Orange Hall, it would be able to withstand the West Indian gales. It has."

Eden's sparkling gaze traveled farther. There were a number of other buildings clustered around the cottage—a guesthouse to provide extra sleeping quarters, a hothouse and summerhouse, the customary detached kitchen, a schoolhouse, and even a plantation hospital. A tabby barn, the servants' quarters, and the stables were but a short distance away. And the cabins used to house the slaves, she noted with pleasure, were large and comfortable looking.

"Where is everyone?" she wondered aloud, hoping to catch a glimpse of some of the people who lived and worked there. The grounds appeared strangely deserted.

"I don't know," Roark murmured with a frown. Determined not to jump to the worst conclusion, he alighted from the carriage and easily swung Eden down beside him. To the much older, craggy-faced driver, he said, "Where is Mr. Handley?"

"Why, he's gone, Captain."

"Gone?"

"Yes, Captain. He took off some three or four weeks back now."

"Then who the devil has been in charge?" Mentally cursing himself for ever having been fool enough to ignore his qualms about the man, he raked the hat angrily from his head and demanded, "Or has everyone else disappeared as well?"

"Not everyone, Captain. Some of the freemen stayed—not more than a dozen, though. And none of the slaves, I'm sorry to say. They either ran away or were carried off by the bast—er, the British who sailed bold as brass right up to the shore and persuaded them to go. It's young George who's been running things since Mr. Handley left." He noisily cleared his throat before adding, "Times have been hard, Captain. And I fear they'll get no better."

"I know, Thomas." A faint smile touched his lips when he met the other man's solemn, regretful gaze. "I thank you for your loyalty."

"Your father, God rest his soul, would have turned over in his grave if I'd done anything less than what I've done." His eyes suddenly twinkled down at Eden. "I have it in mind that he'd be pleased to know you've finally settled with a wife."

"If only he were truly 'settled,' Thomas," responded Eden, her own gaze clouding.

Roark took his wife's arm and led her up the front steps. His blood was boiling at the thought of the enemy setting foot on St. Claire land, and he vowed to do everything in his power to see that it never happened again. Though Eden did not yet know it, his plans for her had just changed.

The interior of the house, she soon discovered, was every bit as charming and unpretentiously comfortable as the outside. It was decorated much the same as the Savannah townhouse, save for the fact that its furnishings were on a slightly larger scale. She much preferred its simple elegance to the overwhelming grandeur of Abbeville Plantation. But her thoughts were, at present, centered on the troubling news her husband had just received.

"Roark, I . . . I am sorry that your homecoming was not more pleasant," she declared as the two of them completed a hasty tour of the downstairs. "I know what a terrible disappointment it must have been for you to learn of your manager's betrayal."

"In truth, it is no worse than I feared. I blame no one but myself." Another sharp frown creased his brow, and his cobalt blue eyes glinted dully. "But I am anxious to speak with George and—"

"Master Roark!" exclaimed a young woman who suddenly came bustling forward into the entrance foyer where they stood. She was quite pretty, with almond-shaped eyes and skin the rich golden color of honey, and her face was lit with obvious joy. "The Lord be praised, Master Roark," she said, quickly drying her hands on her apron, "you're home!"

"Hello, Minerva." He gave her a brief albeit warmly affectionate smile and slipped an arm about Eden's shoulder before announcing, "This is my bride, Minerva, the beautiful English lady I told you about. Eden, I'd like to present Minerva, who has been a sore trial to me since the first day she was born. Her husband, George, and I grew up together. She bedeviled us all the way into manhood, at which time poor George had the misfortune to fall hopelessly in love with her."

"I am very pleased to meet you, Minerva," Eden spoke in earnest, after sending Roark a stern, silent admonishment for his merciless teasing of the young woman.

"I'm so glad that you have come at last, Mistress Eden," replied Minerva. Her voice was soft and melodious, and her brown eyes held a genuine welcome. "We all prayed that Master Roark would find you and bring you home."

"Where is George?" asked Roark, growing serious again.

"He is in the fields. We . . ." Her voice trailed

away, and a shadow crossed the smooth, youthful beauty of her countenance when she explained sadly, "Things are not the same now, Master Roark. We've managed to save less than half the crop. There aren't enough hands to do all the work. My mother and sister and I see to the house, and my little brothers, Neptune and Willie, do their best to keep the grounds, but that leaves only George and a dozen other men to look after the fields."

"Thomas has told me what happened," he revealed grimly. "I'm sorry I couldn't return before now."

"They say the British might be planning to overrun the island any day now." Her eyes filled with dread at the possibility. "Is that true, Master Roark?"

"I'm afraid it might be." He turned to Eden and told her, "I've got to speak with George. I'll leave you in Minerva's care. If there's anything you need—"

"I know," she assured him, well aware of his impatience to be off. "Don't worry. I shall be fine."

Watching as he disappeared outside once more, she remained lost in thought for a few moments. Finally, Minerva gave her new mistress a tentative smile and reached out to gently touch her arm.

"If you'll come this way, Mistress Eden, I'll show you up to your room."

"Thank you, Minerva." Her features relaxed into a smile. "I should like that very much."

Appreciative of the other woman's friendliness, she smiled again and followed her up the curving staircase. Minerva led the way down the landing to the far end of a wide, pastel-toned hallway, then opened a door to reveal a room that was wonderfully light and airy—and connected to no other. At Liberty

380

Point, it was fully expected that the master and his wife should sleep in the same bed. A delightful American custom, mused Eden, and one for which she was prepared to offer her wholehearted approval.

"I'll send my sister, Juno, up with some water for your bath," proclaimed Minerva. "And if you'd like something to eat—"

Eden declined, shaking her head. "No, thank you. I am not the least bit hungry. There is something I require, however."

"Yes, Mistress Eden?"

"I should like for us to come to an understanding, Minerva. You are terribly shorthanded here at Liberty Point, and I really must insist that we dispense with the usual formalities. I intend to do whatever I can to help. I've little doubt my husband will do the same."

"You mean, you . . . you are going to *work?*" the other woman asked in shocked amazement. She had heard that all English ladies did nothing but sit around and drink tea and spend hours on end with their embroidery.

"I am indeed," Eden confirmed with a quiet laugh. "Come now, even you must see that no other arrangement will do."

"But, Master Roark—"

"*Master Roark* would be the first to agree with me." Her eyes glowed with the proud, spirited determination Roark had come to know so well. "I am no hothouse rose, Minerva. And I should like it above all else if you and I were to become good friends. I shall have to rely upon your advice a great deal, you see."

"I can see why Master Roark went to such lengths to find you," observed Minerva, her own gaze sparkling with wry amusement. "All right, Mistress Eden. Friends we will be."

"Good! Now that that's settled, there is one more thing I want you to know. But first you must give me your word that you'll not tell my husband."

"I have always been good at keeping secrets," Minerva remarked. It was clear that the idea of keeping Eden's appealed to her.

"I do not know how long it will be before my husband sets sail again, but I do know he intends that I should remain here and wait for him. *I* am of the mind to accompany him, and I shall require your help when the time comes."

"I have never gone against Master Roark," Minerva replied doubtfully. "And it is a woman's duty to obey her husband."

"Yes, I am well aware of that," Eden said with a touch of exasperation. "But surely there are exceptions to every rule!" Noting that Minerva appeared far from convinced, she decided to employ another tactic. "You want to see Roark happy, do you not?"

"Yes."

"Well then, how happy can he be if we must face yet another long separation? Please, Minerva, if you love your own husband even half as much as I love mine, you will agree to help me! Even if you refuse, I shall find a way to go with him. I will not be left behind!" She studied the other woman's face closely, praying that her reaction would be favorable. It was.

"All right," Minerva capitulated, though she did so with obvious reluctance. "I will do what I can when the time comes. Only, please, Mistress Eden, do not ask me to lie to Master Roark. Secrets, I am good at, but lying is a talent I have never quite mastered—especially with him.'' A soft, lopsided smile of remembrance tugged at the corners of her mouth. "George could never see through my deception, but Master Roark could.''

"I give you my word you'll not find it necessary to lie to him.'' She hadn't the faintest notion exactly how she would keep that promise, but she would keep it nonetheless. So long as she was sure of Minerva's assistance, everything else would fall into place. She would not allow herself to doubt it.

It was quite some time, long after she had had her bath and helped Minerva and Juno—and their mother, Adelie—with the preparations for supper, before Eden saw her husband again. Night had already crept over the island, bringing with it a cool southeasterly wind and a sky full of stars.

"The fields are in better shape than I had expected,'' Roark reported with a faint smile of satisfaction.

Slipping off his shirt in order to exchange it for a clean one, he crossed to the wardrobe. Eden sat perched on the edge of the bed, her eyes softly aglow while she watched him change.

"Thank God for George,'' he added. "The place would have fallen into complete disrepair if not for him.''

"When do I get to meet the 'infamous' George?''

"Tonight. He's to dine with us.'' His gaze narrowed imperceptibly. "I didn't think you'd mind. It's a special occasion. And George is much more than a servant."

"Why, of course I do not mind! It might interest you to know that Minerva and I have already come to an agreement. No more life of leisure for me, Captain St. Claire. I am to be the true mistress of all I survey," she asserted with playful loftiness as she rose to her feet beside the bed.

"Are you?" He turned and gave her a warm, roguishly challenging look that made her legs go weak and her heart beat like mad. "Have you not heard it said that every man wants his wife to behave like a mistress? Part angel and part wanton. Aye, sweet vixen, that will suit me well."

"Pray, sir, how am I to know *which* occasion demands *what?*" she parried, her face becomingly flushed.

"The difference is the same as day and night." He began advancing upon her with slow, purposeful steps. An almost predatory gleam shone in the brilliant blue depths of his eyes, and his mouth curved into a tender yet decidedly wayward smile when he stood towering above her. "But of course, it is a husband's prerogative to get the two confused."

Eden smiled seductively up at him and slid her hands beneath the edges of his unbuttoned clean, white linen shirt. As usual, her touch set him afire. She parted her lips ever so slightly, while her eyes issued an undeniable invitation to passion.

"Well then, I can see I shall have to set you straight." Straining on tiptoe, she dropped a pert kiss upon his waiting mouth and added saucily, "But not until I've had my supper!"

She spun away, setting a course for the door, but

was unable to escape a swift and judicious punishment. A startled gasp broke from her lips when a hard, familiar smack landed upon her backside.

"It's you who will be set straight this night, you little spitfire," vowed Roark.

Eden turned and dared to fling him yet another vixenish challenge.

"Are all you Americans so boastful?" she inquired in a voice smooth as silk.

"Only if we are prepared to substantiate our boasts." The look in his eyes promised a sweet revenge. "And I, my love, am fully prepared."

Eden colored at that and made a hasty retreat. Roark joined her in the dining room a few minutes later. George entered soon thereafter, but Minerva stubbornly insisted upon remaining in the kitchen. The war may have changed some things at Liberty Point, but she was determined to hold on to as many traditions as she could. And breaking bread at the same table with the master, be he friend or foe, was simply not right.

"Eden, this is George," Roark dutifully made the introductions as he drew her forward. "George, this is my wife."

"I am happy to meet you at last, George," said Eden, smiling warmly up at the tall, broad-shouldered young man before her. Dressed in a dark blue coat and trousers, he was quite attractive, and there was no denying the intelligence reflected in his steady brown gaze. He appeared to be the perfect match for the lovely Minerva, she mused. "It seems we owe you a considerable debt of gratitude."

"Welcome to Liberty Point, Mistress Eden," he

responded with an answering smile. His eyes were full of approval when he met Roark's gaze again. "But there are no debts between us."

They sat down to the evening meal, which was served by the sixteen-year-old Juno. She giggled whenever offering food to George, and was quite impervious to the quelling looks he sent her. Eden suppressed a dozen smiles, though her green eyes were alight with humor. She noticed that Roark was finding it equally difficult to conceal his amusement. Finally, when they had eaten their fill of the supper—chicken soup, shrimp pie, crab cakes, fresh vegetables from the plantation's own garden, and a dessert of orange marmalade tartlets—they wandered into the large, brightly lit drawing room. George remained only a short while before excusing himself with the announced intention of making sure the horses had been secured in the stables for the night.

"You were right, you know," Eden confessed to her husband once they were alone. Her emerald gaze fastened upon him as he stood before the fireplace, absently scrutinizing the glass of brandy in his hand. "Things *are* completely different here. No one in Barbados—or England, for that matter—would ever consider inviting one of the servants to dine with them. But of course, George truly is so much more than that, isn't he? I like him, Roark, and Minerva and Juno and Adelie as well. They are fiercely loyal to you."

"They are that," he agreed, a faint smile touching his lips at the thought. His handsome features grew solemn in the next moment, and he set the glass atop the mantelpiece before revealing, "I'm afraid I won't be able to leave you here after all."

"You . . . you are going to take me with you?" she stammered in disbelief. Her eyes sparkled with triumphant joy. Rising to her feet, she flew across the room to embrace him. "Oh, Roark! Thank God you—"

"No, Eden." He held her at arm's length and shook his head. His penetrating blue gaze burned down into the sudden confusion of hers. "I won't be taking you with me. You're going back to Savannah."

"Savannah? But, *why?*"

"Because it's too dangerous for you to stay here. The island is an easy target for the British. And nearly everyone has gone." He released her and frowned, his eyes glinting dully. "I had thought to place you under the protection of my friends and neighbors. As it is, I could not leave knowing you were so vulnerable here at Liberty Point. There are but a dozen men left; they could do little if the enemy launched an invasion. No, it will be best if you return to Savannah and wait there."

"But I want to go with you!"

"We'll set sail in two days' time," he continued as if she had not spoken. "Bertha and Patterson will take good care of you. And I'll send you word whenever I am able."

She opened her mouth to argue, but thought better of it. There was no use in provoking him to anger, and well she knew it. The plans had changed, and yet her resolution had not. By all that was holy, she would still find a way to go with him. She *would!*

"What will happen to George and Minerva and all

the others once we have gone?" she asked in a low tone.

"I don't know," he answered truthfully. "I tried to persuade George that they should accompany us to Savannah, but he refused. This is his home, the same as it is mine. He will not leave it." Roark downed the last of his brandy, then moved back to the sideboard and set the glass atop a silver tray. "I doubt they'll suffer any harm. The British have made it a point to refrain from injuring any slaves. It will not matter to the enemy that everyone here is a freeman. Ironically, the color of their skin will protect them in this instance."

"Have you forgotten that I am English? I would be in no danger if—"

"I cannot rely upon that. Damn it, Eden, there are no rules to govern us in wartime. Your own countrymen could well decide to take advantage of your situation."

"I am not afraid of that!" she insisted.

"It does not matter." There was a note of finality in his deep voice now, and his gaze seemed to bore into her very soul. "I'm taking you back to Savannah."

His words effectively put an end to further discussion. Eden returned to the floral silk chaise and sank down upon it with a heavy sigh. Roark's dark mood did not improve until after they had gone upstairs to bed.

The next morning held a pleasant surprise for Eden. Following breakfast, her husband led her outside to the waiting carriage.

"Where are we going?" she asked, her brows knitting together in a frown of puzzlement as Roark handed her up into the open conveyance.

"Thomas knows the way," he answered evasively. He took a seat beside her and instructed the smiling driver to be off.

"Roark St. Claire, why are you being so blasted mysterious?" demanded Eden, her manner sternly reproachful but her eyes dancing with fond amusement.

"Patience, sweet vixen." It was clear he meant to keep her in the dark.

She had no choice but to settle back and wait for enlightenment. Breathing deeply of the cool, fragrant air, she reveled in the feel of the wind against her face and the sight of the never-ending bower of greenery about her. They passed not a single person on horseback or foot, not another carriage. Though it was still quite early, the songbirds were already filling the woods with their sweet, melodious celebration of life. The day promised to be one of extraordinary beauty.

It wasn't long until the carriage turned and headed down a road whose signpost read "Frederica." Eden's gaze shone with curiosity when, a few moments later, she glimpsed an old tabby building surrounded by giant, moss-draped live oaks and standing in the midst of a collection of several other buildings, every one of them in ruins.

Unbeknownst to her, this was all that remained of an early-days fort and settlement. The place had a rather melancholy feel to it, but there was nothing in the least bit gloomy about the one intact structure, which appeared much like a beacon in the shadows when the sun's radiance streamed down through the trees to set it aglow.

"Why, it is a church!" exclaimed Eden, taking note of the small wooden cross atop its roof. She turned to Roark. "Why have you brought me here?"

"We've a wedding to attend, Mrs. St. Claire," he told her. His eyes gleamed with satisfaction.

"A wedding? But . . . *whose?*"

"Our own."

Thomas guided the carriage to a stop in front of the church. Eden, her mind still awhirl as a result of what she had just heard, was scarcely aware of Roark lifting her down. He tucked her hand within the possessive crook of his arm and led her down a stone path toward the church.

"I . . . I do not understand!" she faltered in confusion. "We are already married!"

"That we are," he allowed with a disarming smile. "But we were married on English soil, and I've a mind to speak our vows here in my own country. Call it a safeguard if you will."

"A safeguard?"

"In case your father ever manages to secure an annulment. You're mine, Eden, and I want to make certain the legality of our marriage is never in doubt."

She certainly could not fault the reasoning in that. A whole floodtide of love and emotion coursed through her, and her beautiful eyes told him all that was in her heart.

"Then, by all means, Captain St. Claire, let us proceed with the wedding."

He gave a soft, triumphant laugh and escorted her

through the open doorway to where the parson was waiting. The ceremony which followed took no longer than that first one back in England, but Eden knew that she would never forget it.

As it turned out, the day would forever live in her memory for another reason as well. . . .

She and her twice-wed husband arrived back at the plantation shortly before noon. They had stopped off in the nearby town, where Roark had received a report from the men on watch aboard the *Hornet*. Most of the crew lived there on the southern tip of the island, or just across the sound on the mainland. Only a few of their families had remained.

Anxious to do all he could before the next day's departure, Roark left Eden at the house and strode away to find George again. She knew that he was torn at the prospect of leaving his home once more, especially after so brief a visit, and she vowed to do everything she could to ease his pain once they were at sea. That she would be with him, she would not allow herself to doubt. The trip back to Savannah had at least ensured that she would have some extra time to come up with a plan.

It was late afternoon when she received an unexpected visitor. Clad in one of Minerva's old work dresses, and with her long raven tresses secured beneath a scarf, she was standing outside near the barn when a carriage pulled up in front of the house. She lowered the basketful of eggs to the ground and hastened forward with a bright smile of welcome on her face.

"Jamaica! And Colonel Harding! I am delighted to—"

"Dear God, Eden, they have come!" Jamaica burst

out. Her own face looked ashen, and her eyes were filled with terror as she stepped down and clutched at Eden's arm.

"Who?"

"The enemy!"

"Wha-what are you talking about?"

"It's true," said Colonel Harding. He frowned when Eden's wide, startled gaze moved to him. "Our forces have landed on the island and are on their way here even as we speak."

"Seth barely managed to escape!" Jamaica told her. "He said Roark would know where to find him!"

"*Roark!*" breathed Eden. Her heart leapt in alarm.

"He must get away while he still can!" cautioned Jamaica. "I fear what they will do to him if he is caught!"

"They have seized control of your husband's ship," Colonel Harding informed her. "We have just come from town." He took her hand within the strong, steady warmth of his and said, "Listen to me, Eden. You yourself are in no danger, but your husband is. I speak to you as an old friend now. Were it not for that friendship, I should not care what happened to him. You must find him at once and tell him what is happening."

Eden nodded mutely up at him. Swallowing hard, and feeling sick with dread, she spun about and raced toward the fields. The thought of Roark's capture made her run as she had never run before.

He was talking to George when he caught sight of her. Noting her visible distress, he muttered a curse and hurried forward to meet her.

"What is it, Eden? What's wrong?" he demanded curtly.

"The—the British have landed on the island!" she gasped out. She would have collapsed were it not for his arms about her. "They have taken the *Hornet*!"

"And the crew?"

"I don't know! Jamaica and Colonel Harding have just come with the news!"

He swept her up in his arms and carried her swiftly back to the house. George followed close behind. Once they'd arrived, Colonel Harding told Roark all he knew, while Jamaica and Eden clung to one another and prayed that the worst would not come to pass.

"If you expect to elude them at all, you'd best go now," advised the Englishman. "Mr. Colfax mentioned that the two of you have a safe place to hide."

"We do," confirmed Roark. "But I'm not leaving without Eden."

"Oh, Roark, you must!" she cried adamantly. She flew to his side, her eyes holding a desperate entreaty. "Don't you see? I shall be perfectly safe here! Now, please, before it is too late, *please go!*"

"You can entrust her care to me," Colonel Harding assured him. "I am well known to the Crown, Captain, as is her father, Lord Grayson Parrish. I give you my word she will suffer no mistreatment."

"And you will be needed to help the others!" Eden pointed out. "Your men may . . . they may be hanged if you do not think of a way to free them!"

"You are far more important to me than they!" he ground out, crushing her to him. "By damn, I won't

393

leave you behind!"

"You have no choice!" She drew away and tilted her head back to meet his smoldering gaze squarely. "I would only slow you down! And what will happen to me if you are caught here? Or if we are apprehended elsewhere? I should be judged a traitor to my country!" Drawing in a deep breath, she put the rest of her argument to him more calmly, "But I can pretend ignorance of your whereabouts if I remain here. I can claim to be what I was once—your captive. It is the only way. I would die if anything should happen to you!" Her voice broke as she flung herself upon his broad chest again and fought back the sob which rose in her throat.

"She is right, Master Roark," George surprised everyone by affirming. He did not flinch before the savage gleam in the other man's eyes. "There is no one else to lead your men. If you were caught, you would risk the lives of many."

The dilemma had only one solution, and Roark knew it, but still he hesitated.

"Please, Captain St. Claire!" Jamaica implored him. "What will happen to Seth if you do not go?"

As Eden had said, he had little choice. Jamaica's words only reinforced the decision fate had already made for him.

"All right," he agreed in a low, deceptively even tone. "I'll go."

He swept Eden closer, pressed a hard, near-painful kiss upon her lips, and tore himself from her grasp.

"I'll get word to you somehow!" he promised grimly. Filling his eyes with her beauty once more, he strode from the room.

394

Eden stared after him through a burning rush of tears. Her heart ached terribly, and she dared not let herself think about what would happen if he did not get away in time.

The sound of hoofbeats drew her to the window moments later. She watched in silent anguish as her beloved rode away.

"They will be safe, Eden," Jamaica murmured tremulously beside her. "They *must* be!"

"I pray you are right."

There was nothing to be done now . . . except wait.

Eighteen

The wait was not a long one.

Less than an hour after Roark's departure, the British arrived at Liberty Point. Eden stood proud and silent in front of the house, with Jamaica and Colonel Harding at her side. The enemy—for in truth, she considered them that at present—came marching down the long, tree-lined drive, led by a young officer on horseback.

Drawing to a halt a short distance away from the house, the lone rider dismounted and gallantly doffed his hat. Eden stiffened at his approach.

"I am Lieutenant Davidson," he announced in a clear tone, making her a curt bow. "I have orders to seize this plantation, and to arrest its owner, a man by the name of Captain Roark St. Claire."

"Captain St. Claire is no longer here," Eden informed him with remarkable composure. Her heart was pounding fiercely, and Roark's face swam before her eyes. She would do what she had to do.

"Are you his wife?"

"I am Lady Eden Parrish. My father is Lord Grayson Parrish. Perhaps you are familiar with the name." She calmly turned to indicate the two people with her. "I should like to present Colonel Beauregard Harding, and his daughter, Miss Jamaica Harding."

"Colonel Harding?" the young officer echoed in surprise. Visibly impressed to realize that he was in the presence of a famous war hero, he made Jamaica a bow and stepped forward to accept the older man's outstretched hand. "It is an honor to make your acquaintance, Colonel."

"Lieutenant," said Jamaica's father. Then he demanded gruffly, "What, may I ask, is the meaning of *this?*" He jerked his head toward the waiting column of troops, numbering perhaps twenty-five in all.

"We received information regarding an American privateer. Roark St. Claire is wanted for a number of crimes against His Majesty's ships. I hold in my possession a document calling for his arrest and transport to England, where he will face judgment and in all probablility be sent to Dartmoor Prison," the slender, fair-haired officer concluded with satisfaction.

"That may well be so, Lieutenant, but you stand on American soil," Colonel Harding pointed out. "Your documents are of little significance here. Surely this little invasion of yours was prompted by a good deal more than the desire to find St. Claire."

"Yes, Colonel, it was indeed. We have been planning—" He broke off, as if suddenly realizing he had said too much. When he spoke again, it was in a

397

considerably more pompous and authoritative manner. "I demand to know what the three of you are doing here on this island, and what your connection to Roark St. Claire is!"

"Captain St. Claire and his men abducted us!" Jamaica supplied unexpectedly. A telltale flush had risen to her face, but the young Englishman could not know what had prompted it. She stole a quick, nervous glance at Eden before adding, "We were brought here from Barbados, and . . . and have been held captive ever since!"

"I, on the other hand, have only just arrived, with the express purpose of finding my daughter and taking her home," proclaimed Colonel Harding. He gave the other man an intimidating scowl. "That villain, St. Claire, had already fled like the coward he is by the time I got here."

"Where has he gone?" asked Lieutenant Davidson, looking dubious.

"How the devil should I know?" growled Colonel Harding. "Blast your eyes, boy, do you think I'm not just as anxious as you to see him caught? He certainly gave us no indication of his plans. While we stand here wasting time, he may very well be on his way inland!"

"We have taken his ship. And there are two other detachments guarding the coastline. It will not be possible for him to leave the island," Davidson opined confidently. He turned back to Eden. "I apologize in advance for the inconvenience, Lady Eden, but I have my orders. My men and I will remain quartered here until our operation is completed."

"I understand, Lieutenant Davidson," she deferred in all politeness. She groaned inwardly at the thought of the soldiers at Liberty Point. How would she be able to see Roark or even get word to him with the British watching her every move? Her mind raced to think of a solution to this newest quandary. "Would it not be better if you were to stay in the town?" she suggested. "There, at least, you could—"

"No."

Eden was startled to hear Colonel Harding dispute the suggestion. Her emerald gaze clouded with confusion as it shifted to him.

The merest ghost of a smile appeared on the colonel's face before he explained, "They will be much more comfortable here, my dear. And, since we know the scoundrel's ship to be unavailable to him, it would be foolish to post so many men in town. No, I should expect St. Claire to return to his home. He will not risk going near the harbor."

Eden was uncertain about the older man's reasoning, but she knew that she could trust his motives. He had already proven himself in that respect.

"I quite agree, Colonel," seconded Davidson. "Besides, we have two ships of our own patrolling the immediate waters, and another anchored in the harbor. If St. Claire or any of his men attempt to escape, you can rest assured they will be apprehended."

He still had a number of questions regarding the highly suspicious presence of three British subjects in enemy territory. The tale of abduction sounded more than a trifle far-fetched to his ears. But, he told himself, if Lady Eden truly was the daughter of Lord

Grayson Parrish, and if it was indeed Colonel Beauregard Harding who stood before him, then he had best do nothing to provoke them. The promotion he had long been awaiting would be his at last if only he could bring in Roark St. Claire. And to protect and rescue the daughter of such a highly placed lord of the realm would only further his career. His eyes gleamed with certain triumph at the thought.

"With your permission, Lady Eden, my men will occupy those buildings," he announced, nodding toward the cabins which formerly housed the slaves. "I, myself, of course, will require quarters within the main house."

"Surely that will not be necessary!" Eden blurted out, then colored faintly beneath his close scrutiny. "I beg your pardon, Lieutenant Davidson, but I . . . I am afraid things may become rather crowded. You see, Colonel Harding and Miss Harding must be accommodated as well."

"How many others are living here?" he demanded. His gaze made a hasty but thorough sweep of the area. "And in particular, how many slaves?"

"The slaves have gone," she answered, her eyes kindling with indignation at his arrogance. "There are but a dozen men left, all freemen, and three women and two boys. They have been very kind to us, and I am sure they will cooperate with you in every way possible."

"Very well."

He made her another slight bow, then pivoted about and marched stiffly away to give instructions to the troops. The men broke formation at last and headed obediently toward the cabins. Their eyes strayed toward the two women as they went. Lieutenant Davidson, charging one of the youngest recruits to see to his horse, returned to where Eden stood exchanging a look of silent, helpless frustration with Jamaica.

"Shall we go inside, Lady Eden?" It was more of a command than a request.

"Of course."

Her skirts rustled softly as she led the way up the steps and into the house. Minerva, Juno, and Adelie were waiting just within the doorway. Concealing their mutual dismay at seeing one of the enemy under Master Roark's roof, they said nothing while Davidson ordered them to fetch food and drink for his men, then hurried off to do his bidding.

"It appears that Captain St. Claire's treachery has made him a wealthy man," he remarked disdainfully, his gaze traveling swiftly about the interior of the house. "I should like to inspect the entire property, Lady Eden, in order to see what may be carried with us when we set sail again. I will begin with the house itself."

"You'll find little of interest," Colonel Harding asserted brusquely. Though he shared an unwavering allegiance to the Crown with the lieutenant, he felt anything but kinship with the man at the moment. He told himself it was because his daughter had married an American, but it was more than that. He had always despised the wartime custom of seizure. There was no honor or glory in acting the thief. "I will not allow any plundering, Lieutenant," he decreed.

"I am sorry, Colonel Harding, but I am in

401

command here—not you. My orders are to employ my own powers of discretion and seize anything of value. Captain St. Claire will have no use of his 'plunder' when he is rotting in prison where he belongs."

Eden tensed and suffered a sharp intake of breath. She quickly sought to mask her trepidation with a forced display of hospitality.

"If you will come with me, Lieutenant Davidson, I will show you to your room." She managed a wan smile. "You've only to let us know if there is anything you require. Miss Harding and I will be more than happy to oblige you, will we not, Miss Harding?"

"Yes, of—of course!" Jamaica stammered in a breathless rush.

"Thank you."

The lieutenant's eyes glowed with wholly masculine admiration when he looked to Eden again. He was not immune to her beauty, and although he still had his doubts about the validity of her story, he found himself increasingly enchanted. It had been a long time, too long, since he had been in the company of such a lovely and well-bred young woman. Miss Harding was quite pretty with her blond curls and delicate features, but he much preferred the more voluptuous charms of the raven-haired Lady Eden.

"I am beginning to think," he confided to her in a voice warm with meaning, "that my time here will not be as unpleasant as I had feared. It is my hope that you and I—and Colonel Harding and Miss Harding, too, of course—will become friends."

When hell freezes over, perhaps, Eden mused in

vengeful silence. Forcing another smile to her lips, she moved regally up the staircase with Jamaica in tow.

"We all have our hopes, Lieutenant," she tossed back over her shoulder. She could feel his eyes upon her, and she forced herself to maintain a slow, measured pace as he followed her up the stairs.

The atmosphere at supper that night was quite subdued, at least among three of the diners seated beneath the chandelier's bright glow. Indeed, were it not for the bolstering presence of Jamaica and Colonel Harding, Eden would have found the situation intolerable. As it was, she managed to play the hostess without once betraying her true feelings. It was no easy task, since she could think of little else save Roark.

Lieutenant Davidson did not appear to notice her preoccupation. He told her all about himself, his family, and his ambitions for a successful naval career. He was only slightly evasive when answering Colonel Harding's inquiries regarding his next course of action, and seemed very pleased in general with the way the evening had gone by the time he retired for the night.

Eden breathed a long, ragged sigh when she finally escaped to the privacy of her own room. She threw herself upon the bed, her heart crying out to Roark.

"Where are you now?" she whispered. Tears stung against her eyelids, and she clutched at the pillow beneath her head.

Tormented by visions of his capture, she could only pray he did not try to return to Liberty Point. The thought of him out there in the darkness of the woods, with the British all around, was enough to provoke a rising tide of panic deep within her.

Sleep eluded her until well after midnight, and even then offered a far too unsatisfying respite from her troubles.

Unfortunately, the following day proved to be every bit as much of a trial by fire for her courage and fortitude.

"I heard him say that they will not be leaving until they have captured all of the privateers!" Jamaica revealed when they were alone in Eden's bedroom. She had eavesdropped upon the young officer's conversation with one of his men after breakfast that morning, but she was not feeling the least bit penitent. "Oh, Eden," she murmured despondently, "do you suppose Seth and Captain St. Claire are aware of what is happening here?"

"I don't know. But you can be sure George will do everything in his power to warn them. He has promised to let me know the very moment he hears from Roark." She frowned as she tucked her hair beneath Minerva's red cotton scarf and adjusted the folds of the simple work dress. "In the meantime, I shall go mad if I do not find a way to keep myself occupied—and as far as possible from the overly attentive Lieutenant Davidson!"

"What are you planning to do?" asked Jamaica, eyeing her curious attire.

"I am going to town."

"Like that? But . . . why?"

"Perhaps I can discover something which might be of importance to Roark. At the very least, I should be able to assess the situation with the *Hornet* and the condition of the men who were captured when she was seized. And I do not wish to call attention to myself."

"Well then, I shall go with you!"

"No, Jamaica. You must stay here. I have instructed George to come to you with any news in my absence."

"But it will be far too dangerous for you to go alone!"

"I am not going alone. Your father has consented to take me. And Lieutenant Davidson," she added with an involuntary shudder at the memory of the look in that man's eyes, "has given his permission for the outing."

"Do you . . . do you really think there is any hope of their escaping?" the petite blonde faltered, her thoughts returning to her beloved Seth again.

"If it can be done, you can rest assured Roark St. Claire will see that it is!" avowed Eden, the confidence in her voice belying the dull ache in her heart.

A short time later, she allowed Colonel Harding to assist her down from the carriage after Thomas had drawn up near the wharf. The town looked no different than it had two days ago, save for the fact that there was a British ship anchored in the harbor. Few people were about, and even the tavern appeared empty. Her gaze fell upon the *Hornet*. She saw a dozen uniformed Englishmen on deck, but there was no sign of the members of the ship's last watch.

"They are imprisoned within the old storehouse," Colonel Harding disclosed, as if reading her thoughts. He gave her a faint smile and remarked engimatically, "I have my own methods."

"Do you know how many were captured?"

"Seven." He paused briefly, his gaze narrowing as it moved to the British ship. "It has come to my attention that the gallant lieutenant intends to remain until your husband and the others have been apprehended."

"Yes," she murmured in a low voice full of dread. "Jamaica told me."

"It might be possible to convince him to leave sooner." He turned back to her and grew quite solemn. "Your husband will never be able to escape so long as the British remain here." His eyes filled with compassion as he watched her face pale. "I do not tell you this to frighten you, my dear, but to make you accept reality. Were it only myself involved, I would damned well let your husband—and yes, Jamaica's as well—be taken! I am an Englishman, after all, and we are in the midst of a war. I have little doubt of their guilt. What I have done and am still doing is nothing short of treason. But I am not the heartless bastard some have termed me. I want no part of destroying my daughter's life, or yours, for that matter."

Eden started to question him, her desperation mounting. "Then what—"

"I suggest you speak to the lieutenant at once. Plead with him to take you home. To England."

"But I have no intention of going home! Indeed, Colonel Harding, I am determined to remain with my husband!"

"Your determination will do you no good," he insisted firmly. "Not if Captain St. Claire is captured. No, child, there is little hope of saving your husband's life if the lieutenant cannot be persuaded to cut short his time here on the island. Each hour brings St. Claire closer to discovery. Yes, and the others as well."

"How would it be possible for Lieutenant Davidson to leave?" she argued. "He has his orders, does he not? And what makes you so certain he would be willing to return to England, when—"

"Three reasons," Harding broke in to pronounce. "First, the young stripling's admiration for you has been laid out for anyone with eyes to see. Second, he is well aware of the gratitude he would be shown if he returned Lord Grayson Parrish's daughter to the loving bosom of her family. Third, and perhaps most important of all, I have it on good authority that he will soon be ordered back to England anyway."

"How can you know that?"

"I told you. I have my methods."

Eden's head spun dizzily as she contemplated all she had just heard. The prospect of another long separation from Roark was as grievous as ever. And yet, she would do anything to save him. *Anything*.

"The decision must be made at once," Colonel Harding prompted. "I will do all I can to help."

"Why?" she asked, her eyes full of mingled confusion and unhappiness. "Why are you so willing to help men who are your enemies? Is it because of Jamaica, because of her marriage to Seth?"

"It is. You see," he explained with another brief hint of a smile, "I am guilty of the worst kind of treason—I love my daughter more than my country. And by damn, I will not see her heart broken."

"If . . . if I were to return to England, would you and Jamaica be coming along as well?"

"No. I have promised her that we will stay on St. Simons. If circumstances dictate otherwise, if Mr. Colfax is caught, then we will return to Barbados." He studied her face closely before adding, "The separation would only be a temporary one, my dear. If I've learned one thing about St. Claire thus far, it's that he is not the sort of man to let anything keep him from what he has set his mind to. He'll find a way to bring you back. Of that, I am certain."

Eden drew in a deep, steadying breath. Her troubled gaze moved back to her husband's ship. It pained her almost beyond endurance to think of leaving Roark. But, what else was she to do? *God help me, how am I going to bear it?*

"Well?" demanded her gruff but kindly companion. "What is it to be? Do you risk letting St. Claire be caught, or do you choose to make the sacrifice?"

"You know the answer," she replied in a low, quavering tone that was scarcely more than a whisper. Her eyes were bright with unshed tears when she faced him again, but her spirit was as indomitable as ever. "I shall speak to Lieutenant Davidson at once."

"Good." He frowned and said, "I'll not tell Jamaica yet. I fear she would not understand."

"No. She . . . she need not know," murmured Eden, her voice threatening to break. She fiercely blinked back the tears and took one last look at the *Hornet*. Misery welled up within her, and a sense of such overwhelming loss that she found it difficult to breathe. "I want no one else, no one at all, to know of this, Colonel Harding. It is . . . it is best if we keep the secret between ourselves."

"Agreed." His hand gripped her arm. "I think we should return to Liberty Point now. There is nothing more to be done here."

Nodding mutely, she allowed him to assist her back up into the carriage. The journey homeward seemed at once endless and too short. Her heart ached terribly, and her head throbbed with the dilemma before her. She dared not think about what Roark's reaction would be when he discovered her gone. Oh my love, please try to understand, she beseeched silently. She would come back. No matter what happened, she would find a way to come back!

She went in search of Lieutenant Davidson as soon as she had changed into one of her prettiest gowns. Now that her decision had been made, she was anxious to put the plan into action. She could only hope and pray that it worked. Roark's very life depended on her powers of persuasion; she would give a performance such as no other.

Gathering her courage about her—and holding strong to her vow to be reunited with her beloved once the current danger had passed—she forced a smile to her lips and hailed the young British officer as he strode away from the stables.

"Lieutenant Davidson?"

"Lady Eden!" His eyes lit with pleasure when he saw her, while a delighted smile spread across his fair, smoothly aristocratic countenance. He pulled the hat from his head and quickened his approach. "I did not know you had returned. I trust you enjoyed your little excursion?"

"Yes. It was . . . quite illuminating." Noting his mild frown of bemusement, she gave a soft laugh and moved to tuck her hand about his arm. "Come, Lieutenant, let us stroll about the grounds. I should like to have a word with you."

"Of course," he eagerly consented.

They set off together at a leisurely pace. Eden staunchly ignored the way her stomach turned as she sent a bright, dazzling smile up at her escort. Schooling her voice to melodious warmth, she decided to get right to the point.

"I was so dreadfully unhappy until you came along, Lieutenant." She feigned a shudder of revulsion and told him, "I cannot begin to tell you what indignities I have suffered at the hands of Captain St. Claire. Although I was not harmed in any way, it was nonetheless humiliating beyond belief to be held captive by such an arrogant rogue. He was no gentleman like you. If you had not come along when you did, I do not know what I should have done!"

"You need say no more, Lady Eden," he responded quietly. "Your ordeal is at an end now."

"No, I am afraid it is not."

"What do you mean?"

"I have not seen my family for many months," she revealed with a dramatic sigh. She once more raised wide, luminous green eyes to the adoring steadiness of his gaze. "I was sent to live with an uncle in Barbados, and he—he was not at all kind to me. And then, when Captain St. Claire came along and carried me off, I began to fear that I would never see my home again. I am desperate to return to England,

Lieutenant. I am quite desperate indeed! Please, I beg of you, will you not take me there?"

"Take you to England?' he repeated, visibly incredulous.

"Yes!" The single tear which coursed down the flushed smoothness of her cheek was genuine. "You are my only hope! If you will not agree to take me, then I shall simply have to find someone else to do so! Why, there must be a captain somewhere who would be glad of the opportunity to collect the reward my father will no doubt offer him for my safe return. There are probably even some Americans who would do it. All manner of vessels are on the seas, in spite of our own country's efforts at a blockade. Perhaps I can travel to Savannah and make inquiries—"

"No, no, you must not do that!" he hastened to caution her. A frown of indecision creased his brow. It was obvious that her request had thrown him into a quandary. "It so happens that I was planning to return to England after my duties here had been completed—after Captain St. Claire had been taken into custody, that is. But I do not see how I could possibly set sail before the mission has been accomplished."

"Can you not simply report that he has eluded capture? He has, you know!" she stated on sudden impulse. Giving an inward grown at the waywardness of her tongue, she realized in the next instant that the impulse had not been such a misguided one after all.

"How can you be sure of that?" the Englishman demanded sharply, drawing to an abrupt halt and turning to face her. His gaze narrowed with renewed suspicion as it sought to bore into hers. "Do you possess information about the man's whereabouts, Lady Eden?"

"I . . . I most certainly do!" Having stumbled upon the idea, she quickly embellished it. "I would have told you sooner, only I had no desire to be the bearer of such ill-favored news! Colonel Harding and I overheard a group of islanders talking when we were in town. It seems Captain St. Claire and the majority of his men have already left St. Simons!"

"Impossible!" His features tightened with anger, and his eyes glinted dully. "What exactly did you hear?"

"They were congratulating one another on the successful flight of their friends!" she lied with remarkable ease. "One of them said it was a good thing St. Claire got wind of the British invasion in time, and another mentioned something about a plan involving some other men in—in Savannah!"

"And you say Colonel Harding heard all this as well?"

"Yes!" She nodded her head for emphasis and forced another smile to her lips. "So you see, there is indeed no use in your remaining here! We can set sail for England at once!"

"Those men you overheard must be questioned without delay," he decreed tersely. He took her arm in a firm grip and said, "Come, Lady Eden. You and I are going to find Colonel Harding and see if he bears out your story!"

"But, that is not at all necessary!" she protested, her heart sinking. Sweet Saint Christopher, what had she done? Pretending righteous indignation, she jerked her arm free and exclaimed, "How dare you, sir! How dare you doubt my word! Conduct an investigation if you will, but do *not* make the mistake of offering me such an insult again!"

"I beg your pardon," he apologized somberly. His pulses leapt at the sight of her magnificent, stormy beauty. "Truly, I meant no disrespect, Lady Eden. It is only that I must make certain—"

"Of course you must!" Her eyes blazed reproachfully up at him. "And I suppose you must also do everything in your power to alienate me!" She assumed a wounded air and said in a cool, stiffly composed tone of voice, "I had thought we were better friends than that, Lieutenant. Indeed, I had hoped—"

She broke off and sighed again. Casting a surreptitious glance up at the young officer from beneath her eyelashes, she was satisfied to view the contrite expression on his face.

"You have my most humble apologies, Lady Eden," he offered sincerely, clasping her hand within the warmth of his. "I would never willingly do anything to hurt you."

"I know. I . . . I should not have lost my temper," she murmured. Sending him a soft, conciliatory smile, she suggested, "Why do we not venture into town? If the men are still there, I can point them out to you."

"Your assistance would be greatly appreciated," he told her in heartfelt gratitude. Already half in love with her, he found himself increasingly tempted to grant her request of a homeward voyage.

Fortunately, Eden was able to have a word alone

with Colonel Harding before she accompanied the lieutenant to town. The colonel praised her quick thinking, and agreed to substantiate her tale of escape if her gallant admirer decided to brave her wrath and question him.

"Unless I miss my guess, you will be on your way by this time tomorrow," he predicted.

She was torn between joy and sorrow at the thought. Her mind told her she was doing the right thing. But her heart knew only its own voice. *Roark.* Where was he?

The loose-tongued islanders from her story were never located, of course. Lieutenant Davidson was quite disappointed with the results of their search, and Eden could tell that he was beginning to doubt the wisdom of prolonging his occupation of St. Simons. Those doubts increased tenfold when, upon arriving at the plantation once more, he received a message from the commanders of the other two detachments which had spread out across the island.

"There has been no sign of either St. Claire or his men, Lieutenant," reported the fresh-faced young recruit.

"Has the search been a thorough one?"

"Yes, Lieutenant." The young soldier hesitated for a moment, looking uncomfortable before adding, "Even if they were here, it would be next to impossible to find them."

"And why is that?" the officer demanded curtly.

"Because, Lieutenant, the woods are too thick and the marshes are . . . well, they are impassable."

"Nevertheless, my orders are to continue the search!"

Davidson scowled darkly as the hapless message bearer mounted up and rode away. His gaze softened when it fell upon Eden, who had just that moment emerged from the house. She stood smiling at him from the front verandah, looking lovelier than ever in a gown of pale rose silk. He would never have guessed at her inner turmoil, for her outward appearance was one of almost regal calm.

"Bad news, Lieutenant?" she queried sympathetically.

"Yes, I'm afraid so." He declined to elaborate, instead choosing to offer her his arm and remark with a negligent glance toward the cloud-dotted sky, "It will be dark soon. Perhaps you would care to continue our stroll now?"

She graciously accepted. "Certainly, Lieutenant. Tell me, have you given any further thought to my suggestion regarding an immediate return to England?" she asked before they had traveled far. She tried to keep the impatience from her voice.

"I have."

"And?"

"And I think there is some merit to your suggestion." Drawing her hand even more possessively through the crook of his, he smiled down at her and confessed, "I, too, am anxious to return home. I have been given to think there is a promotion awaiting me. By the time we have won this war, I may well be a captain myself."

"Are we truly going to win?"

"Of course," he answered, his gaze fondly indulgent. "It may interest you to know that the other two ships, at present patrolling the island's coastline, will shortly be ordered to Baltimore to aid in an attack upon Fort McHenry. I expect an end to the conflict by Christmas at the latest."

"But, how can you know that?" she asked. Hope sprung within her breast at his words. Christmas, she echoed silently. Dear God, let him be right.

"I know a good many things," he boasted pompously. "Once we have beaten these insolent savages, I shall make it a point to call upon you often and let you judge the extent of my knowledge and capabilities for yourself. With your permission, of course," he added, a significant gleam in his eye.

"Granted," said Eden. She sent him a coyly encouraging look before frowning a bit. "But, I must admit, sir, that I would look more favorably upon a continuation of our 'friendship' if you were to agree to take me home."

"A tempting proposition, Lady Eden." He smiled and led her toward a stone bench set amidst the gardens. "Perhaps I will soon be able to secure your happiness in that regard."

He indicated for her to take a seat, then sat down beside her. They exchanged a few more pleasantries, but all Eden could think about was that night was fast approaching . . . another night without Roark. Finally, just as she was about to excuse herself and return to the house, her ardent, would-be suitor suddenly took it upon himself to embrace her.

"Lieutenant Davidson!" she gasped in startlement. Then surprise gave way to indignation. She struggled within his grasp and demanded furiously, "Let go of me!"

Disregarding her vehement protests, he pulled her

416

closer and pressed a kiss of controlled passion upon her lips. A vision of Roark immediately flashed across her mind. She forced herself to go pliant against the young officer, realizing that the only way she could hope to achieve her objective was by playing her role to the finish. The kiss was of mercifully brief duration.

"I am sorry, my dearest Lady Eden," said the Englishman, releasing her as if the contact had burned him. He had the grace to look shamefaced in the extreme as he rose abruptly to his feet and explained, "I . . . I was overcome by such extravagance of emotion that I quite forgot myself!"

"Indeed, sir, you most certainly *did!*" Drawing herself upright before him, she did her best to look as if she were wavering between maidenly outrage and secret delight. Her eyes flashed their brilliant emerald fire, which only served to further enchant him, while a becoming rosiness stained her cheeks. "We shall speak no more about it, Lieutenant."

"May I at least have the assurance of your forgiveness?" he pleaded, catching her hand with his.

"Very well." She allowed a soft smile to briefly touch her lips. "I must return to the house now," she announced, dropping her eyes in a gesture that could easily be construed as flirtatious.

She did not wait for a response before pulling her hand away and sweeping back across the beautiful, twilight-cloaked grounds. It would have given strength to her sorely tested courage if she had known of the lieutenant's determination to have her for his own. Because of that, he was no longer plagued by indecision. He would take her to England—and to hell with that slippery rogue, Captain Roark St. Claire.

Eden retired early that night. Her heart sank at the prospect of even one more hour without word from Roark. She had questioned George again after supper, only to learn that he had still heard nothing, and she was beginning to feel as though she had been cast into some terrible, earthbound purgatory from which there was no escape.

"Oh, Roark!" she breathed raggedly, trying in vain to find a comfortable position in the loneliness of their bed.

Muttering an unladylike oath, she flung back the covers and slid from atop the feather mattress. She padded barefoot to the open window, where she folded her arms tightly across her breasts and stared toward the softly crashing, starlit depths of the sea. The sight gave her no comfort, for she was once again reminded of those precious, all too few days with Roark aboard the *Hornet*. Memories of their time together were bittersweet.

"Nothing will ever part us again," she murmured.

Hot, anguished tears sprang to her eyes when she recalled the vow he had made her. He had intended to leave her behind at Liberty Point and return to the war . . . and yet, she could not blame him for that. As he had once tried to make her understand, he could do no less. He was in truth a man of honor.

An honorable pirate, she mused with loving irony. A heavy sigh escaped her lips, and she wandered unhappily back to the bed. She slipped beneath the covers again, plagued by a rare weakness of spirit which made her want to abandon her scheme altogether. More and more of late, she found herself battling the urge to dissolve into a stormtide of weeping.

A sudden noise at the window caused her to start in alarm. Her eyes flew wide. Experiencing a sharp twinge of *déjà vu*, she had done no more than sit up in the bed when a dark figure climbed through the window.

Nineteen

"*Roark!*"

"Quiet, my love!" he cautioned in a vibrant whisper. He climbed all the way inside and lowered the window.

"Dear God, wha—what are you doing here?" demanded Eden, torn between joyful relief and dawning trepidation. She sprang from the bed and was immediately surrounded by his strong arms. "You must get out at once! The British are here! If you are seen—"

"No one saw me," he assured her. His arms tightened about her, molding her soft curves with fierce, loving possessiveness to his hard-muscled warmth. "And I know all about the British."

She wound her arms about his neck and held him as though she would never let him go. Her fears were vanquished by his presence, and her heart soared at the realization that he was unharmed.

"Oh, Roark!" she murmured feelingly. "I have been out of my mind with worry on your account!"

"I'm sorry I couldn't get word to you before now."

"Where have you been? And what about Seth—and the others?" she asked in a breathless rush. She could not see the faint, mocking smile that played about his lips.

"The British don't know the island as we do. We've had little trouble in keeping ourselves concealed." He scooped her up in his arms and carried her to the bed. Taking a seat on the edge, he cradled her on his lap. "Our hiding place is not far from here. We could stay there without fear of detection for a long time, if need be. But I've no intention of remaining idle."

"Seven of your men are imprisoned in the storehouse in town!" she suddenly remembered to tell him. "Colonel Harding and I were there only this morning. I do not know exactly how many British have been stationed aboard the *Hornet*, but I am quite sure she is being well guarded. And there are two more enemy ships patrolling the coastline!"

"It seems there is another St. Claire with the talent of spying," teased Roark. Then he grew serious again. "We're planning to free the prisoners before this night is through. If all else goes well, the *Hornet* will be ours again by morning." He studied her face as closely as possible in the darkness. "George told me you are being well treated."

"Yes! I . . . I am fine." She faltered, a guilty flush rising to her face. "As are the others."

For a few blissful moments, she had completely forgotten about Lieutenant Davidson and her plans to return to England with him. That may not be necessary now, an inner voice pointed out to her. If Roark was indeed successful in regaining possession

421

of his ship, then it was quite possible her sacrifice would not be needed. Her pulses raced at the thought.

"He also told me the commanding officer, a young lieutenant by the name of Davidson, has been particularly attentive to you." There was no denying the jealousy in his low, deep-timbred voice.

"He has indeed," admitted Eden, then hastened to add, "but only because he is so far away from home and relieved to be in the company of an English-woman."

"Then why the devil isn't he paying the same attention to Jamaica?" Roark's arms tightened about her again. "By damn, if he dares to lay one hand on you—"

"No! No, he has been nothing short of a perfect gentleman!" she lied.

She sighed and shifted her hips about a little. Even through her nightgown and his trousers, she was aware of the undeniably masculine heat of his body. His nearness sent liquid fire coursing through her. The thought of the danger he was in, combined with her own fear of separation from him, only served to heighten her passion.

She pulled his head down to hers and gave him a kiss of such sweet, tantalizing boldness that he groaned. His tongue thrust between her parted lips, while his hand swept downward to curve about her thinly clad buttocks. He startled her when he suddenly cupped her face with his hands and put an end to the kiss.

"Damn it, woman, you'll be the death of me yet!" he growled in mock reproach. He burned to possess her, but he knew there was no time to love her as he longed to do. Mentally cursing the British, and himself as well, he proclaimed in a tone edged with raw emotion, "I'm sorry, Eden, but my men are waiting for me."

"You mean you . . . you are going to leave me already?" she stammered. The disappointment and longing in her voice were almost too much for him to bear.

"I must." He stood and set her on her feet, though he kept his arms about her. "I shouldn't have come at all, but I had to see you." Smiling softly down at her in the darkness, he exhorted, "Have courage, my love. It will all be over soon."

"What are you planning to do?" she was almost afraid to ask.

"Don't worry, sweet vixen. I'll exercise great caution," he answered in a characteristically evasive manner.

He swept her up against him once more and brought his lips crashing down upon the soft willingness of hers. When he finally released her, she was warm all over and her senses were reeling.

"I'll be back for you as soon as I can, my love," he vowed. He opened the window again and tossed a quick but thorough glance about the darkened grounds. "If you need me for any reason, just tell George. He'll know where to find me."

"Roark!" she called out in a hoarse whisper.

But it was too late. He was already gone.

She flew to the window, her heart pounding in her ears as she tried to catch a glimpse of him. It was useless; he had disappeared into the night. Were it not for the lingering reaction of her body, she might have thought the whole thing had been nothing more than a dream.

She crossed distractedly to the bed again and sank down upon it. Her thoughts and emotions were in utter chaos. Musing that it was much the same every time Roark St. Claire saw fit to climb in through her bedroom window, she collapsed back against the pillows and closed her eyes against a fresh wave of tears.

It will all be over soon. His words echoed throughout the turbulence of her mind. Still wondering what he was planning to do, she prayed that he would keep his promise to be careful, however offhandedly it had been given. He had most certainly offered her renewed hope; his success would make it possible for her to remain with him. Yes, she told herself once more, if he were somehow able to get away, she would not have to go to England after all.

"Please, God, let it be so!" she murmured tremulously. "Let it be so!" Still holding fast to this fervent entreaty, she finally drifted off to sleep.

Some time later, a series of loud, earth-shattering *booms* split the cool silence of the night.

Eden awakened with a start. She hesitated only a moment before sliding from the bed and flinging a dressing gown about her shoulders. Hurrying out into the hallway, she discovered Jamaica, Colonel Harding, and Lieutenant Davidson emerging from their rooms as well.

"What the bloody hell was *that?*" thundered Colonel Harding. He and the younger man exchanged looks full of surprise and alarm.

424

Jamaica immediately ran to Eden's side.

"Oh, Eden, wasn't it dreadful? Whatever could have made such a noise?"

"Sweet Saint Christopher, I don't know!" she exclaimed. In the next instant, however, she realized the truth. *Roark.* He had said he was going to do something.

"Colonel Harding, stay here with the ladies!" ordered the lieutenant. Having already donned his boots and trousers, he buttoned his shirt while on his way down the staircase.

"I suspect this has something to do with that husband of yours!" Colonel Harding remarked to Eden once the other man had gone.

"So do I!" she readily concurred. "As a matter of fact, I received a visit from Roark this very night!"

"Did he speak of Seth?" demanded Jamaica.

"He assured me they were all in a safe place," Eden told her. "He also made mention of the fact that they were planning to free the others being held in town, and that they hoped to regain possession of the *Hornet*! I can only suppose that what we have just heard has something to do with that!"

"Get dressed at once," Jamaica's father suddenly commanded. "By damn, we may well find ourselves in the midst of a battle before this night is through!"

They hurried off to do as he had instructed, while he took himself downstairs to see if he could find out what had happened. He stepped out onto the front verandah just in time to watch Lieutenant Davidson and perhaps half a dozen men ride across the fields toward the nearby town. His gaze was drawn to the eerie glow which lit the sky in that direction.

Obviously something was on fire; he could only guess what it might be.

George, Minerva, and all the other inhabitants of Liberty Point were soon gathered in front of the house. Eden wanted more than anything to head into town and ascertain for herself if Roark had been involved, but Colonel Harding firmly insisted that she remain at the plantation.

The waiting seemed endless. Finally, Lieutenant Davidson and his men returned with the startling news—their ship had been blown up.

"The devil you say!" exclaimed Colonel Harding. He had not expected anything quite so drastic. His eyes gleamed with a begrudging admiration for Roark. "How the deuce did it happen?"

"Someone loaded a raft with gunpowder, floated it out to my ship, and positioned it directly underneath the starboard bow!" the young officer related in tight, angrily measured tones. "It was discovered only moments beforehand! I can only thank God the men on watch were able to abandon ship in time!"

The result had been a spectacular explosion and fire; all that was left of the vessel still burned uncontrollably. The British had been able to do nothing more than stand and watch in helpless rage as a proud member of His Majesty's gallant fleet was reduced to nothing more than a smoldering pile of wreckage.

"It requires little intelligence to deduce who is responsible for this treachery!" Lieutenant Davidson ground out. Torches had been lit and placed on the verandah, so his vengeful fury was all too visible. "My men fired upon the cowards, but they escaped into the woods! And the prisoners are gone as well!" He turned to Eden and remarked in a low, simmering tone, "It appears that the information you overheard was wrong, does it not? Captain St. Claire is still here!"

"You cannot be sure of that!" she argued. Her own gaze shone with a triumphant glow, but she schooled her features to reveal nothing of her secret pleasure. "Why, it could just as well have been someone else!"

"It was St. Claire," he maintained grimly. "And by all that is holy, he will be made to pay!"

"What are you going to do?" Jamaica asked in a small, fearful voice.

"I am going to see that he and the other villains are found, Miss Harding. They will soon discover what happens to those who are foolish enough to incur the wrath of the Royal Navy!" He turned back to Colonel Harding and disclosed, "I have increased the watch upon St. Claire's ship. If he tries to take it, we will spring the trap!"

"Do you think that wise, Lieutenant?" challenged Eden. She was the very picture of sweet serenity when he rounded on her. "After all, if the man is audacious enough to blow up *your* ship, would he not be equally bold when making an attempt to regain control of his own? I fear your men would be in very grave danger if such proved to be the case."

His only response was to order everyone back to bed. Eden turned to follow his bidding along with the others, only to find herself detained by the pressure of his hand upon her arm.

"One moment, Lady Eden."

"Yes, Lieutenant?"

"I did not wish to speak of this in front of everyone else," he began with a frown. His hand fell back to his side, and he visibly hesitated before confessing, "I am beginning to think my time here is being wasted. Captain St. Claire is proving to be more resourceful than I had believed. My superiors will be greatly displeased when they learn of the loss of my ship." He quickly drew her along with him into the shadows at the far end of the verandah. "I have it in mind to avenge myself against St. Claire and further my own cause at the same time!"

"And how are you planning to do that?" prompted Eden. Her throat constricted in alarm.

"You will find out soon enough. Suffice it to say that I want you to pack your belongings and have them ready at a moment's notice."

"Why? Good heavens, are you . . . are you saying that you have decided to leave the island *now?*" she faltered in disbelief.

"I can offer you no more details until my plan has been perfected," was his mysterious reply. "But, I will tell you this—Captain Roark St. Claire will not have the last laugh!"

Without another word, Davidson led her inside the house and up the stairs.

She was greatly troubled by what he had told her, and could think of little else but that—and Roark—throughout the following day. Her husband's plan to liberate his ship had either failed or been postponed; she could only hope that he did not make another attempt just yet. Immediately after breakfast that morning, she had instructed George to warn Roark of the increased guard aboard the *Hornet*.

The warning turned out to be unnecessary. The fates had decided it was time to put an end to the dilemma. . . .

It all began shortly after supper. Eden had just said good night to Jamaica and Colonel Harding and was on her way upstairs. The lieutenant had excused himself some time earlier.

"Mistress Eden?"

She was in the process of raising a slippered foot to the bottom step when she heard George's voice behind her. Anxious to learn if he had spoken with Roark, she turned and flew back across the entrance foyer.

"Tell me, George, did you talk to him?" she asked in a hushed, breathless tone.

"Yes, Mistress Eden. And I have a message for you."

She urged him along with her to a small, secluded space beneath the stairwell. Casting a hasty glance about, she smiled and prompted him to give her Roark's reply.

"What did he say?"

"He said you were to be ready tonight. He will come for you at midnight."

"Come for me?" she echoed in surprise. "But I . . . I don't understand!"

"He is planning to set sail," George explained with a brief smile of his own.

"You mean he has already seized the *Hornet*?

"No, Mistress Eden. But he will before this night is through. And he will not leave you behind when he goes."

"Nor will I let him!" she avowed. "I shall be ready,

George!" She frowned at a sudden thought, and her eyes were full of genuine concern when she asked, "What will happen to you and Minerva and the others once we are gone?"

"You need not worry about us," he reassured her kindly. His expressive brown eyes were alight with determination. "We will always remain at Liberty Point. And we will survive, Mistress Eden."

"I know you will." A wealth of affection and gratitude filled her heart. Pressing an impulsive kiss upon his cheek, she gave him one last smile, then turned and hurried up the stairs.

She was tempted to tell Jamaica and Colonel Harding of the plan, but decided against it. It would be better to leave them a note explaining her absence; if they were aware of what was about to take place, they would only worry and perhaps even caution her against going. It would be dangerous, but she knew Roark would keep her safe. She would not be dissuaded!

The night deepened. As midnight approached, Eden paced restlessly about her bedroom. Her belongings were secured within a single carpetbag, and she had flung a light woolen cloak about her shoulders to aid in concealment as well as warmth. No lamp burned within her room.

"Please come soon, my love!" she entreated aloud, though in a soft whisper.

She crossed back to the window and fixed her bright, sparkling emerald gaze upon the darkness below. Her mind drifted back over all the many dangers the night could hold, but she dared not allow herself to dwell upon them for long. She could not, however, completely ignore the knot of anxiety tightening in her stomach whenever she thought of the risk her husband faced in coming for her. Heaven forbid, if he were captured now . . .

A quiet but insistent knock sounded on her bedroom door.

Inhaling sharply, she whirled about. Roark? she thought, her eyes growing very round. But no, she chided herself sternly, he would not come to the door. It must be Jamaica, or even Minerva. Whoever it was, she would have to get rid of this person quickly!

She hastened to light the lamp, then slipped off the cloak and flung it across the foot of her bed. Snatching up a book from the dressing table, she disregarded the fierce pounding of her heart and did her best to look composed. The knock sounded again.

"Yes, what—" she started to question as she finally swung open the door. She broke off with a startled gasp, her face paling at the sight of the tall, uniformed man who stood frowning down at her. "Lieutenant Davidson!" she breathed in dismay.

"The time has come, Lady Eden!" he decreed with an air of great urgency. "We are leaving at once!"

"Leaving?" she echoed dazedly.

"Yes, at this very moment!" He brushed past her and, spying her carpetbag, seized hold of it. "You had best wear that cloak, for the night is cool!" He took the liberty of fetching it for her, then took a firm grip on her arm. "Come, we haven't much time!"

"But, why . . . why are we going now?" she stammered, instinctively holding back. "And why are you in such a hurry to—"

431

"I will explain everything to you later!"

She cast a look full of confusion and alarm and heartache toward the window. It was almost midnight. Roark would be coming for her at any moment. Dear God, she could not let him be caught! What was she to do?

"Please come quietly, Lady Eden! I do not wish to disturb the household!"

Eden found herself wracked with painful indecision. She was sorely tempted to call for help, to fight against the lieutenant and somehow prevent the inevitable. But in truth, she had little choice, and she knew it. She had to save Roark. Tearing her gaze from the window, she offered no further resistance as the young officer led her from the room and down the stairs.

They hurried outside, where she was surprised to see that a number of the other Englishmen were waiting on horseback. Unbeknownst to her, the remainder of the detachment had been sent ahead on foot. She turned to Lieutenant Davidson in bafflement.

"What is going on? Why—"

"We are ending our occupation of the island!" he announced. He propelled her along with him to his own horse, tossed her up into the saddle, then mounted behind her. "Just as I had suspected, the other ships have been ordered to Baltimore!"

"You mean everyone is . . . is gone?"

"They are indeed, Lady Eden! And so shall we be in an hour's time!"

Raising his hand in a silent command, he reined about and urged his mount across the fields while his men followed. He clamped an arm about Eden's waist, pulling her tightly back against him as the horse carried them toward town. Stunned by what was happening, she was unaware of the fact that Colonel Harding and Jamaica had come flying out of the house to watch helplessly as she was spirited away. George, meanwhile, had already hurried off to find Roark.

Upon their arrival in town, Lieutenant Davidson dismounted and tugged Eden down beside him. It was the first opportunity she'd had to question him since they had made the wild flight from Liberty Point, and she seized full advantage of it.

"I demand an explanation!" she proclaimed hotly. "If the other ships have already sailed away, then how in heaven's name can you be planning for us to leave?"

"It is quite simple, really," he answered with infuriating smugness. He turned his head and nodded toward the lone ship still docked at the wharf. "We are going to take Captain St. Claire's infamous *Hornet*!"

"What?" she gasped in disbelief. Her eyes flew to the ship before moving back to his face. Several lamps burned along the wharf area, so that the proceedings were all too visible. "Surely you are not serious!"

"I told you I would find a way to achieve both my objectives!" he reminded her triumphantly. "My superiors will be delighted with such a prize, and St. Claire will be paid back in kind for the loss of my ship!"

"But, you cannot!" she protested. She shook her

head in emphatic denial of his plans, while Roark's face swam before her eyes. "You cannot do this, Lieutenant! Why, it is nothing short of piracy!"

"Call it what you will, Lady Eden, but we are going to sail the *Hornet* back to England!" He took her arm, but she jerked it free.

"No! I shall not be going with you!" she asserted, her manner one of proud defiance. Her eyes blazed venomously up at him. "I will have no part of this . . . this despicable plunderage of yours!"

She shuddered at the realization of just how close she had come to disaster. Roark will come soon, she told herself; he will save me. Now that he and his men were not so greatly outnumbered, she had every confidence that he would emerge victorious!

"Why should it matter so much to you?" the lieutenant demanded in growing suspicion, and more than a touch of anger. He seized her arm again, his fingers biting into her soft flesh with near-bruising force. "What is St. Claire to you?"

"Nothing!" Struggling within his grasp, she exclaimed furiously, "How dare you! Let go of me!"

"No, Lady Eden! You are coming with me, willingly or *not!*"

She cried out when he suddenly bent and tossed her facedown over his shoulder. Oblivious to her protests, and to the pounding of her fists upon his back, he bore her quickly down the wharf and aboard the *Hornet*. He set her on her feet once they were on deck, but his arm remained locked like a band of iron about her waist.

"Make ready to sail!" he ordered his men sharply.

"Damn you, let me go!" cried Eden.

Bringing her hand up, she slapped him across the face as hard as she could. He cursed and grew visibly enraged, though he managed to fight down the urge to strike her in return.

"There *is* something between you and St. Claire, isn't there?" he accused, seizing her arms and forcing them behind her back. "Why else would you suddenly display such reluctance to—"

"I have told you why! I refuse to sail aboard this ship! And if you persist in holding me captive, I shall see that my father 'rewards' you for your unforgivably churlish behavior!" she threatened with a toss of her raven curls. "He will have your head for this!"

"Your father will offer me nothing but gratitude once I have returned you to him!" the Englishman disputed confidently. "If you have indeed become involved with that American scoundrel in some way, then Lord Grayson Parrish will be doubly grateful for my intervention!"

"You are much mistaken!" *Dear God, where is Roark?* "Now let me disembark, or I shall be forced to—"

"You will do nothing, do you hear?" he hissed, bringing his face menacingly close to hers. "We are going to sail for England, my dearest Lady Eden, and you may as well accustom yourself to that fact here and now! It matters not what your connection is to Captain St. Claire, nor what treason you may be guilty of! You are the daughter of a lord of the realm, and I will not leave you behind!"

She struggled furiously against him, but to no avail. Her wide, horrified gaze swept across the lamplit deck as the men made their final preparations

435

to set sail.

"Cast off!" her self-appointed rescuer directed them in a curt, angry tone of voice.

"Please, Lieutenant, do not do this!" Eden now tried pleading. She was desperately stalling for time, trying to find some way to escape before it was too late. Her heart cried out to Roark as she choked back hot, bitter tears of defeat. "If you will only let me go, I shall send word to my father and ask him to help you secure the promotion of which you spoke! He is highly placed within the government, as you well know, and I am quite certain he will be able to help you!"

"I am an officer in His Majesty's Royal Navy," Davidson parried loftily. "You cannot bribe me into an abandonment of duty!" This was not entirely true; he had been willing enough to bend the rules of duty and honor when he'd believed Eden could be his. But now that his suspicions about her had returned to plague him, he once again cloaked himself in the responsibilities of his position. "Come!" he told her. "You are going below!"

Eden renewed her struggles when he began pulling her across the deck toward the companion-way.

A gunshot suddenly rang out. It was followed by another and another, then two more in rapid succession. Darkness fell upon the shore, for the street lamps had been shattered.

"Let her go, Davidson!" a familiar, deep-timbred voice thundered from the nearby darkness.

Roark! Eden called his name silently. Flooded with relief, her eyes flew to the man beside her.

436

"Douse those lights!" Lieutenant Davidson ordered tersely. In a matter of seconds, the deck of the *Hornet* was cast into darkness as well. The men readied themselves for battle, taking up their positions at the rail and making sure their weapons were at hand.

"Release her and you'll go free!" Roark called out.

"Who are you?" demanded the lieutenant, his gaze narrowing in an attempt to catch a glimpse of the voice's owner. He could see nothing at present.

"I am the man you seek—Captain Roark St. Claire!"

"It's the devil himself!" one of the men aboard the *Hornet* muttered in surprise.

Lieutenant Davidson tensed. His fury-laced gaze shot to Eden, who stood silent and still beside him in the cool, starlit darkness. Her outward composure belied the turmoil raging within her. Fear for Roark made her legs grow perilously weak.

"What is Lady Eden to you, St. Claire?" the English officer finally countered.

"It's me you want, not her! Now let her go!"

"Come forward and show yourself, Captain St. Claire! I will deal with no man who skulks about in the shadows!"

"No!" Eden impulsively cried out. Oblivious to the lieutenant's searing glare, she gasped when Roark sauntered from the woods. She could not quite make out his face, but she knew with a certainty that it was her beloved who stood so tall and proud and unafraid before his enemies. "Roark, no!" she exclaimed in a choked voice, panic coursing through her. "Go back! Dear God, *go back!*"

"For the last time, Davidson, let her go!" Roark

instructed with deadly calm.

"Perhaps, Captain St. Claire, you would be interested in an exchange!" the other man suggested. He forced Eden back to the rail with him. "Her freedom for your own!"

"No!" she breathed in horror.

"Well, Captain?" Davidson prompted with a furious, mocking air. He knew the other Americans were somewhere close by. He also knew that, with Eden aboard, they would not dare an attack. *They will not risk harming her,* he told himself. Clenching his jaw at the realization that she was apparently St. Claire's woman after all, he demanded, "What is it to be? Do you return to England as my prisoner, or will it be the beautiful Lady Eden who enjoys my company?"

"Release her now, and I will go with you," came Roark's steady reply.

"Please, Roark, no!" Eden cried once more. She could not believe what was happening. "You must not do this! I will be all right! I will come back—"

"Quiet!" snapped Davidson. He jerked her roughly in front of him and clamped a hand across her mouth.

"Take your hands off her, you bastard!" Roark ground out. "You've got what you came for—*now let her go!*"

"Not until you and your men come aboard!"

"My men were not part of the bargain!"

"Those are my terms, Captain! Either you and all of your men surrender, or we set sail with Lady Eden!" To emphasize the point, he gave the order for the sails to be hoisted. "Your time is up!" he told

Roark. "What is it to be?"

"I say we kill every last one of the fancy-coated bastards!" a coarse voice sang out from the concealing darkness of the woods.

"Aye, kill them all!" seconded another.

"Hold your fire, damn it!" Roark cautioned his men. "You might well hit Eden!" His eyes darkened with a savage gleam, while his handsome features became a grim mask of fury. "Whatever else I may have thought of you English, Davidson, I would not have expected you to hide behind a woman's skirts!" he taunted derisively, hoping to provoke the young lieutenant to recklessness.

"Shut up, you ill-mannered savage!" growled the aristocratic officer. His hand fell away from Eden's mouth to curl about the hilt of his sword.

"I begin to see, Lieutenant," Roark continued in the same contemptuous vein, "that you and your men are not above using any means at hand to save your own hides! If you're going to behave like cowards, then by damn, you—"

Without warning, a single shot rent the air.

Roark ground out a curse and clutched at his left shoulder. A shrill scream broke from Eden's lips. At the same time, Lieutenant Davidson rounded furiously upon the young recruit who had fired.

"*Roark!*" Eden choked out, her heart twisting at the sight of his pain. "Dear God, no!"

She suddenly pushed against her captor with all her might. Taken off-guard by the violence of her actions, he staggered backward.

"Watch out!" one of his men yelled, "She's—"

But it was too late. Eden scrambled to the top of the

rail and cast herself overboard. The very moment she disappeared beneath the black waters, the Americans opened fire upon the British.

Lieutenant Davidson faced even more of a dilemma now than he had anticipated. He hastily gave the order for his men to return the enemy's fire, but it was no use. They might as well have been shooting at phantoms, for the Americans had the advantages of darkness and concealment. The British, on the other hand, provided too easy a target. Several of them had already been hit, and it soon became clear that the casualties would mount if they remained any longer.

They had little choice but to put to sea with all haste.

"Weigh anchor!" Lieutenant Davidson roared above the din. His eyes were full of hatred as he looked to where Roark was making his way toward Eden. Taking careful aim with his own weapon, he was about to pull the trigger—but never got the chance.

A strangled cry of pain was torn from him as a bullet suddenly ripped across his chest. He fell heavily to his knees upon the quarter-deck, the gun slipping from his grasp before someone helped him to his feet again.

The battle had ended as abruptly as it had begun. With the wind filling her sails and the familiar waters of the sound churning beneath her sleek wooden hull, the *Hornet* glided swiftly toward the Atlantic.

Eden stumbled to the shore, where Roark caught her before she fell. He gathered her close with his uninjured arm, and she clung weakly to him, chilled and shaking, but filled with the most profound joy she had ever known.

"Oh, Roark!" she murmured tremulously. "I . . . I thought I had lost you!"

"You'll not get rid of me so easily, sweet vixen." His mouth curved into a faint smile of irony. "You have a talent for getting carried off, don't you, Mrs. St. Claire?"

"Your ship!" She drew away to look up at him. A shadow of mingled sadness and anger crossed her beautiful face, and her emerald gaze was bright with tears. "Sweet Saint Christopher, they have taken the *Hornet*!"

"It doesn't matter." He gritted his teeth against the burning pain in his shoulder and swept her close again. "Everything I hold dear, I am holding now."

Seth and the others came hurrying forward to join them. Roark finally, reluctantly, let Eden go. Someone placed a coat about her shoulders, while Seth pressed a makeshift bandage to Roark's wound.

"Let's go home, Captain," he said quietly.

Roark grasped Eden's hand, covering it with the strong warmth of his. His warm, magnificent blue eyes told her everything that was in his heart.

"Home," he repeated for her ears alone.

Together, they walked toward the horses. The future was as yet an uncertain one, but they knew it would hold more than enough love to see them through. Indeed, fate had willed it to be so, on a starry, long-ago London night. . . .

Twenty

Six months later . . .

Eden released a long, pent-up sigh and shifted her weight about on the satin-upholstered chaise, trying in vain to find a more comfortable position.

"Eight weeks," she murmured aloud. "Sweet Saint Christopher, only eight weeks more!"

She smoothed a loving hand across her rounded belly. Thinking of the child whose heart beat as one with hers, she smiled to herself. At least, thank God, she'd had the baby to give her comfort and strength these past six months.

Six months. It had seemed like an eternity.

"Oh, Roark!" she whispered brokenly, fresh tears starting to her eyes.

She had seen him only once in all this time, shortly before she had left Savannah and returned to St. Simons. That had been more than three months ago. His visit had been unmercifully brief, and he had warned her that he might not be able to come back for a number of weeks, or even months. His warning had proven all too necessary.

Her eyes clouded with remembrance as she thought about all that had happened following her husband's swift recovery from his wound. There had, as usual, been no reasoning with him.

Only three days after Lieutenant Davidson had made off with the *Hornet*, Roark had taken her to Savannah. The task of procuring another ship had been accomplished with ease; she selfishly wished it had not been so. Were it not for the baby, she would have followed through on her determination to sail with him. But she had already begun to suspect her condition, and a conversation with Bertha McManus had confirmed her suspicions. In the end, she had stayed behind . . . and Roark had sailed off to war. The memory of it still brought a sharp pain slicing through her heart.

Jamaica had written often. Seth had been persuaded that his wife would be safe enough at his own plantation with her father. Ironically, another British force had invaded St. Simons a month later. They had occupied the island for nearly three weeks, plundering the estates and carrying off food, cotton, cattle, and even slaves when they sailed away. The Colfax plantation had been spared, due to the commanding presence of Colonel Harding, but Liberty Point had not. A great many things had either been taken or destroyed.

At least George and Minerva and the others were safe, she thought, once more giving silent thanks for that. There was plenty to eat, due to the fact that the British had not discovered the hidden cache of food and supplies beneath the barn, and George had seen to it that the vegetable gardens and cotton fields were tended religiously. The joint efforts of everyone at Liberty Point had ensured that it would not only survive, but would prosper once more. Roark would be pleased, mused Eden, and so very proud as well.

She heaved another faint, dispirited sigh. Placing a hand upon the back of the chaise, she slowly pushed herself to her feet and wandered to the fireplace. She raised her eyes to the mantelpiece, where a small, framed likeness of her mother had been added to the collection of St. Claire ancestry.

She had written to both her mother and father, relating to them the startling events of the past several months and informing them that they were soon to be grandparents. But no reply had as yet been received. She could only hope that the lack of it was due to the war and not to any lingering anger on their part. Someday, she vowed to herself, she would be reunited with them. God willing, they would see her child, and they would know of the love she and Roark shared.

Feeling a strange recklessness, she turned and crossed back to the chaise. She changed her mind about resuming her seat, however, and continued onward to the window. Her preoccupied gaze fastened on the majestic avenue of live oaks in the near distance. Twilight had already cloaked the early spring landscape. The night promised to be clear and cool and lit with the moon's soft radiance.

"You've changed a bit, sweet vixen." The familiar, splendidly resonant voice came from behind her.

Her eyes flew wide. *Dear God, Roark!*

She whirled about, her heart leaping wildly and a small cry of joy escaping her lips. Her legs suddenly threatened to give way beneath her, but Roark was across the room in two long strides to catch her. His strong arms slipped about her, gathering her close to his hard-muscled warmth. Their lips met in a long, sweetly compelling kiss that left them both shaken.

"By damn, I've missed you!" he murmured hoarsely, burying his face in the shimmering thickness of her hair.

"Oh, my love, why did you not tell anyone you were coming? How long can you stay?" she asked in a breathless rush. She lifted her head from his chest and gazed up at him with eyes so full of love that he felt truly humbled. "How did you know where—"

"Where to find you?" he finished for her. He gave her a smile that sent warm color flying to her cheeks. "I didn't. Not until I received the news of your whereabouts from Bertha—firsthand, I might add. I seem to recall, Mrs. St. Claire, that you were instructed to remain in Savannah." He frowned down at her, only half-serious in his reproach.

"I . . . I tried to, Roark, I truly did!" she faltered guiltily, her green eyes falling before the piercing blue intensity of his. "But I thought it best that our child be born here at Liberty Point."

"Damn it, woman, will you never do as you're told?" he asked, then chuckled quietly as he led her to the chaise, took a seat, and drew her down upon his lap.

"Oh, but I am much too heavy now!" she protested.

"You are more beautiful than ever," he spoke in all

sincerity. He rested a gentle hand upon the undeniable evidence of his affection. His eyes glowed warmly. "My son appears to be hale and hearty."

"Your daughter," she saw fit to correct. Her silken brow creased into a frown when she pointed out, "You have not yet answered my question. How long will you be able to stay this time?"

"Forever."

"Forever?" she echoed in stunned disbelief.

"The war is over at last, Eden," he told her solemnly.

"But . . . we have heard nothing of it!"

"The news has traveled slowly. We sailed to Washington before heading back down to Savannah, else I might not have known of it myself. The treaty was in fact signed before Christmas, but it wasn't ratified until a few weeks ago. I fear it will be quite some time yet before the ships at sea get wind of it."

"I can scarcely believe it," murmured Eden, her head spinning as realization began to sink in. "Oh, Roark, did we surrender after all?" she questioned sadly.

"Who the devil is the *we* you are referring to?" he challenged. A disarming smile tugged at his lips in the next moment, and his eyes danced with wry amusement. "If you mean the Americans, then no, we did not surrender."

"Good heavens! England has been defeated?" Her own eyes grew quite round at the thought.

"No." He shook his head and explained, "In truth, my love, there was no victor. But we have finally secured for ourselves the freedom of the seas. There will be no more impressment, and no more interference with trade. Neither side wants a repetition of what happened."

"So you really are home to stay?" asked Eden, seeking confirmation of the truth. "You will never go away again?"

"Never," he promised.

He captured her lips with his once more, and did not relinquish his fiercely loving possession of them until she was melting against him and he was burning with the white-hot desire she never failed to provoke within him.

"We've a lot of time to make up for," he decreed, his deep-timbred voice sending another shiver of enchantment down her back. "And a lot of work to do. I mean to see to it that Liberty Point is the finest plantation in all of Georgia."

"It shall be," Eden asserted confidently. She wound her arms more tightly about his neck. A soft gasp broke from her lips.

"What is it?" Roark demanded with a frown.

"I do believe, my dearest Captain, that your son is impatient to meet his father. He just kicked me in the boldest manner imaginable!" It did not strike her as significant that she had referred to the child as *he;* she would realize soon enough how prophetic her comment had been.

"He has the true St. Claire spirit."

"God help the poor woman who one day falls in love with him," she remarked with a dramatic sigh.

Roark smiled.

"Well spoken, sweet vixen." He brought his mouth close to hers once more and whispered, "God help her indeed."

447

"I love you," she breathed, closing her eyes against the sweetness of the moment.

"And I you."

Their lips met, their hearts soared together as one . . . and a lifetime of happiness lay before them.

Adam Parrish St. Claire was born precisely nine months after his mother was first carried aboard the *Hornet*. And if the talk among the islanders is to be believed, he proved to be every bit as masterful, determined, and devastatingly handsome as his father.